HELLBOY

AND THE

BUREAU FOR PARANORMAL · RESEARCH AND DEFENSE ·

1956

Created by MIKE MIGNOLA

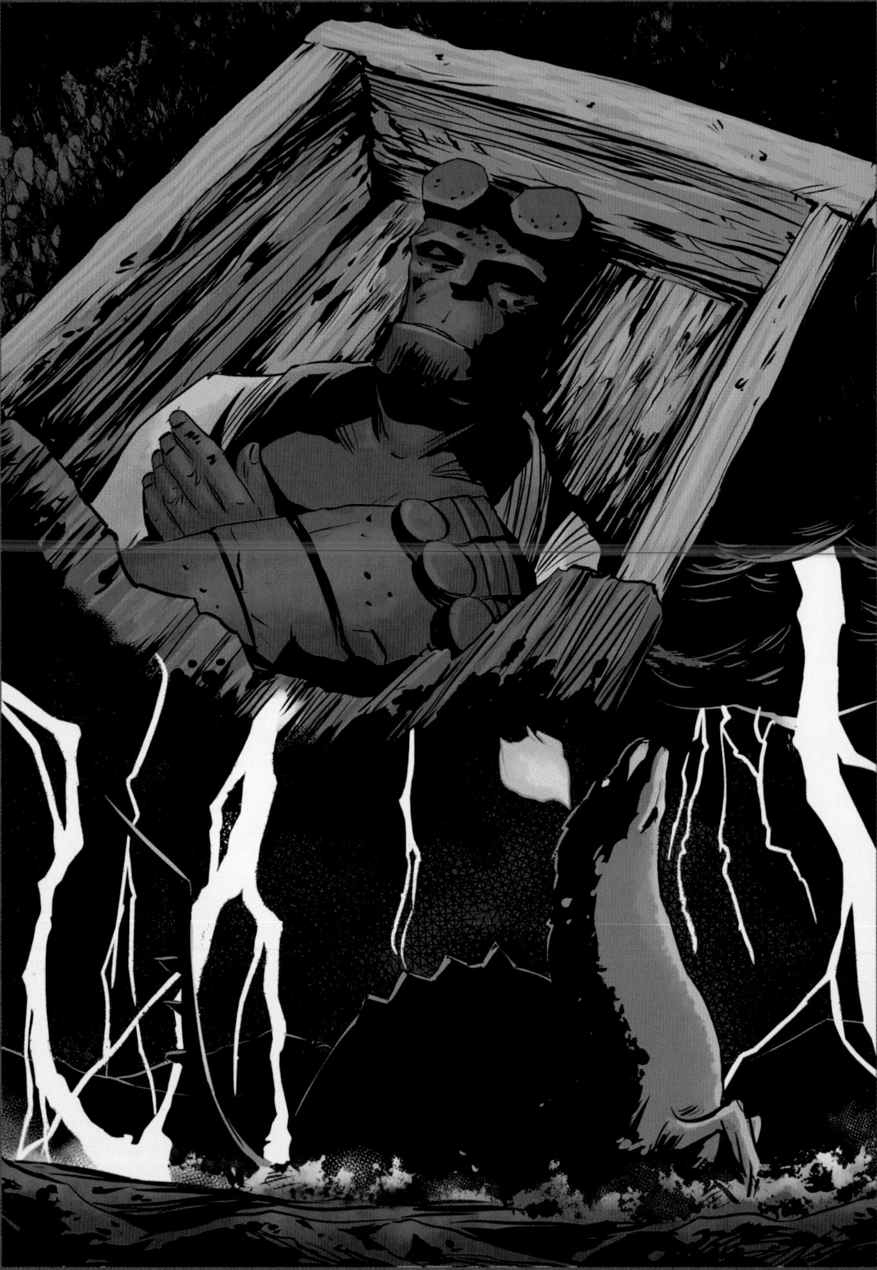

MIKE MIGNOLA'S

HELLBOY™

AND THE B.P.R.D. 1956

Stories by
MIKE MIGNOLA & CHRIS ROBERSON

HELLBOY AND THE B.P.R.D.: 1956

Art by

MIKE NORTON
Chapter #1 pages 2-13
Chapter #2 pages 1-3, 10-17
Chapter #3 pages 1-9, 20-22
Chapter #4 pages 1-5, 17-22
Chapter #5 pages 1-20

YISHAN LI
Chapter #1 pages 14-18
Chapter #2 pages 4-9
Chapter #3 pages 15-19
Chapter #4 pages 12-16
Chapter #5 page 22

MICHAEL AVON OEMING
Chapter #1 pages 19-23
Chapter #2 pages 18-22
Chapter #3 pages 10-14
Chapter #4 pages 6-11
Chapter #5 page 21

HELLBOY VS. LOBSTER JOHNSON: THE RING OF DEATH

Art by MIKE NORTON ✠ *Colors by* DAVE STEWART

HELLBOY VS. LOBSTER JOHNSON: DOWN MEXICO WAY

Art by PAUL GRIST ✠ *Colors by* BILL CRABTREE

Published by Dark Horse Books
A division of Dark Horse Comics LLC
10956 SE Main Street • Milwaukie, OR 97222

DarkHorse.com
Advertising Sales: (503) 905-2315
Comic Shop Locator Service: ComicShopLocator.com

First edition: September 2019
ISBN 978-1-50671-105-8

1 3 5 7 9 10 8 6 4 2
Printed in China

Hellboy and the B.P.R.D.: 1956

This book collects *Hellboy and the B.P.R.D.: 1956* #1–#5, as well as the one-shot *Hellboy vs. Lobster Johnson: The Ring of Death*.

Library of Congress Cataloging-in-Publication Data

Names: Mignola, Mike, author. | Roberson, Chris, author. | Norton, Mike,
  artist. | Li, Yishan, 1981- artist. | Oeming, Michael Avon, artist. |
  Stewart, Dave, colourist. | Robins, Clem, 1955- letterer.
Title: Hellboy and the B.P.R.D. 1956 / stories by Mike Mignola and Chris
  Roberson ; art by Mike Norton, Yishan Li, Michael Avon Oeming ; colors by
  Dave Stewart ; letters by Clem Robins.
Other titles: At head of title: Mike Mignola's
Description: First edition. | Milwaukie, OR : Dark Horse Books, 2019. | "This
  book collects Hellboy and the B.P.R.D.: 1956 #1-#5, as well as The Ring of
  Death and Down Mexico Way from the Hellboy vs. Lobster Johnson one-shot."
Identifiers: LCCN 2019009286 | ISBN 9781506711058
Subjects: LCSH: Comic books, strips, etc.
Classification: LCC PN6728.H3838 M295 2019 | DDC 741.5/973--dc23
LC record available at https://lccn.loc.gov/2019009286

CHAPTER ONE

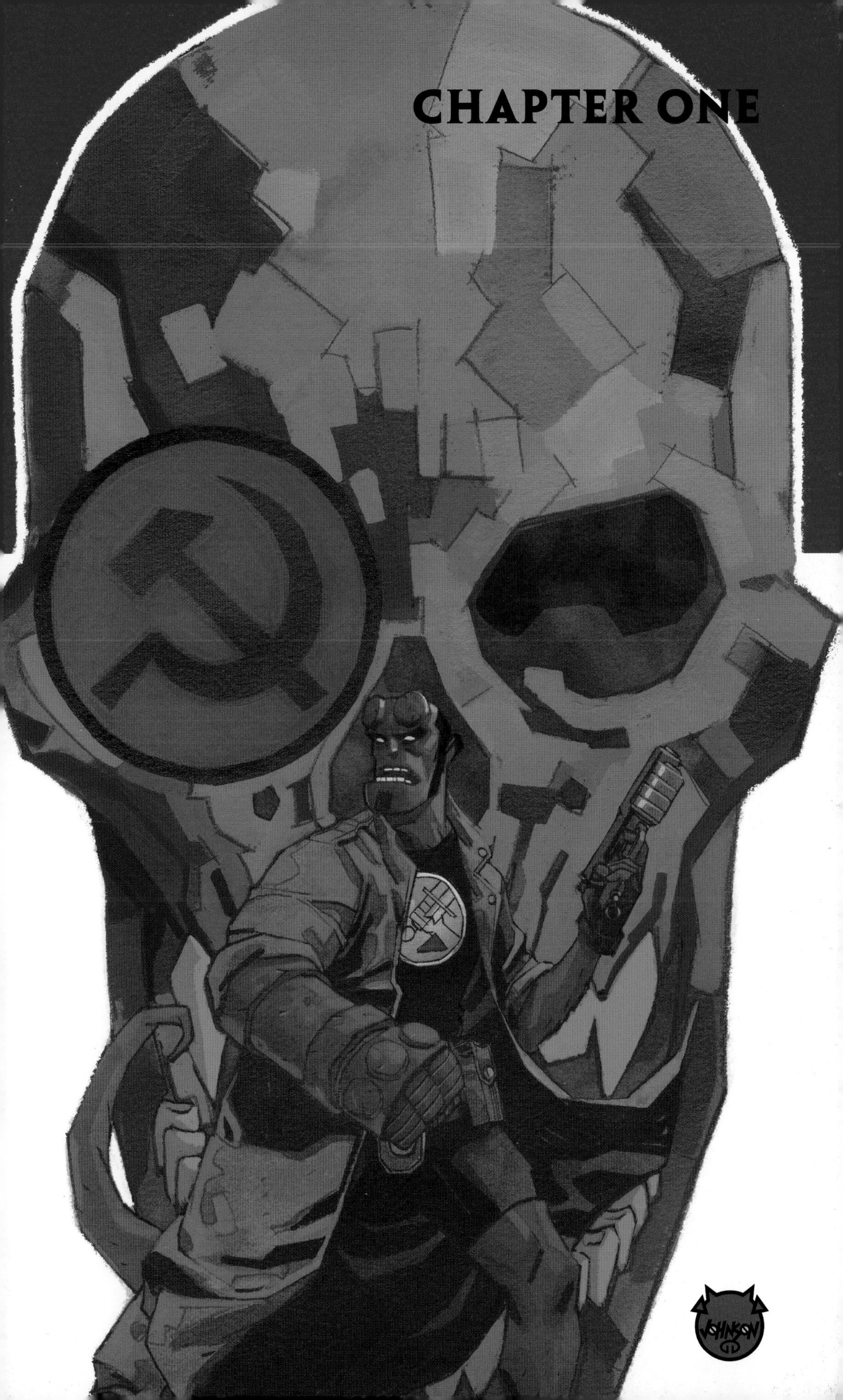
JOHNSON

BUREAU FOR PARANORMAL RESEARCH AND DEFENSE

TO: ALL BUREAU PERSONNEL

FROM: T. BRUTTENHOLM, DIRECTOR

SUBJECT: ORGANIZATIONAL STRUCTURE

MATERIEL & EQUIPMENT

STAFFING LEVELS

DATE: APRIL 15, 1956

I have been made aware that there is still some confusion and uncertainty about recent changes in our organizational structure, and in particular the role and function of the newly established Intelligence division. I am confident that our new consultant Myron Linneberg will be able to address many of your concerns when he transfers over from the Central Intelligence Agency next month, but in the meantime please continue to direct any inquiries to Margaret Laine.

In her capacity as the newly promoted Assistant Director of Operations, Miss Laine will be overseeing the recruitment of new field agents in our attempt to increase staff levels to projected goals, which should have the effect of reducing the workload that I know many of you are struggling with. She is currently in the process of reviewing applicants, and referrals of potential recruits are always welcome. Some of you may be asked to assist in training the new recruits, and I know I can count on all of you to provide whatever support or assistance is required.

Assistant Director Laine is also spearheading an initiative to upgrade the equipment available to our agents in the field. Since the inception of the Bureau we have made do with military surplus, and equipment failure in the field has become increasingly common. Miss Laine has heard your complaints and feels strongly that with the increased security and heightened scrutiny under which we now labor, more modern and robust options are in order. The necessary budgetary expenditures are currently being reviewed, but I am confident that new field uniforms and armaments will soon be made available.

Now, let us turn our attention to more pressing matters. As I am sure most of you are aware, the unpleasant business in Nebraska at the beginning of this month was the result of an improperly secured exorcism. Fortunately there were no fatalities, and the injured agents are expected to make a full recovery, but at a time when we are already short-staffed as is, we cannot afford to let any more such accidents deplete the number of

(continued)

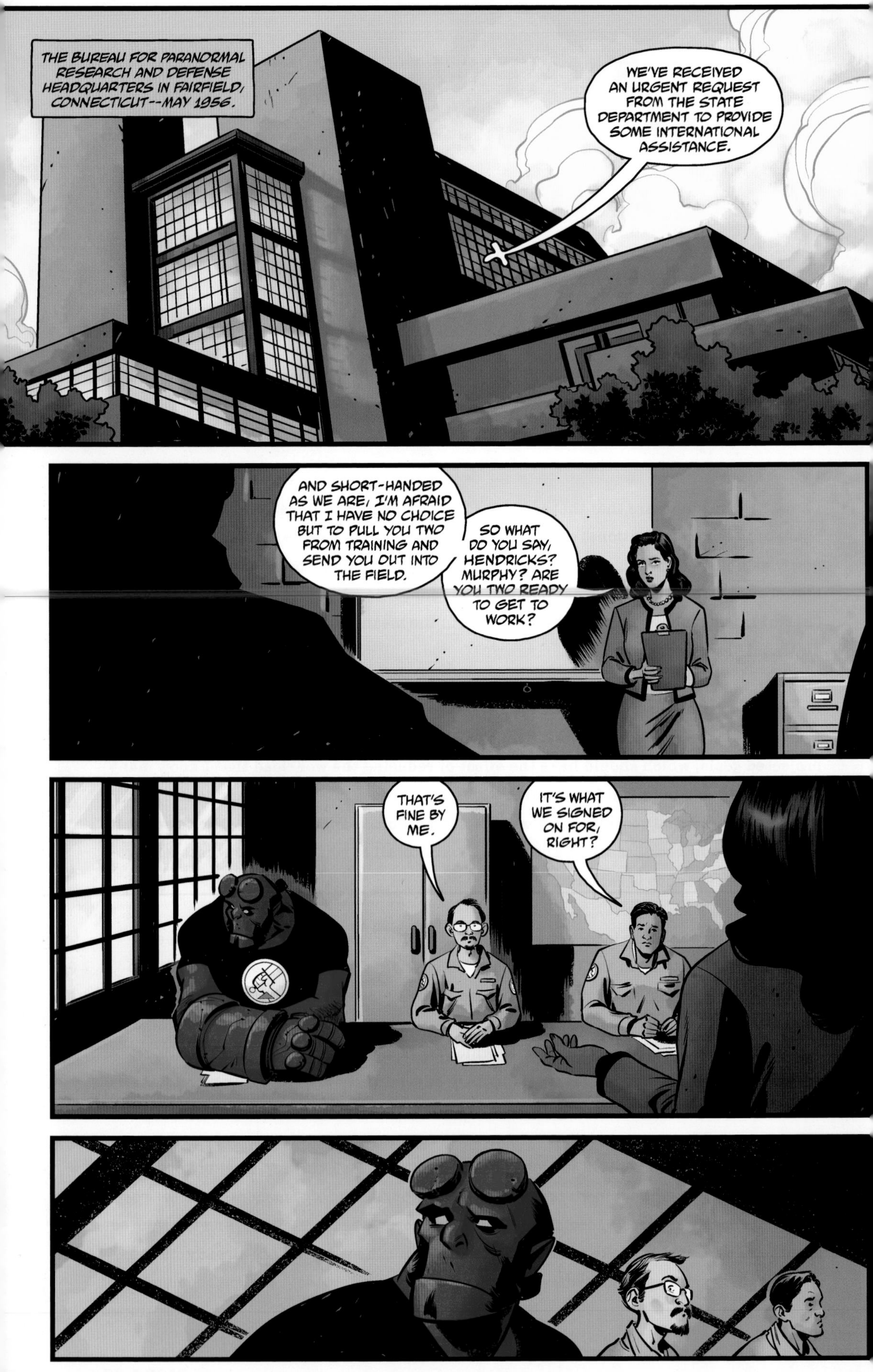
THE BUREAU FOR PARANORMAL RESEARCH AND DEFENSE HEADQUARTERS IN FAIRFIELD, CONNECTICUT--MAY 1956.
WE'VE RECEIVED AN URGENT REQUEST FROM THE STATE DEPARTMENT TO PROVIDE SOME INTERNATIONAL ASSISTANCE.
AND SHORT-HANDED AS WE ARE, I'M AFRAID THAT I HAVE NO CHOICE BUT TO PULL YOU TWO FROM TRAINING AND SEND YOU OUT INTO THE FIELD.
SO WHAT DO YOU SAY, HENDRICKS? MURPHY? ARE YOU TWO READY TO GET TO WORK?
THAT'S FINE BY ME.
IT'S WHAT WE SIGNED ON FOR, RIGHT?

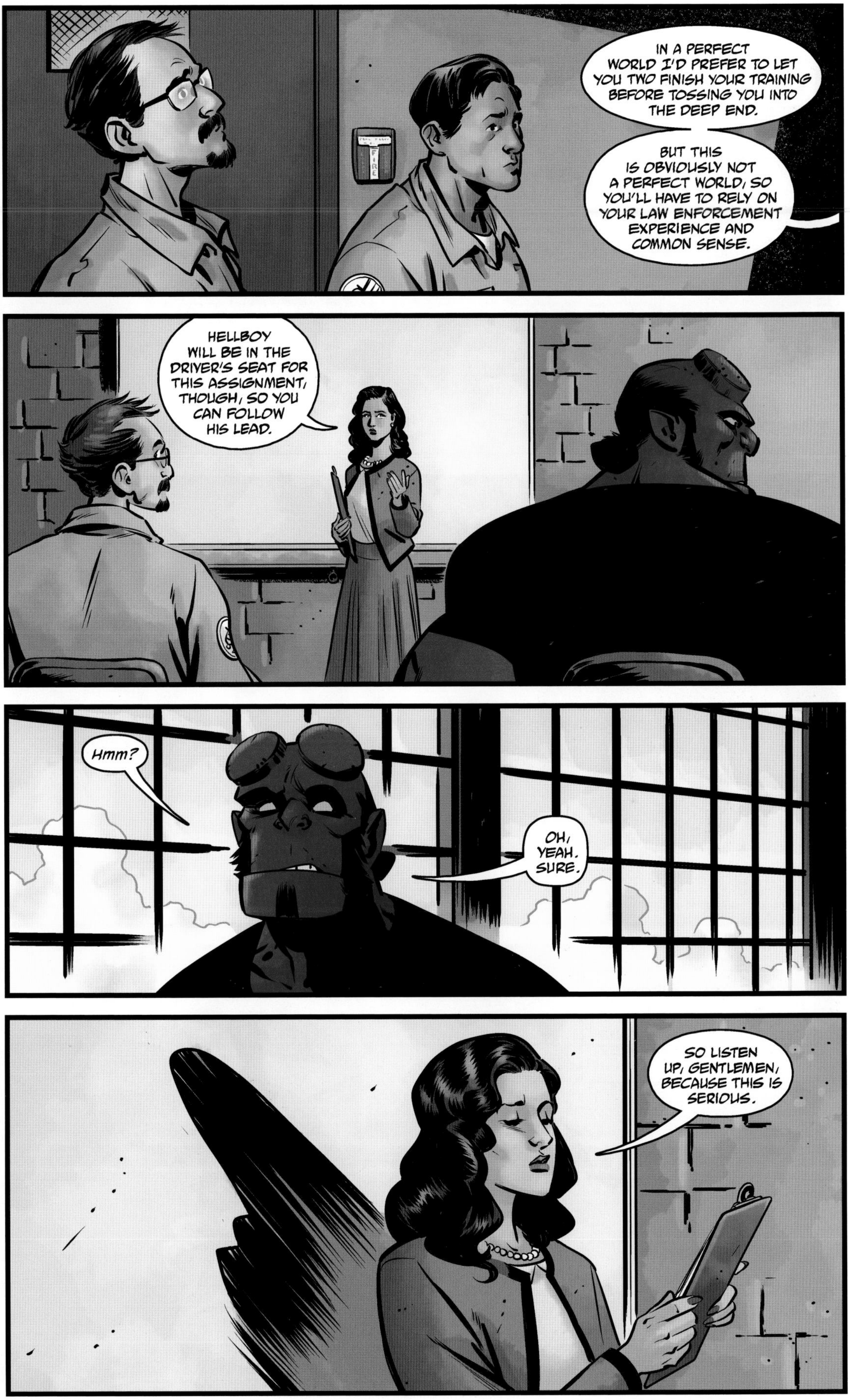
IN A PERFECT WORLD I'D PREFER TO LET YOU TWO FINISH YOUR TRAINING BEFORE TOSSING YOU INTO THE DEEP END.
BUT THIS IS OBVIOUSLY NOT A PERFECT WORLD, SO YOU'LL HAVE TO RELY ON YOUR LAW ENFORCEMENT EXPERIENCE AND COMMON SENSE.
FIRE
HELLBOY WILL BE IN THE DRIVER'S SEAT FOR THIS ASSIGNMENT, THOUGH, SO YOU CAN FOLLOW HIS LEAD.
Hmm?
OH, YEAH. SURE.
SO LISTEN UP, GENTLEMEN, BECAUSE THIS IS SERIOUS.

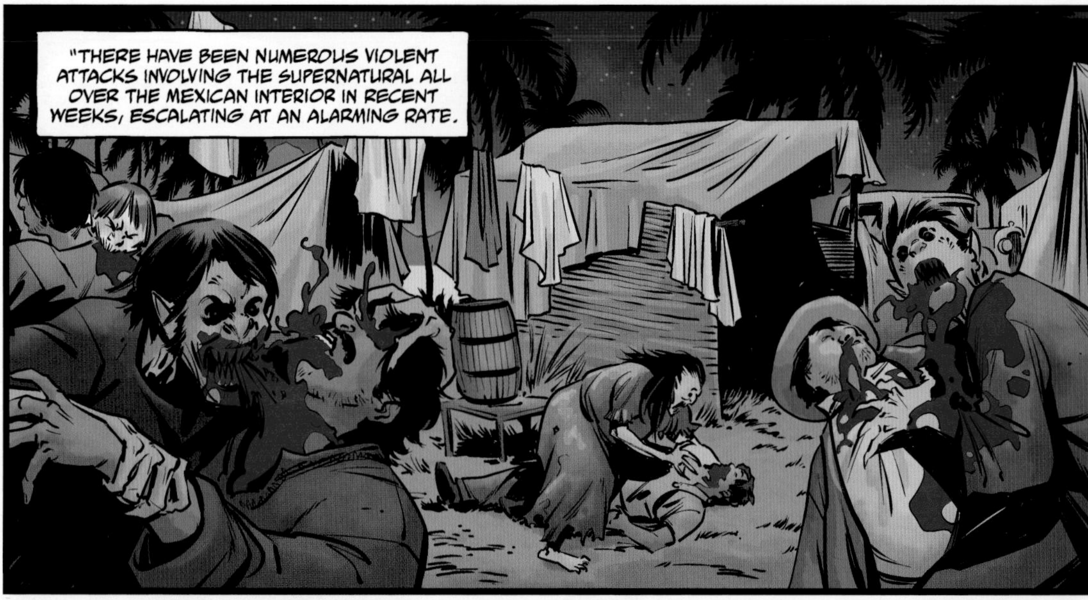
"THERE HAVE BEEN NUMEROUS VIOLENT ATTACKS INVOLVING THE SUPERNATURAL ALL OVER THE MEXICAN INTERIOR IN RECENT WEEKS, ESCALATING AT AN ALARMING RATE.

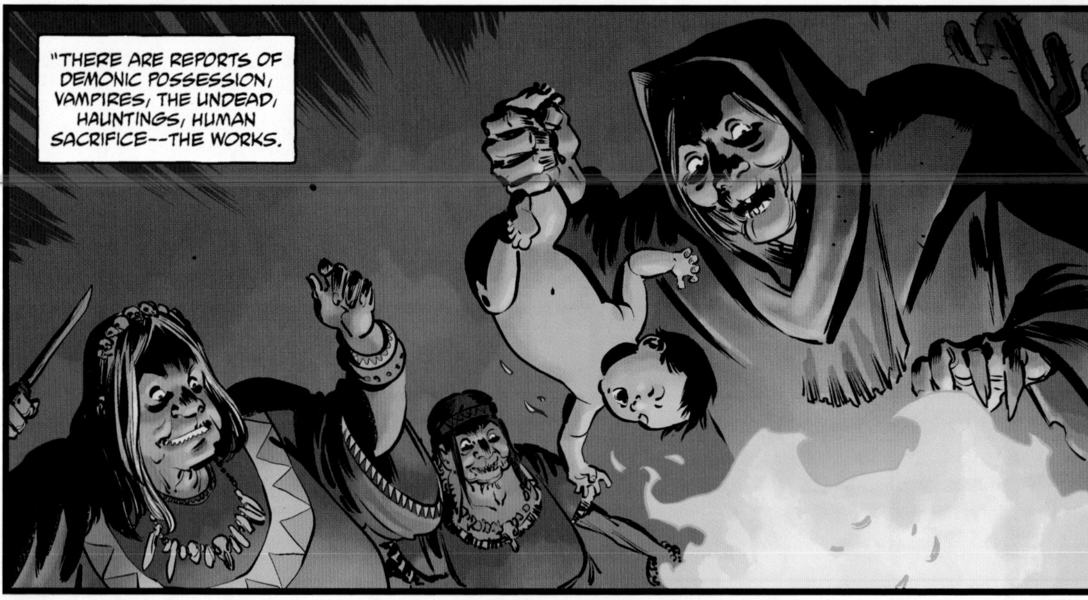
"THERE ARE REPORTS OF DEMONIC POSSESSION, VAMPIRES, THE UNDEAD, HAUNTINGS, HUMAN SACRIFICE--THE WORKS.

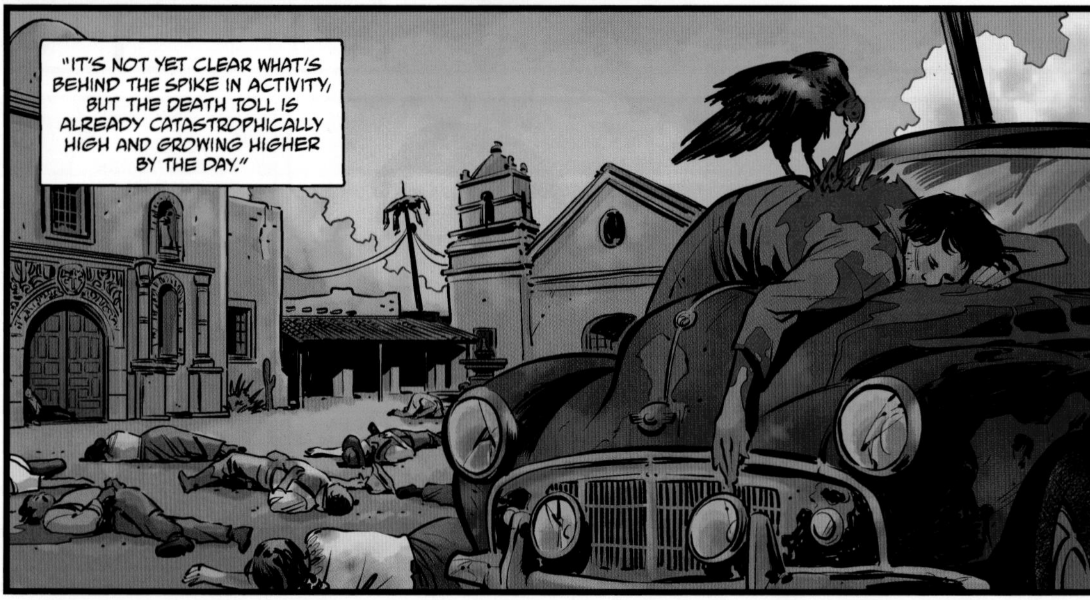
"IT'S NOT YET CLEAR WHAT'S BEHIND THE SPIKE IN ACTIVITY, BUT THE DEATH TOLL IS ALREADY CATASTROPHICALLY HIGH AND GROWING HIGHER BY THE DAY."

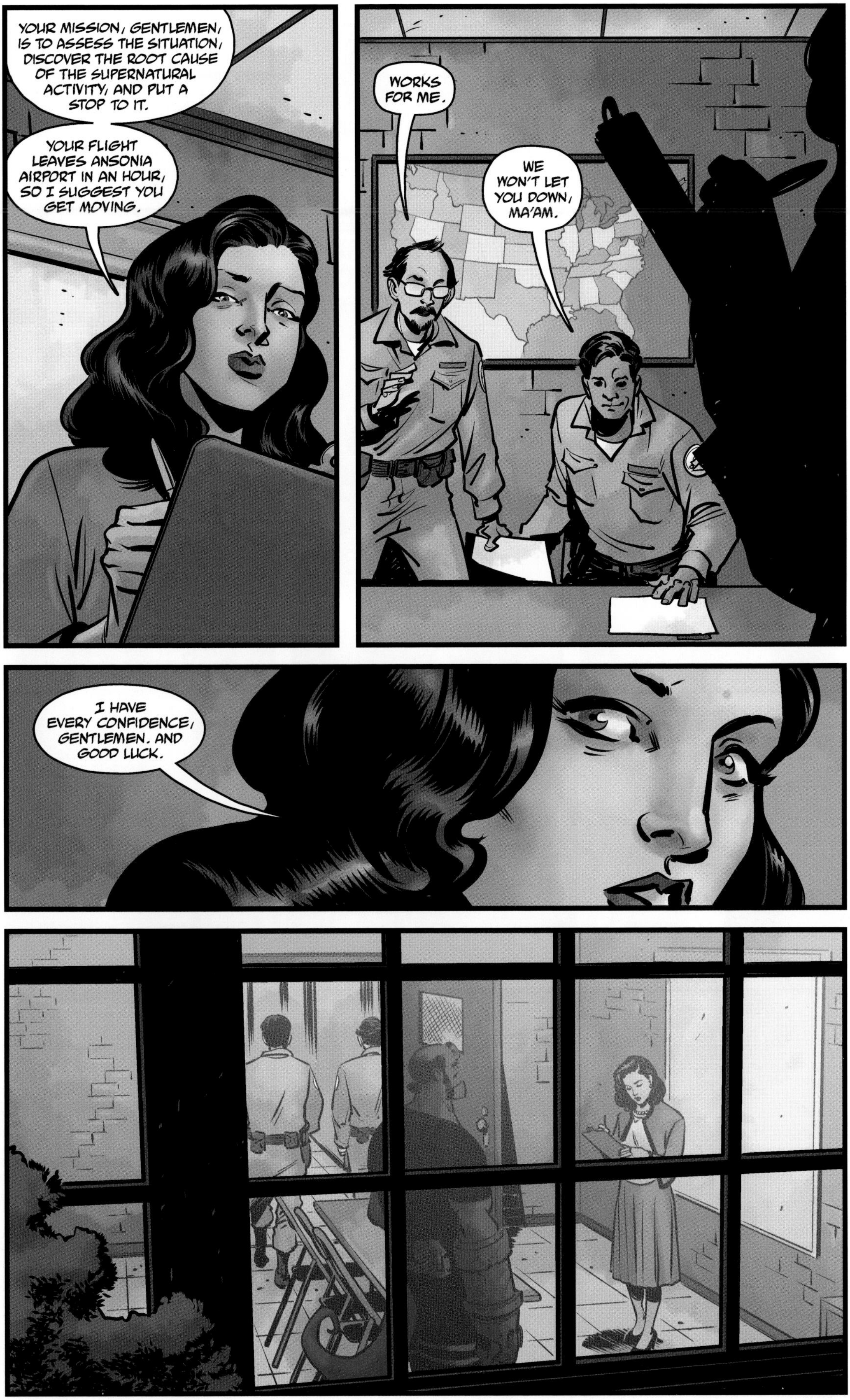
YOUR MISSION, GENTLEMEN, IS TO ASSESS THE SITUATION, DISCOVER THE ROOT CAUSE OF THE SUPERNATURAL ACTIVITY, AND PUT A STOP TO IT.
YOUR FLIGHT LEAVES ANSONIA AIRPORT IN AN HOUR, SO I SUGGEST YOU GET MOVING.
WORKS FOR ME.
WE WON'T LET YOU DOWN, MA'AM.
I HAVE EVERY CONFIDENCE, GENTLEMEN. AND GOOD LUCK.

Um... Margaret? I wanted to... see, it's about Mac.

Well, with the professor away and Archie and the rest of the gang out in the field, there's not really anyone else I can--

I'm sorry, Hellboy, but my hands are full.

Maybe one of the office staff can look after your dog while you're away? I don't think I'll be able to find the time.

Yeah, but I...I really need someone to talk--

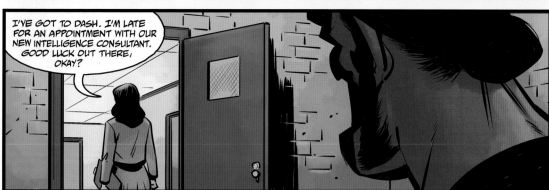

I've got to dash. I'm late for an appointment with our new intelligence consultant. Good luck out there, okay?

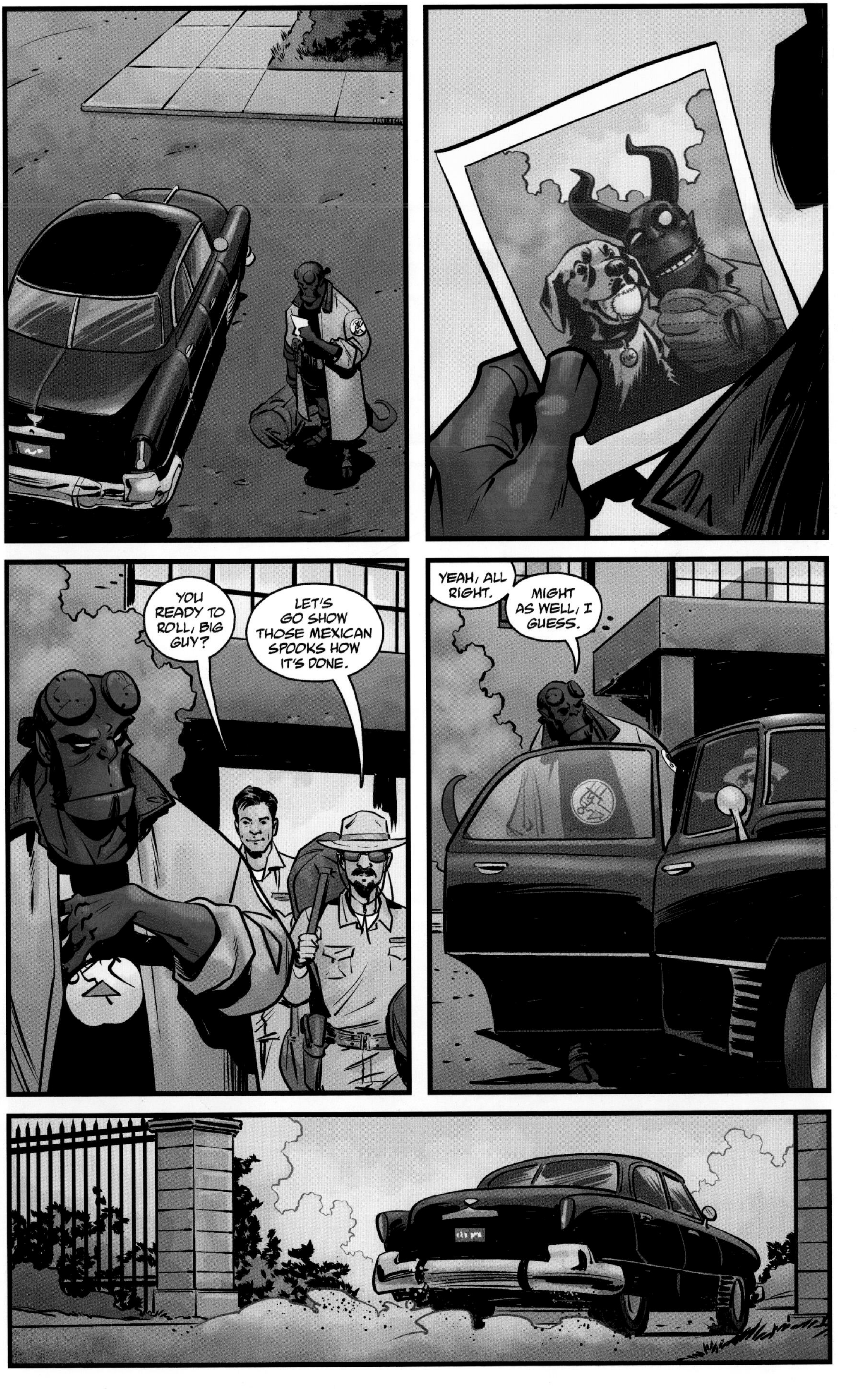
YOU READY TO ROLL, BIG GUY?
LET'S GO SHOW THOSE MEXICAN SPOOKS HOW IT'S DONE.
YEAH, ALL RIGHT.
MIGHT AS WELL, I GUESS.

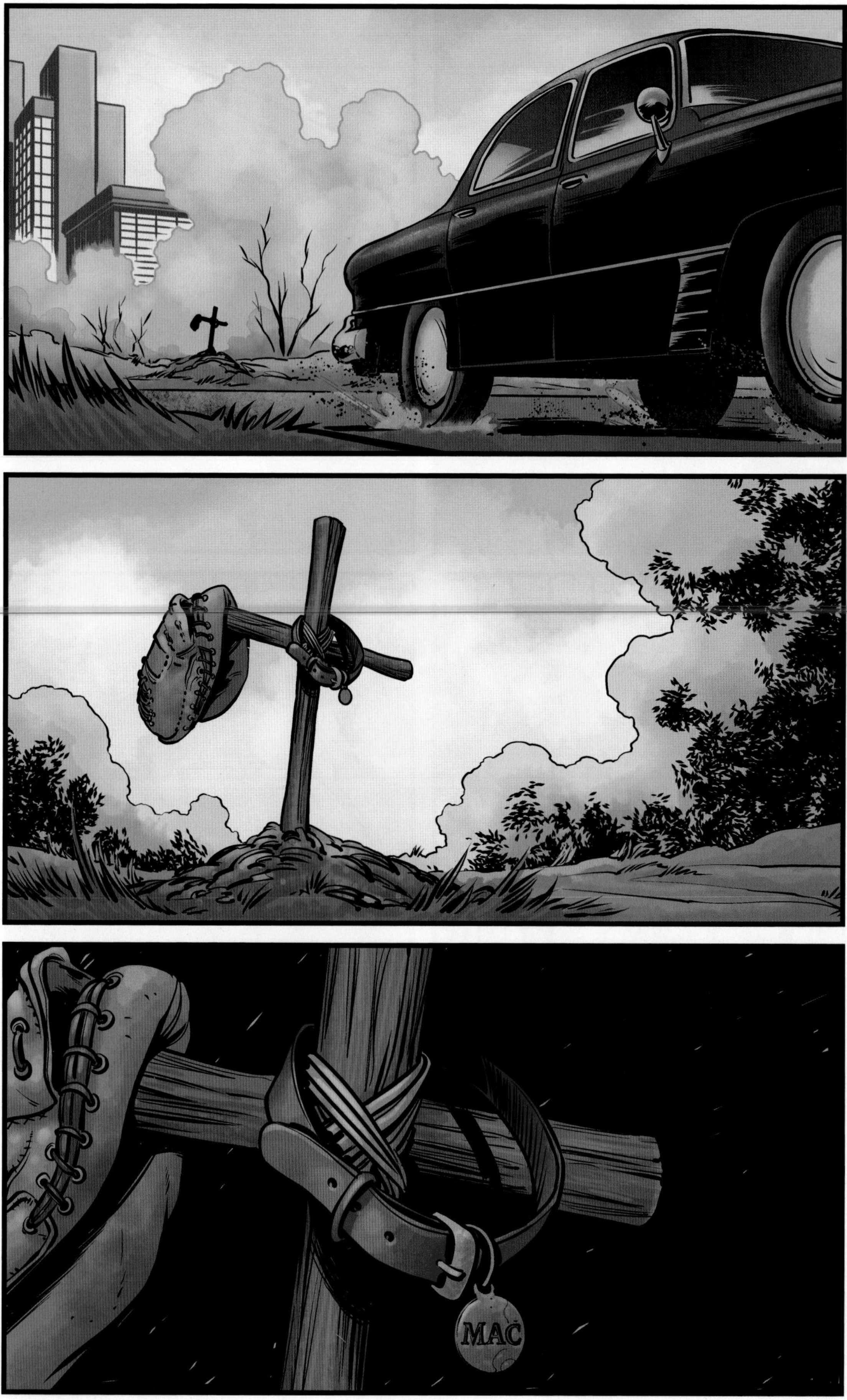
MAC

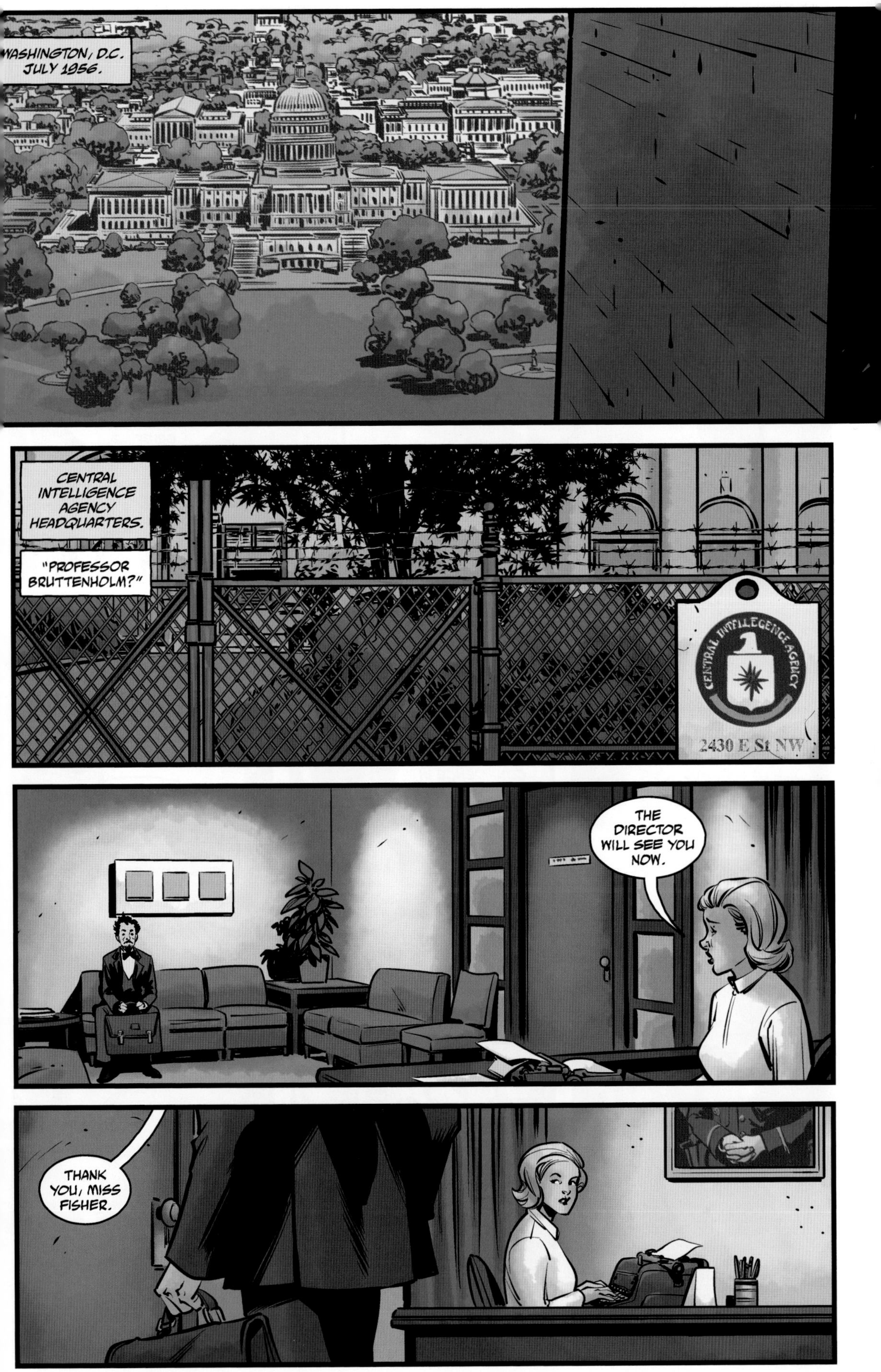
WASHINGTON, D.C. JULY 1956.
CENTRAL INTELLIGENCE AGENCY HEADQUARTERS.
"PROFESSOR BRUTTENHOLM?"
CENTRAL INTELLIGENCE AGENCY
2430 E St NW
THE DIRECTOR WILL SEE YOU NOW.
THANK YOU, MISS FISHER.

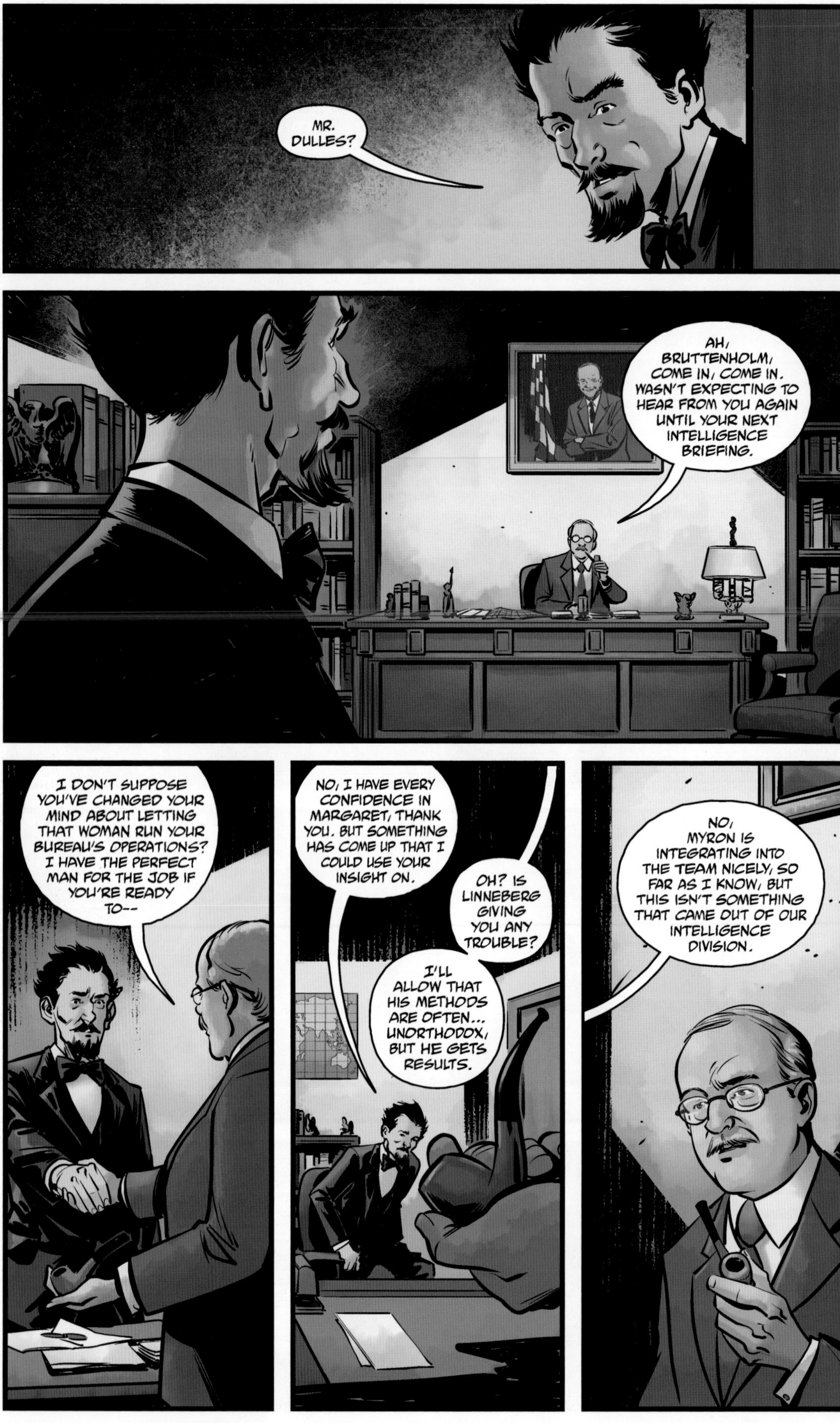
MR. DULLES?
AH, BRUTTENHOLM, COME IN, COME IN. WASN'T EXPECTING TO HEAR FROM YOU AGAIN UNTIL YOUR NEXT INTELLIGENCE BRIEFING.
I DON'T SUPPOSE YOU'VE CHANGED YOUR MIND ABOUT LETTING THAT WOMAN RUN YOUR BUREAU'S OPERATIONS? I HAVE THE PERFECT MAN FOR THE JOB IF YOU'RE READY TO--
NO, I HAVE EVERY CONFIDENCE IN MARGARET, THANK YOU. BUT SOMETHING HAS COME UP THAT I COULD USE YOUR INSIGHT ON.
OH? IS LINNEBERG GIVING YOU ANY TROUBLE?
I'LL ALLOW THAT HIS METHODS ARE OFTEN... UNORTHODOX, BUT HE GETS RESULTS.
NO, MYRON IS INTEGRATING INTO THE TEAM NICELY, SO FAR AS I KNOW, BUT THIS ISN'T SOMETHING THAT CAME OUT OF OUR INTELLIGENCE DIVISION.

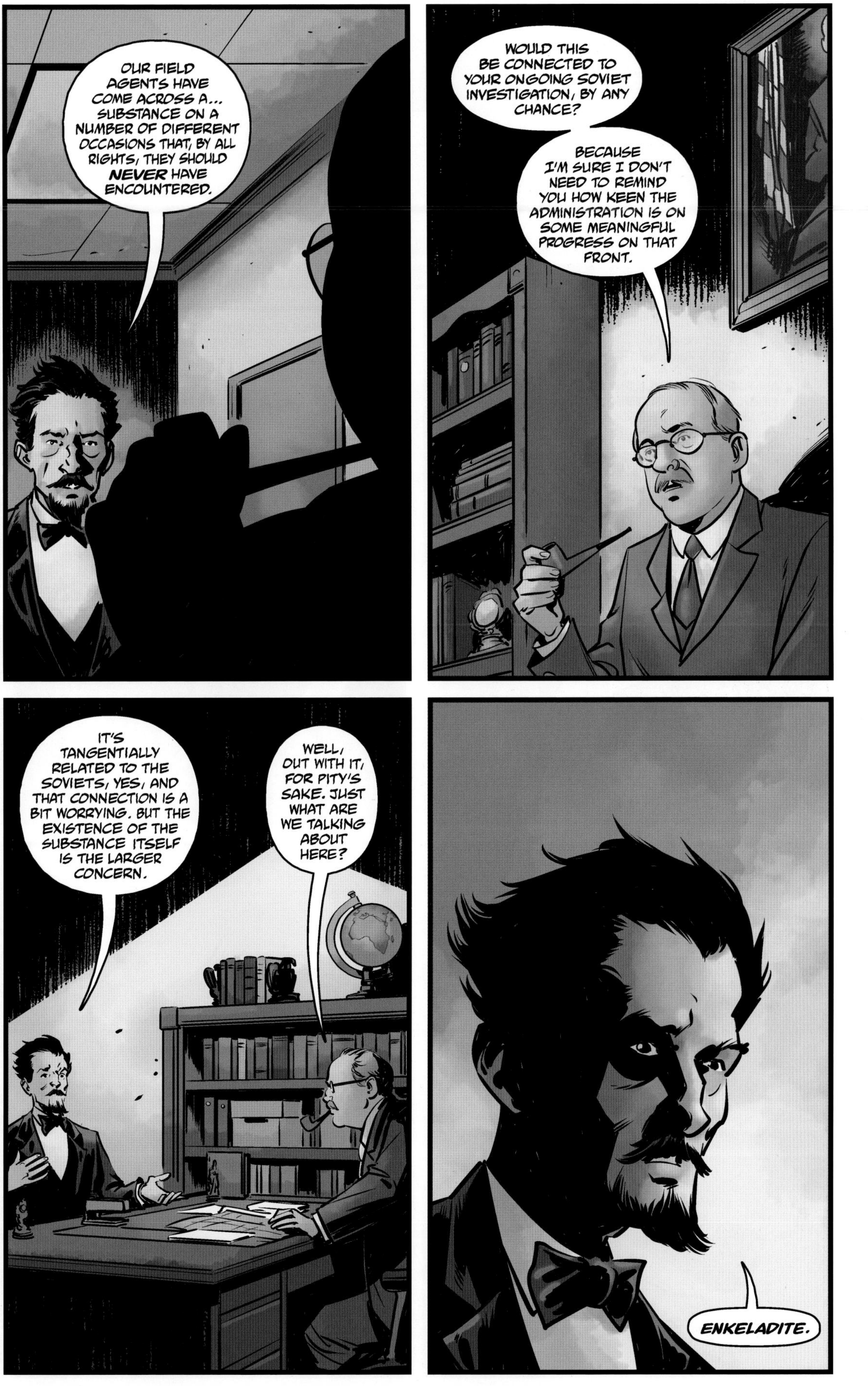
OUR FIELD AGENTS HAVE COME ACROSS A... SUBSTANCE ON A NUMBER OF DIFFERENT OCCASIONS THAT, BY ALL RIGHTS, THEY SHOULD NEVER HAVE ENCOUNTERED.
WOULD THIS BE CONNECTED TO YOUR ONGOING SOVIET INVESTIGATION, BY ANY CHANCE?
BECAUSE I'M SURE I DON'T NEED TO REMIND YOU HOW KEEN THE ADMINISTRATION IS ON SOME MEANINGFUL PROGRESS ON THAT FRONT.
IT'S TANGENTIALLY RELATED TO THE SOVIETS, YES, AND THAT CONNECTION IS A BIT WORRYING. BUT THE EXISTENCE OF THE SUBSTANCE ITSELF IS THE LARGER CONCERN.
WELL, OUT WITH IT, FOR PITY'S SAKE. JUST WHAT ARE WE TALKING ABOUT HERE?
ENKELADITE.

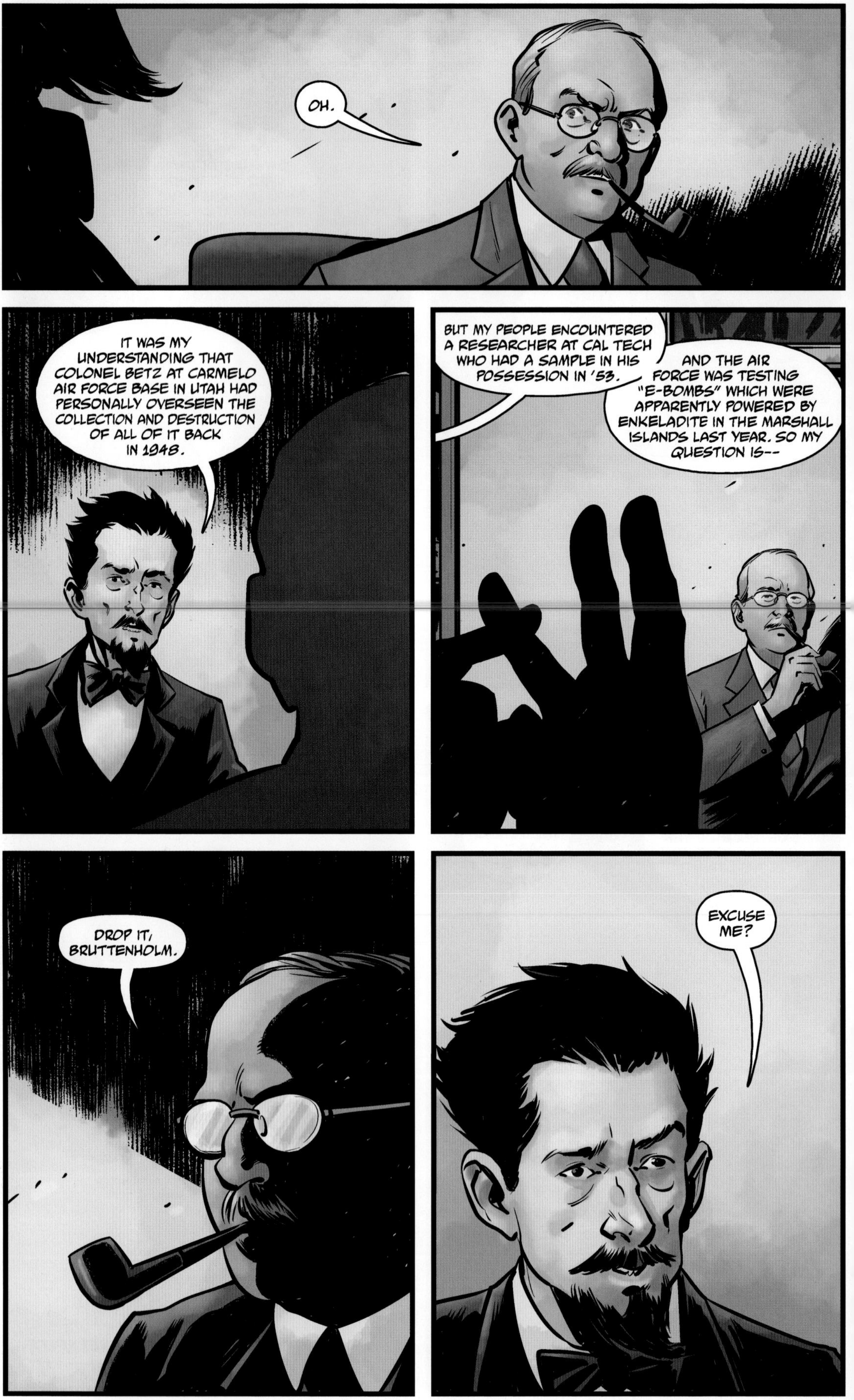
OH.
IT WAS MY UNDERSTANDING THAT COLONEL BETZ AT CARMELO AIR FORCE BASE IN UTAH HAD PERSONALLY OVERSEEN THE COLLECTION AND DESTRUCTION OF ALL OF IT BACK IN 1948.
BUT MY PEOPLE ENCOUNTERED A RESEARCHER AT CAL TECH WHO HAD A SAMPLE IN HIS POSSESSION IN '53.
AND THE AIR FORCE WAS TESTING "E-BOMBS" WHICH WERE APPARENTLY POWERED BY ENKELADITE IN THE MARSHALL ISLANDS LAST YEAR. SO MY QUESTION IS--
DROP IT, BRUTTENHOLM.
EXCUSE ME?

WE HAVE MORE PRESSING CONCERNS THAN CASES THAT WERE CLOSED YEARS AGO.

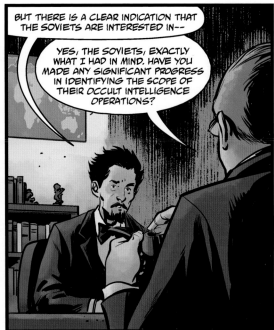

BUT THERE IS A CLEAR INDICATION THAT THE SOVIETS ARE INTERESTED IN--

YES, THE SOVIETS, EXACTLY WHAT I HAD IN MIND. HAVE YOU MADE ANY SIGNIFICANT PROGRESS IN IDENTIFYING THE SCOPE OF THEIR OCCULT INTELLIGENCE OPERATIONS?

AND I TRUST THAT YOU DON'T HAVE MYRON DOWN THERE TWIDDLING HIS THUMBS WHILE YOU OBSESS OVER OLD BUSINESS.

WITH THE TAXPAYER DOLLARS NOW BEING FUNNELED INTO YOUR BUREAU, WE EXPECT RESULTS. AND IF RESULTS AREN'T FORTHCOMING, THAT FUNDING MIGHT BE CALLED INTO QUESTION.

I ASSURE YOU, MR. LINNEBERG HAS OUR COMPLETE SUPPORT, AND THE UNDIVIDED ATTENTION OF THE AGENT THAT I'VE ASSIGNED TO ASSIST HIM.

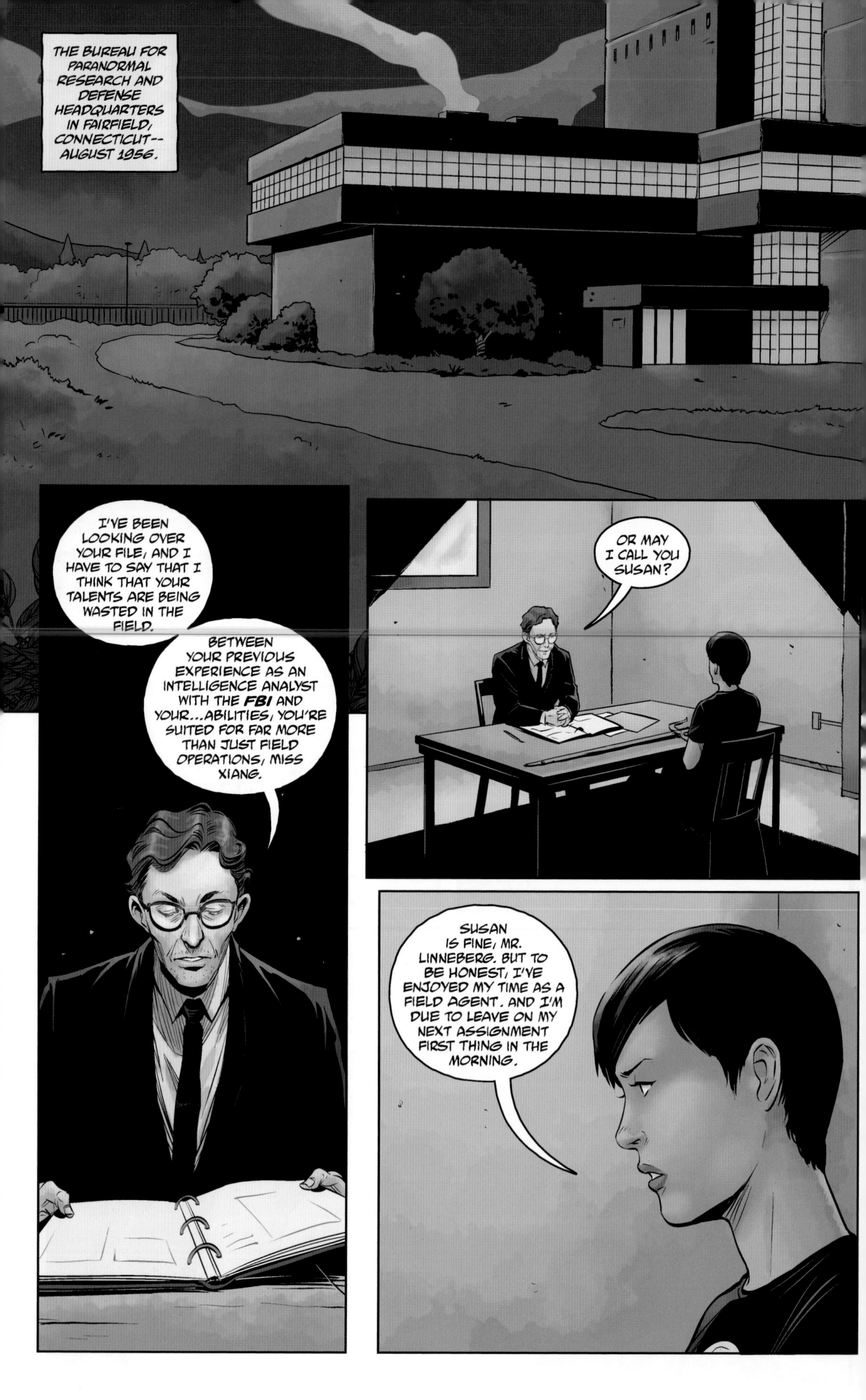
THE BUREAU FOR PARANORMAL RESEARCH AND DEFENSE HEADQUARTERS IN FAIRFIELD, CONNECTICUT-- AUGUST 1956.
I'VE BEEN LOOKING OVER YOUR FILE, AND I HAVE TO SAY THAT I THINK THAT YOUR TALENTS ARE BEING WASTED IN THE FIELD.
BETWEEN YOUR PREVIOUS EXPERIENCE AS AN INTELLIGENCE ANALYST WITH THE FBI AND YOUR...ABILITIES, YOU'RE SUITED FOR FAR MORE THAN JUST FIELD OPERATIONS, MISS XIANG.
OR MAY I CALL YOU SUSAN?
SUSAN IS FINE, MR. LINNEBERG. BUT TO BE HONEST, I'VE ENJOYED MY TIME AS A FIELD AGENT. AND I'M DUE TO LEAVE ON MY NEXT ASSIGNMENT FIRST THING IN THE MORNING.

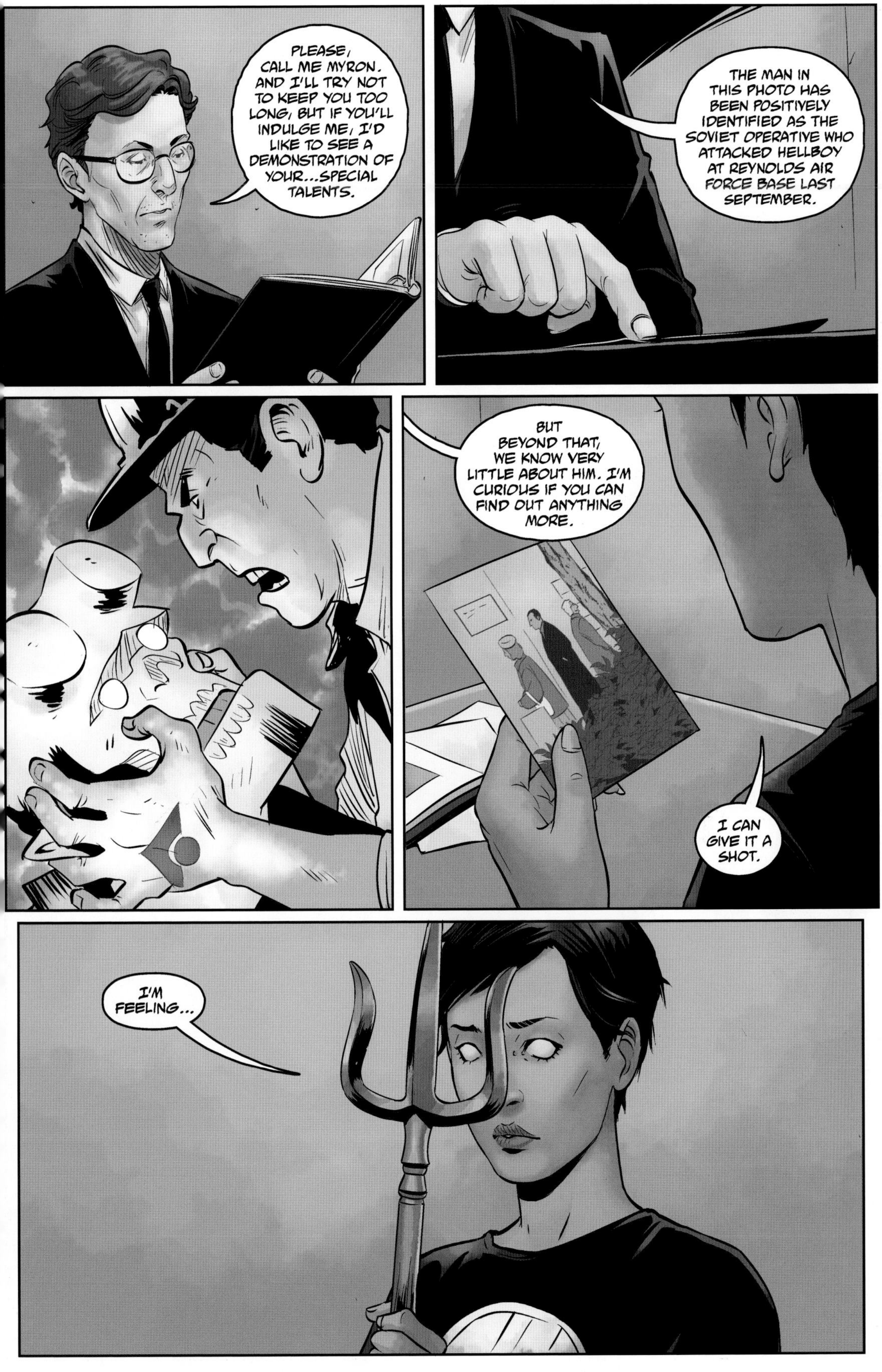
PLEASE, CALL ME MYRON. AND I'LL TRY NOT TO KEEP YOU TOO LONG, BUT IF YOU'LL INDULGE ME, I'D LIKE TO SEE A DEMONSTRATION OF YOUR...SPECIAL TALENTS.
THE MAN IN THIS PHOTO HAS BEEN POSITIVELY IDENTIFIED AS THE SOVIET OPERATIVE WHO ATTACKED HELLBOY AT REYNOLDS AIR FORCE BASE LAST SEPTEMBER.
BUT BEYOND THAT, WE KNOW VERY LITTLE ABOUT HIM. I'M CURIOUS IF YOU CAN FIND OUT ANYTHING MORE.
I CAN GIVE IT A SHOT.
I'M FEELING...

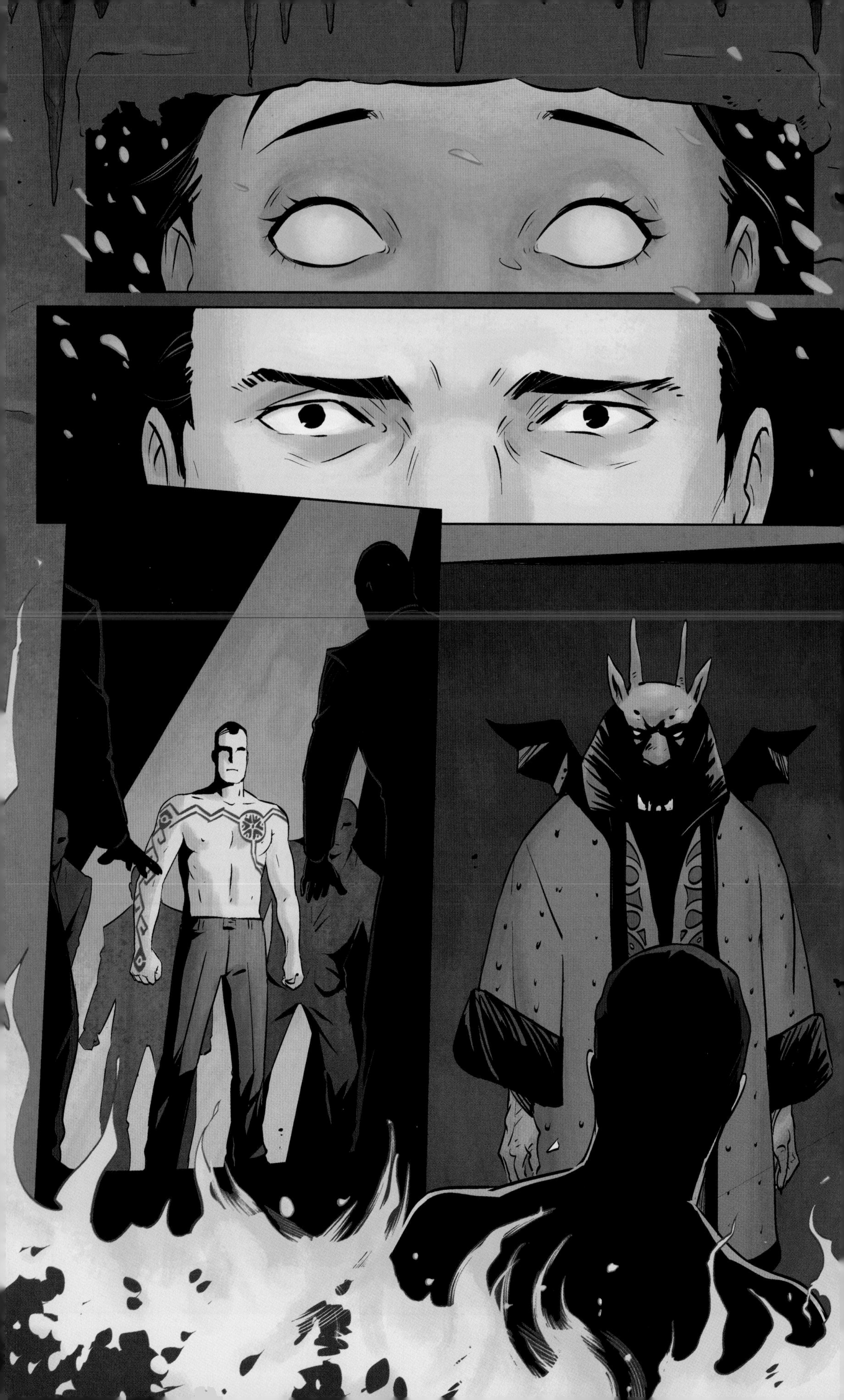

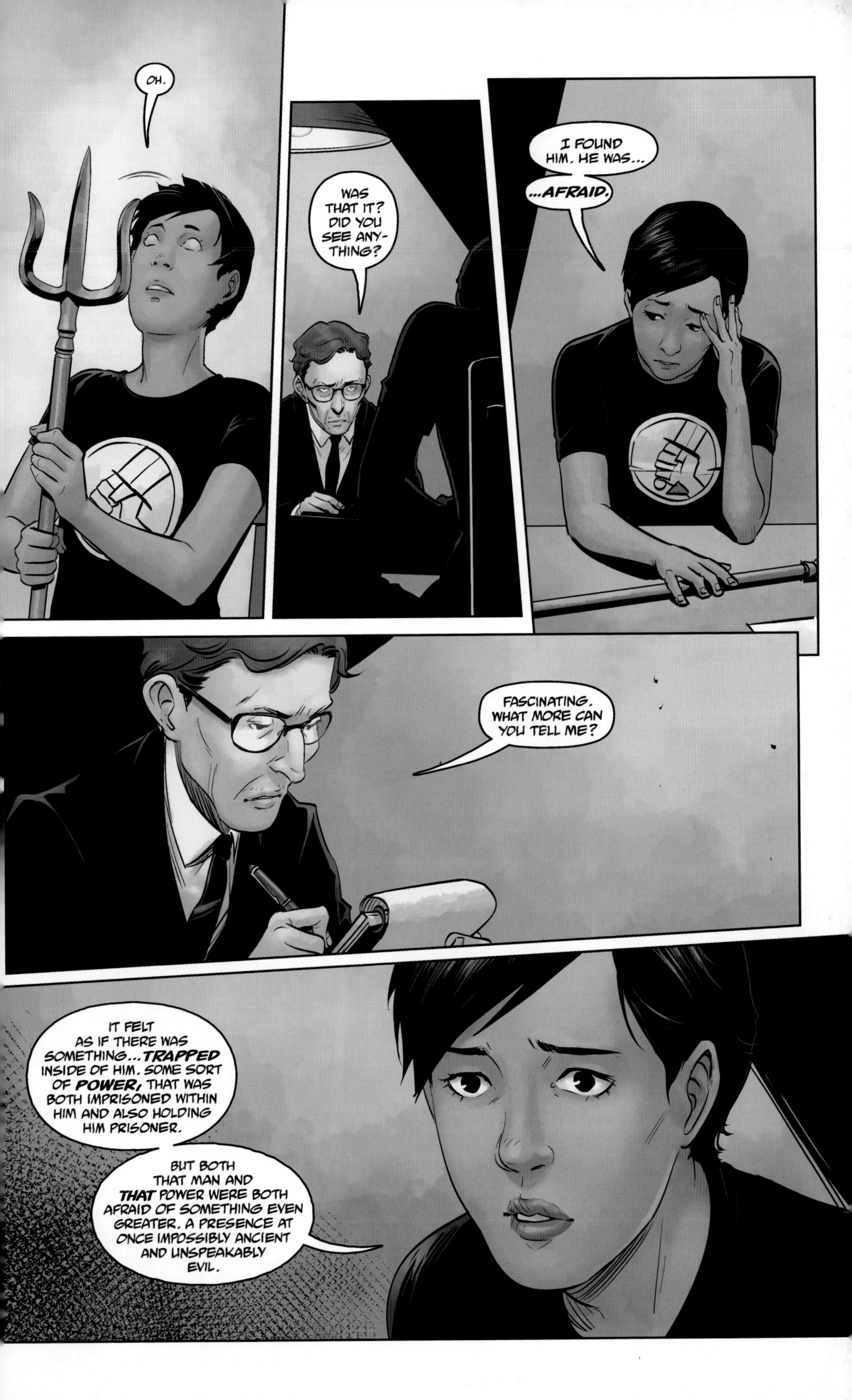

OH.
WAS THAT IT? DID YOU SEE ANYTHING?
I FOUND HIM. HE WAS...
...AFRAID.
FASCINATING. WHAT MORE CAN YOU TELL ME?
IT FELT AS IF THERE WAS SOMETHING... TRAPPED INSIDE OF HIM. SOME SORT OF POWER, THAT WAS BOTH IMPRISONED WITHIN HIM AND ALSO HOLDING HIM PRISONER.
BUT BOTH THAT MAN AND THAT POWER WERE BOTH AFRAID OF SOMETHING EVEN GREATER. A PRESENCE AT ONCE IMPOSSIBLY ANCIENT AND UNSPEAKABLY EVIL.

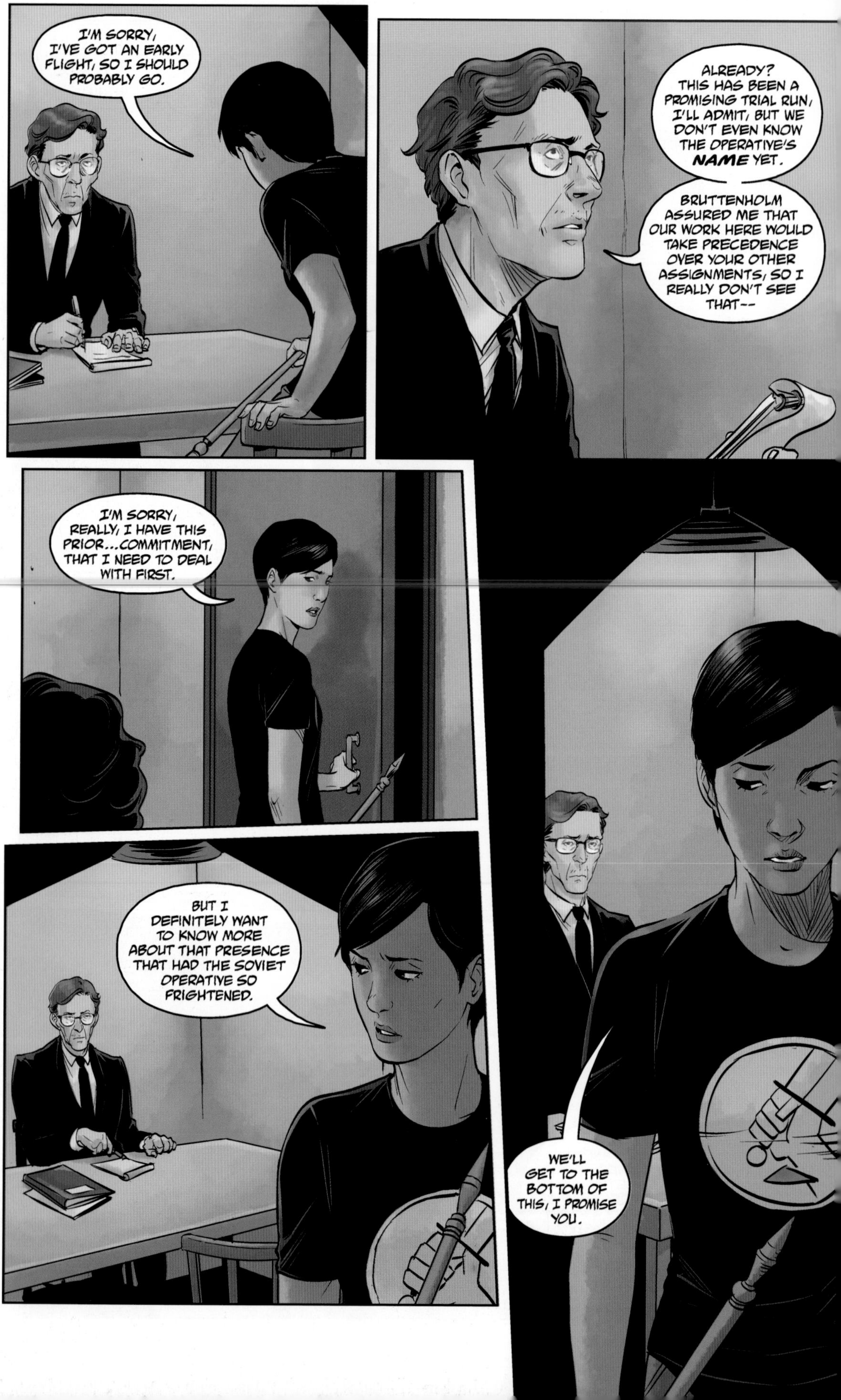

I'M SORRY, I'VE GOT AN EARLY FLIGHT, SO I SHOULD PROBABLY GO.
ALREADY? THIS HAS BEEN A PROMISING TRIAL RUN, I'LL ADMIT, BUT WE DON'T EVEN KNOW THE OPERATIVE'S **NAME** YET.
BRUTTENHOLM ASSURED ME THAT OUR WORK HERE WOULD TAKE PRECEDENCE OVER YOUR OTHER ASSIGNMENTS, SO I REALLY DON'T SEE THAT--
I'M SORRY, REALLY, I HAVE THIS PRIOR...COMMITMENT, THAT I NEED TO DEAL WITH FIRST.
BUT I DEFINITELY WANT TO KNOW MORE ABOUT THAT PRESENCE THAT HAD THE SOVIET OPERATIVE SO FRIGHTENED.
WE'LL GET TO THE BOTTOM OF THIS, I PROMISE YOU.

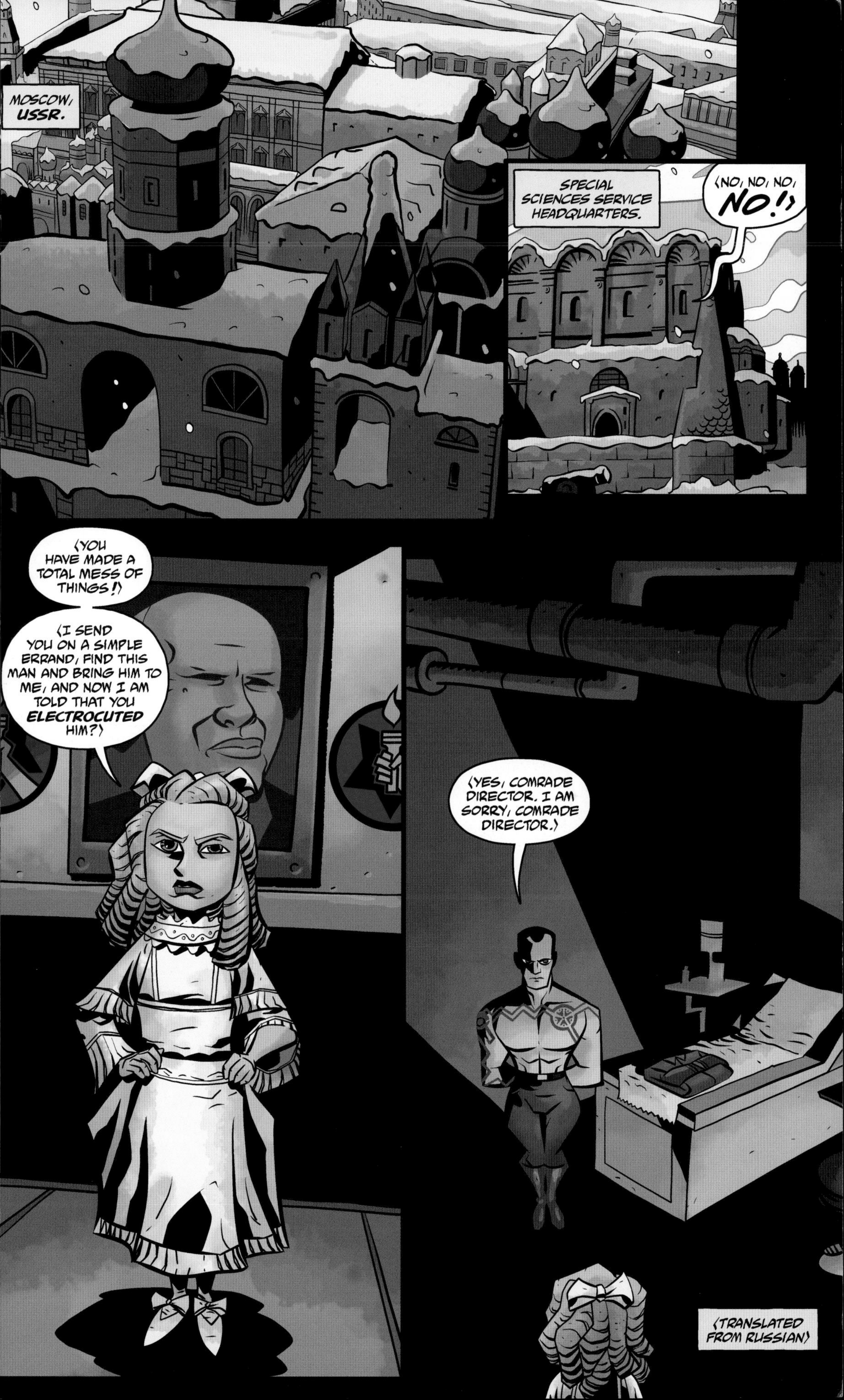
MOSCOW, USSR.
SPECIAL SCIENCES SERVICE HEADQUARTERS.
‹NO, NO, NO, NO!›
‹YOU HAVE MADE A TOTAL MESS OF THINGS!›
‹I SEND YOU ON A SIMPLE ERRAND, FIND THIS MAN AND BRING HIM TO ME, AND NOW I AM TOLD THAT YOU ELECTROCUTED HIM?›
‹YES, COMRADE DIRECTOR. I AM SORRY, COMRADE DIRECTOR.›
‹TRANSLATED FROM RUSSIAN›

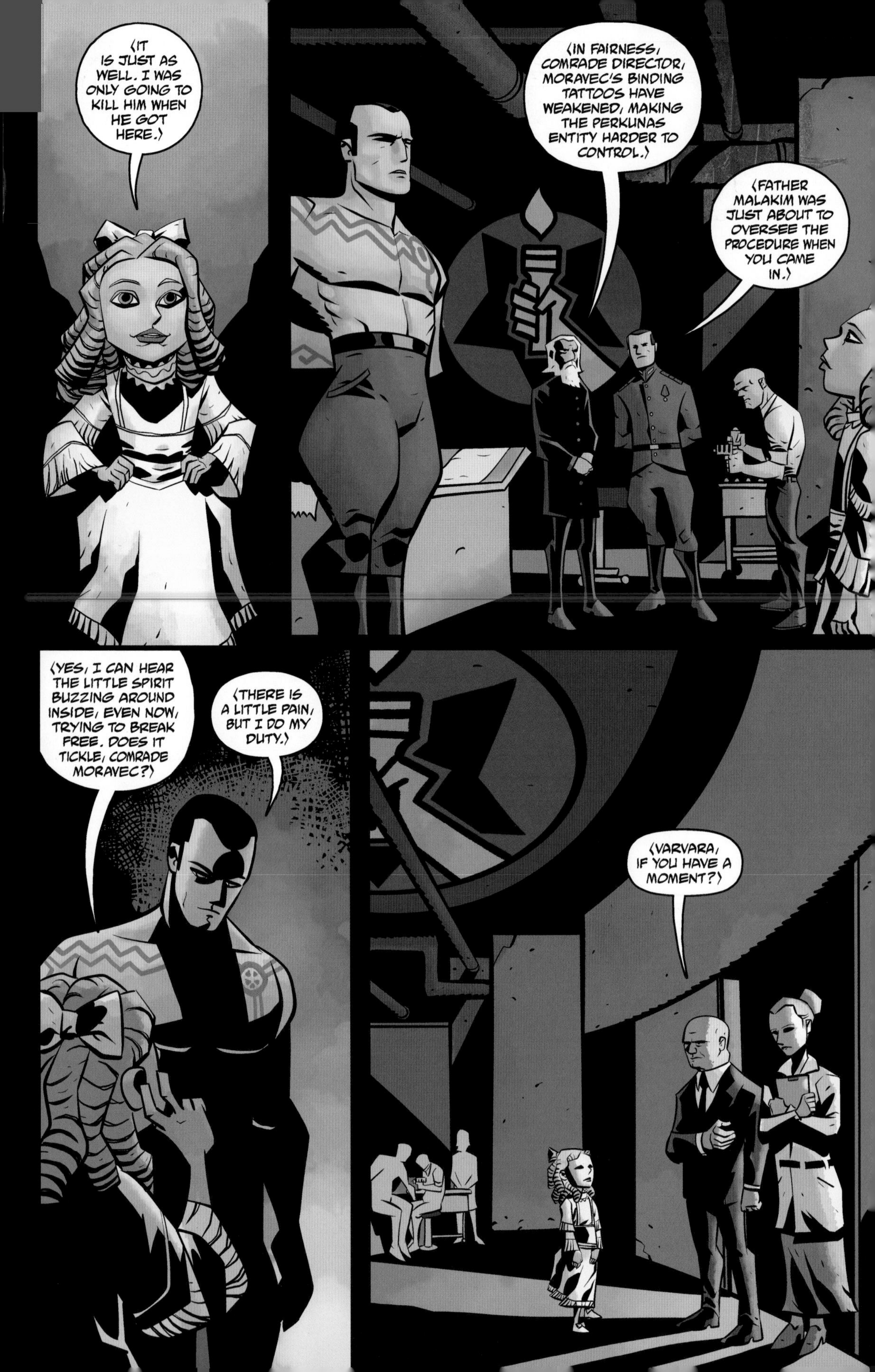
⟨IT IS JUST AS WELL. I WAS ONLY GOING TO KILL HIM WHEN HE GOT HERE.⟩
⟨IN FAIRNESS, COMRADE DIRECTOR, MORAVEC'S BINDING TATTOOS HAVE WEAKENED, MAKING THE PERKUNAS ENTITY HARDER TO CONTROL.⟩
⟨FATHER MALAKIM WAS JUST ABOUT TO OVERSEE THE PROCEDURE WHEN YOU CAME IN.⟩
⟨YES, I CAN HEAR THE LITTLE SPIRIT BUZZING AROUND INSIDE, EVEN NOW, TRYING TO BREAK FREE. DOES IT TICKLE, COMRADE MORAVEC?⟩
⟨THERE IS A LITTLE PAIN, BUT I DO MY DUTY.⟩
⟨VARVARA, IF YOU HAVE A MOMENT?⟩

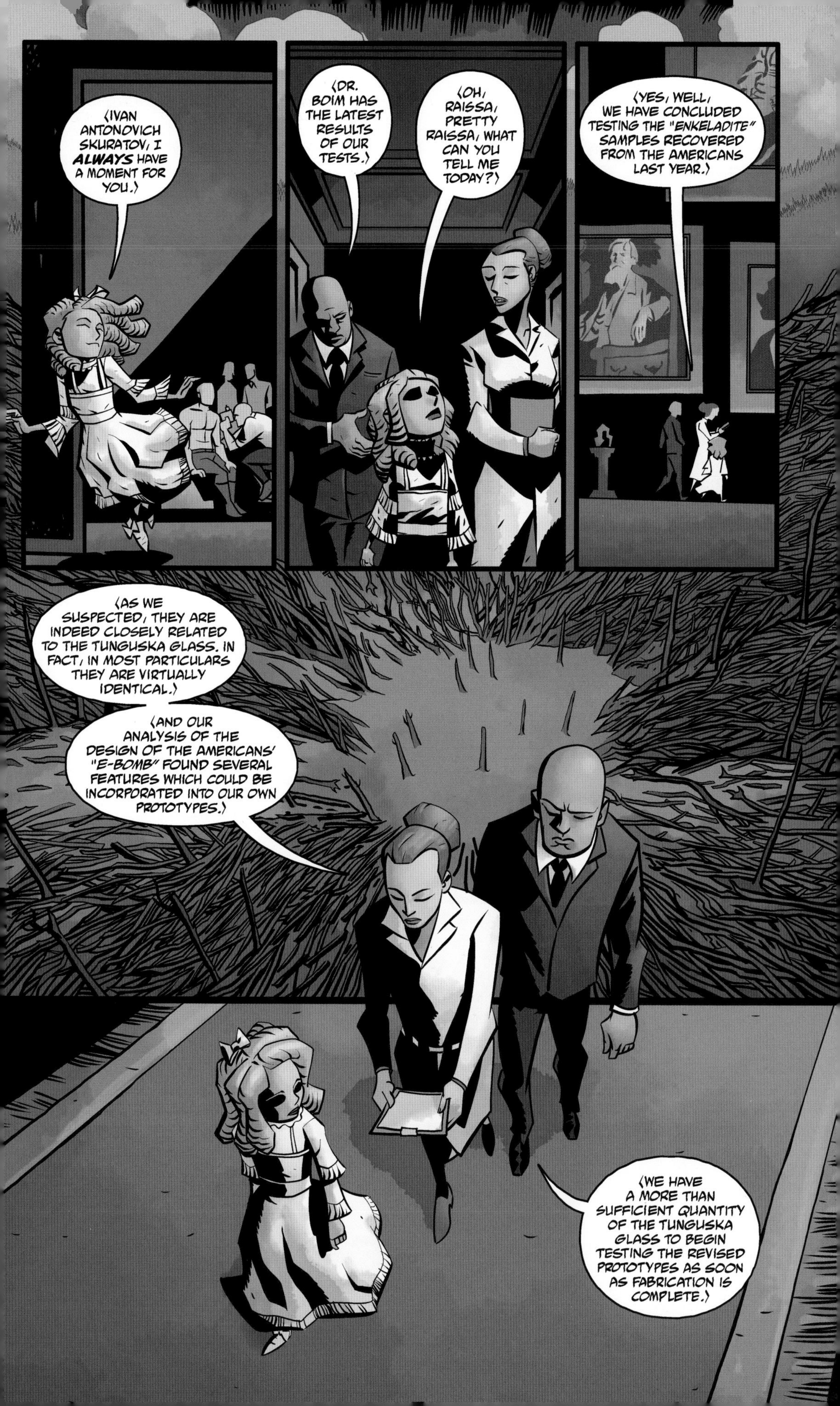
⟨IVAN ANTONOVICH SKURATOV, I ALWAYS HAVE A MOMENT FOR YOU.⟩
⟨DR. BOIM HAS THE LATEST RESULTS OF OUR TESTS.⟩
⟨OH, RAISSA, PRETTY RAISSA, WHAT CAN YOU TELL ME TODAY?⟩
⟨YES, WELL, WE HAVE CONCLUDED TESTING THE "ENKELADITE" SAMPLES RECOVERED FROM THE AMERICANS LAST YEAR.⟩
⟨AS WE SUSPECTED, THEY ARE INDEED CLOSELY RELATED TO THE TUNGUSKA GLASS. IN FACT, IN MOST PARTICULARS THEY ARE VIRTUALLY IDENTICAL.⟩
⟨AND OUR ANALYSIS OF THE DESIGN OF THE AMERICANS' "E-BOMB" FOUND SEVERAL FEATURES WHICH COULD BE INCORPORATED INTO OUR OWN PROTOTYPES.⟩
⟨WE HAVE A MORE THAN SUFFICIENT QUANTITY OF THE TUNGUSKA GLASS TO BEGIN TESTING THE REVISED PROTOTYPES AS SOON AS FABRICATION IS COMPLETE.⟩

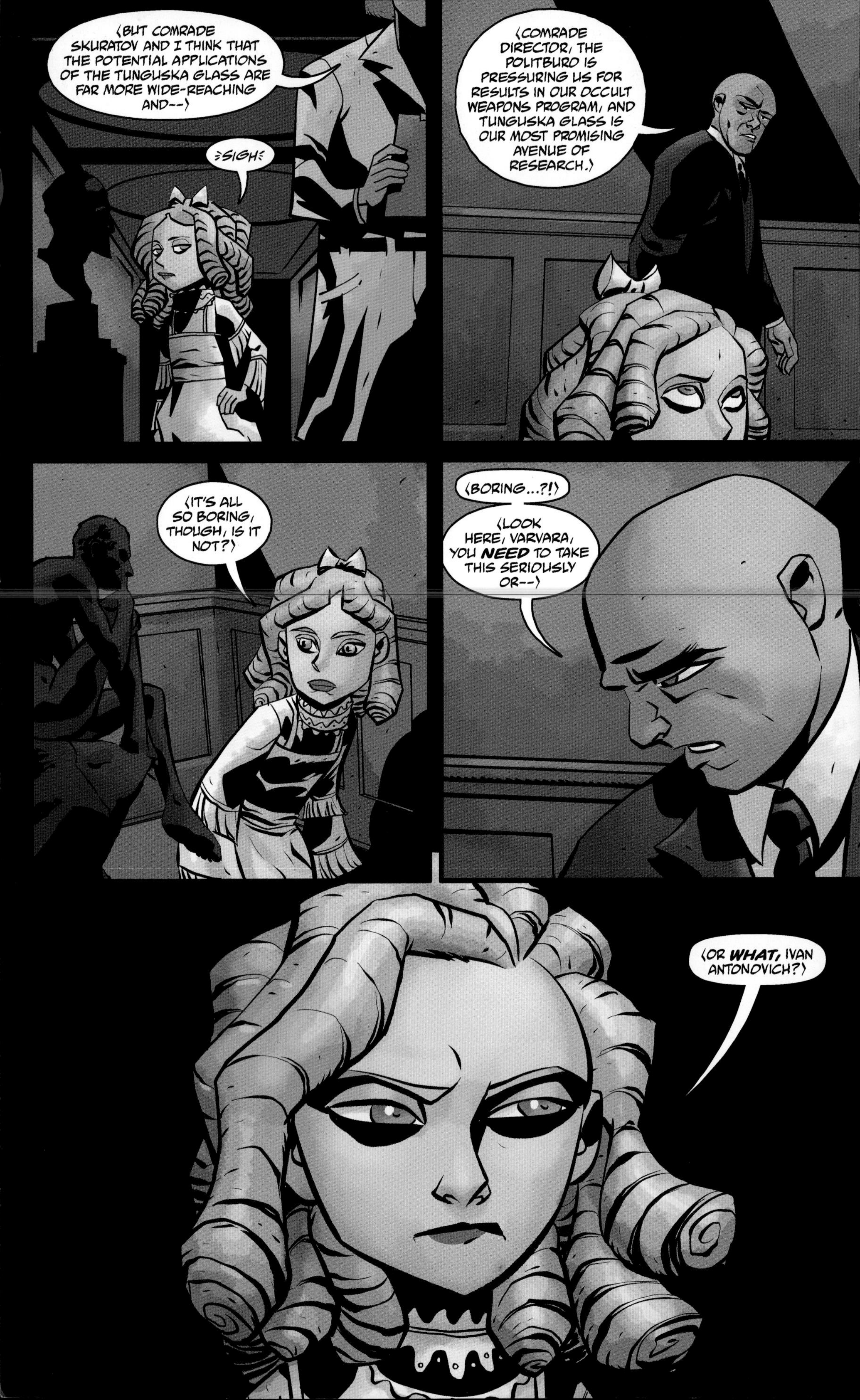
⟨BUT COMRADE SKURATOV AND I THINK THAT THE POTENTIAL APPLICATIONS OF THE TUNGUSKA GLASS ARE FAR MORE WIDE-REACHING AND--⟩
⟨SIGH⟩
⟨COMRADE DIRECTOR, THE POLITBURO IS PRESSURING US FOR RESULTS IN OUR OCCULT WEAPONS PROGRAM, AND TUNGUSKA GLASS IS OUR MOST PROMISING AVENUE OF RESEARCH.⟩
⟨IT'S ALL SO BORING, THOUGH, IS IT NOT?⟩
⟨BORING...?!⟩
⟨LOOK HERE, VARVARA, YOU **NEED** TO TAKE THIS SERIOUSLY OR--⟩
⟨OR **WHAT,** IVAN ANTONOVICH?⟩

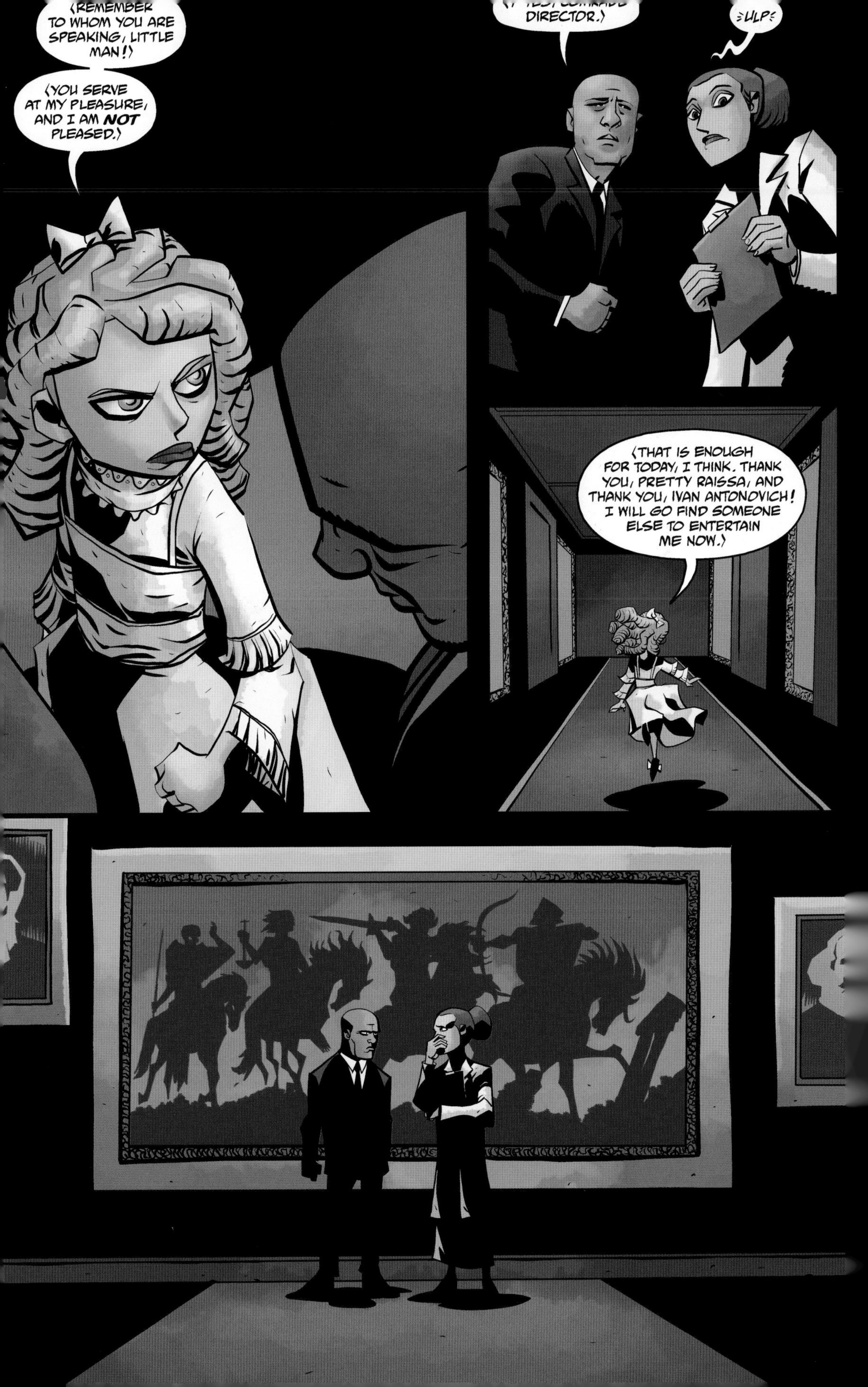

‹REMEMBER TO WHOM YOU ARE SPEAKING, LITTLE MAN!›
‹YOU SERVE AT MY PLEASURE, AND I AM **NOT** PLEASED.›
DIRECTOR.›
ULP
‹THAT IS ENOUGH FOR TODAY, I THINK. THANK YOU, PRETTY RAISSA, AND THANK YOU, IVAN ANTONOVICH! I WILL GO FIND SOMEONE ELSE TO ENTERTAIN ME NOW.›

CHAPTER TWO

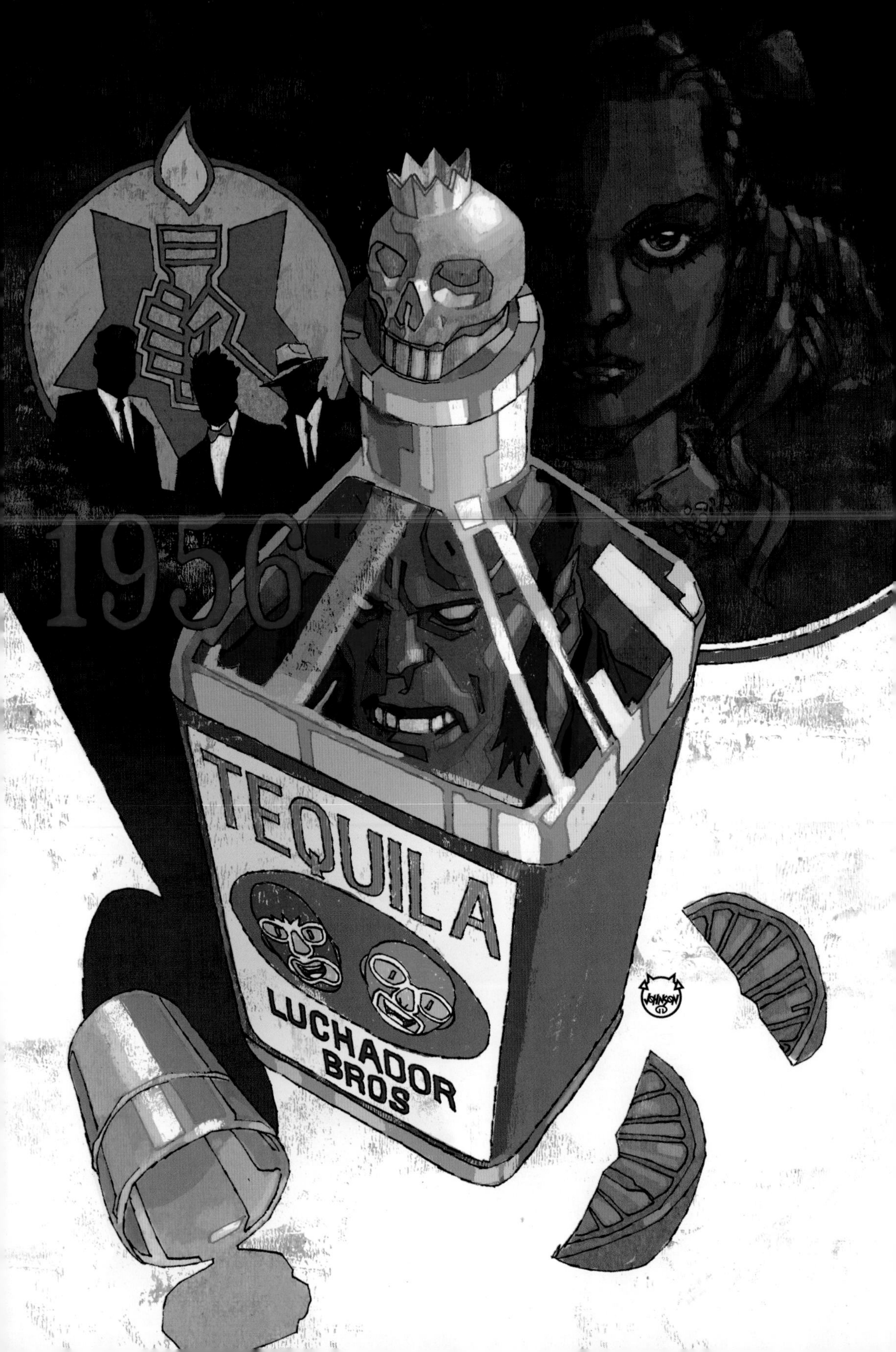
1956
TEQUILA
LUCHADOR BROS
JOHNSON

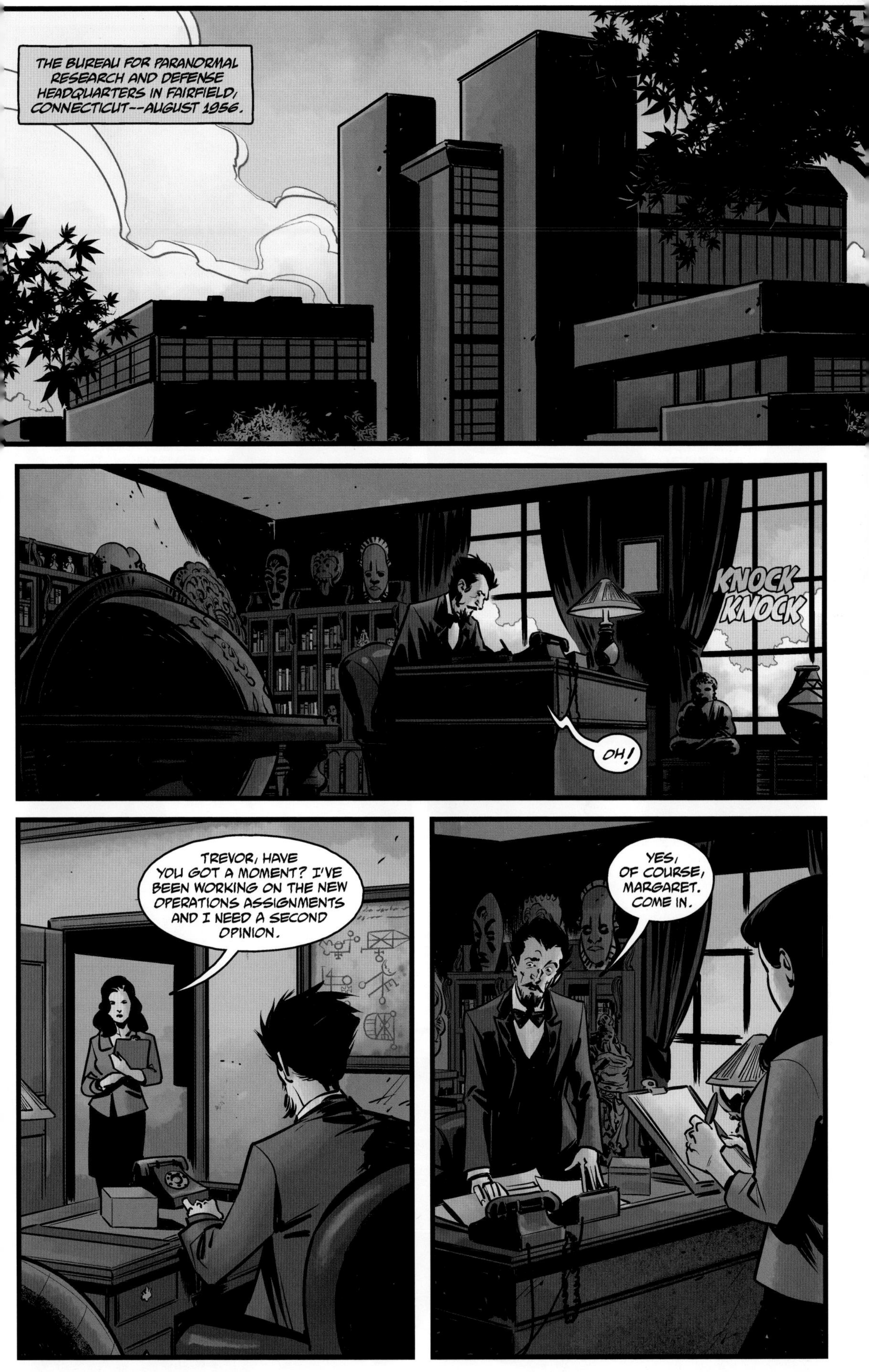
THE BUREAU FOR PARANORMAL RESEARCH AND DEFENSE HEADQUARTERS IN FAIRFIELD, CONNECTICUT--AUGUST 1956.
KNOCK KNOCK
OH!
TREVOR, HAVE YOU GOT A MOMENT? I'VE BEEN WORKING ON THE NEW OPERATIONS ASSIGNMENTS AND I NEED A SECOND OPINION.
YES, OF COURSE, MARGARET. COME IN.

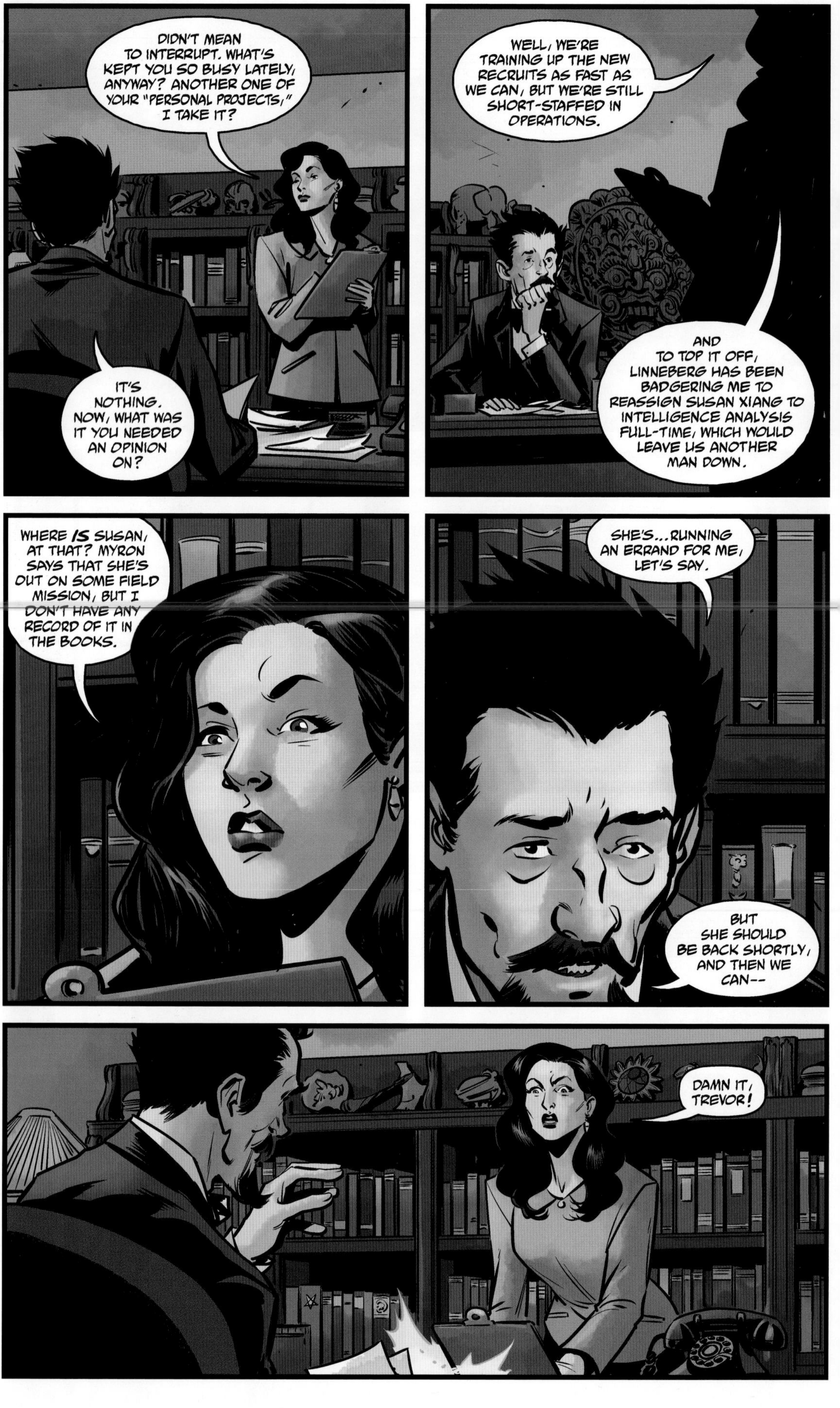
DIDN'T MEAN TO INTERRUPT. WHAT'S KEPT YOU SO BUSY LATELY, ANYWAY? ANOTHER ONE OF YOUR "PERSONAL PROJECTS," I TAKE IT?
IT'S NOTHING. NOW, WHAT WAS IT YOU NEEDED AN OPINION ON?
WELL, WE'RE TRAINING UP THE NEW RECRUITS AS FAST AS WE CAN, BUT WE'RE STILL SHORT-STAFFED IN OPERATIONS.
AND TO TOP IT OFF, LINNEBERG HAS BEEN BADGERING ME TO REASSIGN SUSAN XIANG TO INTELLIGENCE ANALYSIS FULL-TIME, WHICH WOULD LEAVE US ANOTHER MAN DOWN.
WHERE IS SUSAN, AT THAT? MYRON SAYS THAT SHE'S OUT ON SOME FIELD MISSION, BUT I DON'T HAVE ANY RECORD OF IT IN THE BOOKS.
SHE'S...RUNNING AN ERRAND FOR ME, LET'S SAY.
BUT SHE SHOULD BE BACK SHORTLY, AND THEN WE CAN--
DAMN IT, TREVOR!

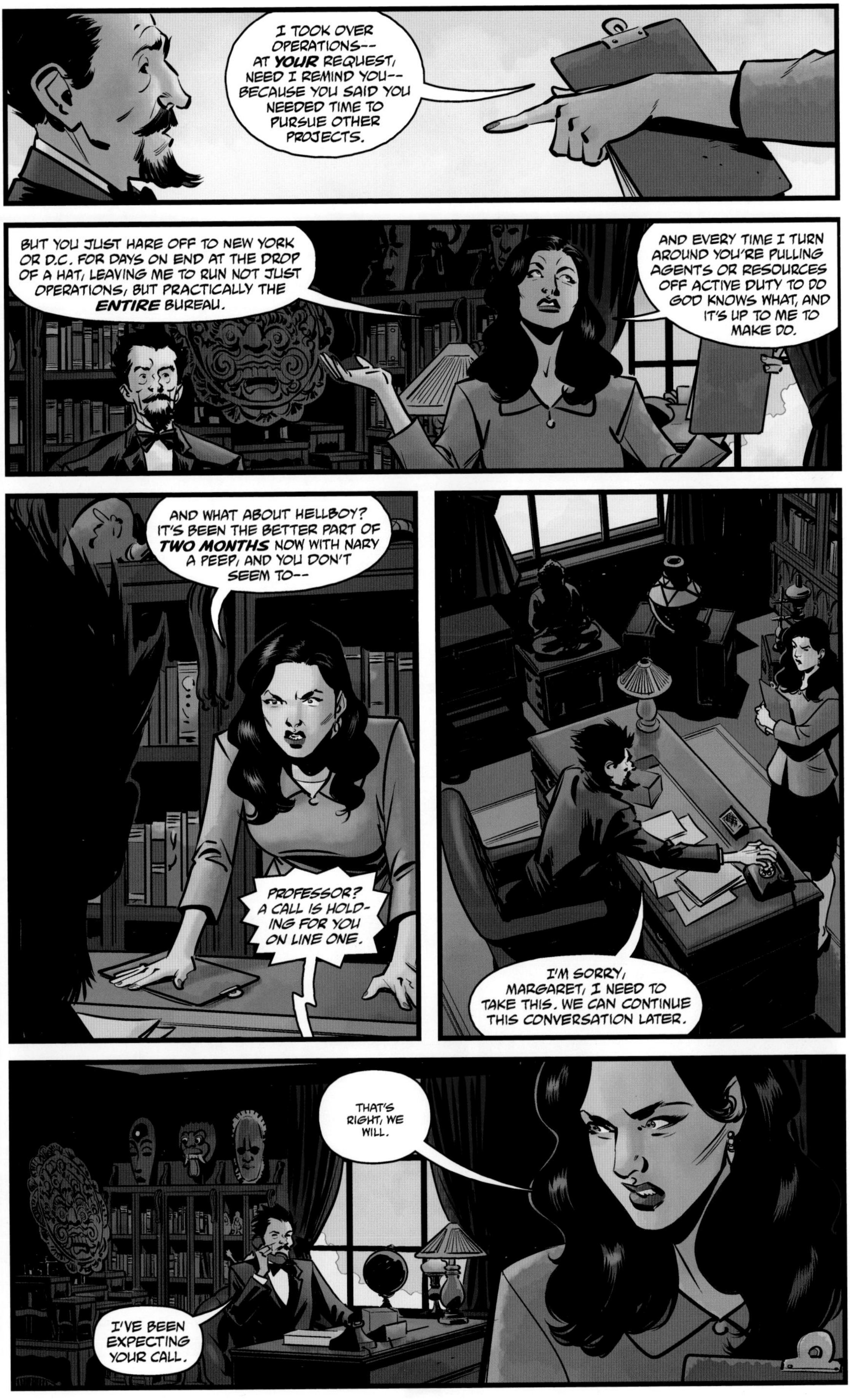
I TOOK OVER OPERATIONS-- AT YOUR REQUEST, NEED I REMIND YOU-- BECAUSE YOU SAID YOU NEEDED TIME TO PURSUE OTHER PROJECTS.
BUT YOU JUST HARE OFF TO NEW YORK OR D.C. FOR DAYS ON END AT THE DROP OF A HAT, LEAVING ME TO RUN NOT JUST OPERATIONS, BUT PRACTICALLY THE ENTIRE BUREAU.
AND EVERY TIME I TURN AROUND YOU'RE PULLING AGENTS OR RESOURCES OFF ACTIVE DUTY TO DO GOD KNOWS WHAT, AND IT'S UP TO ME TO MAKE DO.
AND WHAT ABOUT HELLBOY? IT'S BEEN THE BETTER PART OF TWO MONTHS NOW WITH NARY A PEEP, AND YOU DON'T SEEM TO--
PROFESSOR? A CALL IS HOLDING FOR YOU ON LINE ONE.
I'M SORRY, MARGARET, I NEED TO TAKE THIS. WE CAN CONTINUE THIS CONVERSATION LATER.
THAT'S RIGHT, WE WILL.
I'VE BEEN EXPECTING YOUR CALL.

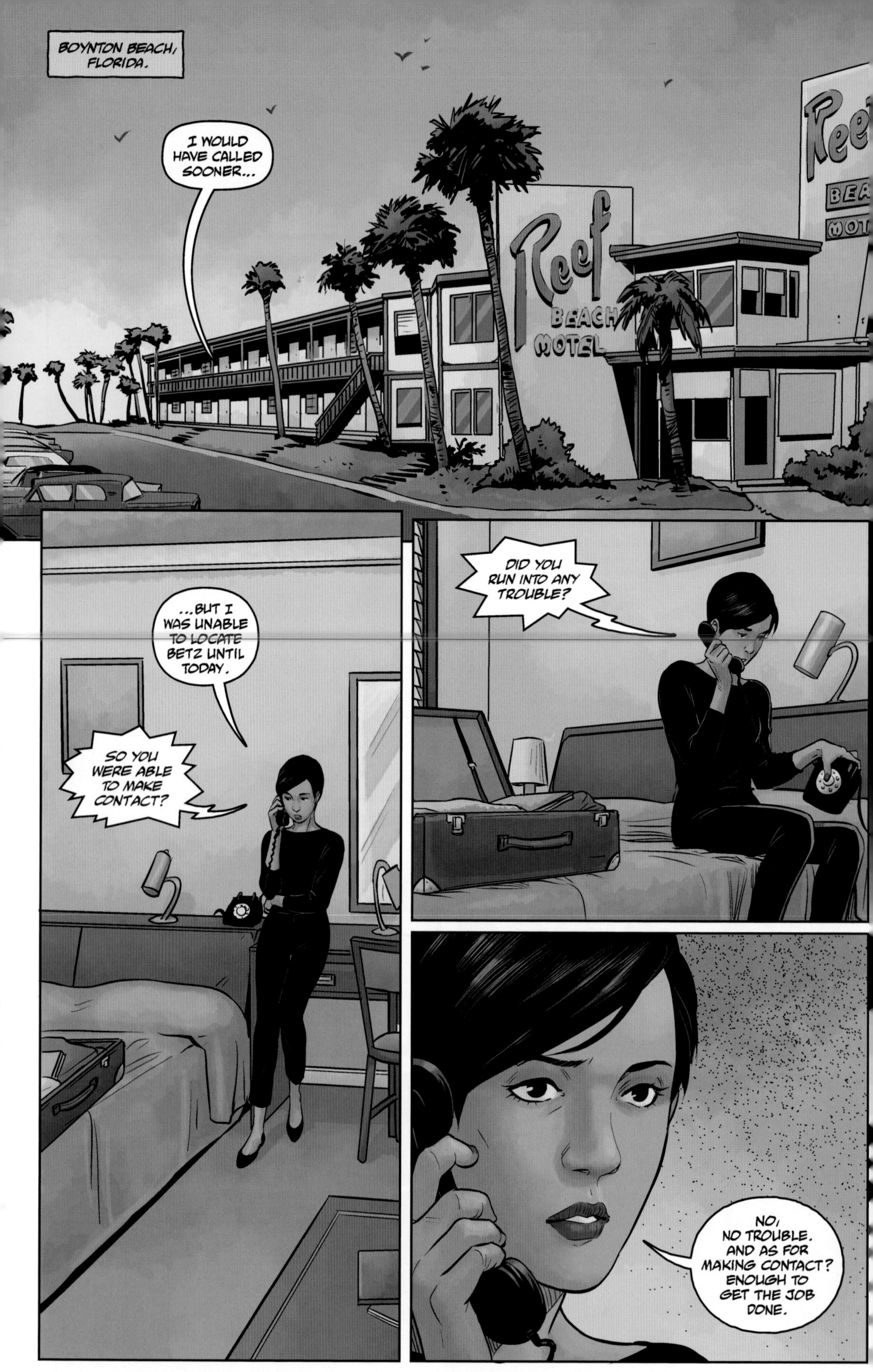
BOYNTON BEACH, FLORIDA.
I WOULD HAVE CALLED SOONER...
Reef BEACH MOTEL
...BUT I WAS UNABLE TO LOCATE BETZ UNTIL TODAY.
SO YOU WERE ABLE TO MAKE CONTACT?
DID YOU RUN INTO ANY TROUBLE?
NO, NO TROUBLE. AND AS FOR MAKING CONTACT? ENOUGH TO GET THE JOB DONE.

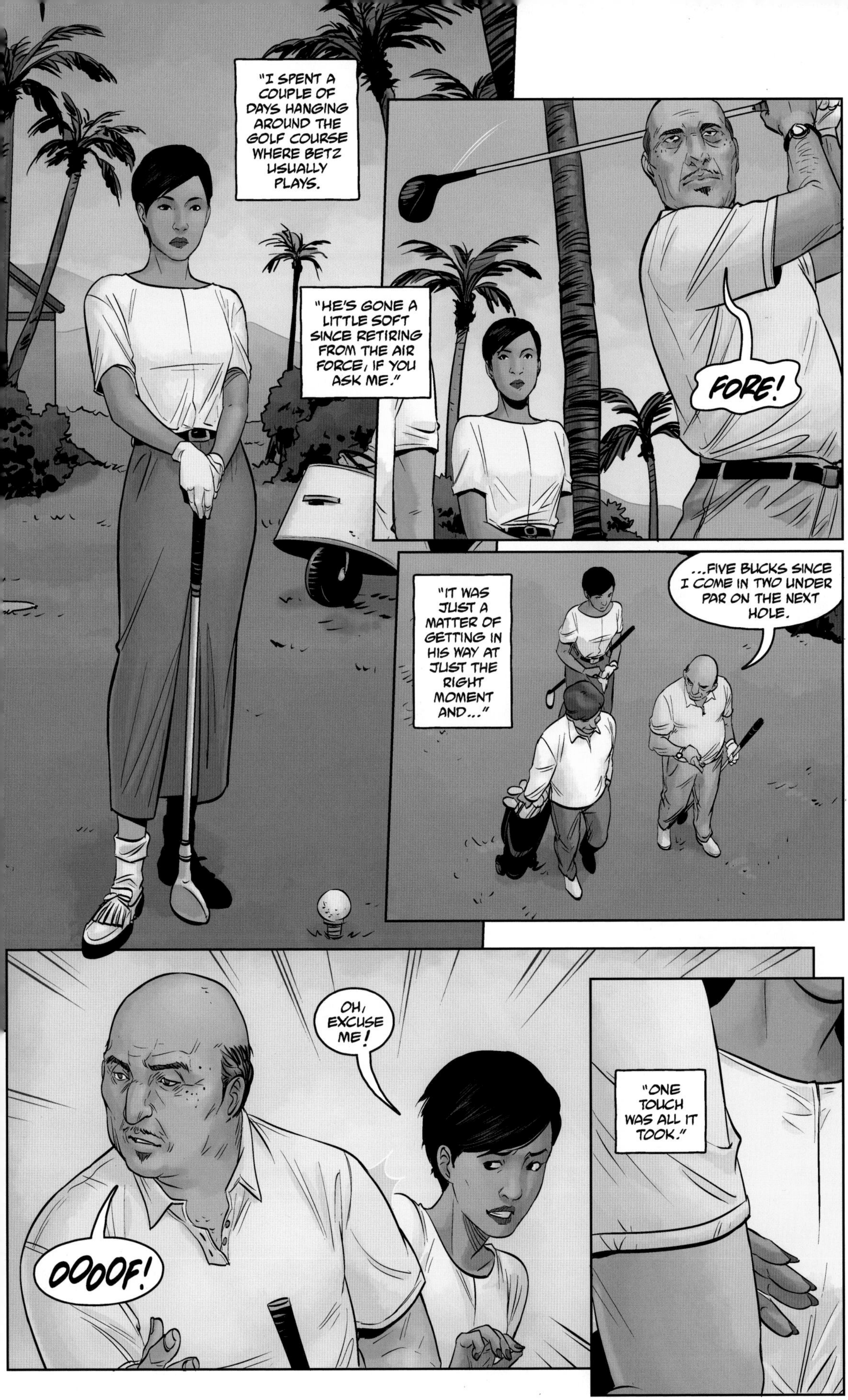
"I SPENT A COUPLE OF DAYS HANGING AROUND THE GOLF COURSE WHERE BETZ USUALLY PLAYS.
"HE'S GONE A LITTLE SOFT SINCE RETIRING FROM THE AIR FORCE, IF YOU ASK ME."
FORE!
"IT WAS JUST A MATTER OF GETTING IN HIS WAY AT JUST THE RIGHT MOMENT AND..."
...FIVE BUCKS SINCE I COME IN TWO UNDER PAR ON THE NEXT HOLE.
OH, EXCUSE ME!
OOOOF!
"ONE TOUCH WAS ALL IT TOOK."

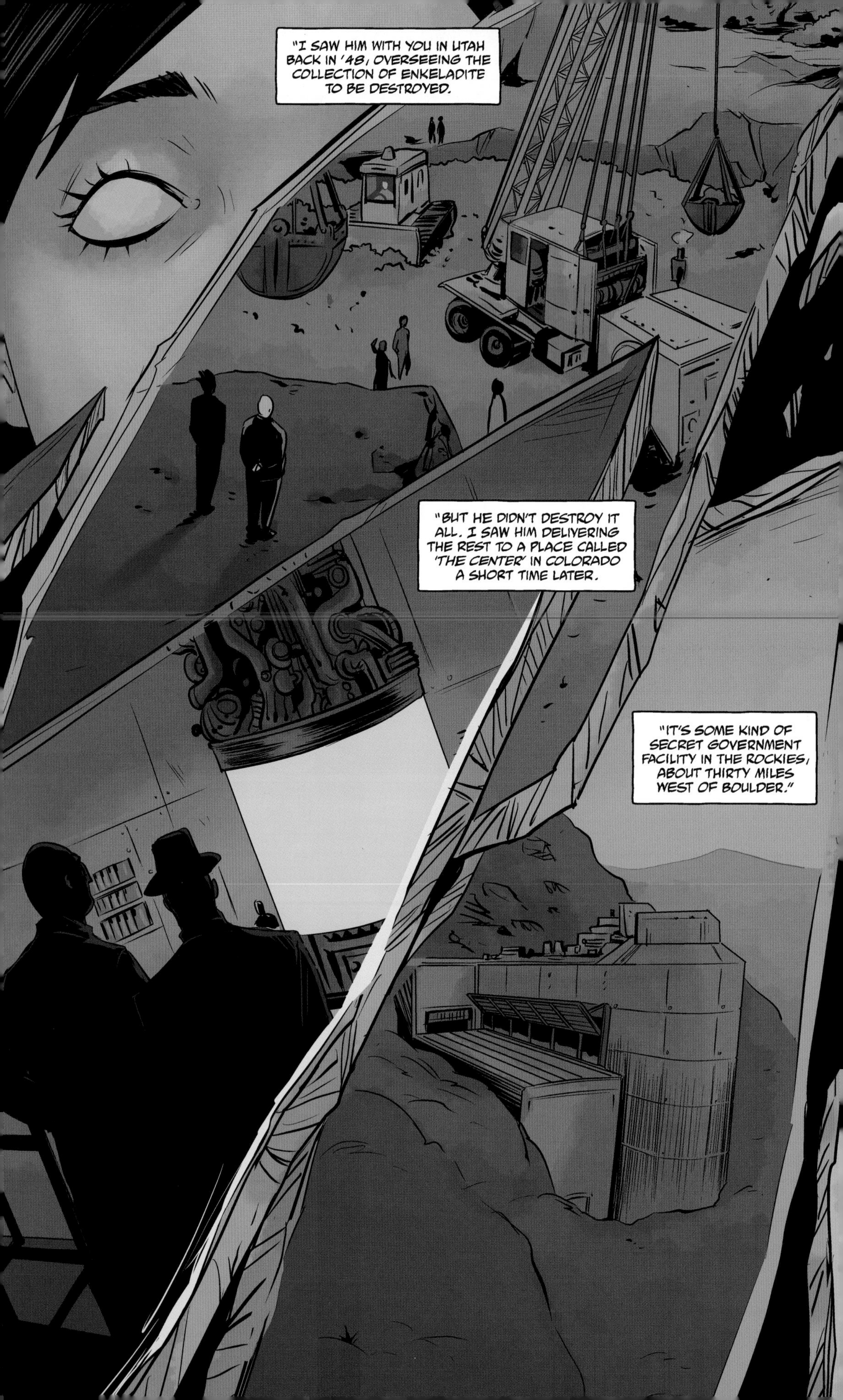
"I SAW HIM WITH YOU IN UTAH BACK IN '48, OVERSEEING THE COLLECTION OF ENKELADITE TO BE DESTROYED.
"BUT HE DIDN'T DESTROY IT ALL. I SAW HIM DELIVERING THE REST TO A PLACE CALLED 'THE CENTER' IN COLORADO A SHORT TIME LATER.
"IT'S SOME KIND OF SECRET GOVERNMENT FACILITY IN THE ROCKIES, ABOUT THIRTY MILES WEST OF BOULDER."

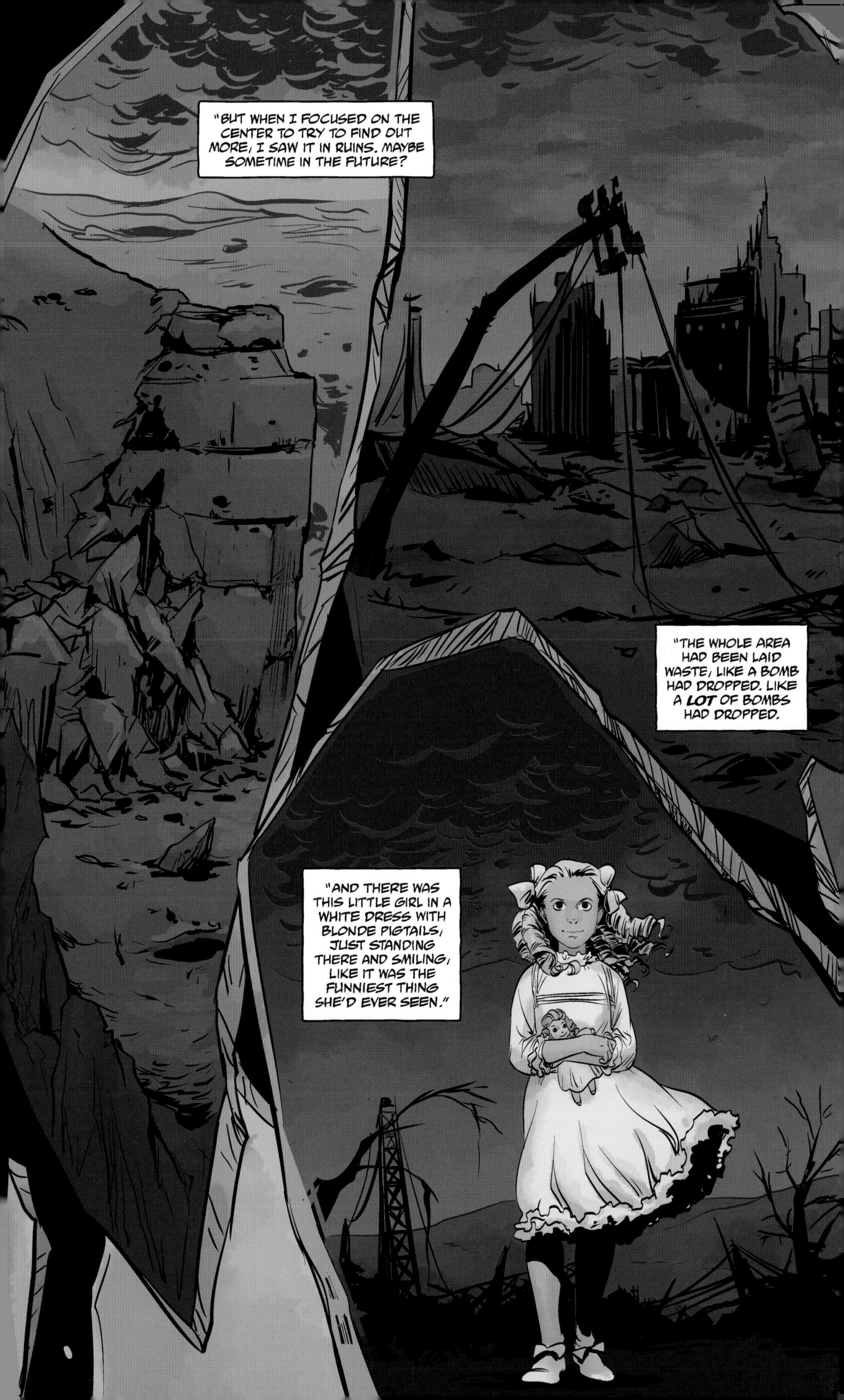
"BUT WHEN I FOCUSED ON THE CENTER TO TRY TO FIND OUT MORE, I SAW IT IN RUINS. MAYBE SOMETIME IN THE FUTURE?
"THE WHOLE AREA HAD BEEN LAID WASTE, LIKE A BOMB HAD DROPPED. LIKE A **LOT** OF BOMBS HAD DROPPED.
"AND THERE WAS THIS LITTLE GIRL IN A WHITE DRESS WITH BLONDE PIGTAILS, JUST STANDING THERE AND SMILING, LIKE IT WAS THE FUNNIEST THING SHE'D EVER SEEN."

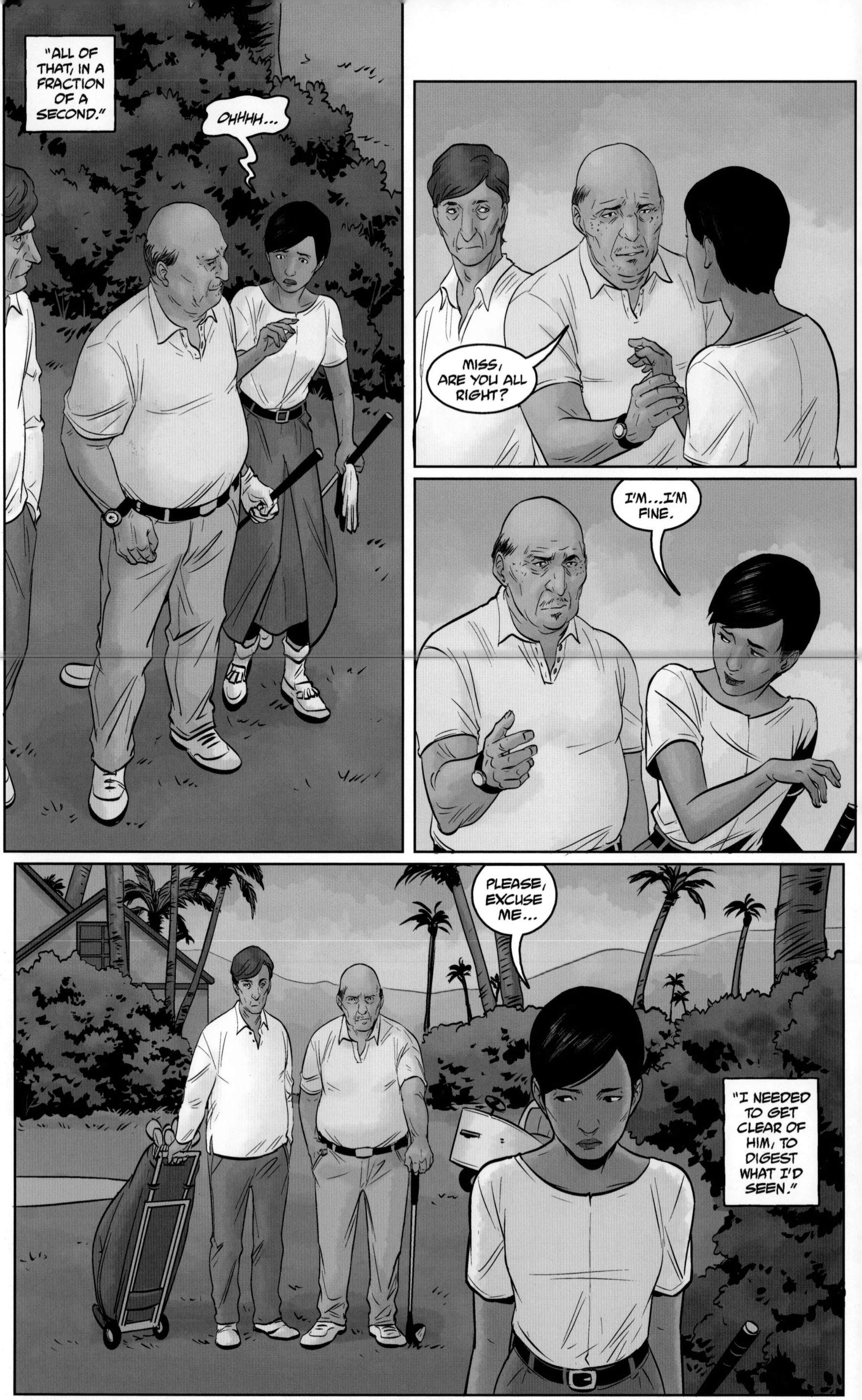
"ALL OF THAT, IN A FRACTION OF A SECOND."
OHHHH...
MISS, ARE YOU ALL RIGHT?
I'M...I'M FINE.
PLEASE, EXCUSE ME...
"I NEEDED TO GET CLEAR OF HIM, TO DIGEST WHAT I'D SEEN."

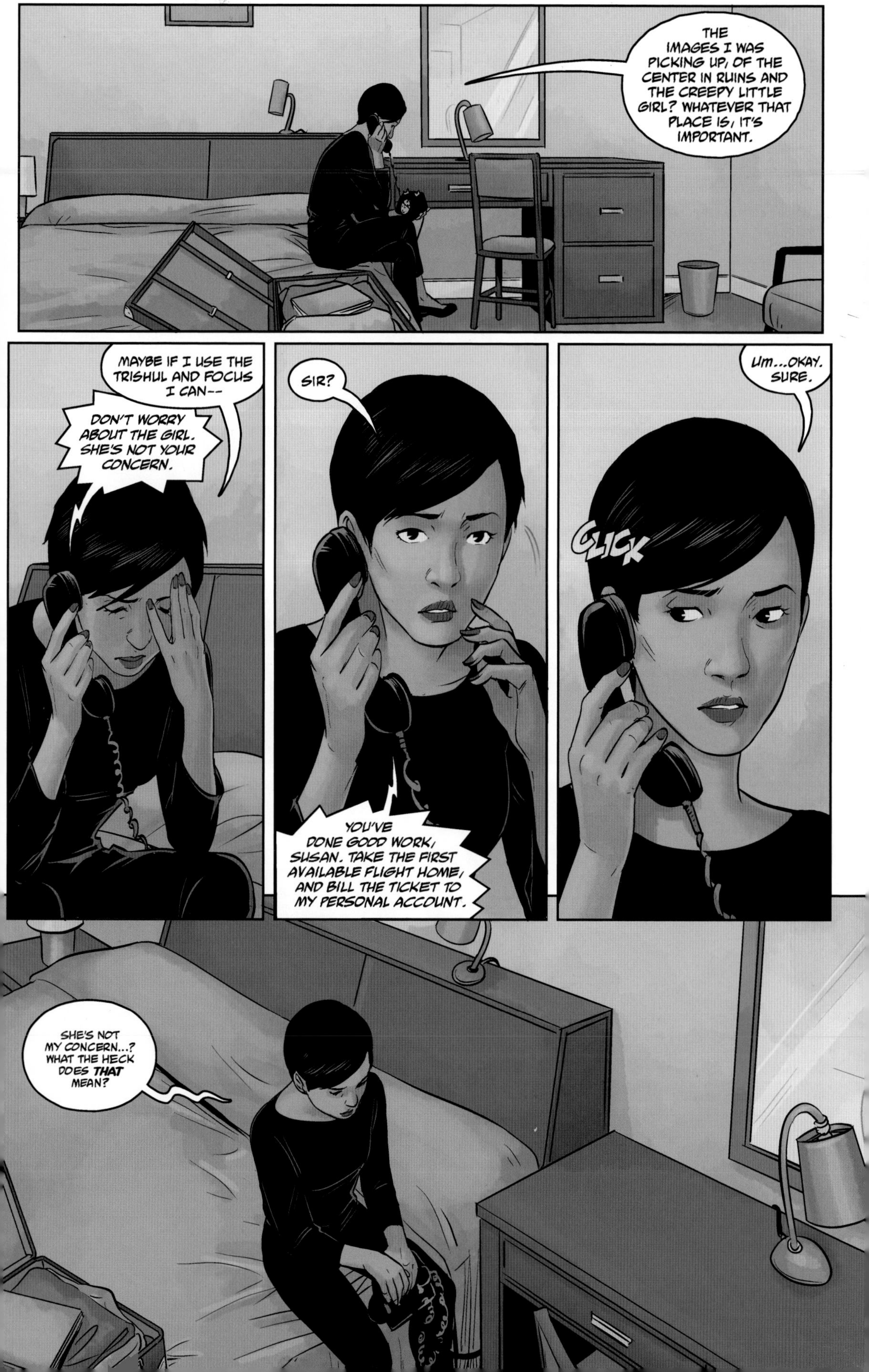
THE IMAGES I WAS PICKING UP, OF THE CENTER IN RUINS AND THE CREEPY LITTLE GIRL? WHATEVER THAT PLACE IS, IT'S IMPORTANT.
MAYBE IF I USE THE TRISHUL AND FOCUS I CAN--
DON'T WORRY ABOUT THE GIRL. SHE'S NOT YOUR CONCERN.
SIR?
YOU'VE DONE GOOD WORK, SUSAN. TAKE THE FIRST AVAILABLE FLIGHT HOME, AND BILL THE TICKET TO MY PERSONAL ACCOUNT.
CLICK
UM...OKAY. SURE.
SHE'S NOT MY CONCERN...? WHAT THE HECK DOES THAT MEAN?

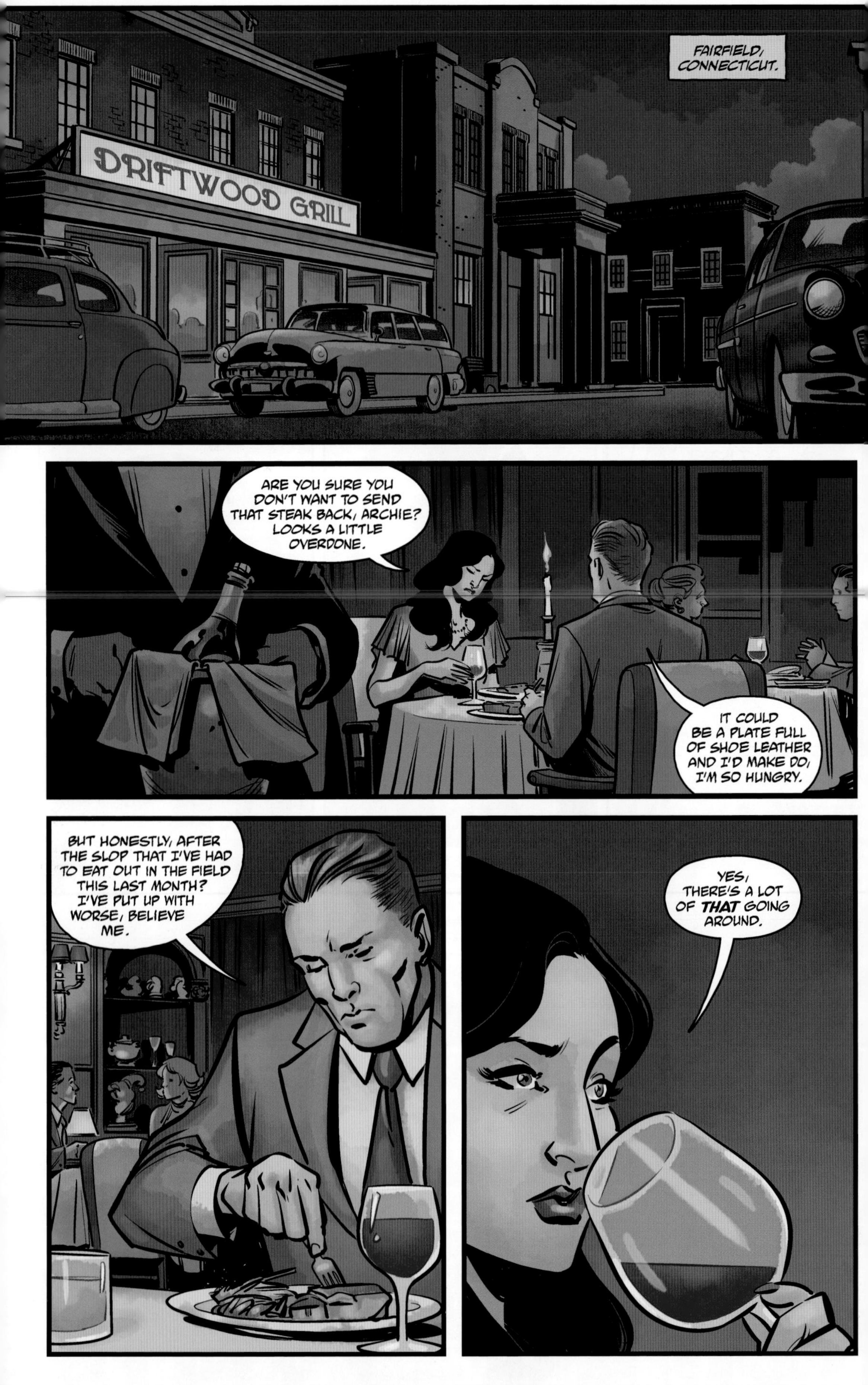
DRIFTWOOD GRILL
FAIRFIELD, CONNECTICUT.
ARE YOU SURE YOU DON'T WANT TO SEND THAT STEAK BACK, ARCHIE? LOOKS A LITTLE OVERDONE.
IT COULD BE A PLATE FULL OF SHOE LEATHER AND I'D MAKE DO, I'M SO HUNGRY.
BUT HONESTLY, AFTER THE SLOP THAT I'VE HAD TO EAT OUT IN THE FIELD THIS LAST MONTH? I'VE PUT UP WITH WORSE, BELIEVE ME.
YES, THERE'S A LOT OF ***THAT*** GOING AROUND.

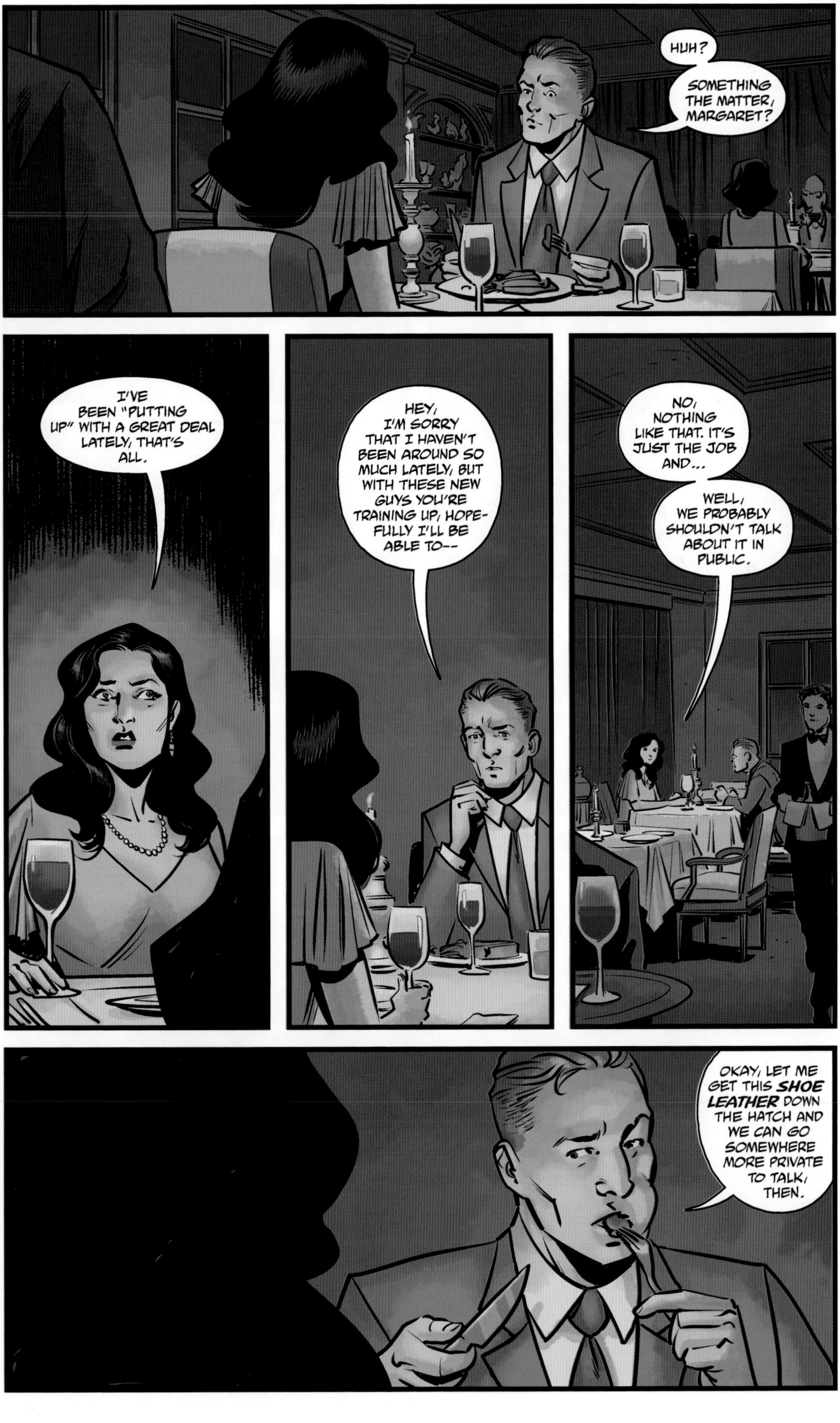
HUH?
SOMETHING THE MATTER, MARGARET?
I'VE BEEN "PUTTING UP" WITH A GREAT DEAL LATELY, THAT'S ALL.
HEY, I'M SORRY THAT I HAVEN'T BEEN AROUND SO MUCH LATELY, BUT WITH THESE NEW GUYS YOU'RE TRAINING UP, HOPE-FULLY I'LL BE ABLE TO--
NO, NOTHING LIKE THAT. IT'S JUST THE JOB AND...
WELL, WE PROBABLY SHOULDN'T TALK ABOUT IT IN PUBLIC.
OKAY, LET ME GET THIS SHOE LEATHER DOWN THE HATCH AND WE CAN GO SOMEWHERE MORE PRIVATE TO TALK, THEN.

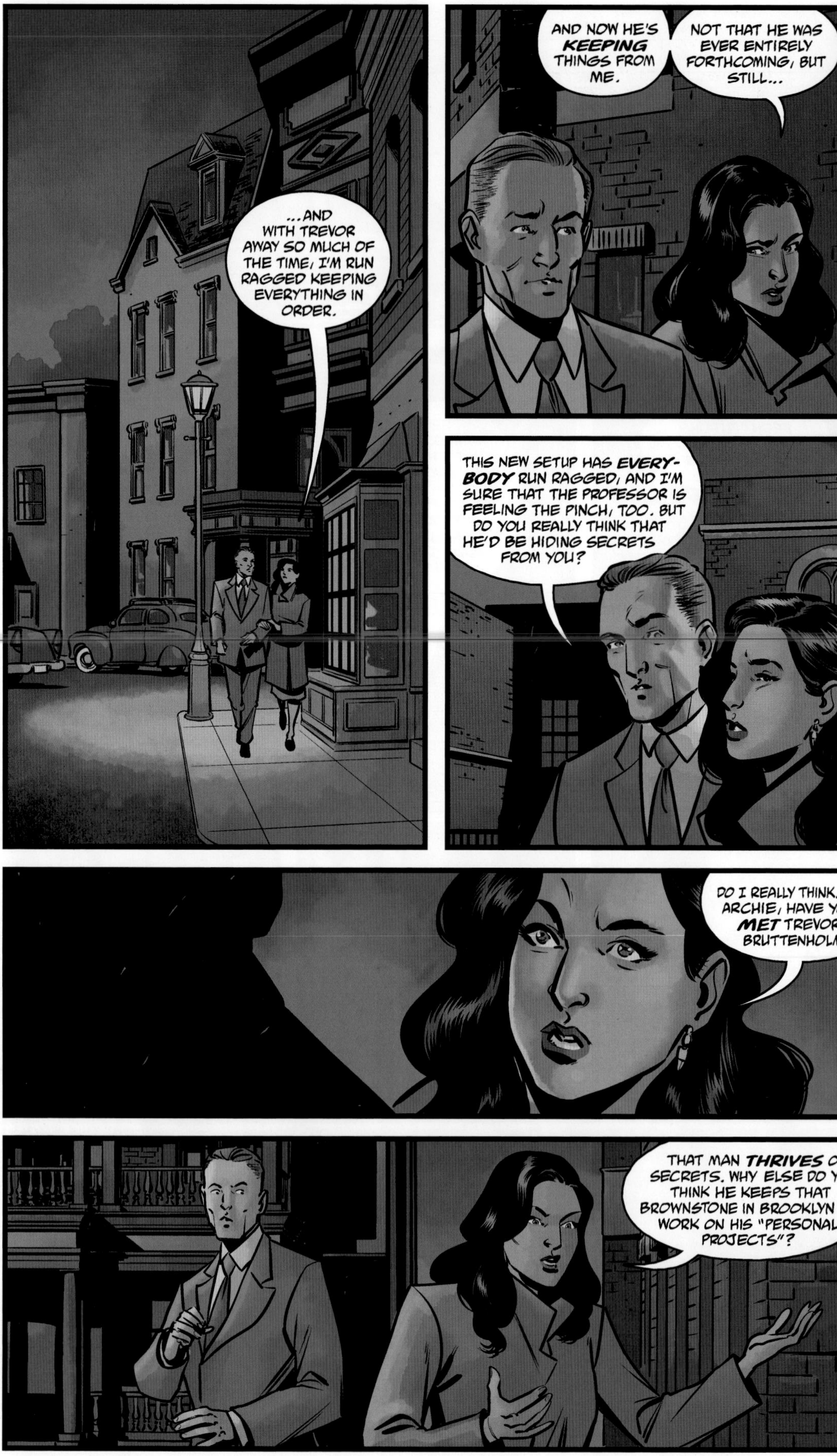
...AND WITH TREVOR AWAY SO MUCH OF THE TIME, I'M RUN RAGGED KEEPING EVERYTHING IN ORDER.
AND NOW HE'S **KEEPING** THINGS FROM ME.
NOT THAT HE WAS EVER ENTIRELY FORTHCOMING, BUT STILL...
THIS NEW SETUP HAS **EVERY-BODY** RUN RAGGED, AND I'M SURE THAT THE PROFESSOR IS FEELING THE PINCH, TOO. BUT DO YOU REALLY THINK THAT HE'D BE HIDING SECRETS FROM YOU?
DO I REALLY THINK...? ARCHIE, HAVE YOU **MET** TREVOR BRUTTENHOLM?
THAT MAN **THRIVES** ON SECRETS. WHY ELSE DO YOU THINK HE KEEPS THAT BROWNSTONE IN BROOKLYN TO WORK ON HIS "PERSONAL PROJECTS"?

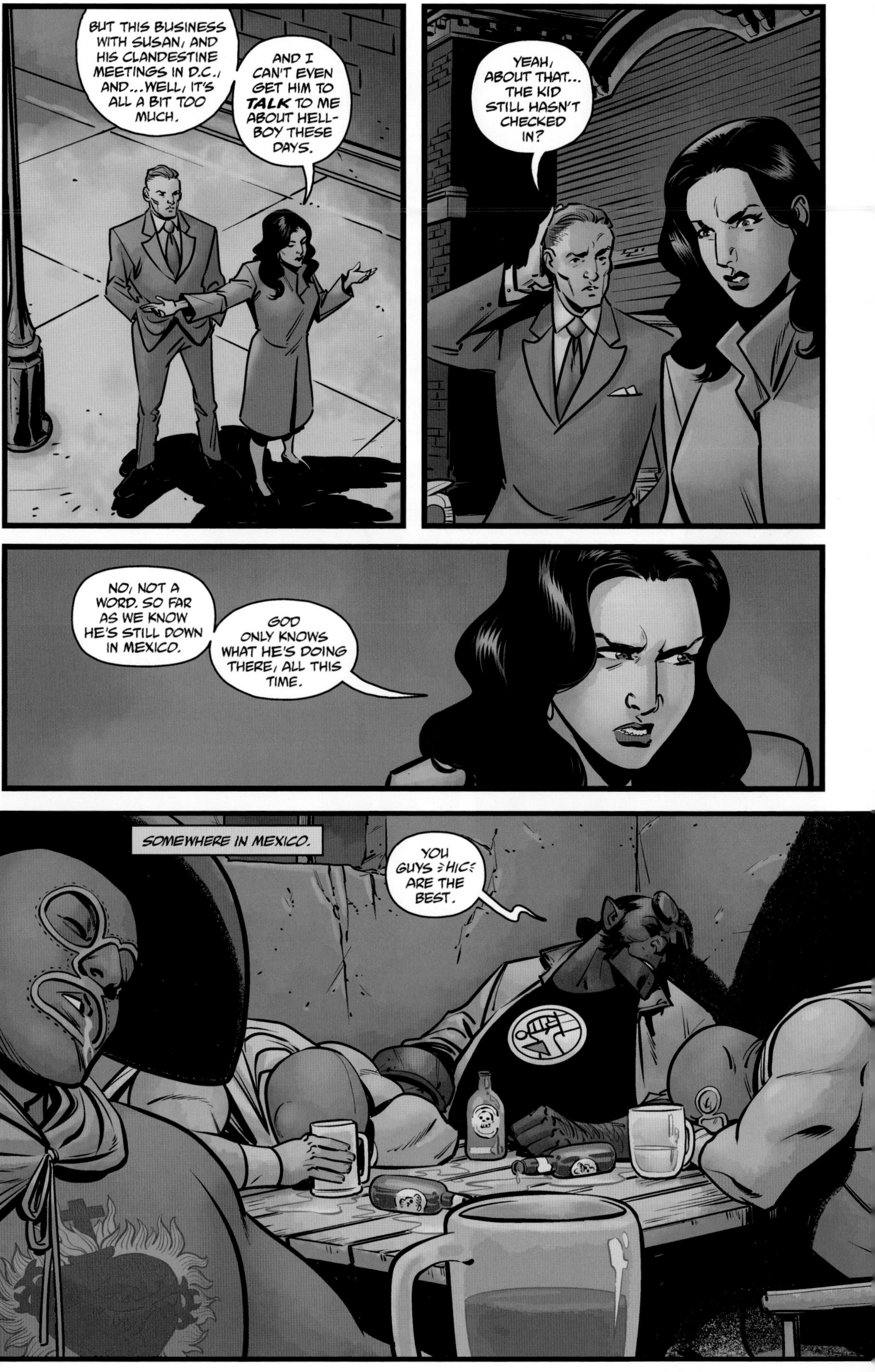
BUT THIS BUSINESS WITH SUSAN, AND HIS CLANDESTINE MEETINGS IN D.C., AND...WELL, IT'S ALL A BIT TOO MUCH.
AND I CAN'T EVEN GET HIM TO TALK TO ME ABOUT HELL-BOY THESE DAYS.
YEAH, ABOUT THAT... THE KID STILL HASN'T CHECKED IN?
NO, NOT A WORD. SO FAR AS WE KNOW HE'S STILL DOWN IN MEXICO.
GOD ONLY KNOWS WHAT HE'S DOING THERE, ALL THIS TIME.
SOMEWHERE IN MEXICO.
YOU GUYS ≥HIC≤ ARE THE BEST.

BROOKLYN, NEW YORK.

THANK YOU FOR COMING ON SUCH SHORT NOTICE.

I APOLOGIZE FOR ANY INCONVENIENCE, BUT THERE ARE SO MANY NEW FACES AROUND BUREAU HEAD-QUARTERS, SO MANY PEOPLE WITH CONNECTIONS TO OTHER AGENCIES AND...

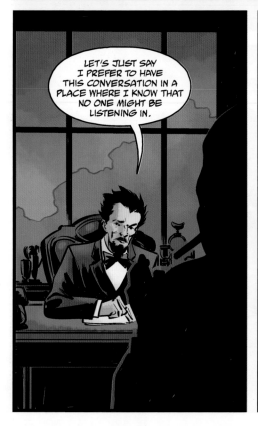

LET'S JUST SAY I PREFER TO HAVE THIS CONVERSATION IN A PLACE WHERE I KNOW THAT NO ONE MIGHT BE LISTENING IN.

WELL, *I'M* LISTENING.

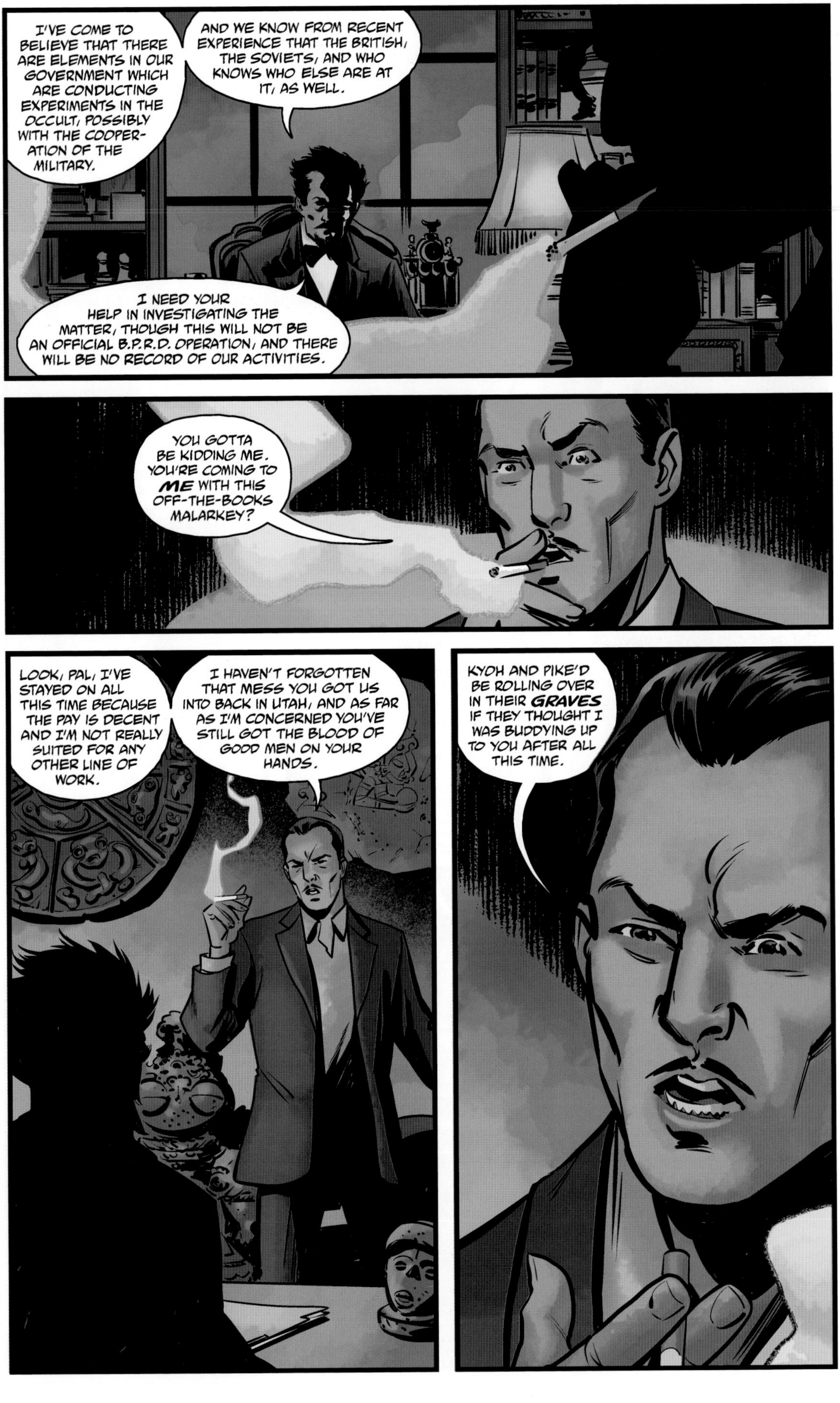
I'VE COME TO BELIEVE THAT THERE ARE ELEMENTS IN OUR GOVERNMENT WHICH ARE CONDUCTING EXPERIMENTS IN THE OCCULT, POSSIBLY WITH THE COOPERATION OF THE MILITARY.
AND WE KNOW FROM RECENT EXPERIENCE THAT THE BRITISH, THE SOVIETS, AND WHO KNOWS WHO ELSE ARE AT IT, AS WELL.
I NEED YOUR HELP IN INVESTIGATING THE MATTER, THOUGH THIS WILL NOT BE AN OFFICIAL B.P.R.D. OPERATION, AND THERE WILL BE NO RECORD OF OUR ACTIVITIES.
YOU GOTTA BE KIDDING ME. YOU'RE COMING TO ME WITH THIS OFF-THE-BOOKS MALARKEY?
LOOK, PAL, I'VE STAYED ON ALL THIS TIME BECAUSE THE PAY IS DECENT AND I'M NOT REALLY SUITED FOR ANY OTHER LINE OF WORK.
I HAVEN'T FORGOTTEN THAT MESS YOU GOT US INTO BACK IN UTAH, AND AS FAR AS I'M CONCERNED YOU'VE STILL GOT THE BLOOD OF GOOD MEN ON YOUR HANDS.
KYOH AND PIKE'D BE ROLLING OVER IN THEIR GRAVES IF THEY THOUGHT I WAS BUDDYING UP TO YOU AFTER ALL THIS TIME.

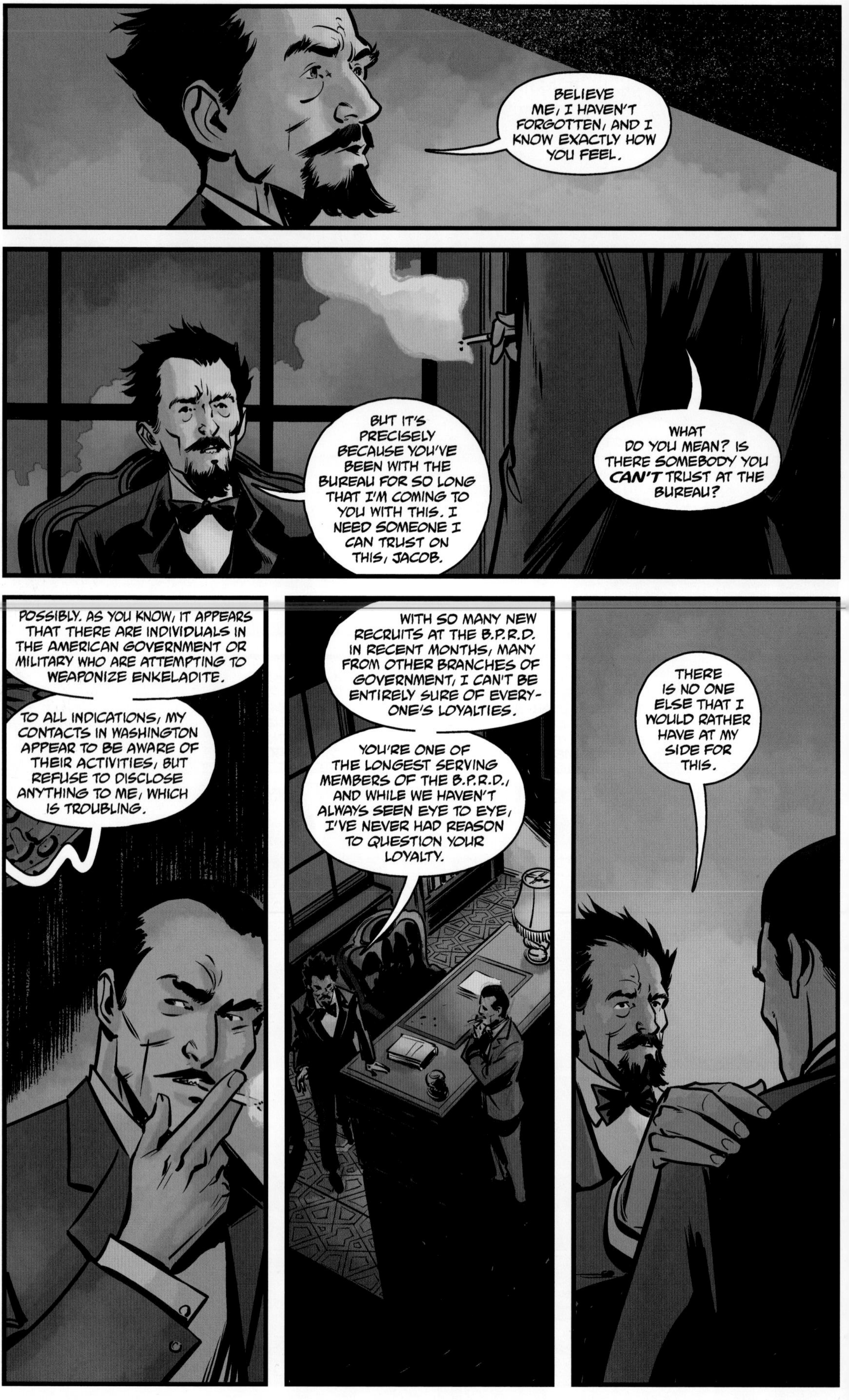
BELIEVE ME, I HAVEN'T FORGOTTEN, AND I KNOW EXACTLY HOW YOU FEEL.
BUT IT'S PRECISELY BECAUSE YOU'VE BEEN WITH THE BUREAU FOR SO LONG THAT I'M COMING TO YOU WITH THIS. I NEED SOMEONE I CAN TRUST ON THIS, JACOB.
WHAT DO YOU MEAN? IS THERE SOMEBODY YOU CAN'T TRUST AT THE BUREAU?
POSSIBLY. AS YOU KNOW, IT APPEARS THAT THERE ARE INDIVIDUALS IN THE AMERICAN GOVERNMENT OR MILITARY WHO ARE ATTEMPTING TO WEAPONIZE ENKELADITE.
TO ALL INDICATIONS, MY CONTACTS IN WASHINGTON APPEAR TO BE AWARE OF THEIR ACTIVITIES, BUT REFUSE TO DISCLOSE ANYTHING TO ME, WHICH IS TROUBLING.
WITH SO MANY NEW RECRUITS AT THE B.P.R.D. IN RECENT MONTHS, MANY FROM OTHER BRANCHES OF GOVERNMENT, I CAN'T BE ENTIRELY SURE OF EVERYONE'S LOYALTIES.
YOU'RE ONE OF THE LONGEST SERVING MEMBERS OF THE B.P.R.D., AND WHILE WE HAVEN'T ALWAYS SEEN EYE TO EYE, I'VE NEVER HAD REASON TO QUESTION YOUR LOYALTY.
THERE IS NO ONE ELSE THAT I WOULD RATHER HAVE AT MY SIDE FOR THIS.

WELL, DAMN. BUT, WHAT ABOUT HELLBOY? SEEMS LIKE HE'D BE YOUR GUY FOR A CAPER LIKE THIS.

EVEN IF HELLBOY WAS ON HAND, THIS "CAPER" REQUIRES SUBTLETY, WHICH HAS NEVER BEEN HIS FORTE. NO, YOU ARE THE MAN FOR THE JOB.

ALL RIGHT, THEN. COUNT ME IN.

SO, YOU GOT ANY IDEA WHERE WE NEED TO START LOOKING?

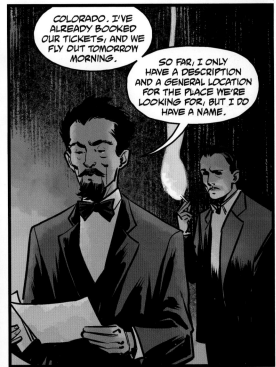

COLORADO. I'VE ALREADY BOOKED OUR TICKETS, AND WE FLY OUT TOMORROW MORNING.

SO FAR, I ONLY HAVE A DESCRIPTION AND A GENERAL LOCATION FOR THE PLACE WE'RE LOOKING FOR, BUT I DO HAVE A NAME.

"THE CENTER."

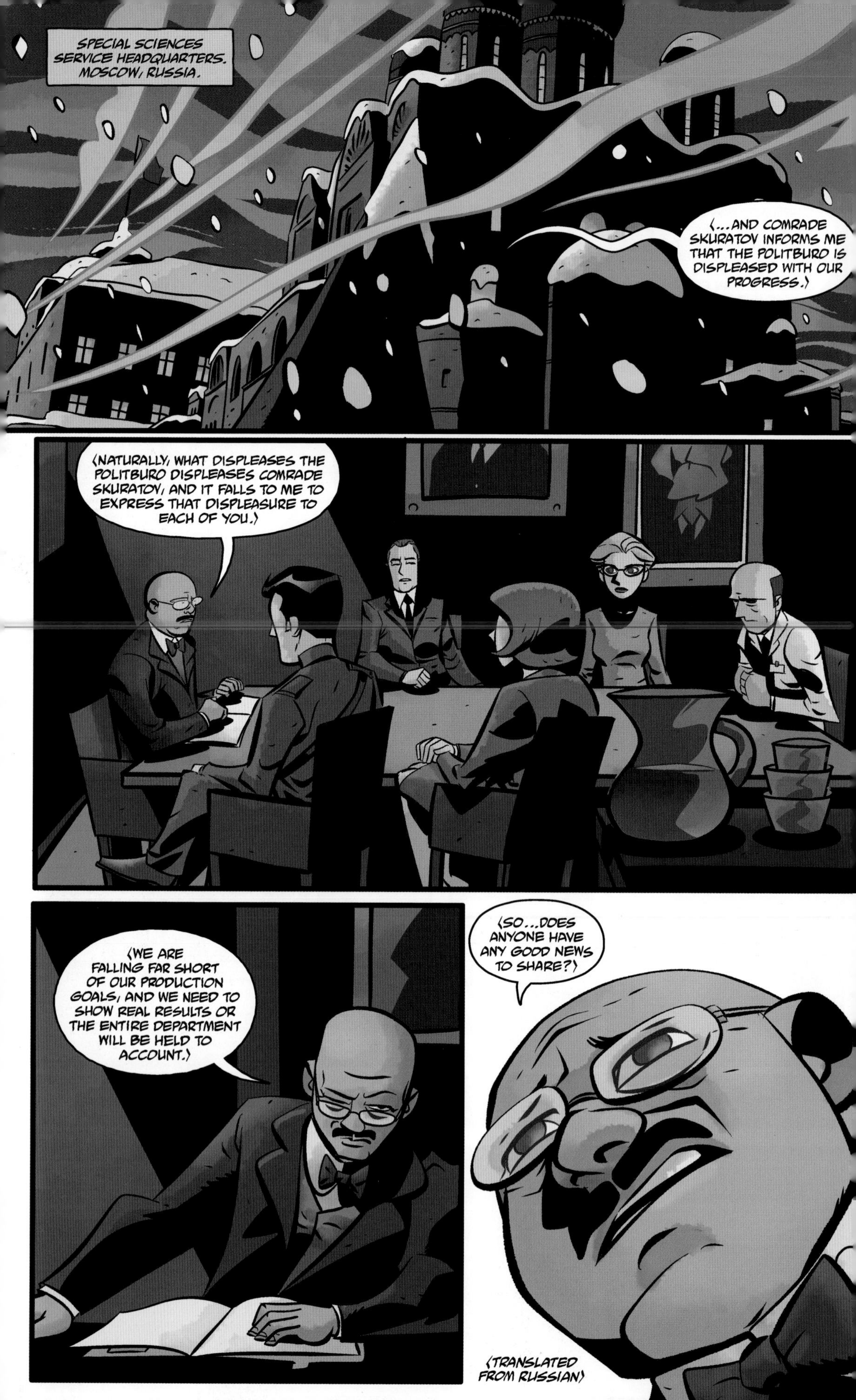
SPECIAL SCIENCES SERVICE HEADQUARTERS. MOSCOW, RUSSIA.
‹...AND COMRADE SKURATOV INFORMS ME THAT THE POLITBURO IS DISPLEASED WITH OUR PROGRESS.›
‹NATURALLY, WHAT DISPLEASES THE POLITBURO DISPLEASES COMRADE SKURATOV, AND IT FALLS TO ME TO EXPRESS THAT DISPLEASURE TO EACH OF YOU.›
‹WE ARE FALLING FAR SHORT OF OUR PRODUCTION GOALS, AND WE NEED TO SHOW REAL RESULTS OR THE ENTIRE DEPARTMENT WILL BE HELD TO ACCOUNT.›
‹SO...DOES ANYONE HAVE ANY GOOD NEWS TO SHARE?›
‹TRANSLATED FROM RUSSIAN›

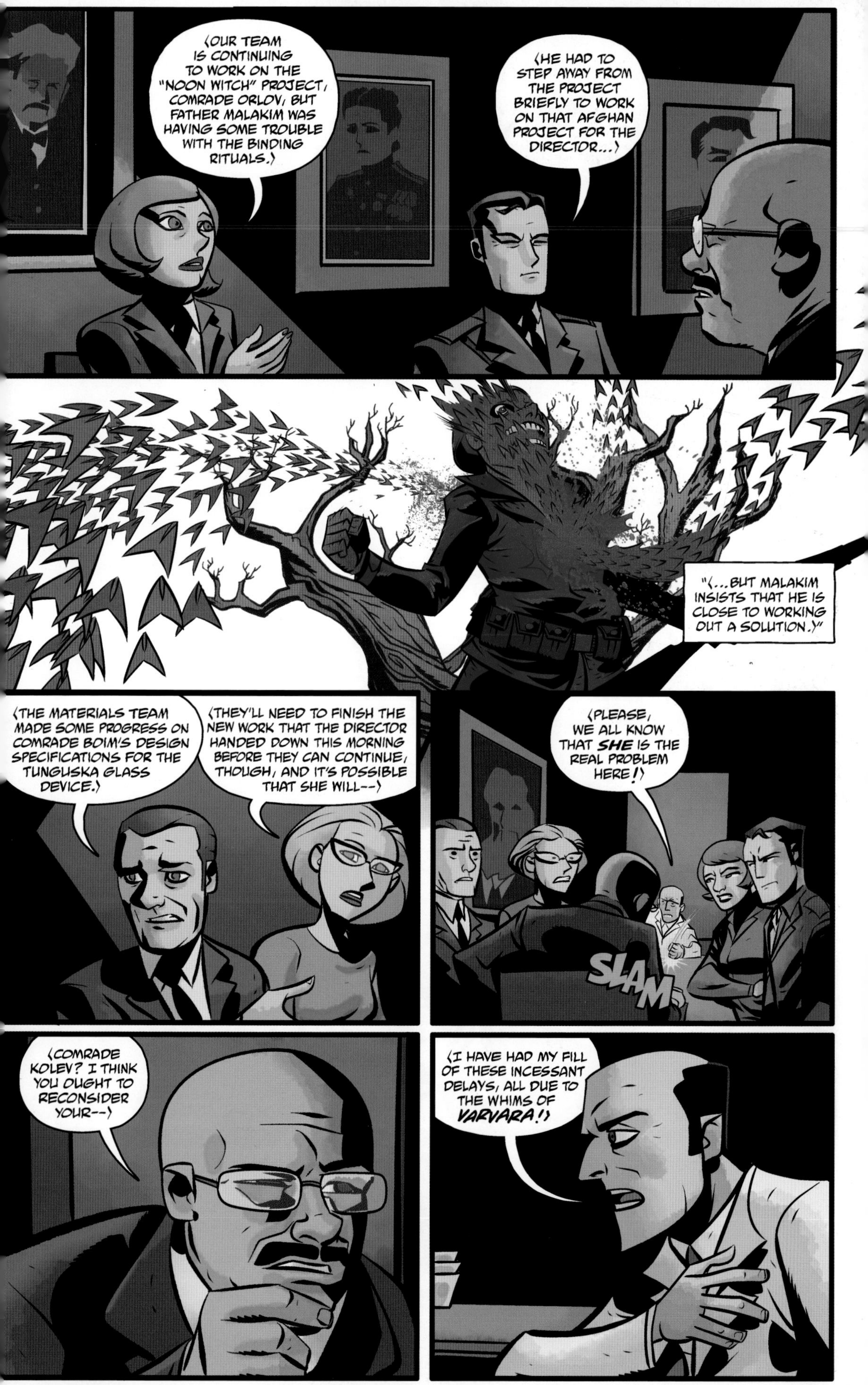

⟨OUR TEAM IS CONTINUING TO WORK ON THE "NOON WITCH" PROJECT, COMRADE ORLOV, BUT FATHER MALAKIM WAS HAVING SOME TROUBLE WITH THE BINDING RITUALS.⟩
⟨HE HAD TO STEP AWAY FROM THE PROJECT BRIEFLY TO WORK ON THAT AFGHAN PROJECT FOR THE DIRECTOR...⟩
"⟨...BUT MALAKIM INSISTS THAT HE IS CLOSE TO WORKING OUT A SOLUTION.⟩"
⟨THE MATERIALS TEAM MADE SOME PROGRESS ON COMRADE BOIM'S DESIGN SPECIFICATIONS FOR THE TUNGUSKA GLASS DEVICE.⟩
⟨THEY'LL NEED TO FINISH THE NEW WORK THAT THE DIRECTOR HANDED DOWN THIS MORNING BEFORE THEY CAN CONTINUE, THOUGH, AND IT'S POSSIBLE THAT SHE WILL--⟩
⟨PLEASE, WE ALL KNOW THAT *SHE* IS THE REAL PROBLEM HERE!⟩
SLAM
⟨COMRADE KOLEV? I THINK YOU OUGHT TO RECONSIDER YOUR--⟩
⟨I HAVE HAD MY FILL OF THESE INCESSANT DELAYS, ALL DUE TO THE WHIMS OF *VARVARA*!⟩

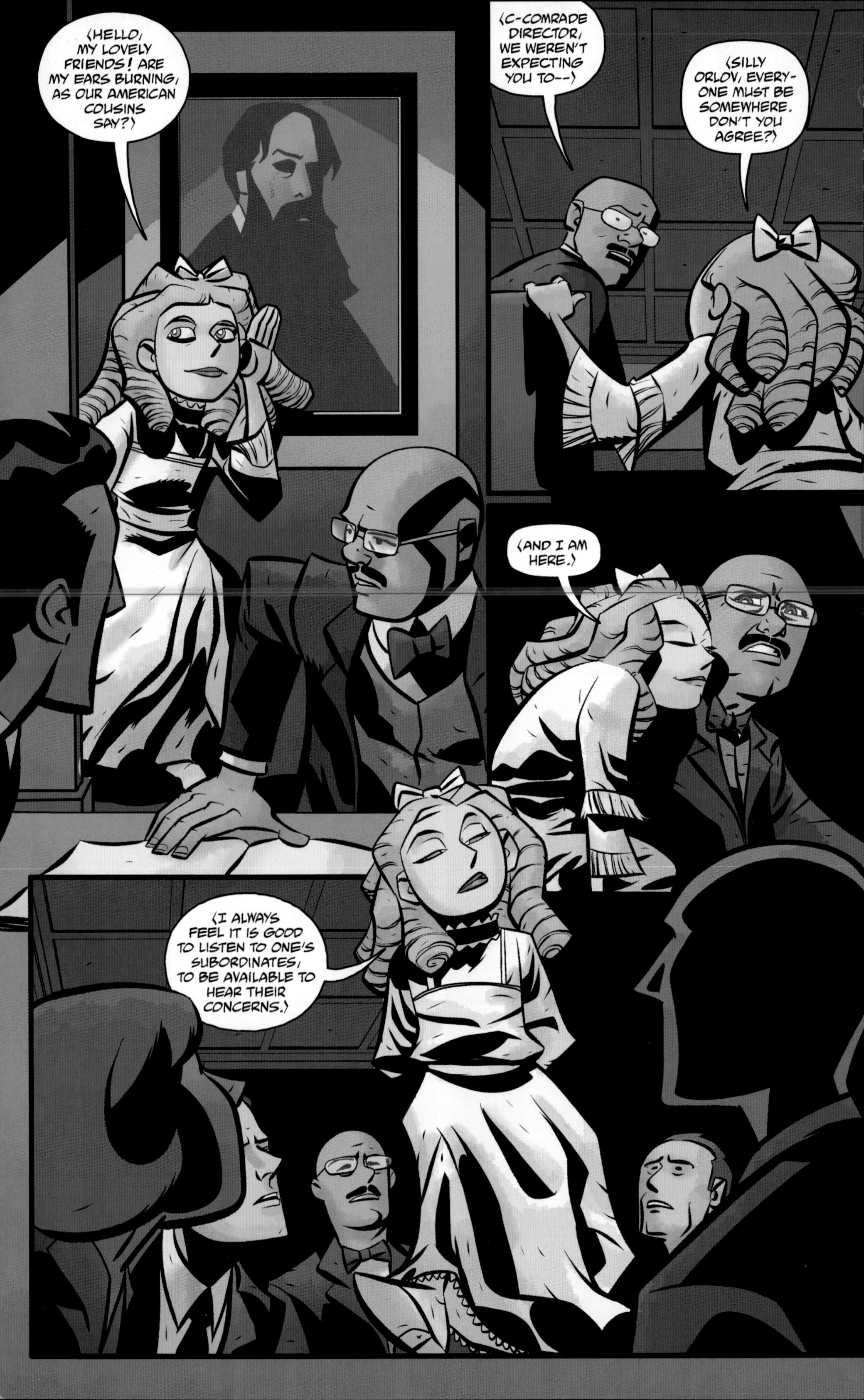

‹HELLO, MY LOVELY FRIENDS! ARE MY EARS BURNING, AS OUR AMERICAN COUSINS SAY?›
‹C-COMRADE DIRECTOR, WE WEREN'T EXPECTING YOU TO--›
‹SILLY ORLOV, EVERY-ONE MUST BE SOMEWHERE. DON'T YOU AGREE?›
‹AND I AM HERE.›
‹I ALWAYS FEEL IT IS GOOD TO LISTEN TO ONE'S SUBORDINATES, TO BE AVAILABLE TO HEAR THEIR CONCERNS.›

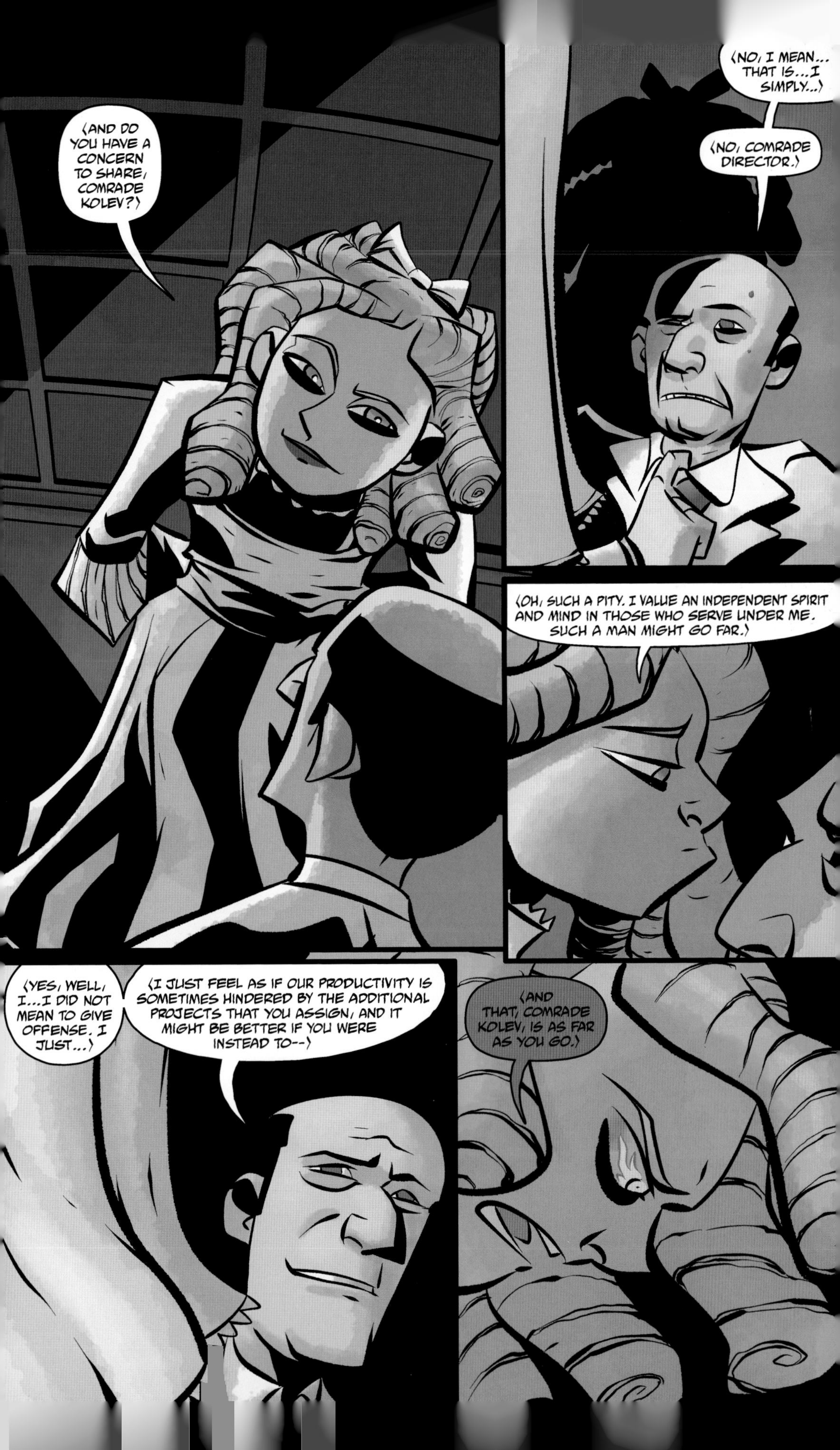

⟨AND DO YOU HAVE A CONCERN TO SHARE, COMRADE KOLEV?⟩
⟨NO, I MEAN... THAT IS...I SIMPLY...⟩
⟨NO, COMRADE DIRECTOR.⟩
⟨OH, SUCH A PITY. I VALUE AN INDEPENDENT SPIRIT AND MIND IN THOSE WHO SERVE UNDER ME. SUCH A MAN MIGHT GO FAR.⟩
⟨YES, WELL, I...I DID NOT MEAN TO GIVE OFFENSE. I JUST...⟩
⟨I JUST FEEL AS IF OUR PRODUCTIVITY IS SOMETIMES HINDERED BY THE ADDITIONAL PROJECTS THAT YOU ASSIGN, AND IT MIGHT BE BETTER IF YOU WERE INSTEAD TO--⟩
⟨AND THAT, COMRADE KOLEV, IS AS FAR AS YOU GO.⟩

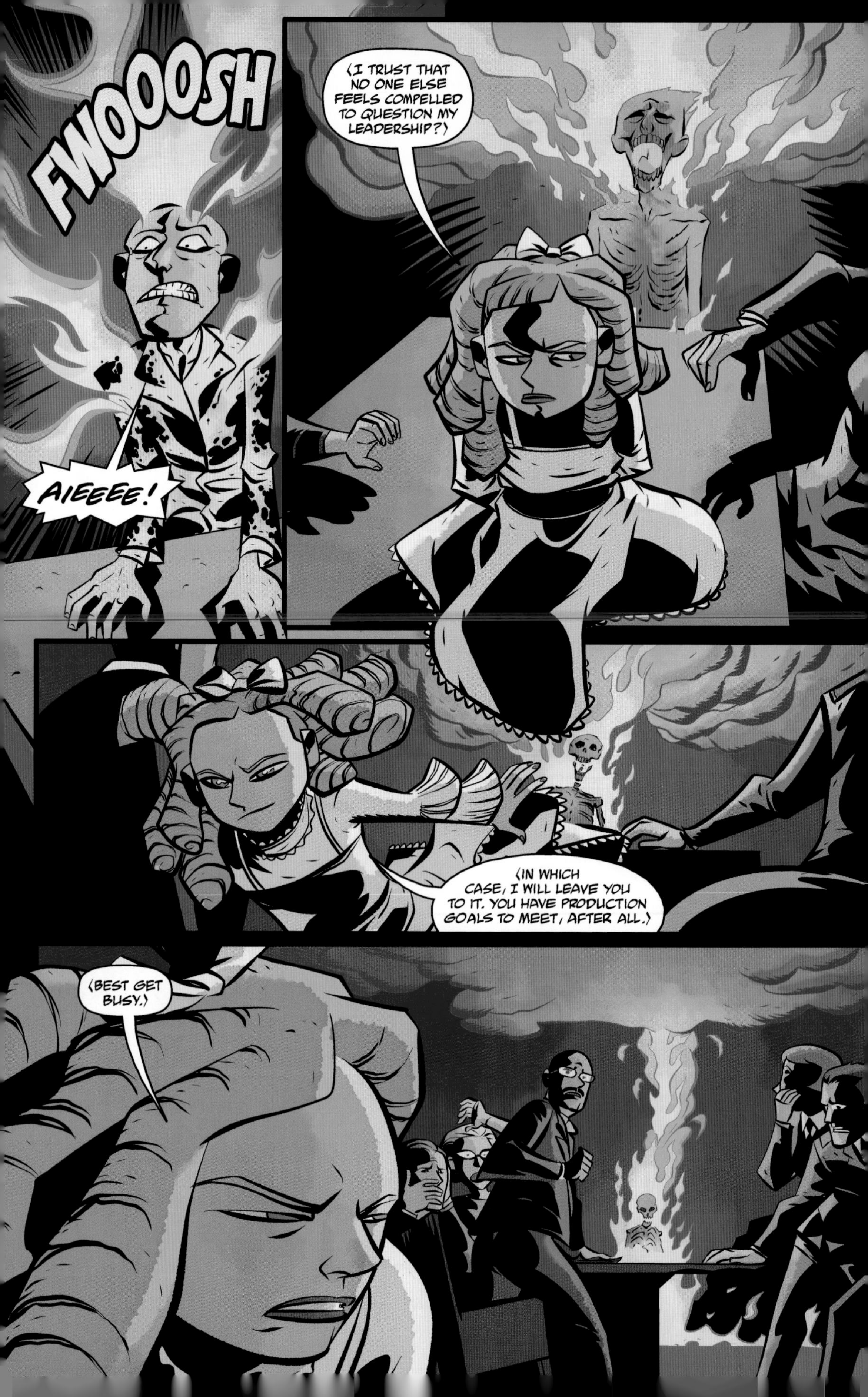
FWOOOSH
AIEEEE!
⟨I TRUST THAT NO ONE ELSE FEELS COMPELLED TO QUESTION MY LEADERSHIP?⟩
⟨IN WHICH CASE, I WILL LEAVE YOU TO IT. YOU HAVE PRODUCTION GOALS TO MEET, AFTER ALL.⟩
⟨BEST GET BUSY.⟩

CHAPTER THREE

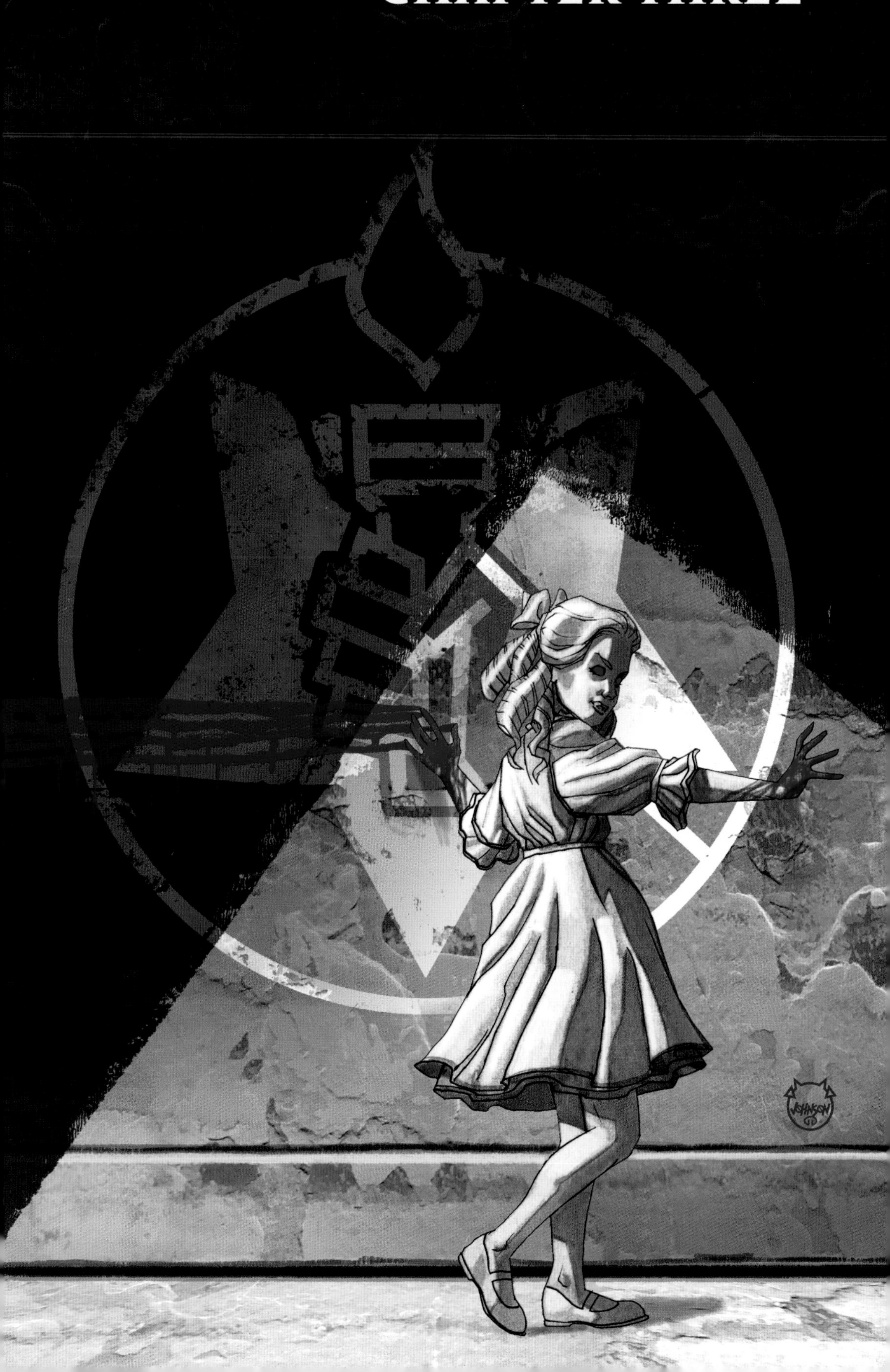
JOHNSON

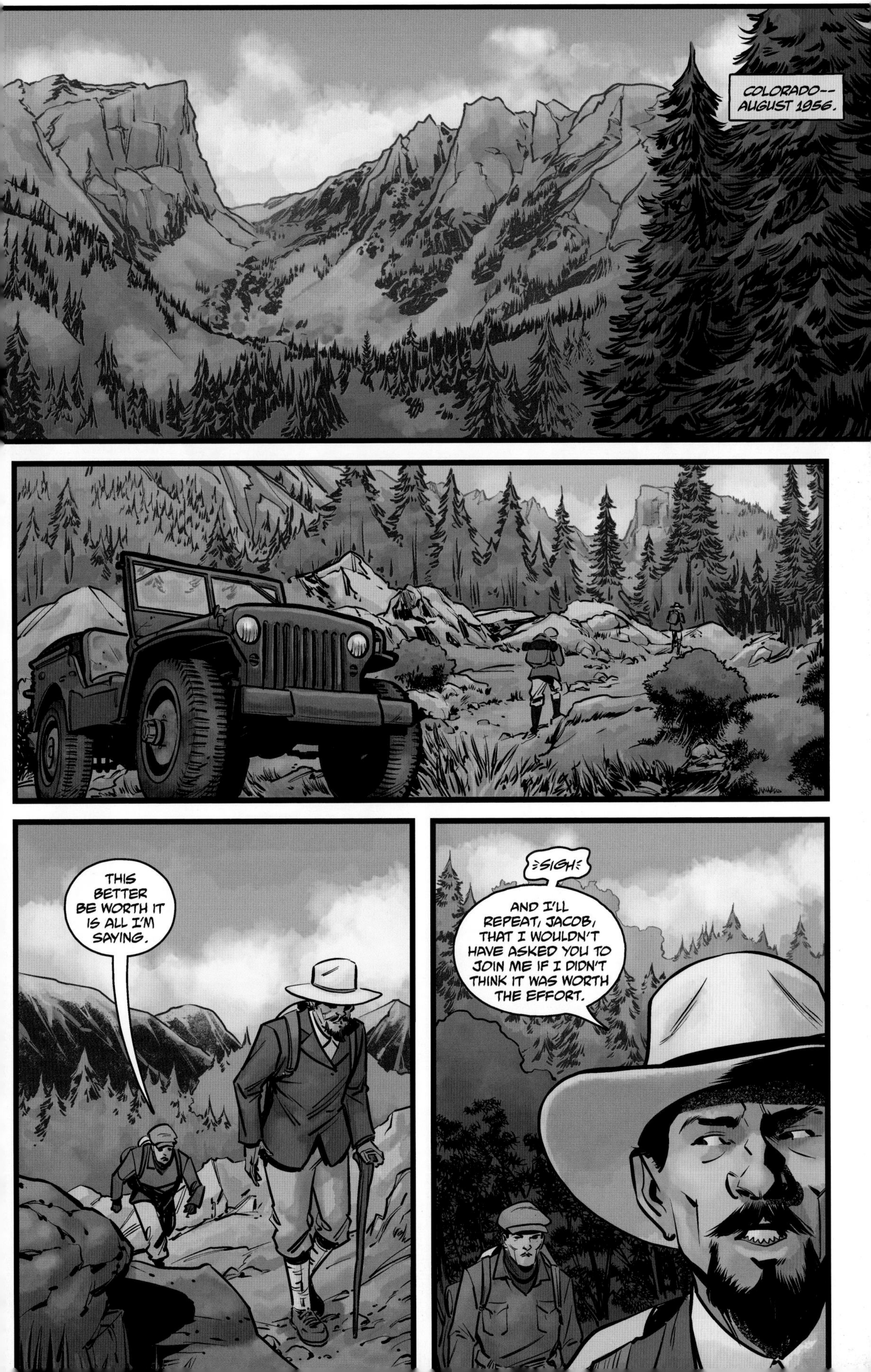
COLORADO--
AUGUST 1956.
THIS BETTER BE WORTH IT IS ALL I'M SAYING.
SIGH
AND I'LL REPEAT, JACOB, THAT I WOULDN'T HAVE ASKED YOU TO JOIN ME IF I DIDN'T THINK IT WAS WORTH THE EFFORT.

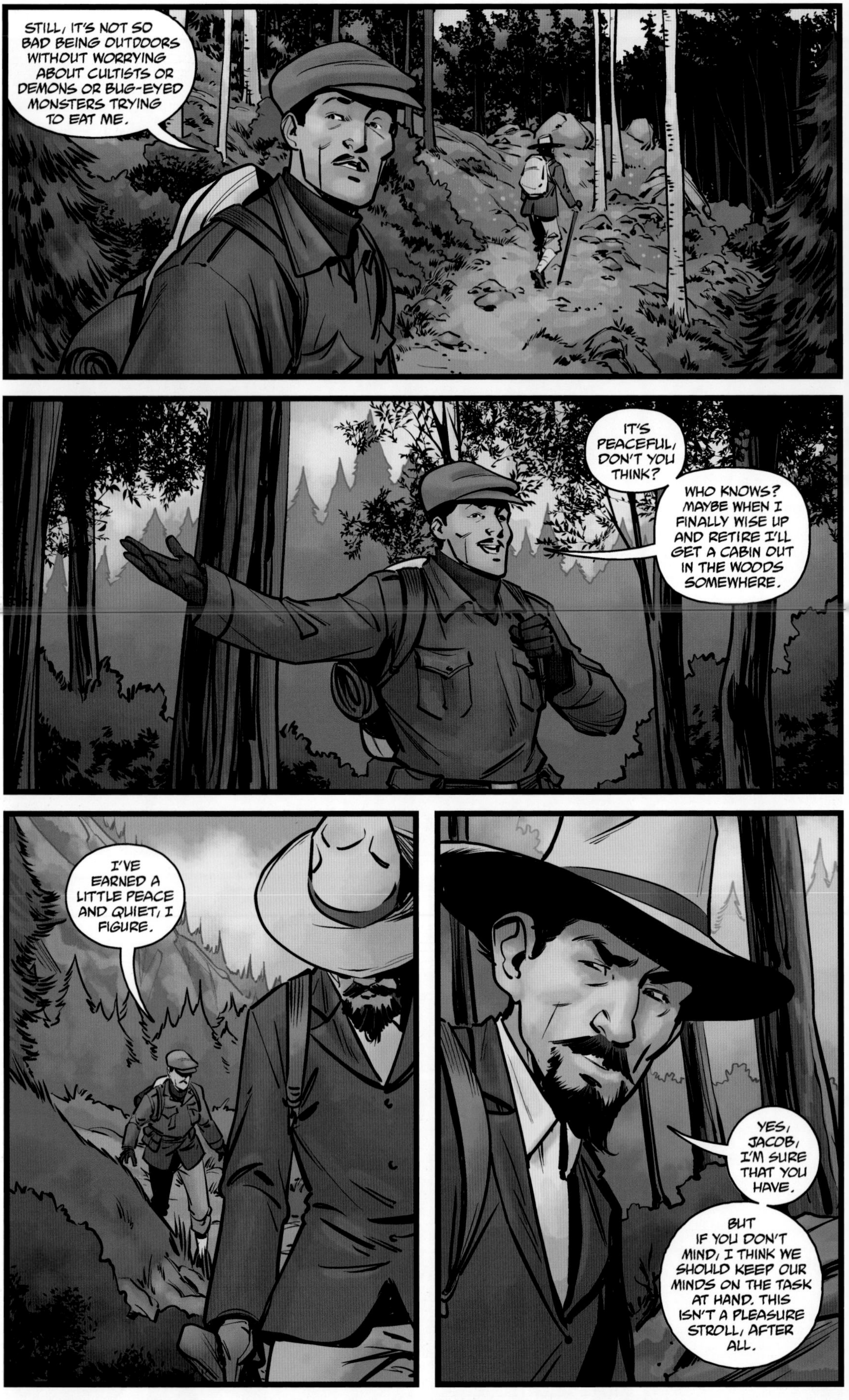
STILL, IT'S NOT SO BAD BEING OUTDOORS WITHOUT WORRYING ABOUT CULTISTS OR DEMONS OR BUG-EYED MONSTERS TRYING TO EAT ME.
IT'S PEACEFUL, DON'T YOU THINK?
WHO KNOWS? MAYBE WHEN I FINALLY WISE UP AND RETIRE I'LL GET A CABIN OUT IN THE WOODS SOMEWHERE.
I'VE EARNED A LITTLE PEACE AND QUIET, I FIGURE.
YES, JACOB, I'M SURE THAT YOU HAVE.
BUT IF YOU DON'T MIND, I THINK WE SHOULD KEEP OUR MINDS ON THE TASK AT HAND. THIS ISN'T A PLEASURE STROLL, AFTER ALL.

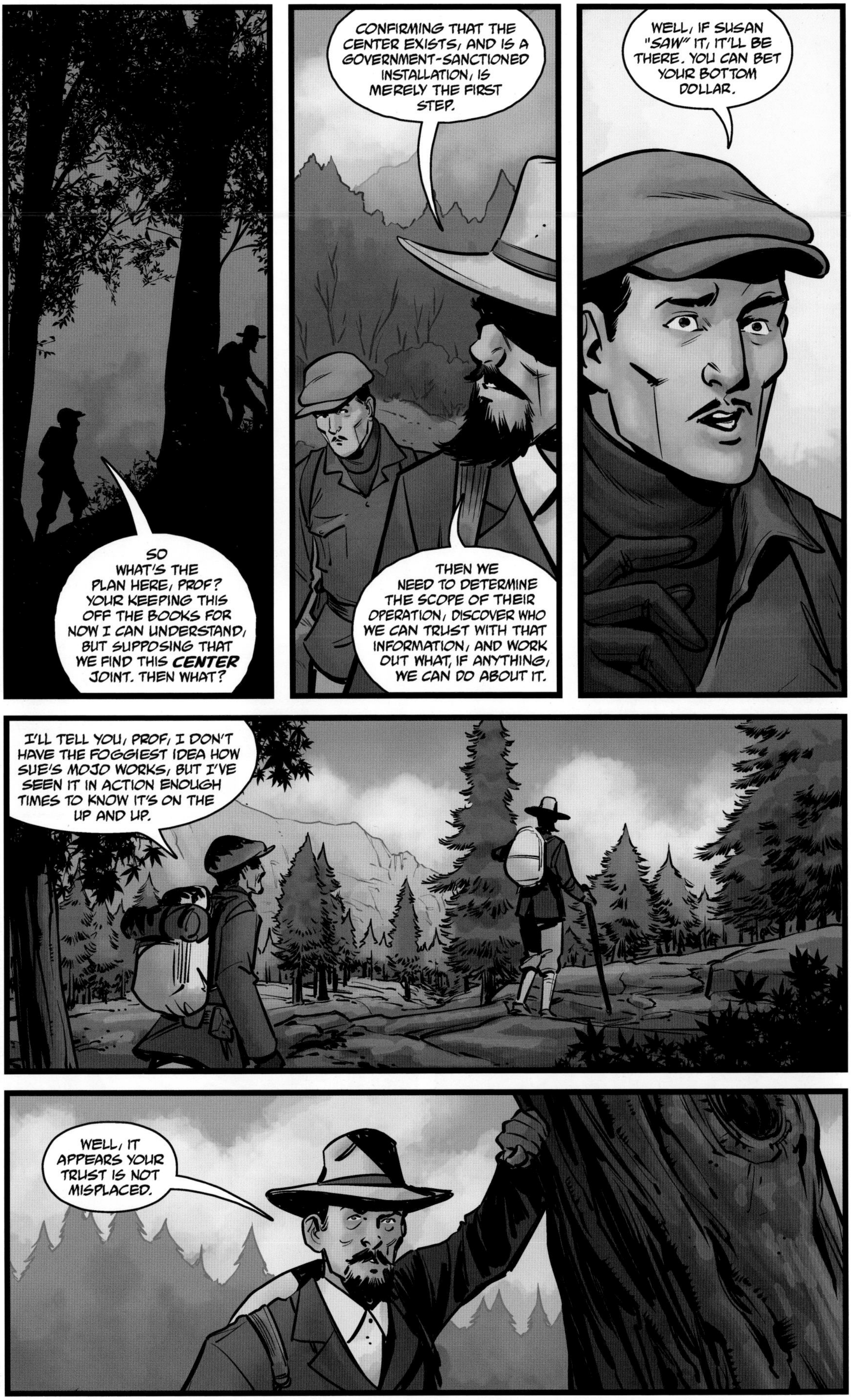
SO WHAT'S THE PLAN HERE, PROF? YOUR KEEPING THIS OFF THE BOOKS FOR NOW I CAN UNDERSTAND, BUT SUPPOSING THAT WE FIND THIS **CENTER** JOINT. THEN WHAT?
CONFIRMING THAT THE CENTER EXISTS, AND IS A GOVERNMENT-SANCTIONED INSTALLATION, IS MERELY THE FIRST STEP.
THEN WE NEED TO DETERMINE THE SCOPE OF THEIR OPERATION, DISCOVER WHO WE CAN TRUST WITH THAT INFORMATION, AND WORK OUT WHAT, IF ANYTHING, WE CAN DO ABOUT IT.
WELL, IF SUSAN "*SAW*" IT, IT'LL BE THERE. YOU CAN BET YOUR BOTTOM DOLLAR.
I'LL TELL YOU, PROF, I DON'T HAVE THE FOGGIEST IDEA HOW SUE'S MOJO WORKS, BUT I'VE SEEN IT IN ACTION ENOUGH TIMES TO KNOW IT'S ON THE UP AND UP.
WELL, IT APPEARS YOUR TRUST IS NOT MISPLACED.

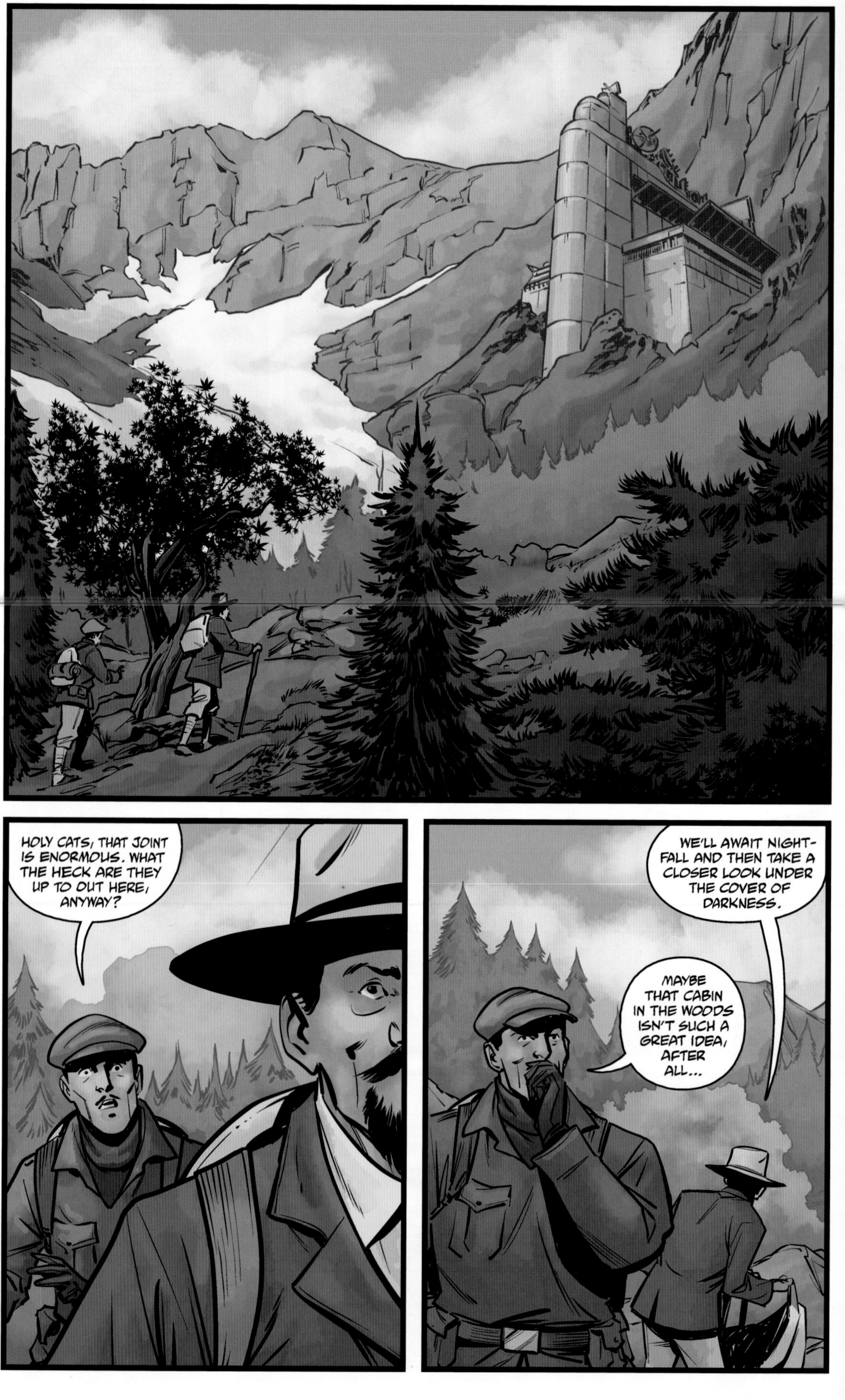
HOLY CATS, THAT JOINT IS ENORMOUS. WHAT THE HECK ARE THEY UP TO OUT HERE, ANYWAY?
WE'LL AWAIT NIGHT-FALL AND THEN TAKE A CLOSER LOOK UNDER THE COVER OF DARKNESS.
MAYBE THAT CABIN IN THE WOODS ISN'T SUCH A GREAT IDEA, AFTER ALL...

THE BUREAU FOR PARANORMAL RESEARCH AND DEFENSE HEADQUARTERS IN FAIRFIELD, CONNECTICUT.

...YOU HAVE TO BE READY FOR ANY EVENTUALITY.

NINE TIMES OUT OF TEN WHEN WE'RE SENT OUT INTO THE FIELD TO INVESTIGATE A REPORT OF PARANORMAL ACTIVITY, WE DON'T HAVE A CLEAR IDEA WHAT WE'RE UP AGAINST.

DEMONIC POSSESSION? HAUNTING? MUTATION? OTHERWORLDLY INTRUSION? CRYPTOZOOLOGICAL SPECIES? WE USUALLY DON'T KNOW UNTIL WE FIND IT.

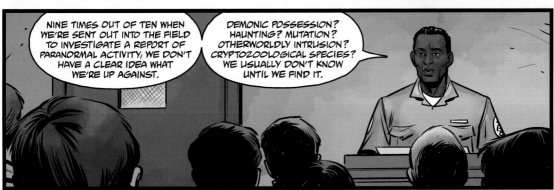

SO AS FIELD AGENTS, YOU'VE GOT TO BE QUICK ON YOUR FEET AND READY TO ADAPT TO WHAT- EVER THE CIRCUMSTANCES MIGHT BE.

COME ON, PULL THE OTHER ONE. I MEAN, HAUNTINGS I CAN BELIEVE, BUT LITTLE GREEN MEN FROM OUTER SPACE?

HEY, DON'T JOKE, GUSTAFSSON. THAT'S A REAL THING.

I'VE SEEN FLYING SAUCERS WITH MY OWN TWO EYES, BACK WHEN I WAS A SHERIFF'S DEPUTY IN MARFA, TEXAS.

WELL, I SAW SOMETHING, ANYWAY.

"PEOPLE'VE BEEN SEEING LIGHTS IN THE SKIES OVER MARFA CLEAR BACK TO THE 1880s. NOBODY'S SURE JUST WHAT THEY ARE, BUT IF YOU ASK ME, IT'S ALIENS."

OH, COME OFF IT, HINOJOSA. HOW COME WHEN ALIENS SUPPOSEDLY COME TO VISIT EARTH, IT'S ALWAYS SOME LITTLE FLYSPECK PODUNK TOWN IN THE MIDDLE OF NOWHERE?

MY HAND TO GOD, IT'S TRUE. YOU DON'T BELIEVE ME, GO ON DOWN THERE AND SEE FOR YOURSELF AND THEN MAYBE YOU'LL--

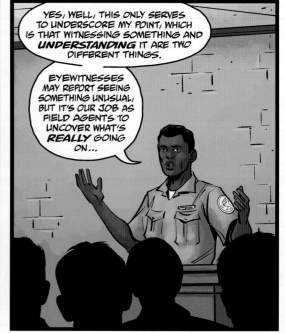

YES, WELL, THIS ONLY SERVES TO UNDERSCORE MY POINT, WHICH IS THAT WITNESSING SOMETHING AND UNDERSTANDING IT ARE TWO DIFFERENT THINGS.

EYEWITNESSES MAY REPORT SEEING SOMETHING UNUSUAL, BUT IT'S OUR JOB AS FIELD AGENTS TO UNCOVER WHAT'S REALLY GOING ON...

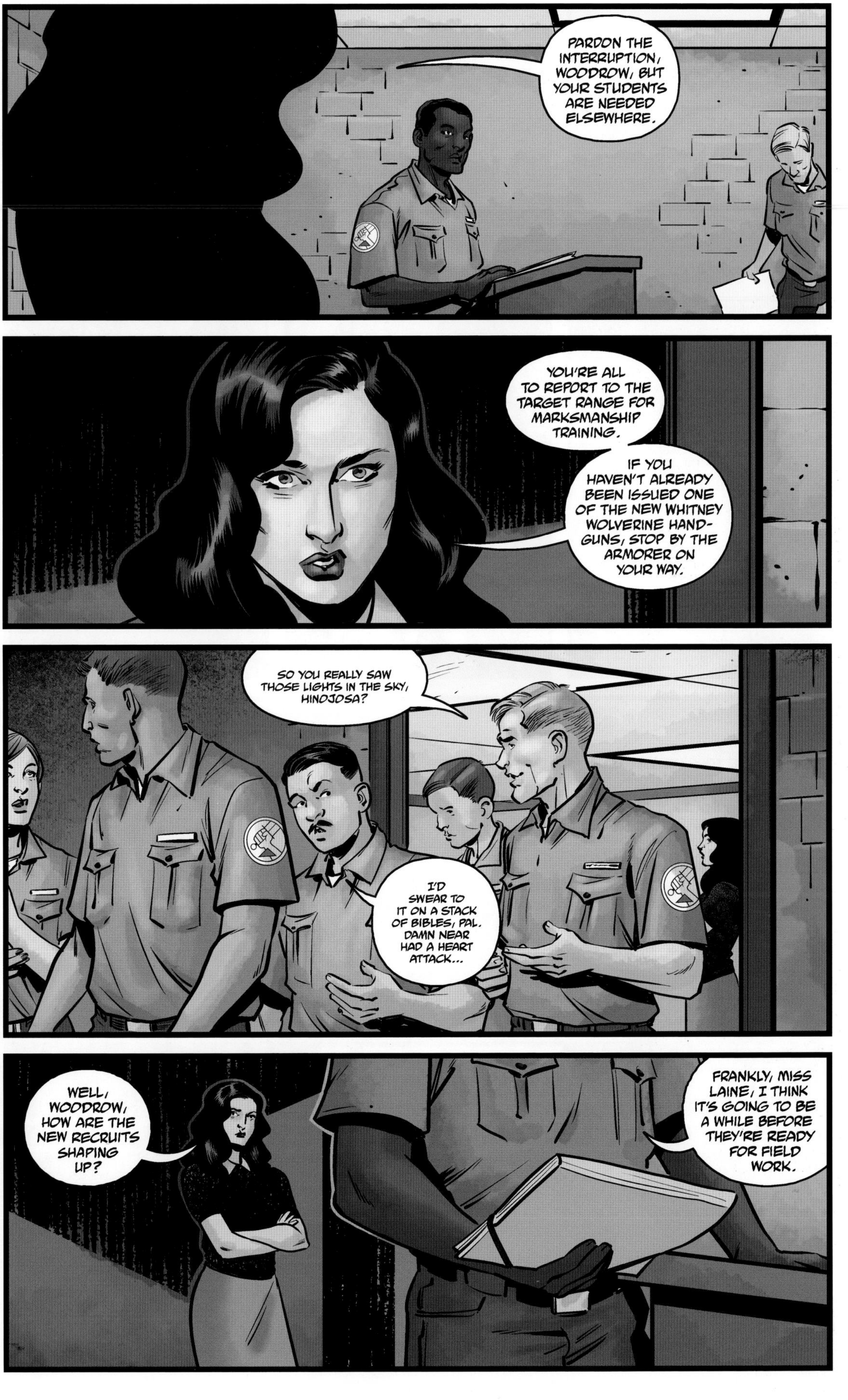
PARDON THE INTERRUPTION, WOODROW, BUT YOUR STUDENTS ARE NEEDED ELSEWHERE.
YOU'RE ALL TO REPORT TO THE TARGET RANGE FOR MARKSMANSHIP TRAINING.
IF YOU HAVEN'T ALREADY BEEN ISSUED ONE OF THE NEW WHITNEY WOLVERINE HAND-GUNS, STOP BY THE ARMORER ON YOUR WAY.
SO YOU REALLY SAW THOSE LIGHTS IN THE SKY, HINOJOSA?
I'D SWEAR TO IT ON A STACK OF BIBLES, PAL. DAMN NEAR HAD A HEART ATTACK...
WELL, WOODROW, HOW ARE THE NEW RECRUITS SHAPING UP?
FRANKLY, MISS LAINE, I THINK IT'S GOING TO BE A WHILE BEFORE THEY'RE READY FOR FIELD WORK.

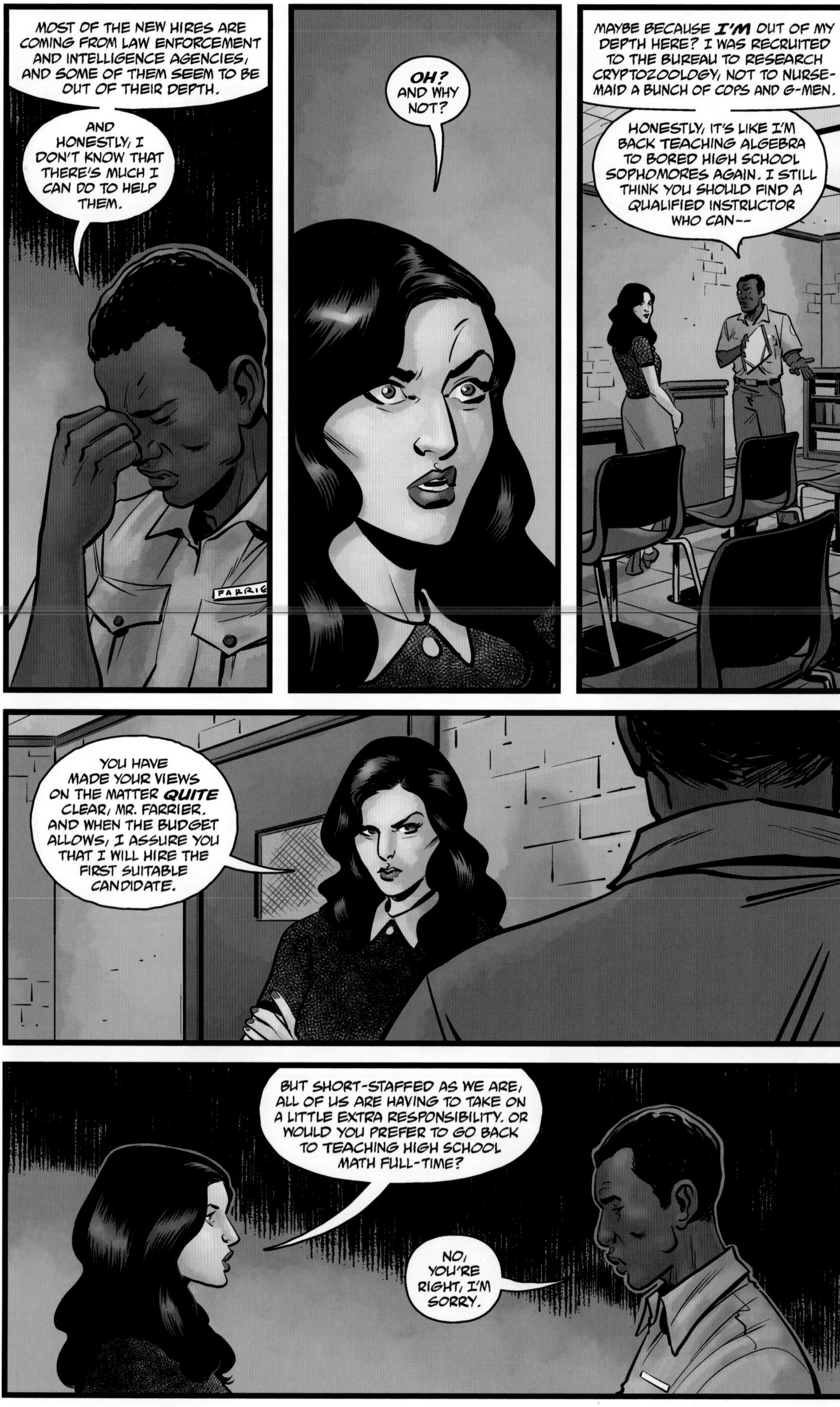
MOST OF THE NEW HIRES ARE COMING FROM LAW ENFORCEMENT AND INTELLIGENCE AGENCIES, AND SOME OF THEM SEEM TO BE OUT OF THEIR DEPTH.
AND HONESTLY, I DON'T KNOW THAT THERE'S MUCH I CAN DO TO HELP THEM.
FARRIE
OH? AND WHY NOT?
MAYBE BECAUSE I'M OUT OF MY DEPTH HERE? I WAS RECRUITED TO THE BUREAU TO RESEARCH CRYPTOZOOLOGY, NOT TO NURSE-MAID A BUNCH OF COPS AND G-MEN.
HONESTLY, IT'S LIKE I'M BACK TEACHING ALGEBRA TO BORED HIGH SCHOOL SOPHOMORES AGAIN. I STILL THINK YOU SHOULD FIND A QUALIFIED INSTRUCTOR WHO CAN--
YOU HAVE MADE YOUR VIEWS ON THE MATTER QUITE CLEAR, MR. FARRIER. AND WHEN THE BUDGET ALLOWS, I ASSURE YOU THAT I WILL HIRE THE FIRST SUITABLE CANDIDATE.
BUT SHORT-STAFFED AS WE ARE, ALL OF US ARE HAVING TO TAKE ON A LITTLE EXTRA RESPONSIBILITY. OR WOULD YOU PREFER TO GO BACK TO TEACHING HIGH SCHOOL MATH FULL-TIME?
NO, YOU'RE RIGHT, I'M SORRY.

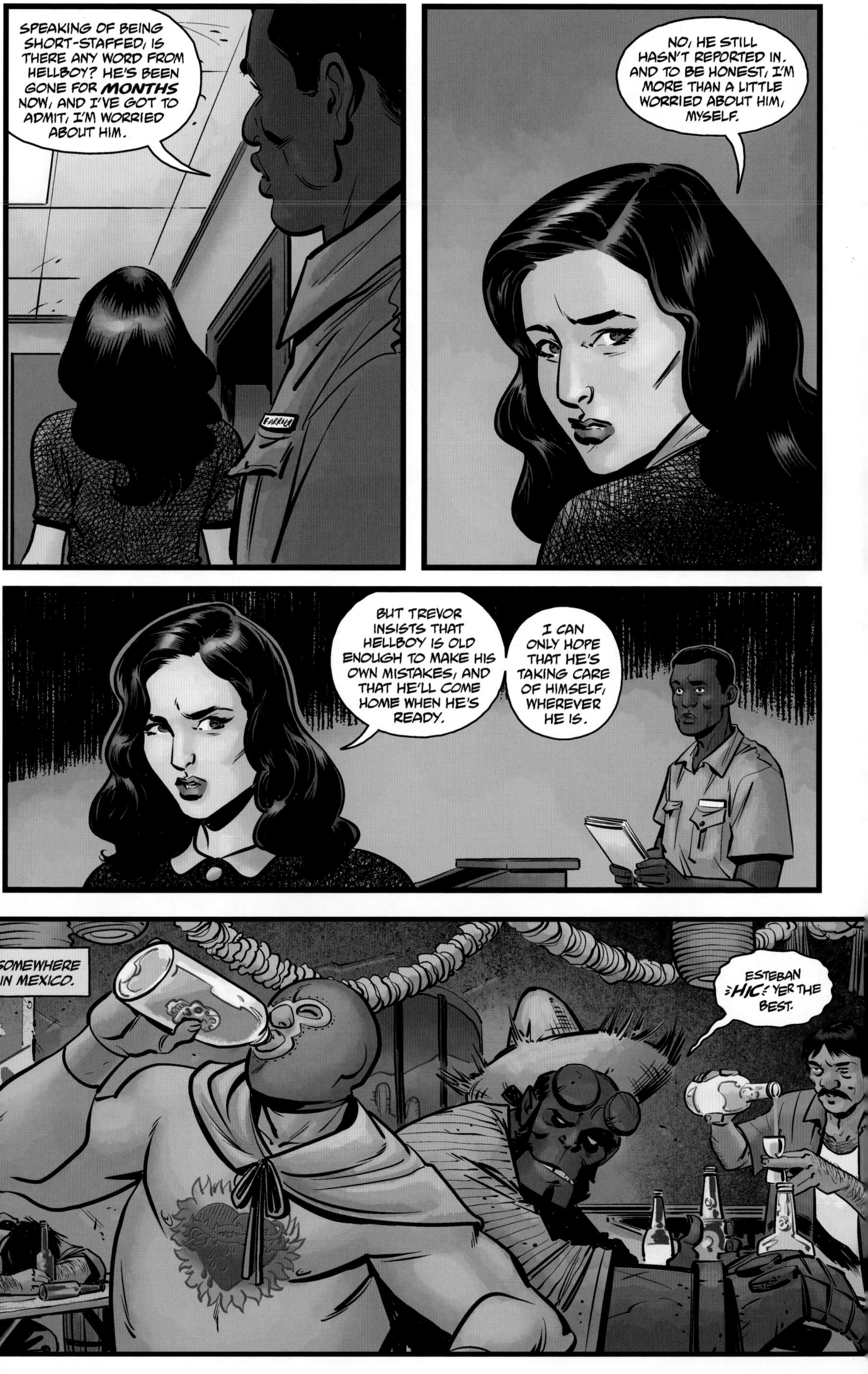
SPEAKING OF BEING SHORT-STAFFED, IS THERE ANY WORD FROM HELLBOY? HE'S BEEN GONE FOR MONTHS NOW, AND I'VE GOT TO ADMIT, I'M WORRIED ABOUT HIM.
FARRIER
NO, HE STILL HASN'T REPORTED IN. AND TO BE HONEST, I'M MORE THAN A LITTLE WORRIED ABOUT HIM, MYSELF.
BUT TREVOR INSISTS THAT HELLBOY IS OLD ENOUGH TO MAKE HIS OWN MISTAKES, AND THAT HE'LL COME HOME WHEN HE'S READY.
I CAN ONLY HOPE THAT HE'S TAKING CARE OF HIMSELF, WHEREVER HE IS.
SOMEWHERE IN MEXICO.
ESTEBAN *HIC* YER THE BEST.

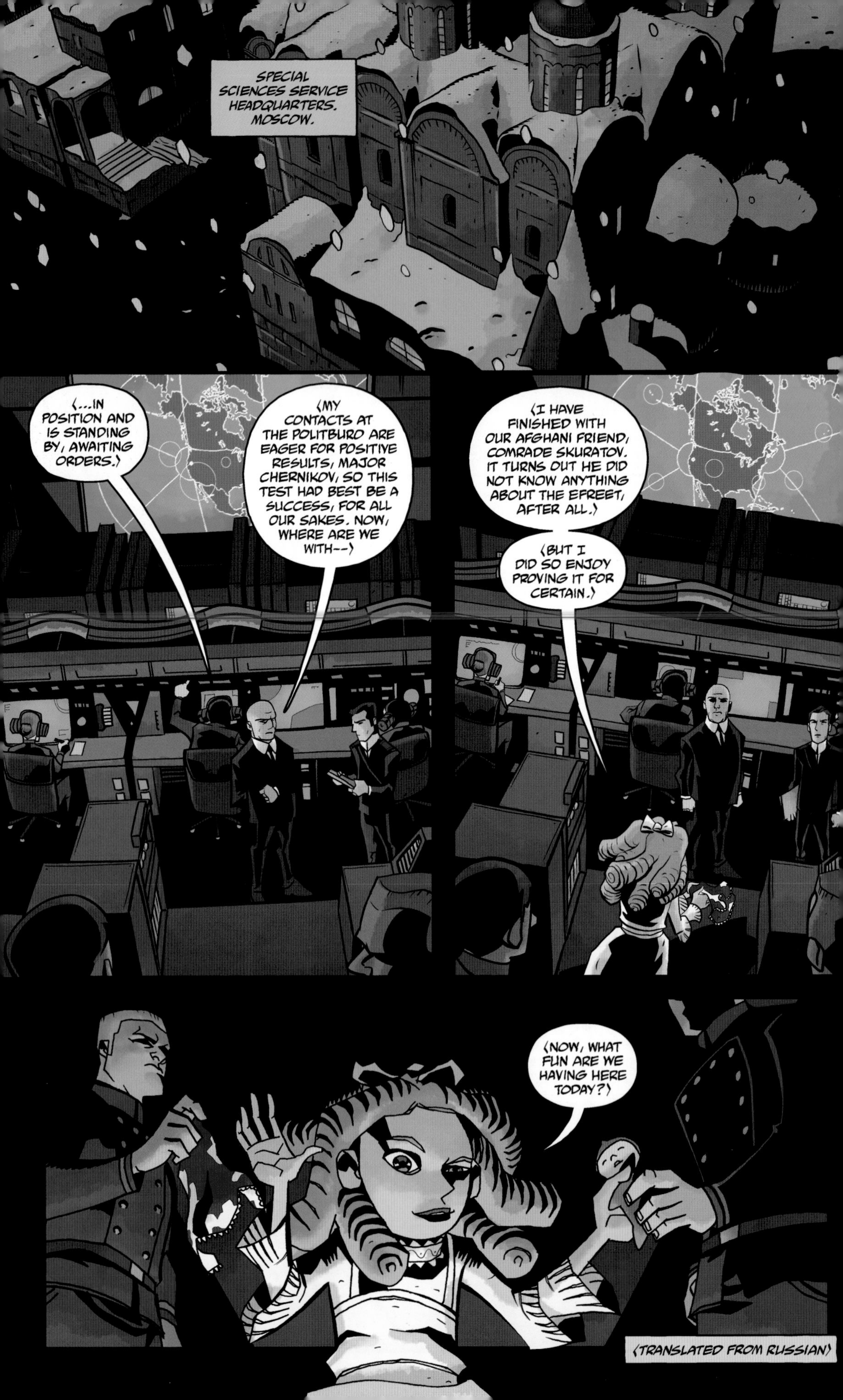
SPECIAL SCIENCES SERVICE HEADQUARTERS. MOSCOW.
⟨...IN POSITION AND IS STANDING BY, AWAITING ORDERS.⟩
⟨MY CONTACTS AT THE POLITBURO ARE EAGER FOR POSITIVE RESULTS, MAJOR CHERNIKOV, SO THIS TEST HAD BEST BE A SUCCESS, FOR ALL OUR SAKES. NOW, WHERE ARE WE WITH--⟩
⟨I HAVE FINISHED WITH OUR AFGHANI FRIEND, COMRADE SKURATOV. IT TURNS OUT HE DID NOT KNOW ANYTHING ABOUT THE EFREET, AFTER ALL.⟩
⟨BUT I DID SO ENJOY PROVING IT FOR CERTAIN.⟩
⟨NOW, WHAT FUN ARE WE HAVING HERE TODAY?⟩
⟨TRANSLATED FROM RUSSIAN⟩

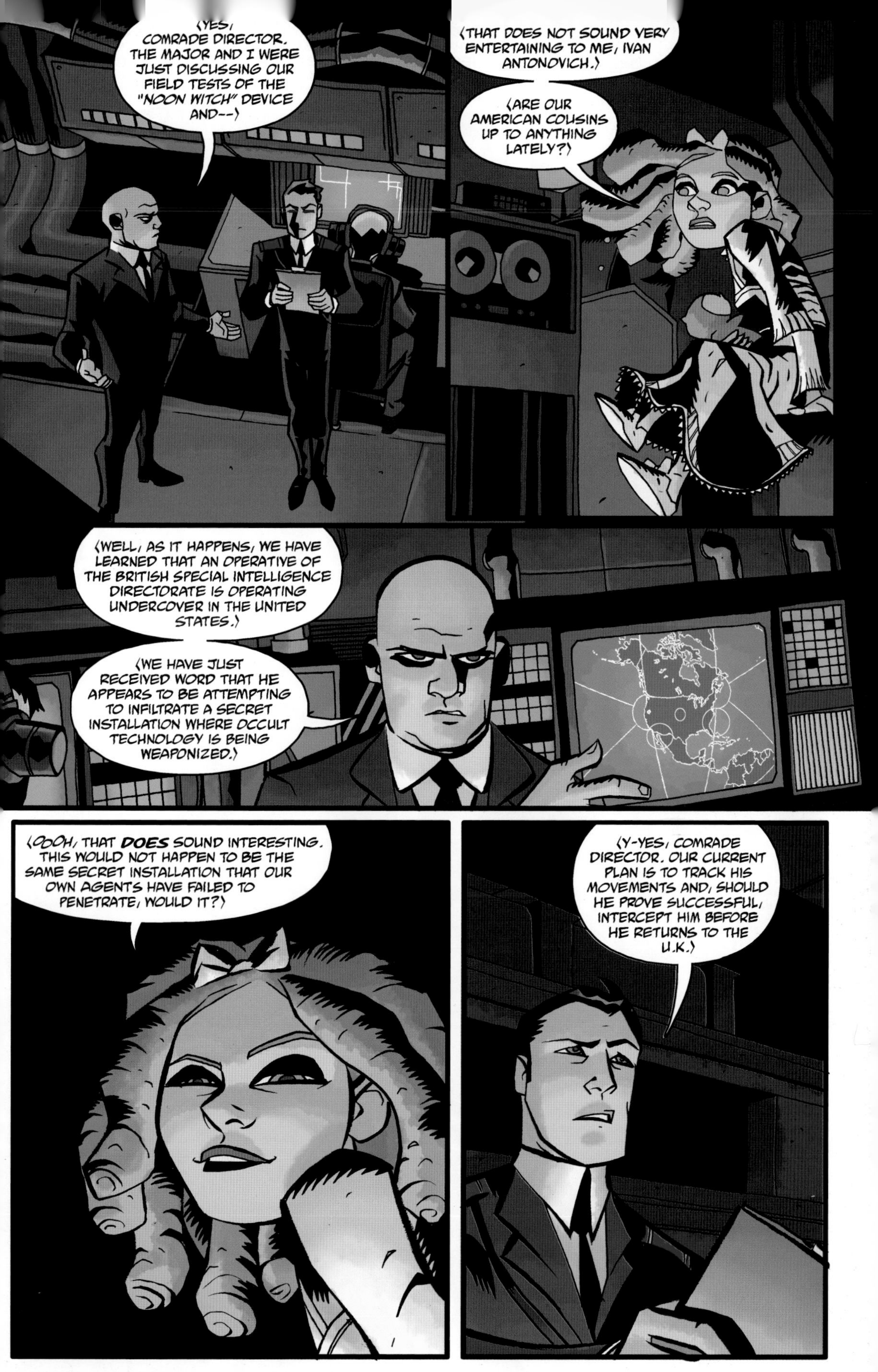

⟨YES, COMRADE DIRECTOR. THE MAJOR AND I WERE JUST DISCUSSING OUR FIELD TESTS OF THE "NOON WITCH" DEVICE AND--⟩
⟨THAT DOES NOT SOUND VERY ENTERTAINING TO ME, IVAN ANTONOVICH.⟩
⟨ARE OUR AMERICAN COUSINS UP TO ANYTHING LATELY?⟩
⟨WELL, AS IT HAPPENS, WE HAVE LEARNED THAT AN OPERATIVE OF THE BRITISH SPECIAL INTELLIGENCE DIRECTORATE IS OPERATING UNDERCOVER IN THE UNITED STATES.⟩
⟨WE HAVE JUST RECEIVED WORD THAT HE APPEARS TO BE ATTEMPTING TO INFILTRATE A SECRET INSTALLATION WHERE OCCULT TECHNOLOGY IS BEING WEAPONIZED.⟩
⟨OOOH, THAT **DOES** SOUND INTERESTING. THIS WOULD NOT HAPPEN TO BE THE SAME SECRET INSTALLATION THAT OUR OWN AGENTS HAVE FAILED TO PENETRATE, WOULD IT?⟩
⟨Y-YES, COMRADE DIRECTOR. OUR CURRENT PLAN IS TO TRACK HIS MOVEMENTS AND, SHOULD HE PROVE SUCCESSFUL, INTERCEPT HIM BEFORE HE RETURNS TO THE U.K.⟩

〈WHAT FUN!〉

〈THEN WE CAN LEARN FROM HIM WHATEVER SECRETS HE HAS WHEEDLED FROM THE AMERICANS, AND TAKE ONE OF THE BRITISH PAWNS OFF THE BOARD AT THE SAME TIME.〉

〈ANY NEWS OF OUR *OTHER* BRITISH FRIEND, HMM? WHAT IS DEAR OLD TREVOR GETTING UP TO THESE DAYS, I WONDER...?〉

〈N-NO NEW INTEL ON THAT. BUT...THE "NOON WITCH" IS NEARLY READY FOR ITS FIRST FIELD TEST.〉

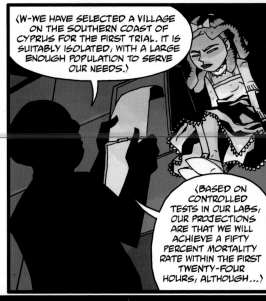

〈W-WE HAVE SELECTED A VILLAGE ON THE SOUTHERN COAST OF CYPRUS FOR THE FIRST TRIAL. IT IS SUITABLY ISOLATED, WITH A LARGE ENOUGH POPULATION TO SERVE OUR NEEDS.〉

〈BASED ON CONTROLLED TESTS IN OUR LABS, OUR PROJECTIONS ARE THAT WE WILL ACHIEVE A FIFTY PERCENT MORTALITY RATE WITHIN THE FIRST TWENTY-FOUR HOURS, ALTHOUGH...〉

〈COMRADE DIRECTOR? IS SOMETHING WRONG...?〉

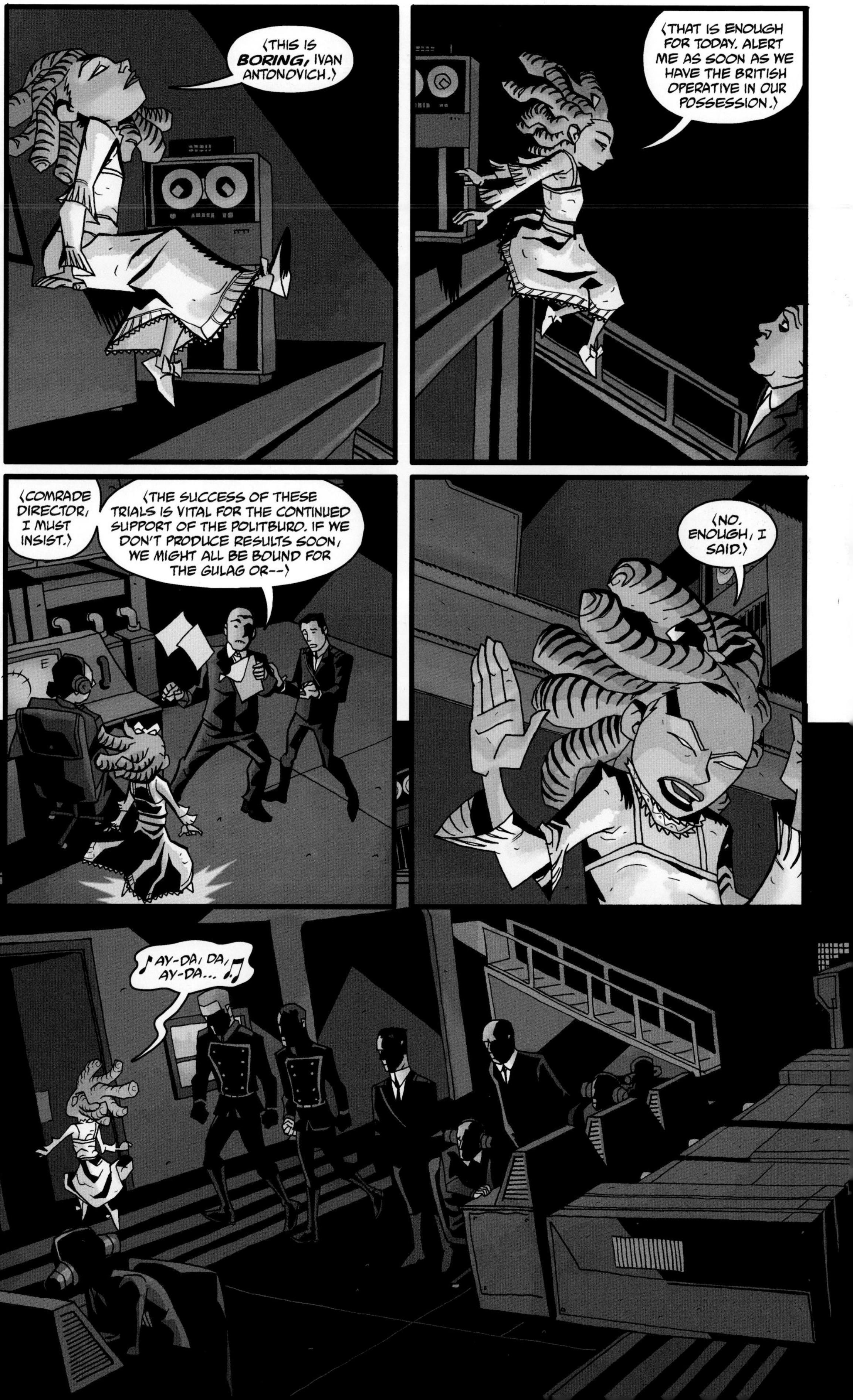

‹THIS IS BORING, IVAN ANTONOVICH.›
‹THAT IS ENOUGH FOR TODAY. ALERT ME AS SOON AS WE HAVE THE BRITISH OPERATIVE IN OUR POSSESSION.›
‹COMRADE DIRECTOR, I MUST INSIST.›
‹THE SUCCESS OF THESE TRIALS IS VITAL FOR THE CONTINUED SUPPORT OF THE POLITBURO. IF WE DON'T PRODUCE RESULTS SOON, WE MIGHT ALL BE BOUND FOR THE GULAG OR--›
‹NO. ENOUGH, I SAID.›
♪ AY-DA, DA, AY-DA... ♪♫

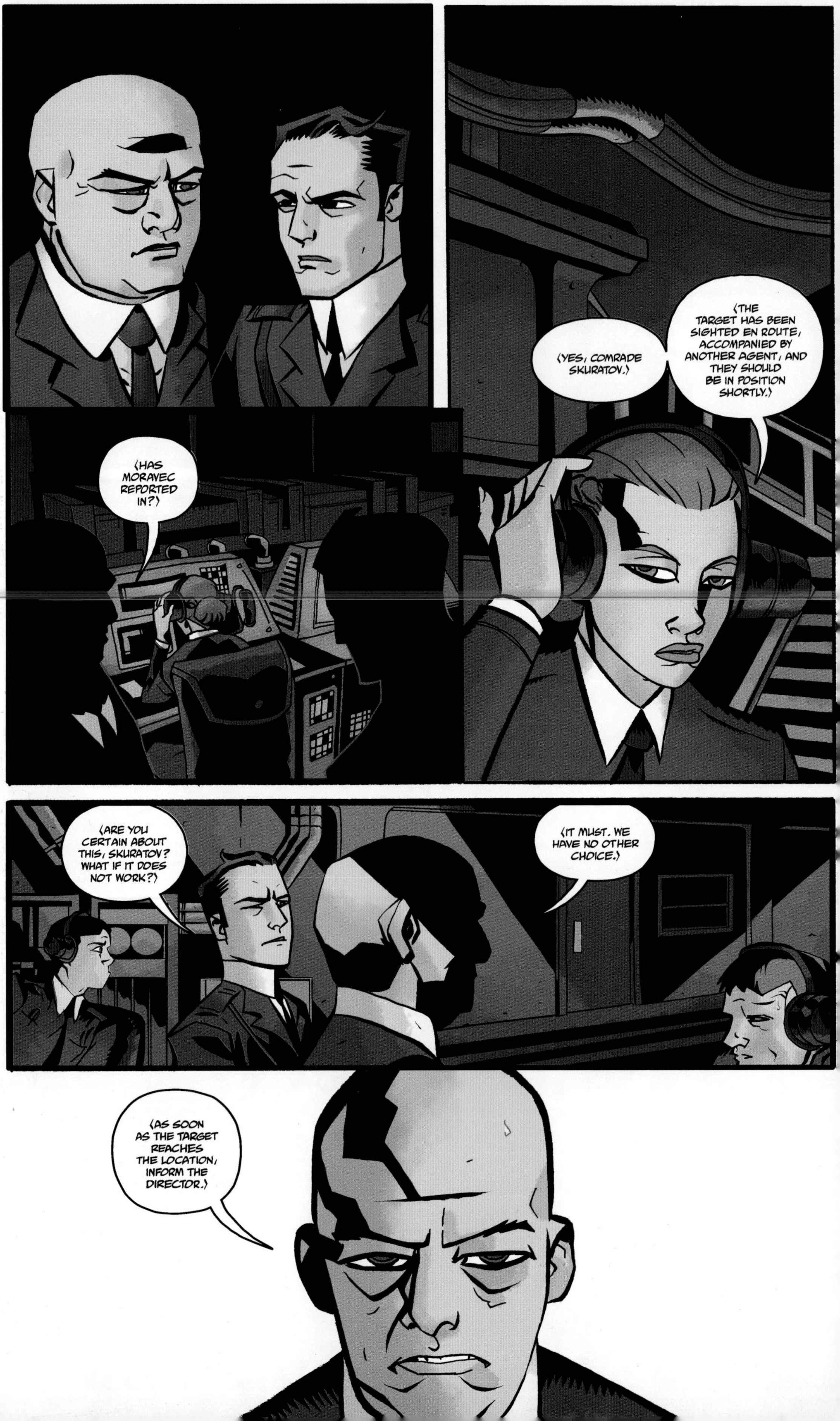

‹YES, COMRADE SKURATOV.›
‹THE TARGET HAS BEEN SIGHTED EN ROUTE, ACCOMPANIED BY ANOTHER AGENT, AND THEY SHOULD BE IN POSITION SHORTLY.›
‹HAS MORAVEC REPORTED IN?›
‹ARE YOU CERTAIN ABOUT THIS, SKURATOV? WHAT IF IT DOES NOT WORK?›
‹IT MUST. WE HAVE NO OTHER CHOICE.›
‹AS SOON AS THE TARGET REACHES THE LOCATION, INFORM THE DIRECTOR.›

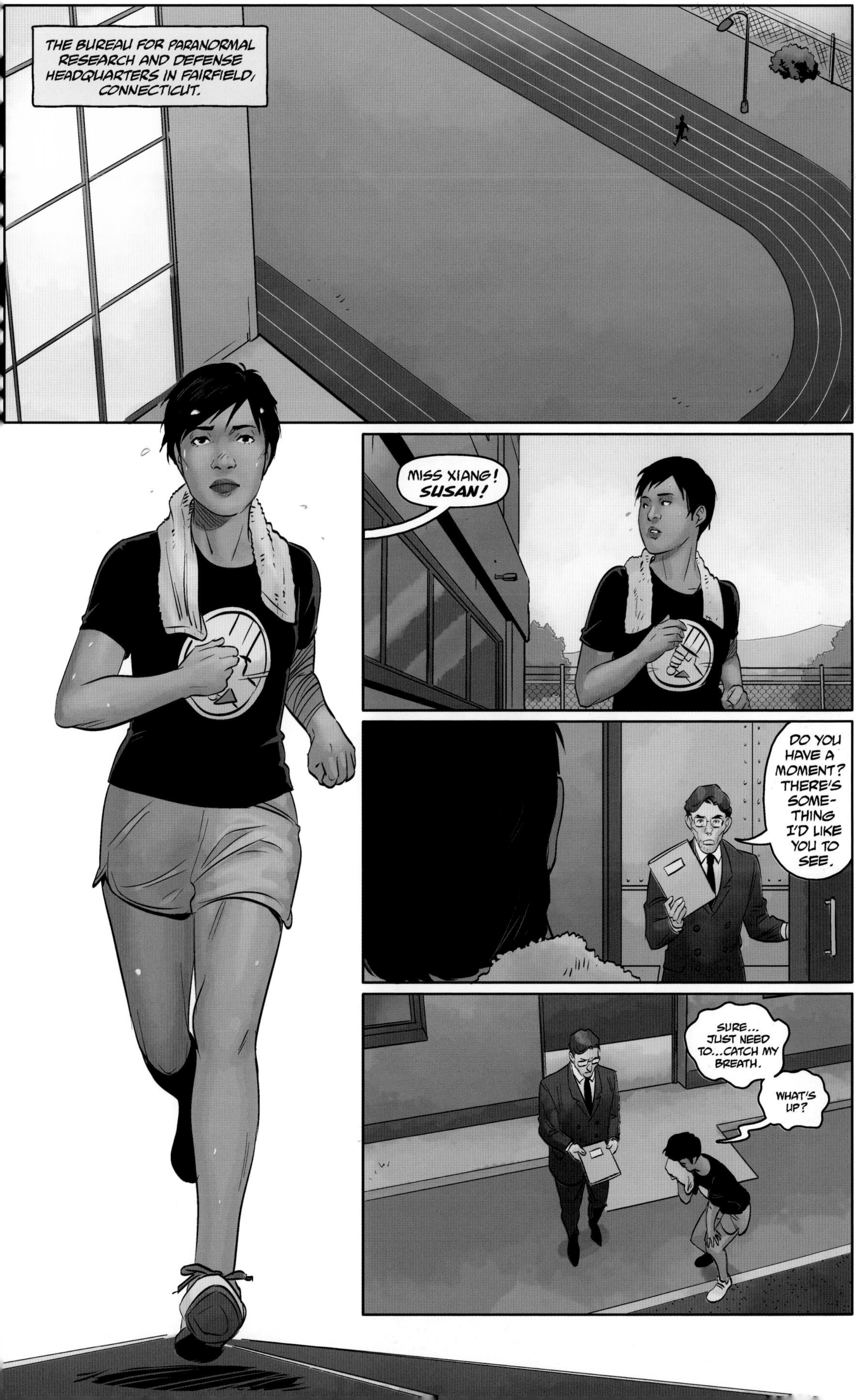
THE BUREAU FOR PARANORMAL RESEARCH AND DEFENSE HEADQUARTERS IN FAIRFIELD, CONNECTICUT.
MISS XIANG! SUSAN!
DO YOU HAVE A MOMENT? THERE'S SOMETHING I'D LIKE YOU TO SEE.
SURE... JUST NEED TO...CATCH MY BREATH.
WHAT'S UP?

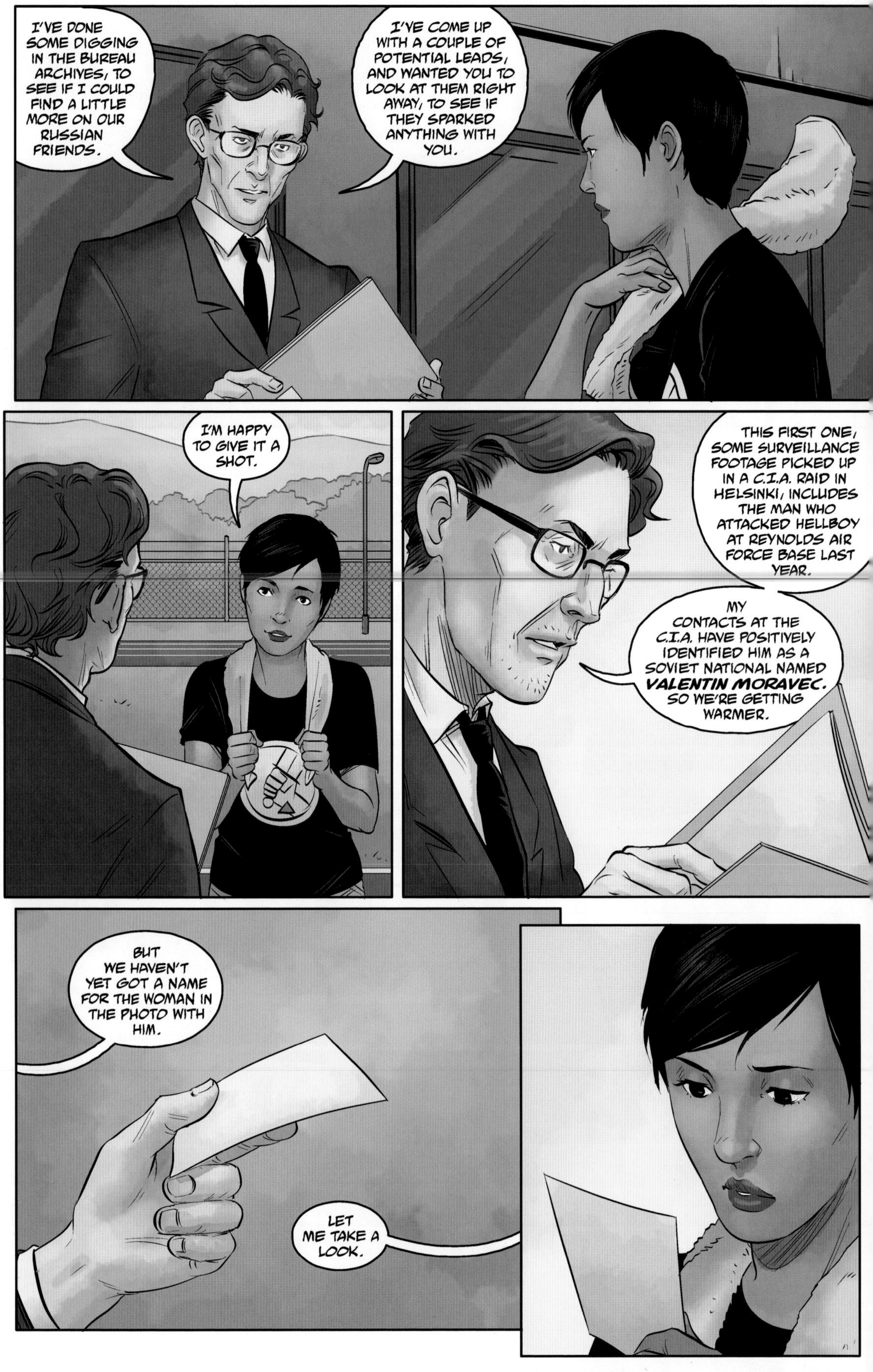
I'VE DONE SOME DIGGING IN THE BUREAU ARCHIVES, TO SEE IF I COULD FIND A LITTLE MORE ON OUR RUSSIAN FRIENDS.
I'VE COME UP WITH A COUPLE OF POTENTIAL LEADS, AND WANTED YOU TO LOOK AT THEM RIGHT AWAY, TO SEE IF THEY SPARKED ANYTHING WITH YOU.
I'M HAPPY TO GIVE IT A SHOT.
THIS FIRST ONE, SOME SURVEILLANCE FOOTAGE PICKED UP IN A C.I.A. RAID IN HELSINKI, INCLUDES THE MAN WHO ATTACKED HELLBOY AT REYNOLDS AIR FORCE BASE LAST YEAR.
MY CONTACTS AT THE C.I.A. HAVE POSITIVELY IDENTIFIED HIM AS A SOVIET NATIONAL NAMED **VALENTIN MORAVEC.** SO WE'RE GETTING WARMER.
BUT WE HAVEN'T YET GOT A NAME FOR THE WOMAN IN THE PHOTO WITH HIM.
LET ME TAKE A LOOK.

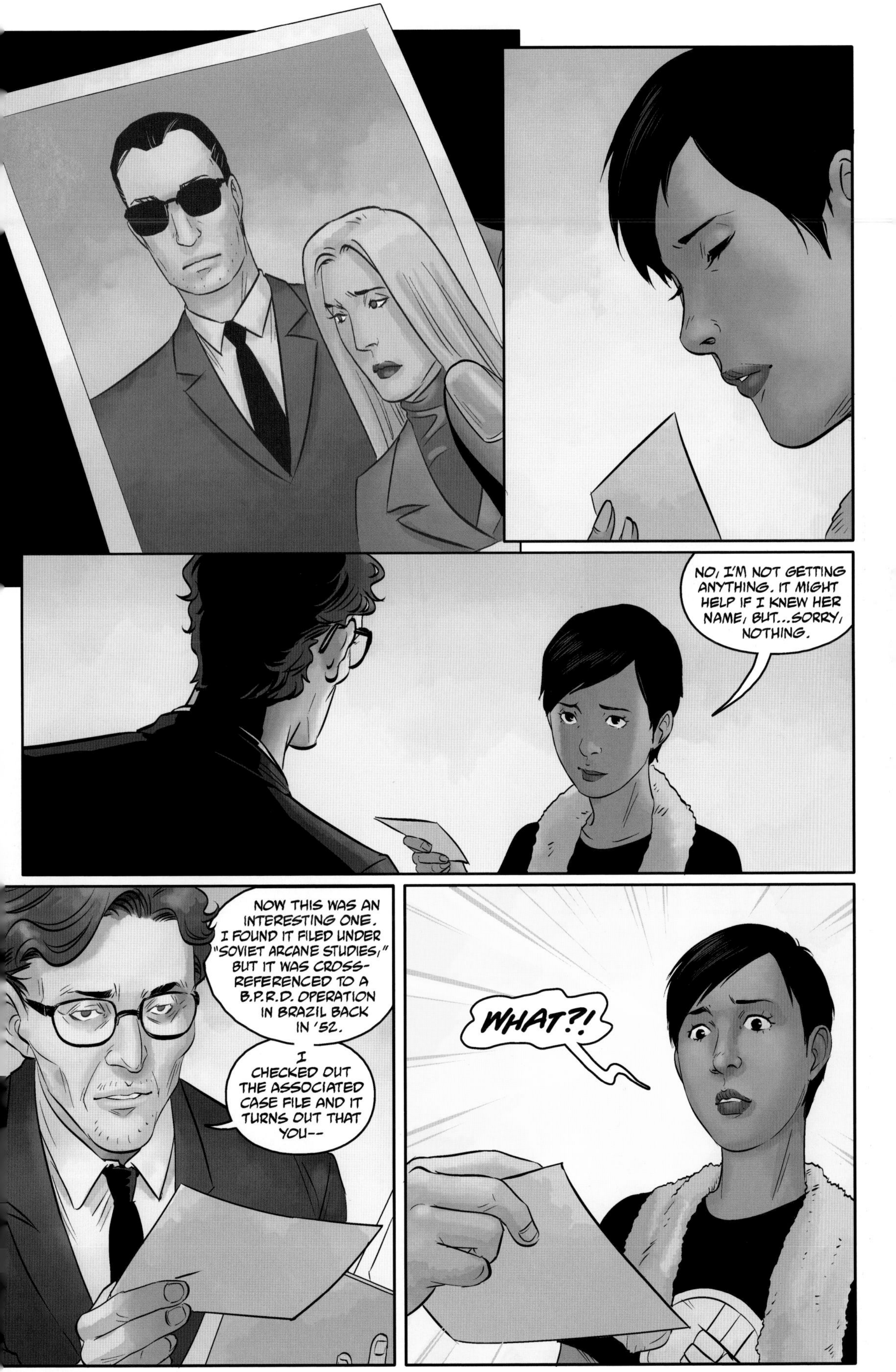
NO, I'M NOT GETTING ANYTHING. IT MIGHT HELP IF I KNEW HER NAME, BUT...SORRY, NOTHING.
NOW THIS WAS AN INTERESTING ONE. I FOUND IT FILED UNDER "SOVIET ARCANE STUDIES," BUT IT WAS CROSS-REFERENCED TO A B.P.R.D. OPERATION IN BRAZIL BACK IN '52.
I CHECKED OUT THE ASSOCIATED CASE FILE AND IT TURNS OUT THAT YOU--
WHAT?!

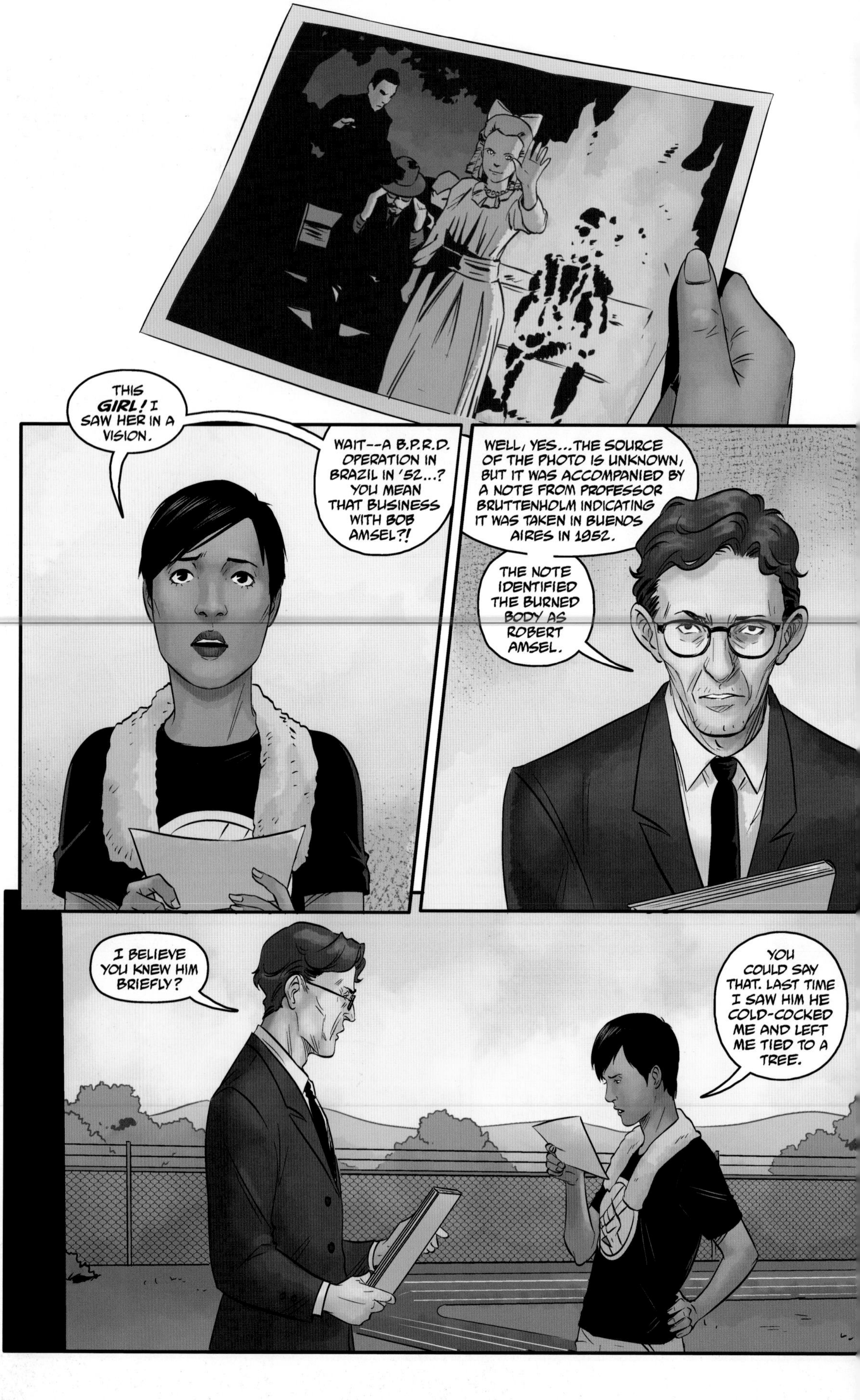
THIS GIRL! I SAW HER IN A VISION.
WAIT--A B.P.R.D. OPERATION IN BRAZIL IN '52...? YOU MEAN THAT BUSINESS WITH BOB AMSEL?!
WELL, YES... THE SOURCE OF THE PHOTO IS UNKNOWN, BUT IT WAS ACCOMPANIED BY A NOTE FROM PROFESSOR BRUTTENHOLM INDICATING IT WAS TAKEN IN BUENOS AIRES IN 1952.
THE NOTE IDENTIFIED THE BURNED BODY AS ROBERT AMSEL.
I BELIEVE YOU KNEW HIM BRIEFLY?
YOU COULD SAY THAT. LAST TIME I SAW HIM HE COLD-COCKED ME AND LEFT ME TIED TO A TREE.

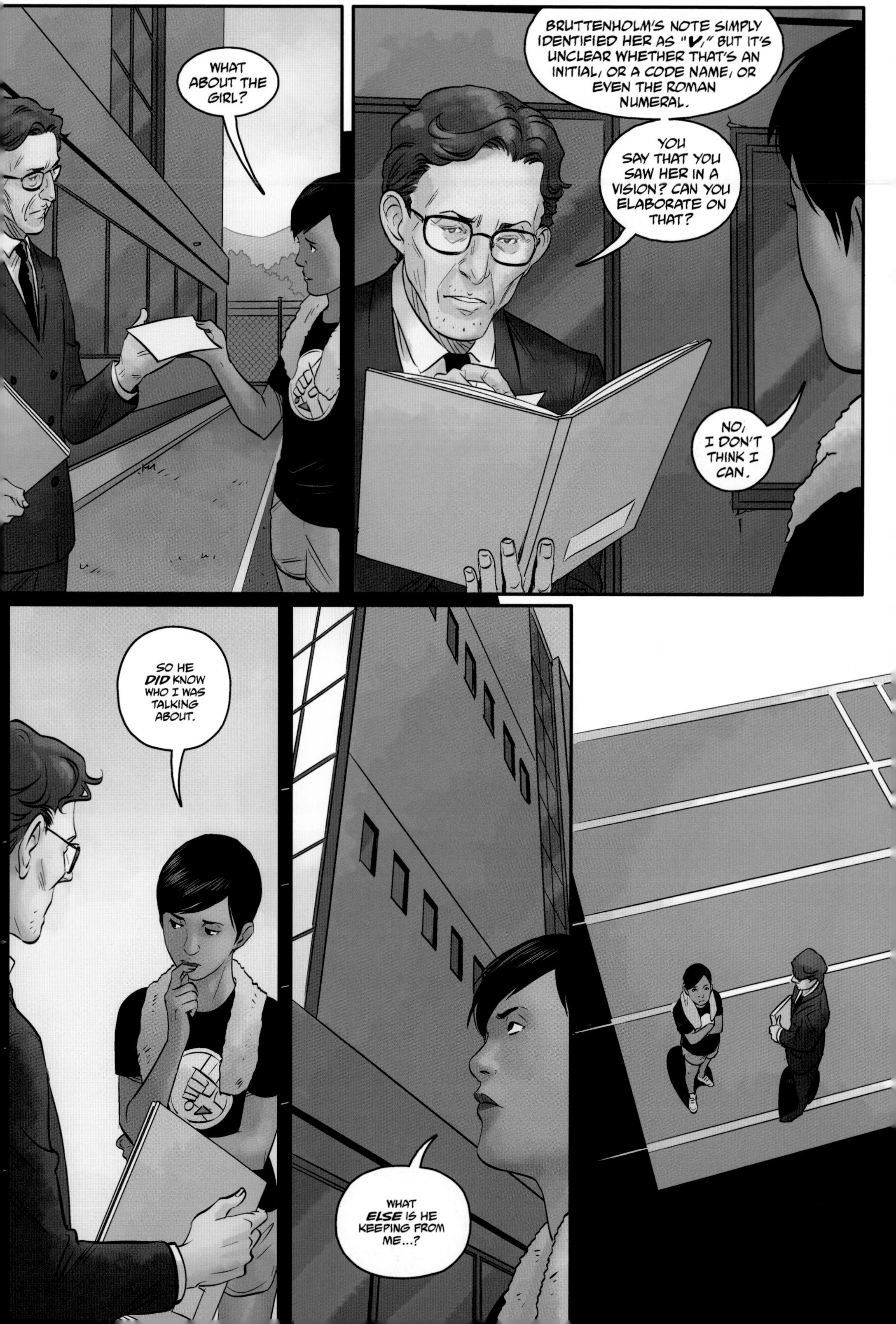
WHAT ABOUT THE GIRL?
BRUTTENHOLM'S NOTE SIMPLY IDENTIFIED HER AS "V," BUT IT'S UNCLEAR WHETHER THAT'S AN INITIAL, OR A CODE NAME, OR EVEN THE ROMAN NUMERAL.
YOU SAY THAT YOU SAW HER IN A VISION? CAN YOU ELABORATE ON THAT?
NO, I DON'T THINK I CAN.
SO HE DID KNOW WHO I WAS TALKING ABOUT.
WHAT ELSE IS HE KEEPING FROM ME...?

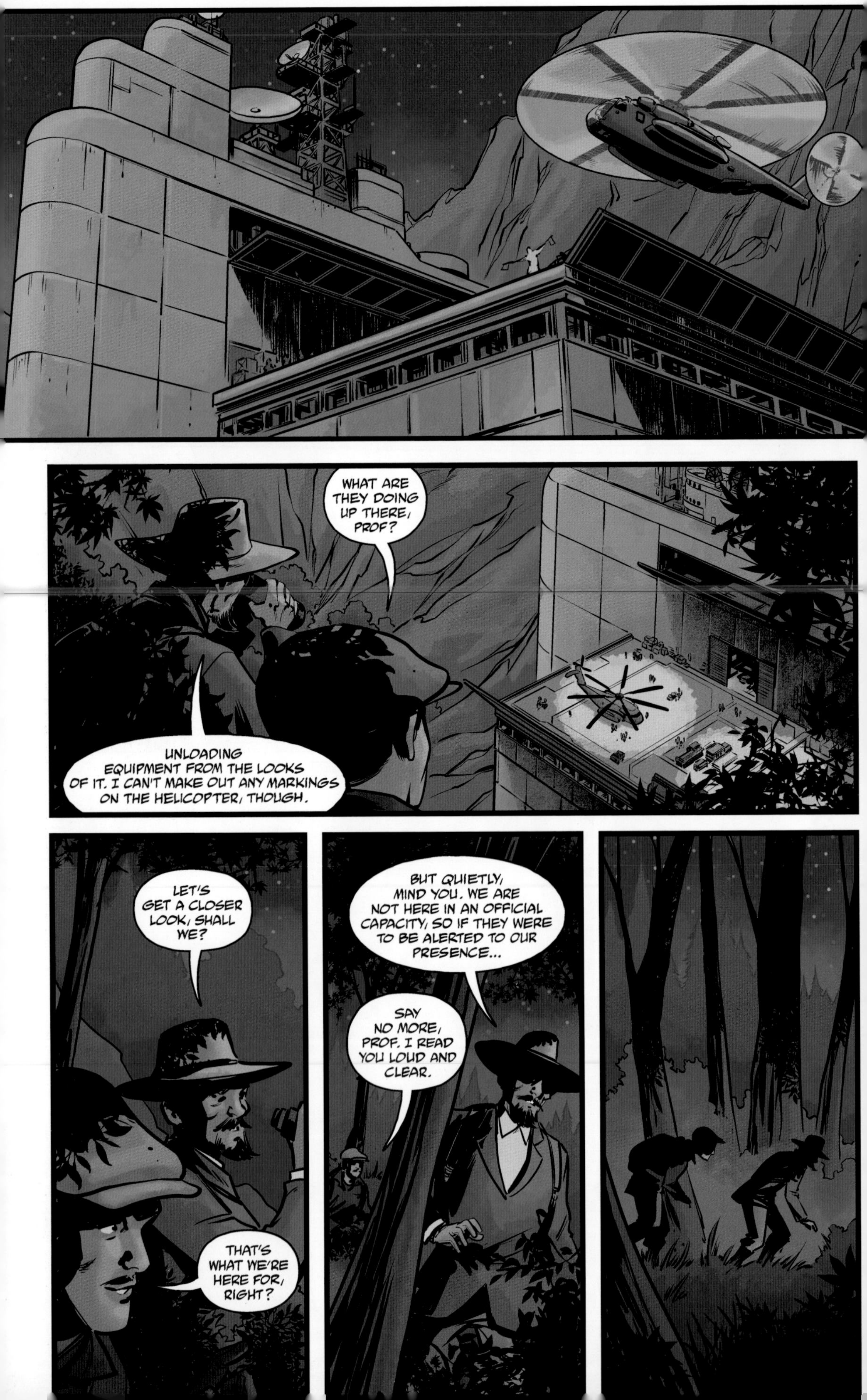
WHAT ARE THEY DOING UP THERE, PROF?
UNLOADING EQUIPMENT FROM THE LOOKS OF IT. I CAN'T MAKE OUT ANY MARKINGS ON THE HELICOPTER, THOUGH.
LET'S GET A CLOSER LOOK, SHALL WE?
THAT'S WHAT WE'RE HERE FOR, RIGHT?
BUT QUIETLY, MIND YOU. WE ARE NOT HERE IN AN OFFICIAL CAPACITY, SO IF THEY WERE TO BE ALERTED TO OUR PRESENCE...
SAY NO MORE, PROF. I READ YOU LOUD AND CLEAR.

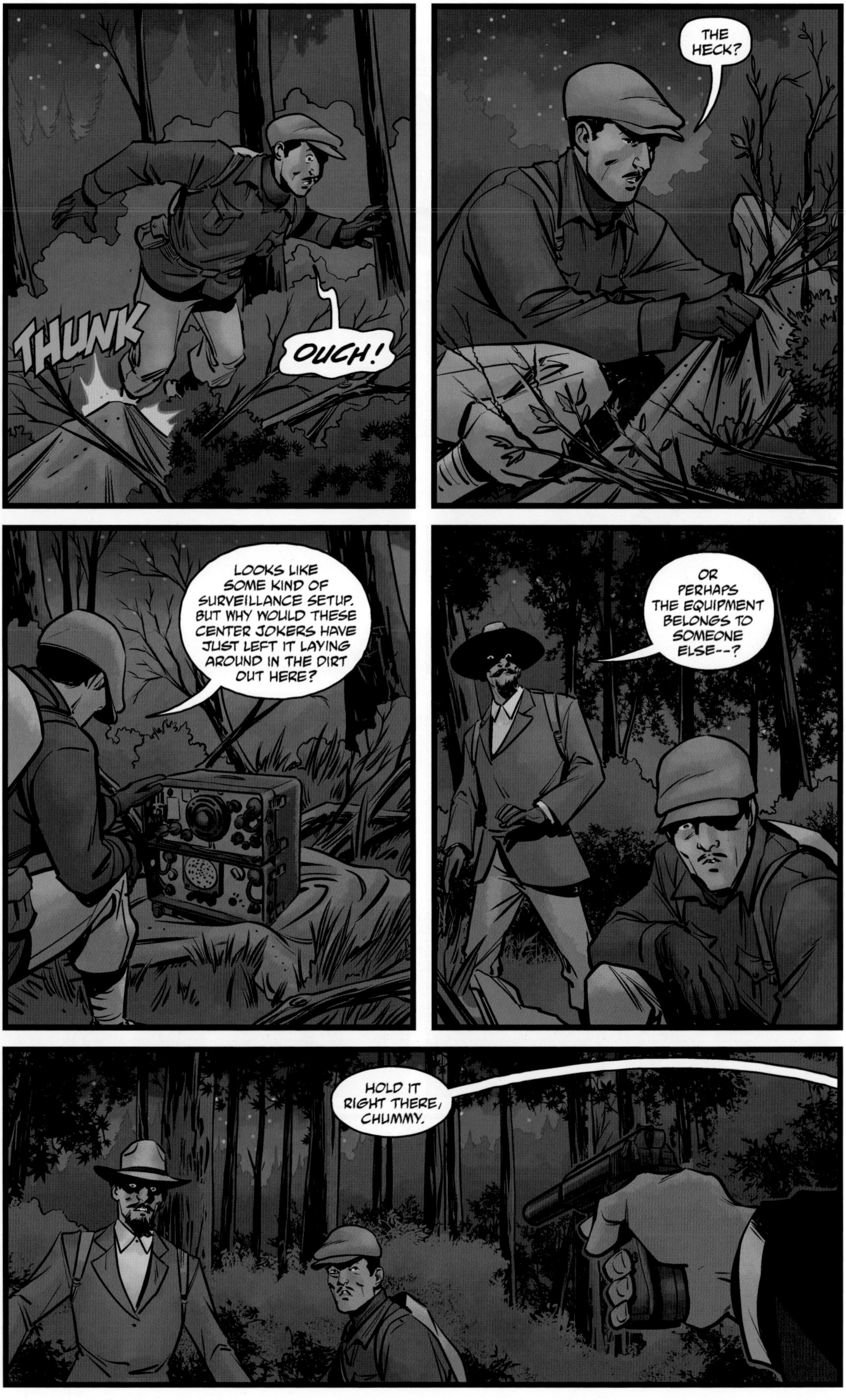
THUNK
OUCH!
THE HECK?
LOOKS LIKE SOME KIND OF SURVEILLANCE SETUP. BUT WHY WOULD THESE CENTER JOKERS HAVE JUST LEFT IT LAYING AROUND IN THE DIRT OUT HERE?
OR PERHAPS THE EQUIPMENT BELONGS TO SOMEONE ELSE--?
HOLD IT RIGHT THERE, CHUMMY.

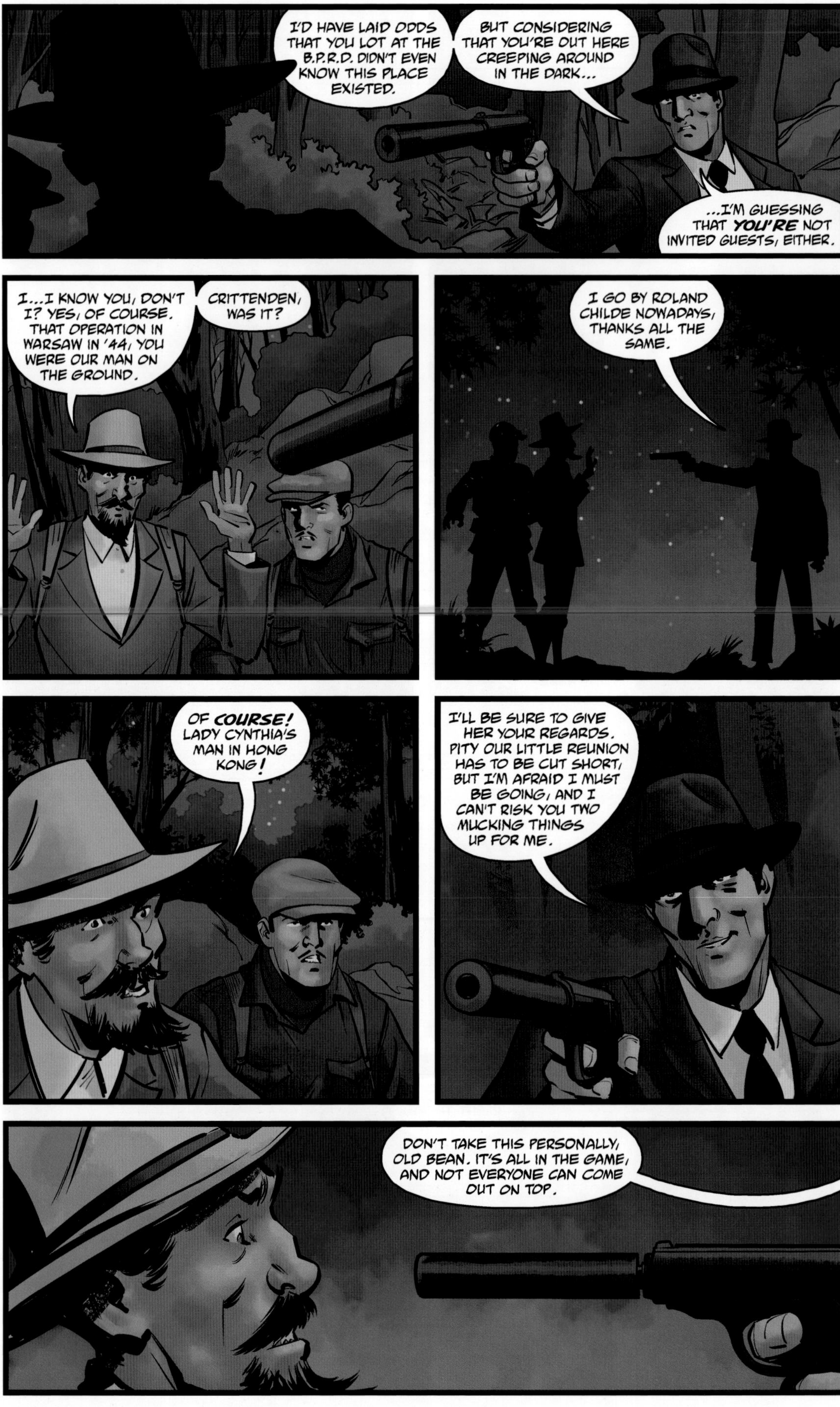
I'D HAVE LAID ODDS THAT YOU LOT AT THE B.P.R.D. DIDN'T EVEN KNOW THIS PLACE EXISTED.
BUT CONSIDERING THAT YOU'RE OUT HERE CREEPING AROUND IN THE DARK...
...I'M GUESSING THAT YOU'RE NOT INVITED GUESTS, EITHER.
I...I KNOW YOU, DON'T I? YES, OF COURSE. THAT OPERATION IN WARSAW IN '44, YOU WERE OUR MAN ON THE GROUND.
CRITTENDEN, WAS IT?
I GO BY ROLAND CHILDE NOWADAYS, THANKS ALL THE SAME.
OF COURSE! LADY CYNTHIA'S MAN IN HONG KONG!
I'LL BE SURE TO GIVE HER YOUR REGARDS. PITY OUR LITTLE REUNION HAS TO BE CUT SHORT, BUT I'M AFRAID I MUST BE GOING, AND I CAN'T RISK YOU TWO MUCKING THINGS UP FOR ME.
DON'T TAKE THIS PERSONALLY, OLD BEAN. IT'S ALL IN THE GAME, AND NOT EVERYONE CAN COME OUT ON TOP.

CHAPTER FOUR

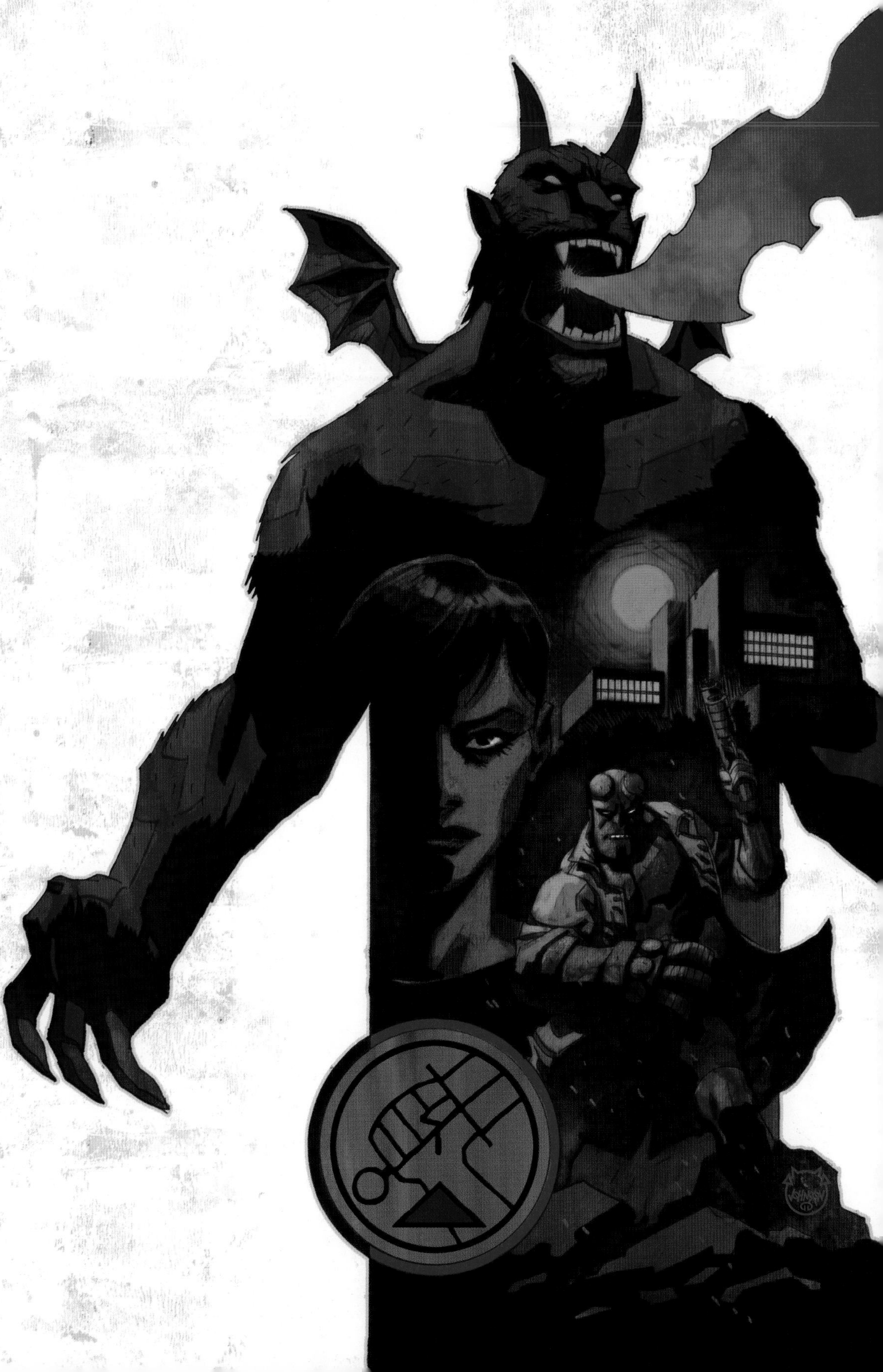

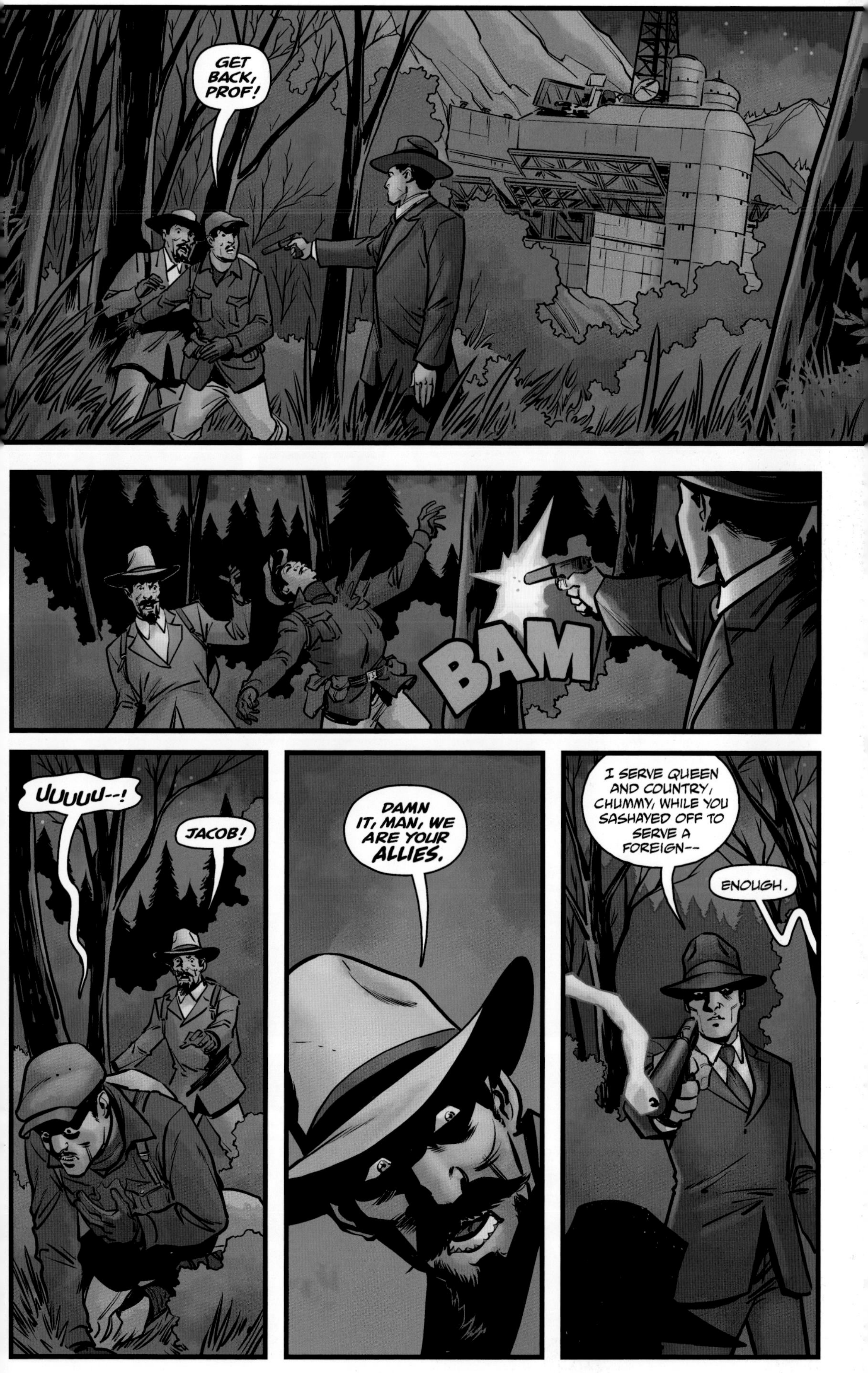
GET BACK, PROF!
BAM
UUUUU--!
JACOB!
DAMN IT, MAN, WE ARE YOUR ALLIES.
I SERVE QUEEN AND COUNTRY, CHUMMY, WHILE YOU SASHAYED OFF TO SERVE A FOREIGN--
ENOUGH.

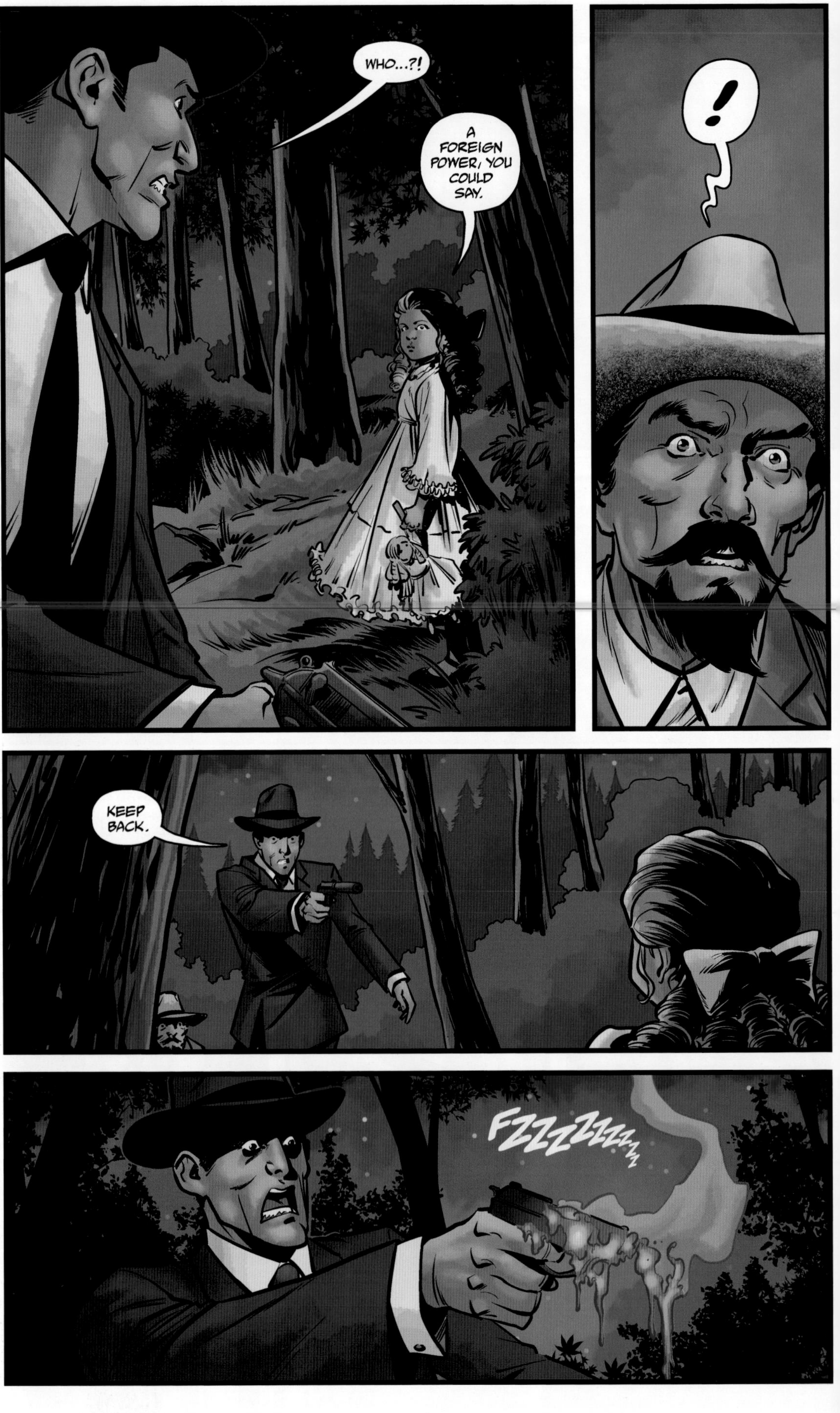
WHO...?!
A FOREIGN POWER, YOU COULD SAY.
!
KEEP BACK.
FZZZZZZZZ

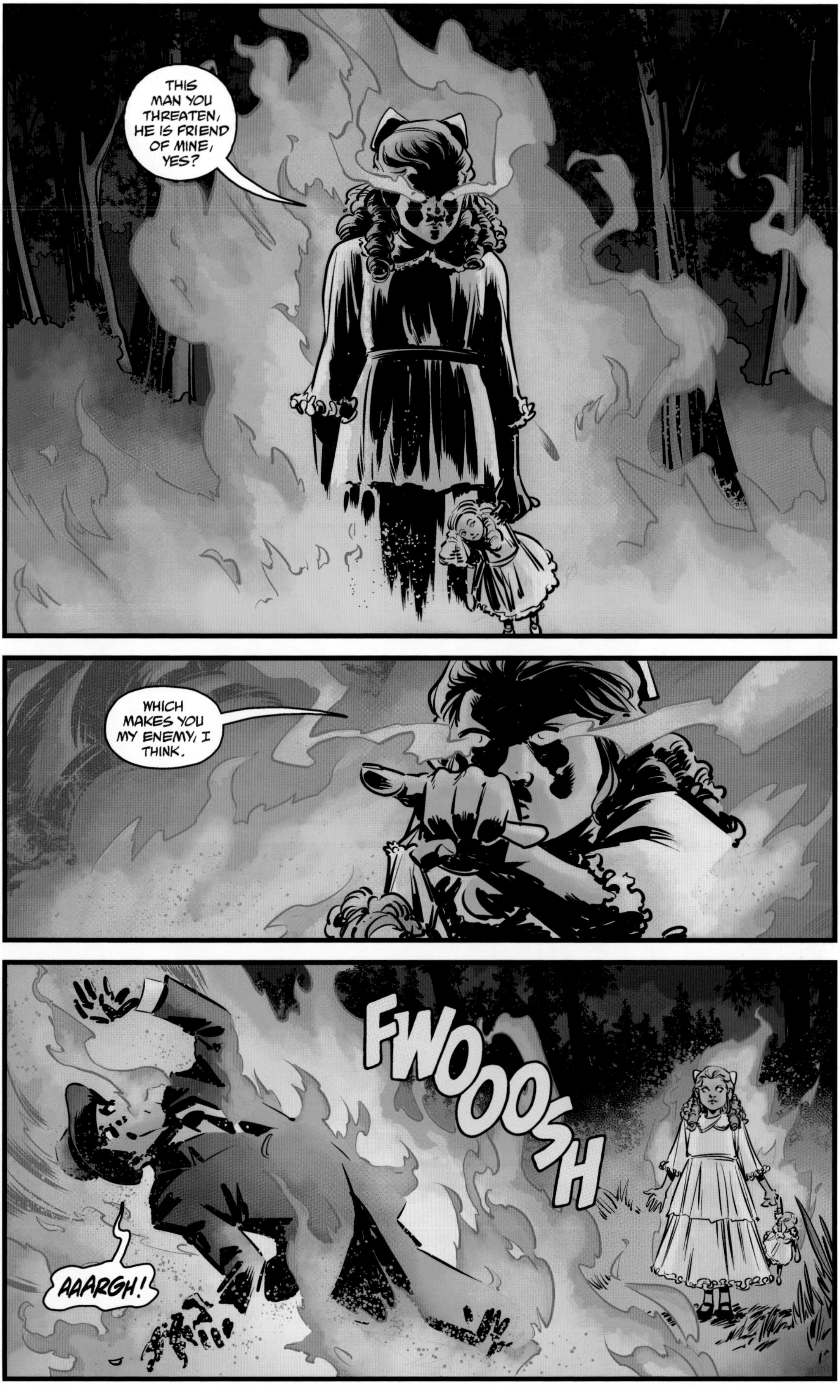
THIS MAN YOU THREATEN, HE IS FRIEND OF MINE, YES?
WHICH MAKES YOU MY ENEMY, I THINK.
FWOOOSH
AAARGH!

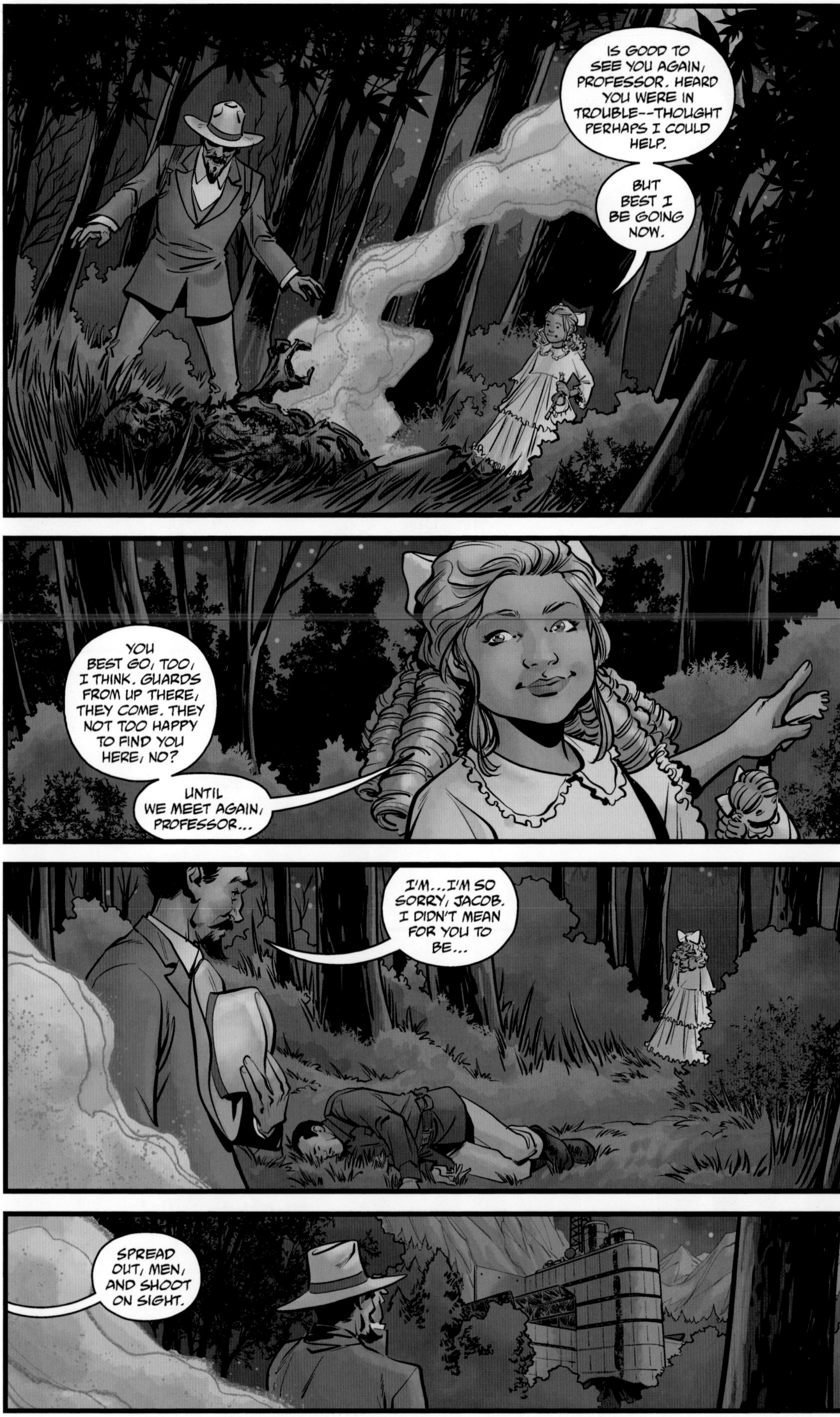
IS GOOD TO SEE YOU AGAIN, PROFESSOR. HEARD YOU WERE IN TROUBLE--THOUGHT PERHAPS I COULD HELP.
BUT BEST I BE GOING NOW.
YOU BEST GO, TOO, I THINK. GUARDS FROM UP THERE, THEY COME. THEY NOT TOO HAPPY TO FIND YOU HERE, NO?
UNTIL WE MEET AGAIN, PROFESSOR...
I'M...I'M SO SORRY, JACOB. I DIDN'T MEAN FOR YOU TO BE...
SPREAD OUT, MEN, AND SHOOT ON SIGHT.

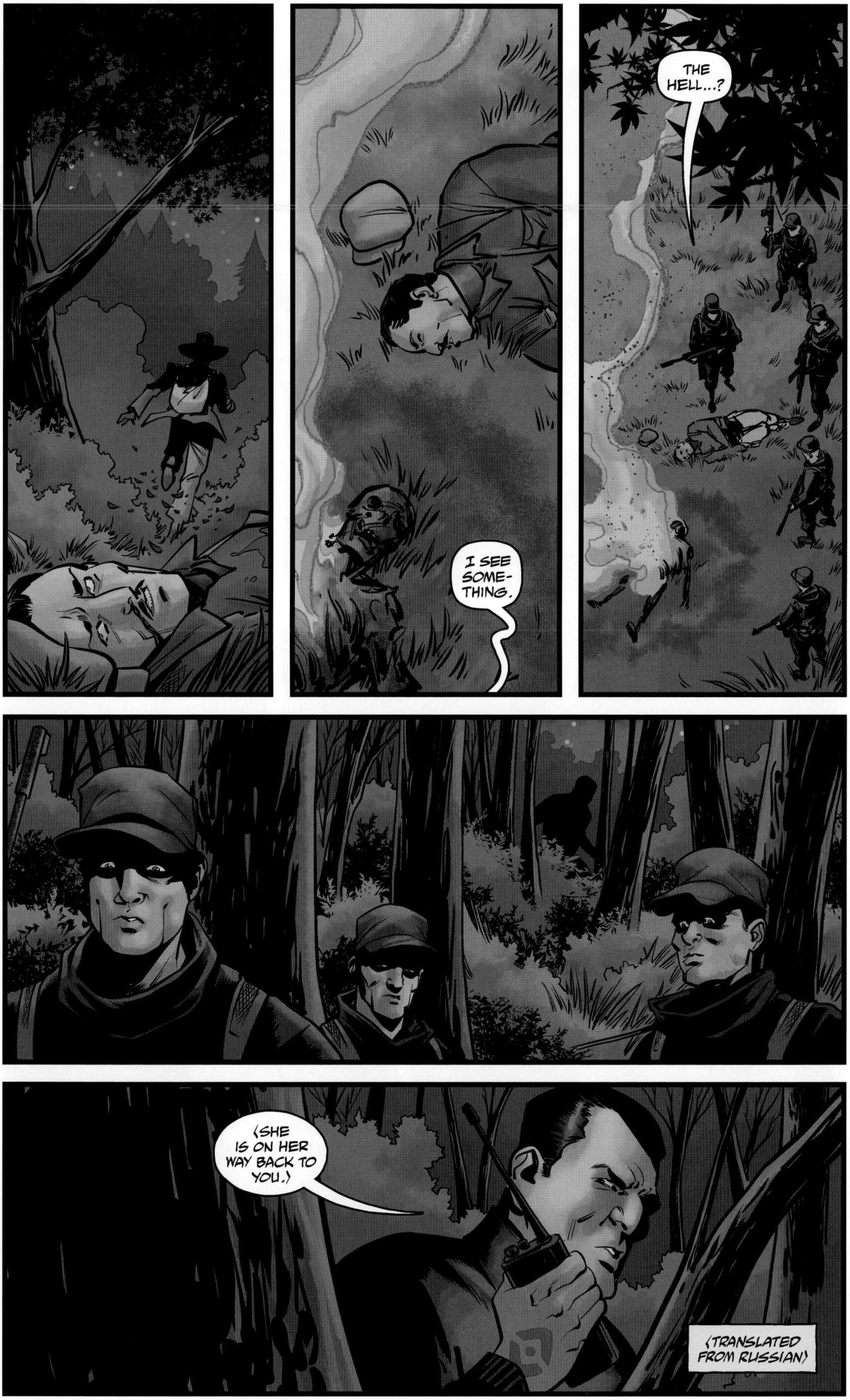
I SEE SOMETHING.
THE HELL...?
⟨SHE IS ON HER WAY BACK TO YOU.⟩
⟨TRANSLATED FROM RUSSIAN⟩

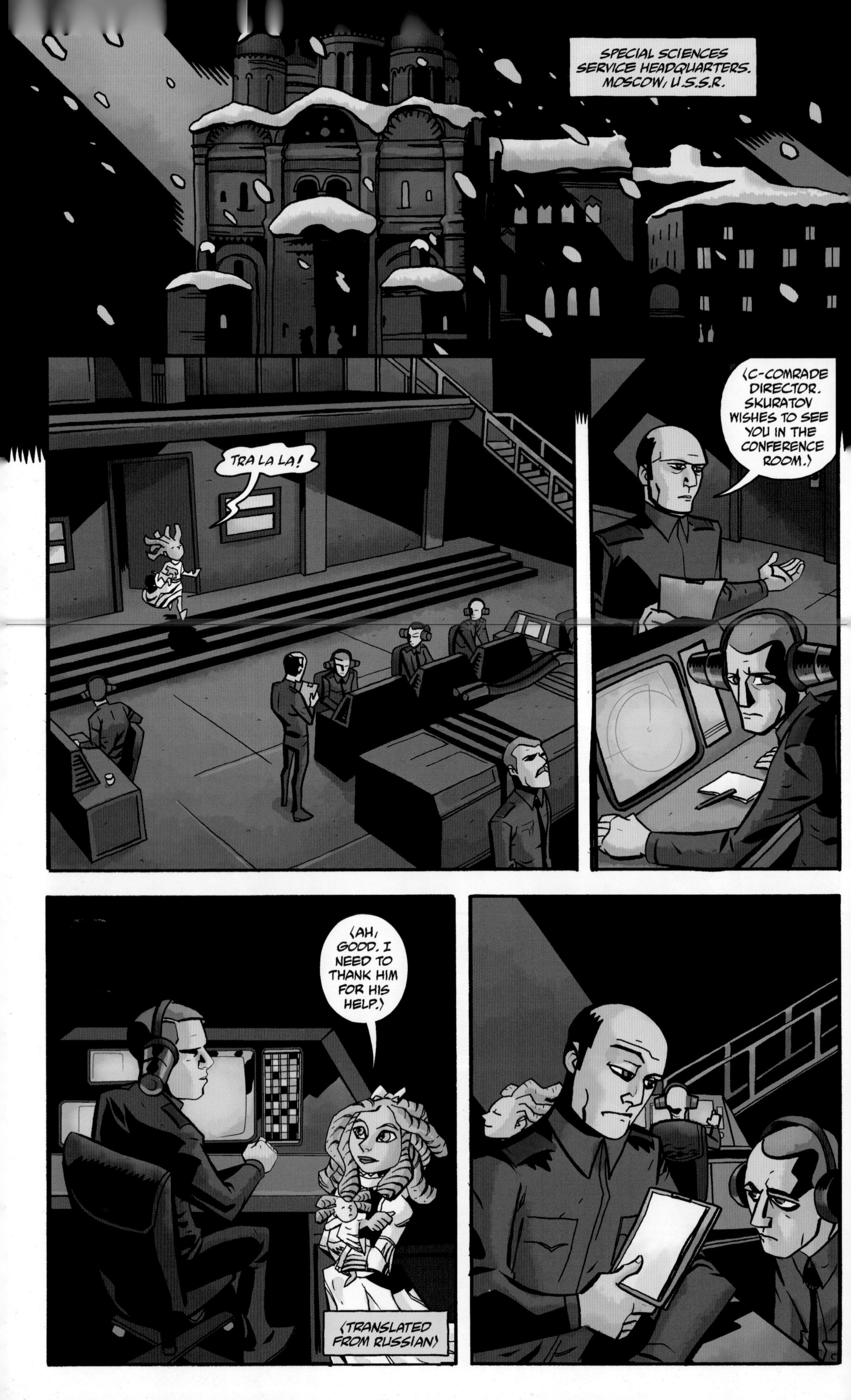
SPECIAL SCIENCES SERVICE HEADQUARTERS. MOSCOW, U.S.S.R.
TRA LA LA!
⟨C-COMRADE DIRECTOR. SKURATOV WISHES TO SEE YOU IN THE CONFERENCE ROOM.⟩
⟨AH, GOOD. I NEED TO THANK HIM FOR HIS HELP.⟩
⟨TRANSLATED FROM RUSSIAN⟩

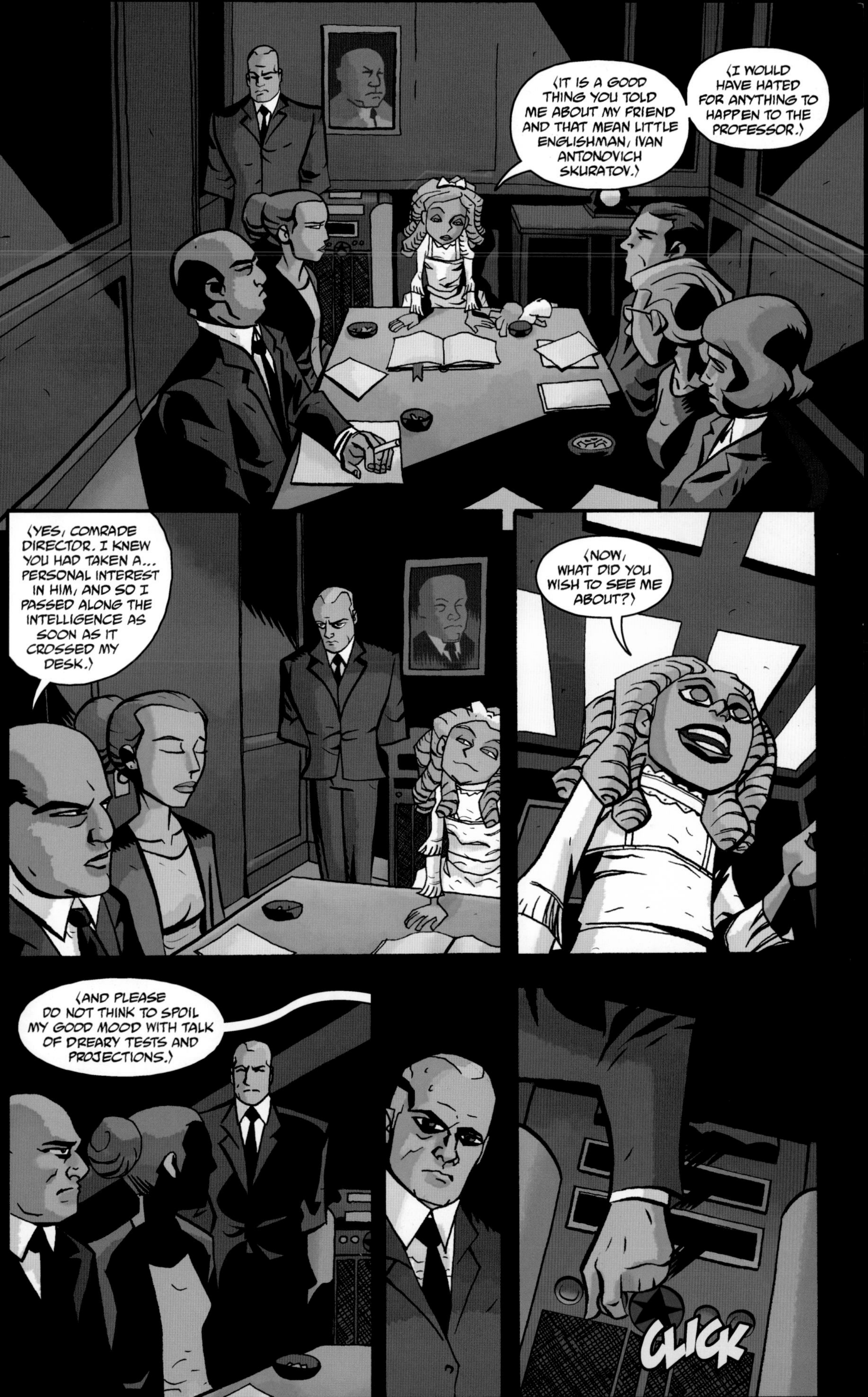
⟨IT IS A GOOD THING YOU TOLD ME ABOUT MY FRIEND AND THAT MEAN LITTLE ENGLISHMAN, IVAN ANTONOVICH SKURATOV.⟩
⟨I WOULD HAVE HATED FOR ANYTHING TO HAPPEN TO THE PROFESSOR.⟩
⟨YES, COMRADE DIRECTOR. I KNEW YOU HAD TAKEN A... PERSONAL INTEREST IN HIM, AND SO I PASSED ALONG THE INTELLIGENCE AS SOON AS IT CROSSED MY DESK.⟩
⟨NOW, WHAT DID YOU WISH TO SEE ME ABOUT?⟩
⟨AND PLEASE DO NOT THINK TO SPOIL MY GOOD MOOD WITH TALK OF DREARY TESTS AND PROJECTIONS.⟩
CLICK

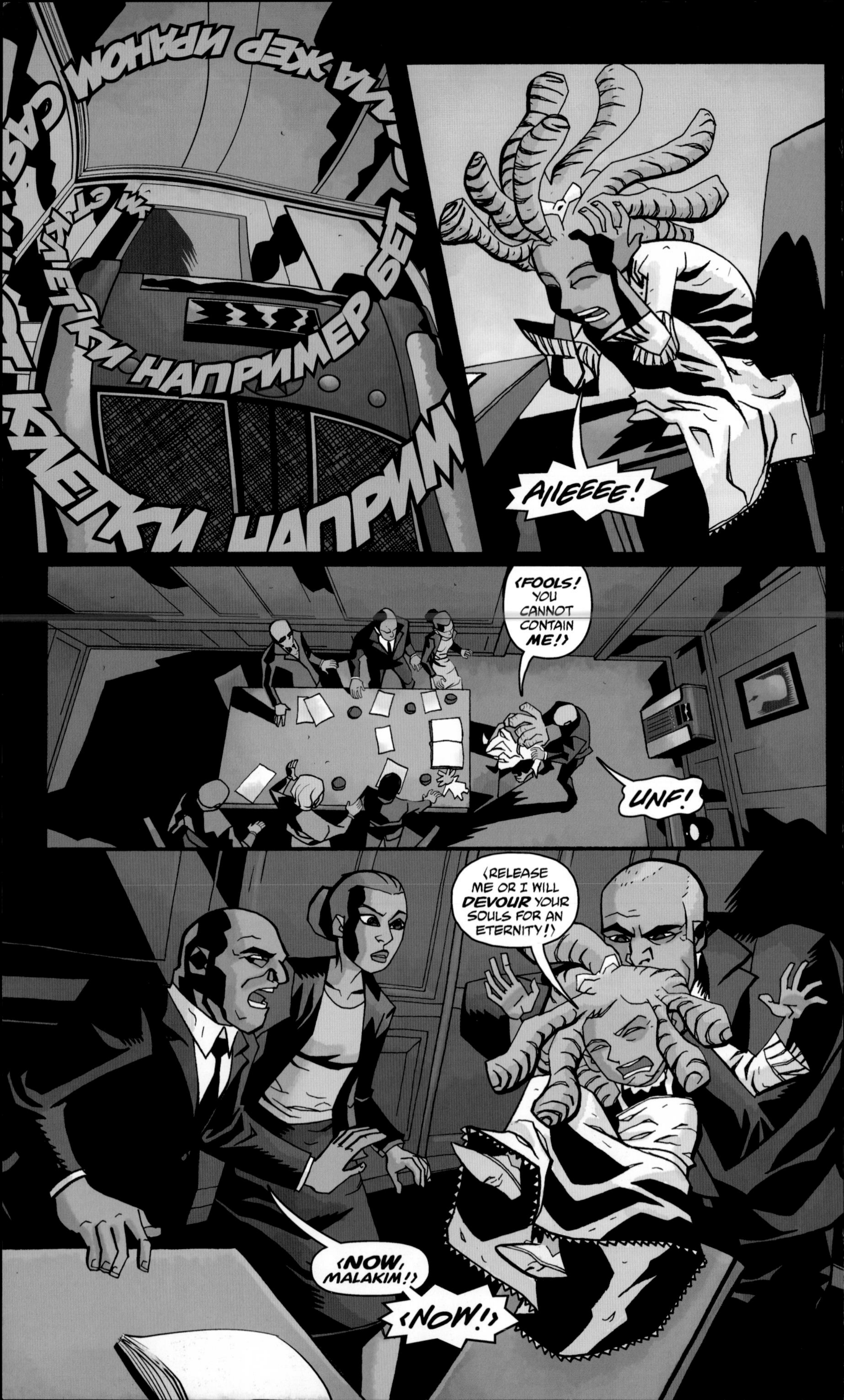

НАПРИМЕР БЕТ
КЛЕТКИ НАПРИМ
AIIEEEE!
‹FOOLS! YOU CANNOT CONTAIN ME!›
UNF!
‹RELEASE ME OR I WILL DEVOUR YOUR SOULS FOR AN ETERNITY!›
‹NOW, MALAKIM!›
‹NOW!›

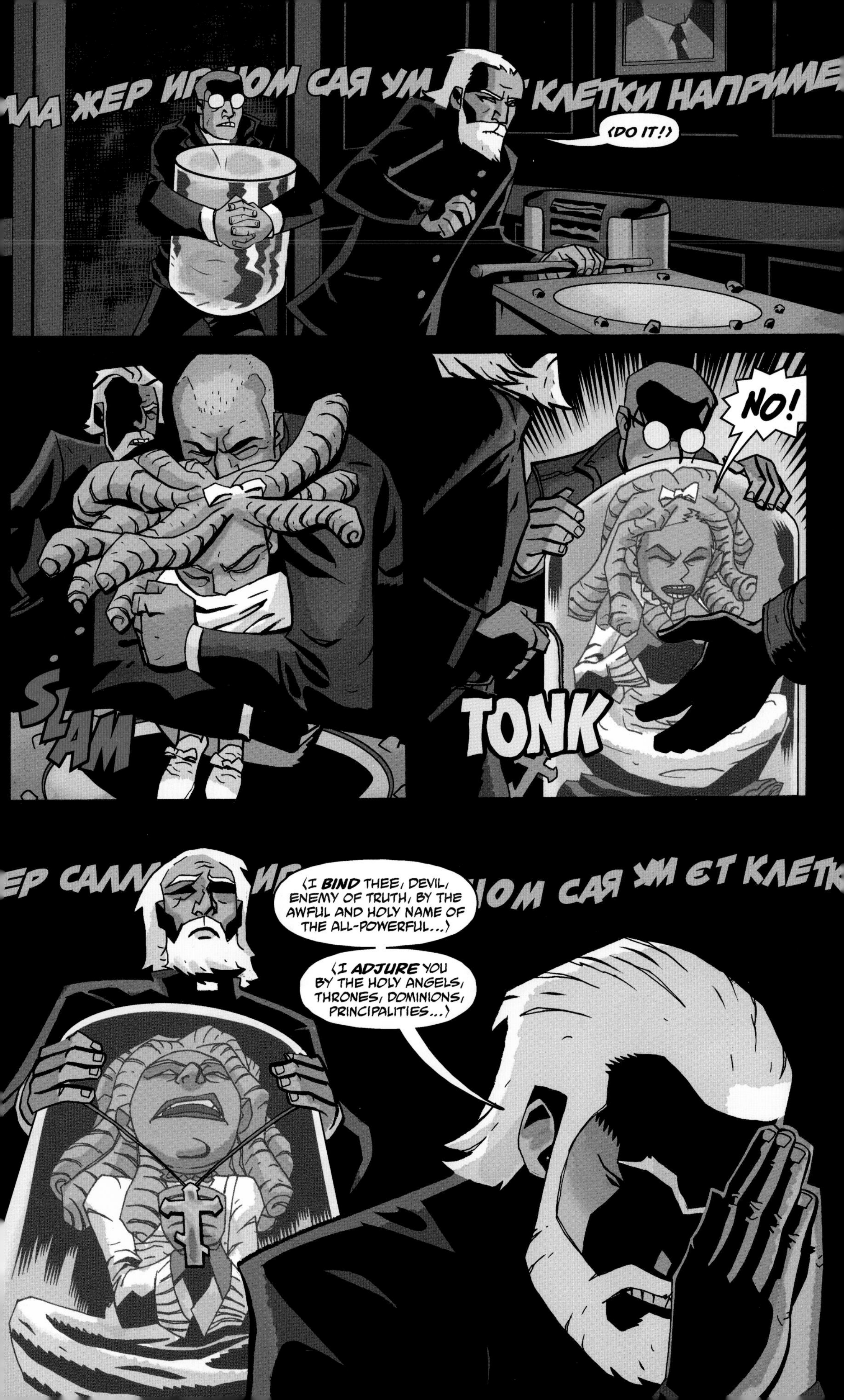
ЛА ЖЕР ИГ ОМ САЯ УМ КЛЕТКИ НАПРИМЕ
<DO IT!>
SLAM
NO!
TONK
ЕР САЛЛ ИГ ОМ САЯ УМ ЄТ КЛЕТК
<I BIND THEE, DEVIL, ENEMY OF TRUTH, BY THE AWFUL AND HOLY NAME OF THE ALL-POWERFUL...>
<I ADJURE YOU BY THE HOLY ANGELS, THRONES, DOMINIONS, PRINCIPALITIES...>

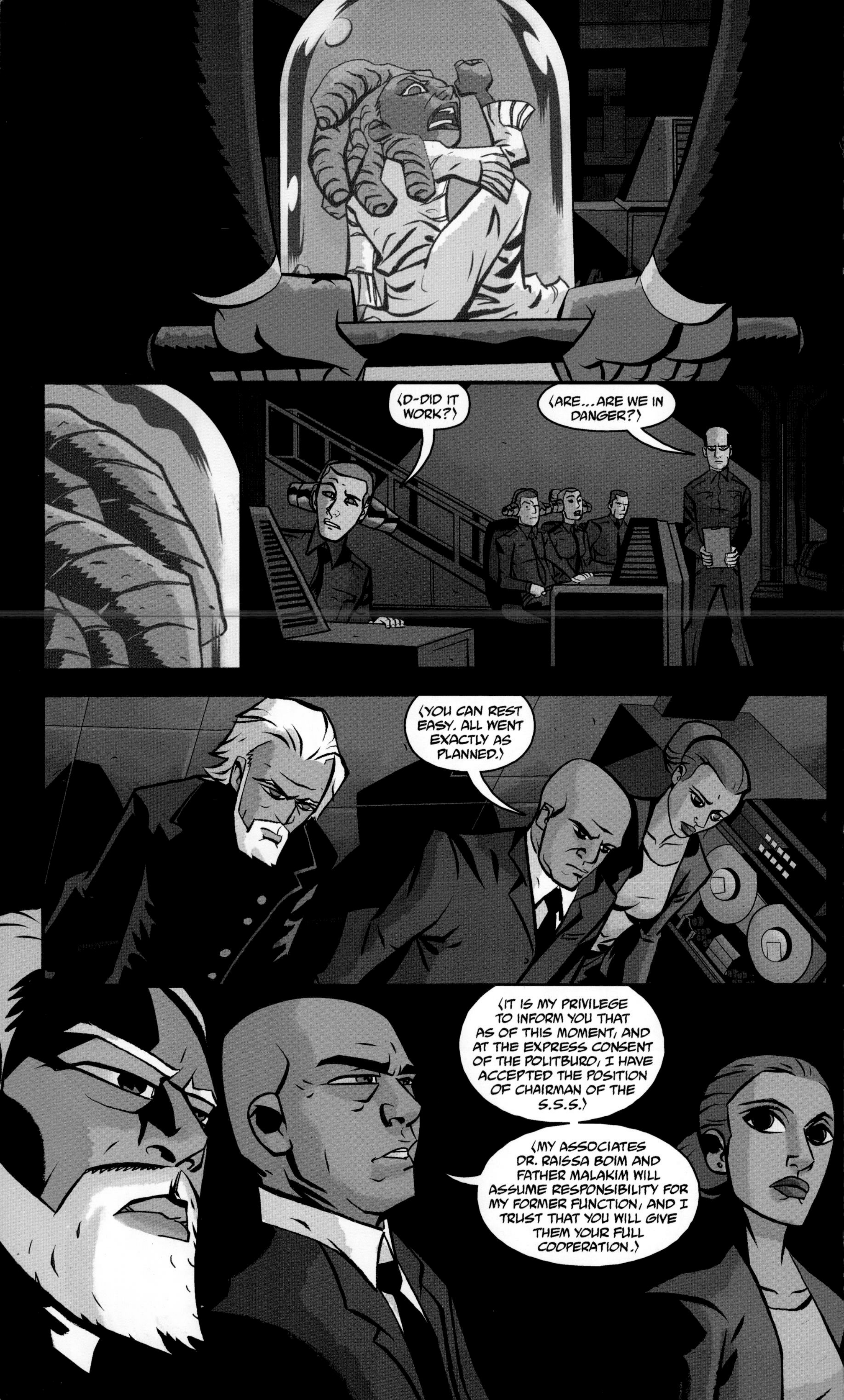
‹D-DID IT WORK?›
‹ARE...ARE WE IN DANGER?›
‹YOU CAN REST EASY. ALL WENT EXACTLY AS PLANNED.›
‹IT IS MY PRIVILEGE TO INFORM YOU THAT AS OF THIS MOMENT, AND AT THE EXPRESS CONSENT OF THE POLITBURO, I HAVE ACCEPTED THE POSITION OF CHAIRMAN OF THE S.S.S.›
‹MY ASSOCIATES DR. RAISSA BOIM AND FATHER MALAKIM WILL ASSUME RESPONSIBILITY FOR MY FORMER FUNCTION, AND I TRUST THAT YOU WILL GIVE THEM YOUR FULL COOPERATION.›

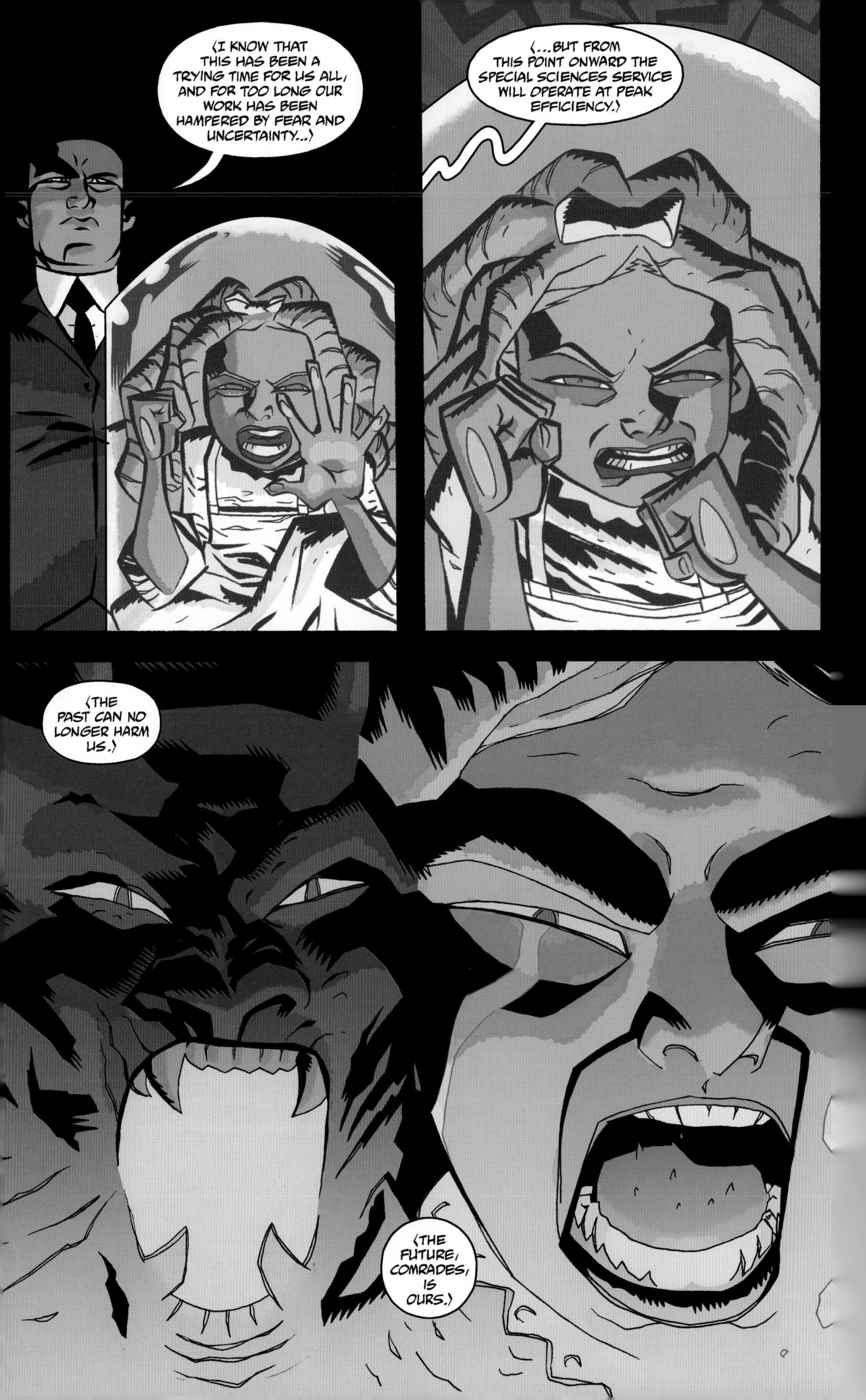
⟨I KNOW THAT THIS HAS BEEN A TRYING TIME FOR US ALL, AND FOR TOO LONG OUR WORK HAS BEEN HAMPERED BY FEAR AND UNCERTAINTY...⟩
⟨...BUT FROM THIS POINT ONWARD THE SPECIAL SCIENCES SERVICE WILL OPERATE AT PEAK EFFICIENCY.⟩
⟨THE PAST CAN NO LONGER HARM US.⟩
⟨THE FUTURE, COMRADES, IS OURS.⟩

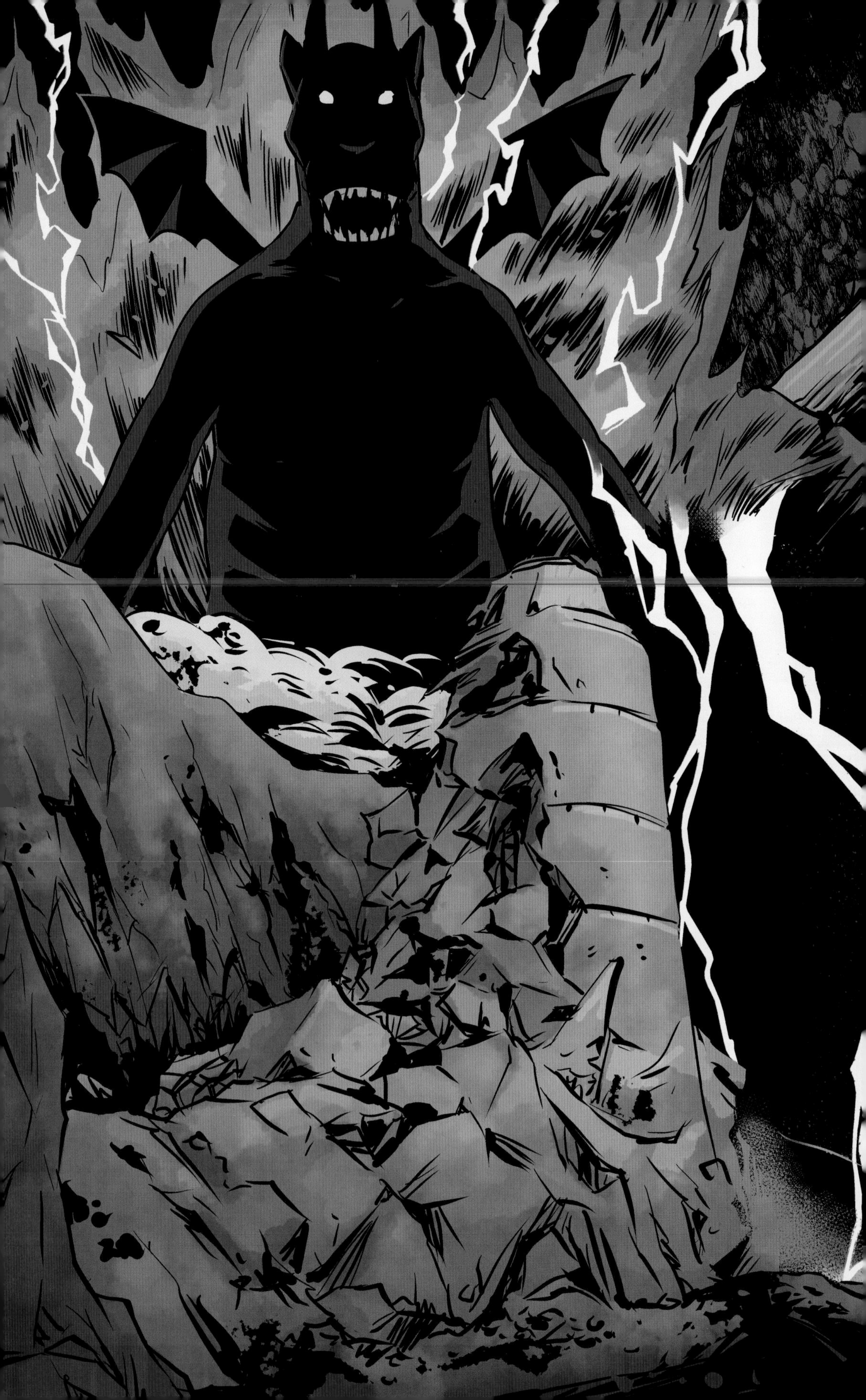

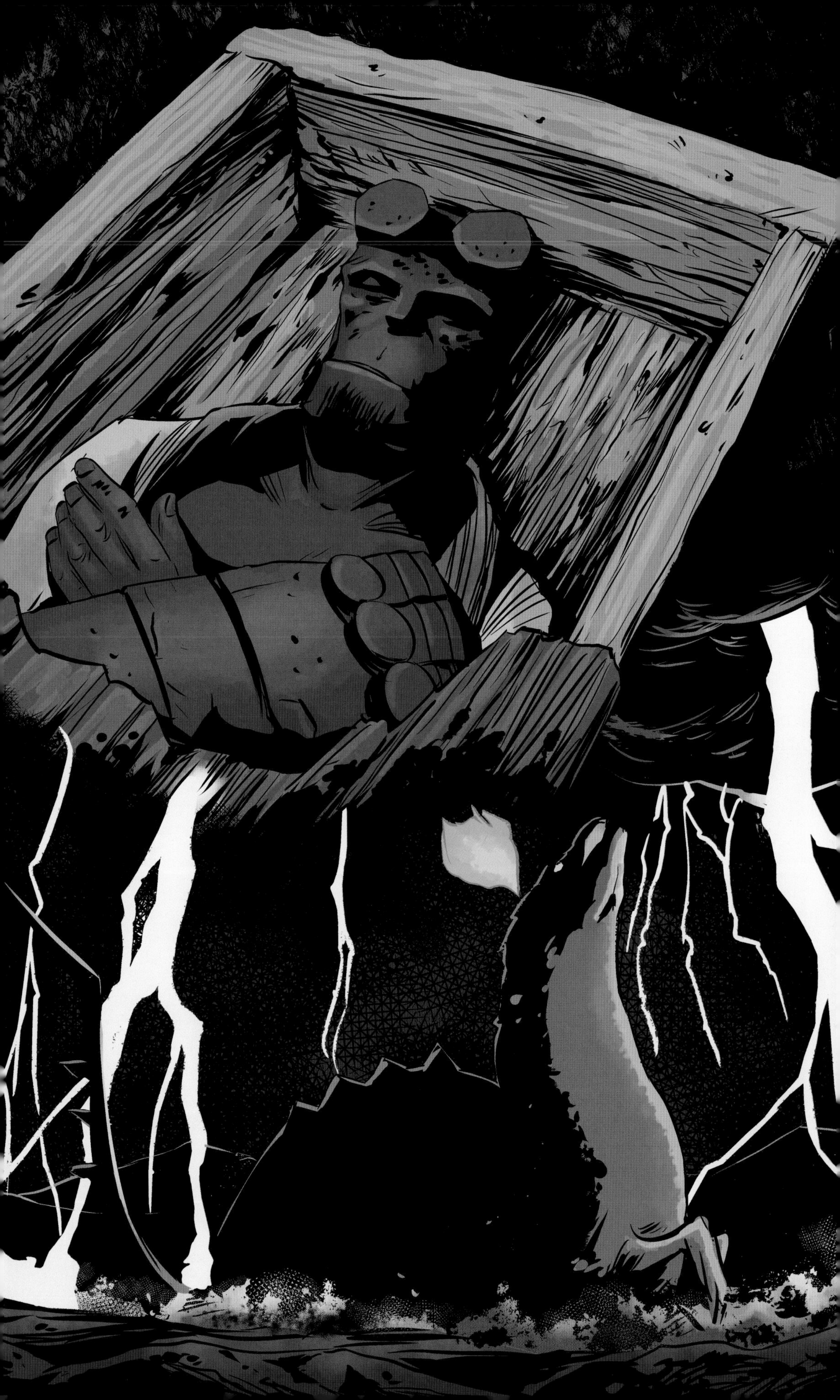

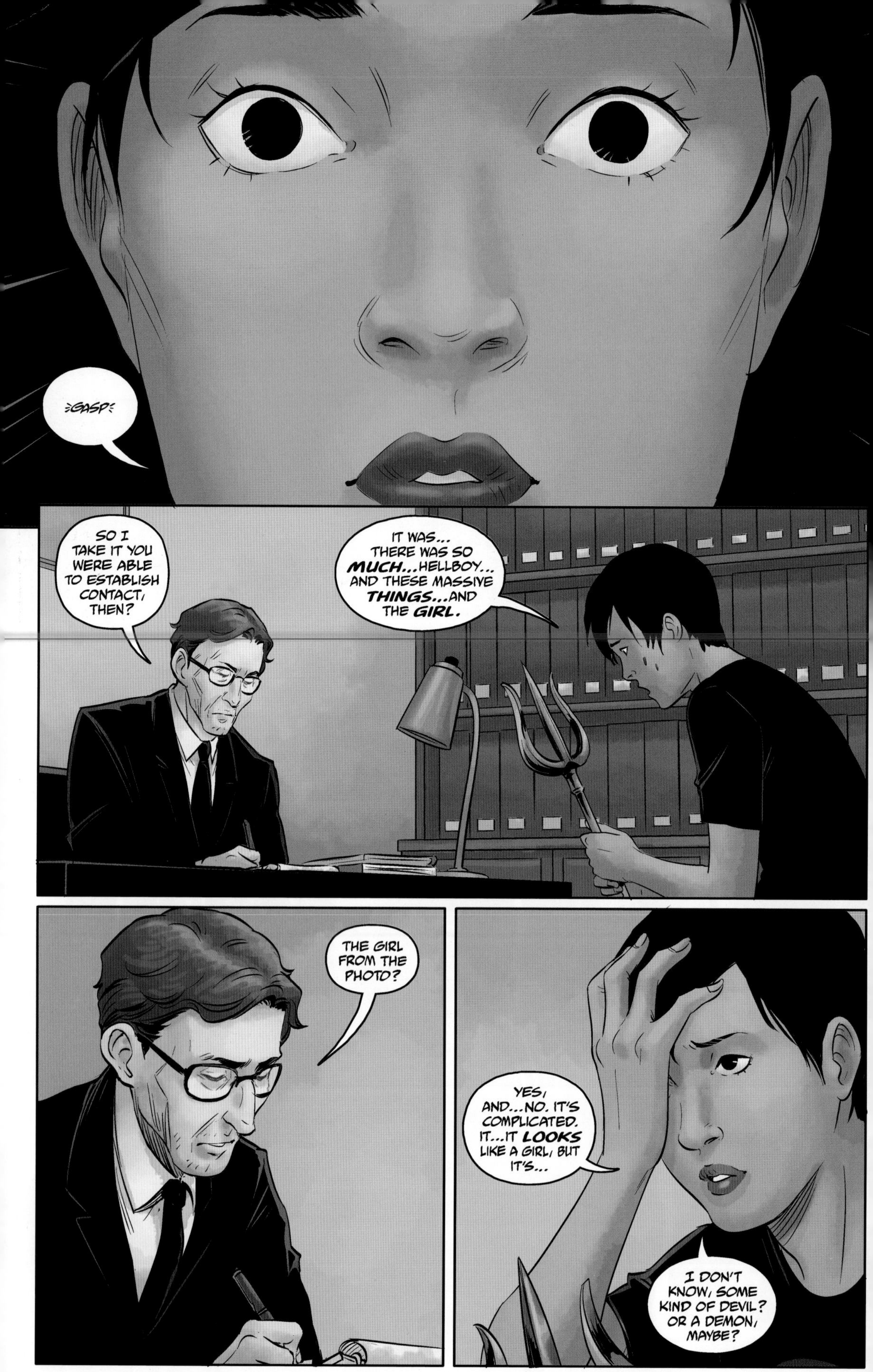

GASP
SO I TAKE IT YOU WERE ABLE TO ESTABLISH CONTACT, THEN?
IT WAS... THERE WAS SO MUCH...HELLBOY... AND THESE MASSIVE THINGS...AND THE GIRL.
THE GIRL FROM THE PHOTO?
YES, AND...NO. IT'S COMPLICATED. IT...IT LOOKS LIKE A GIRL, BUT IT'S...
I DON'T KNOW, SOME KIND OF DEVIL? OR A DEMON, MAYBE?

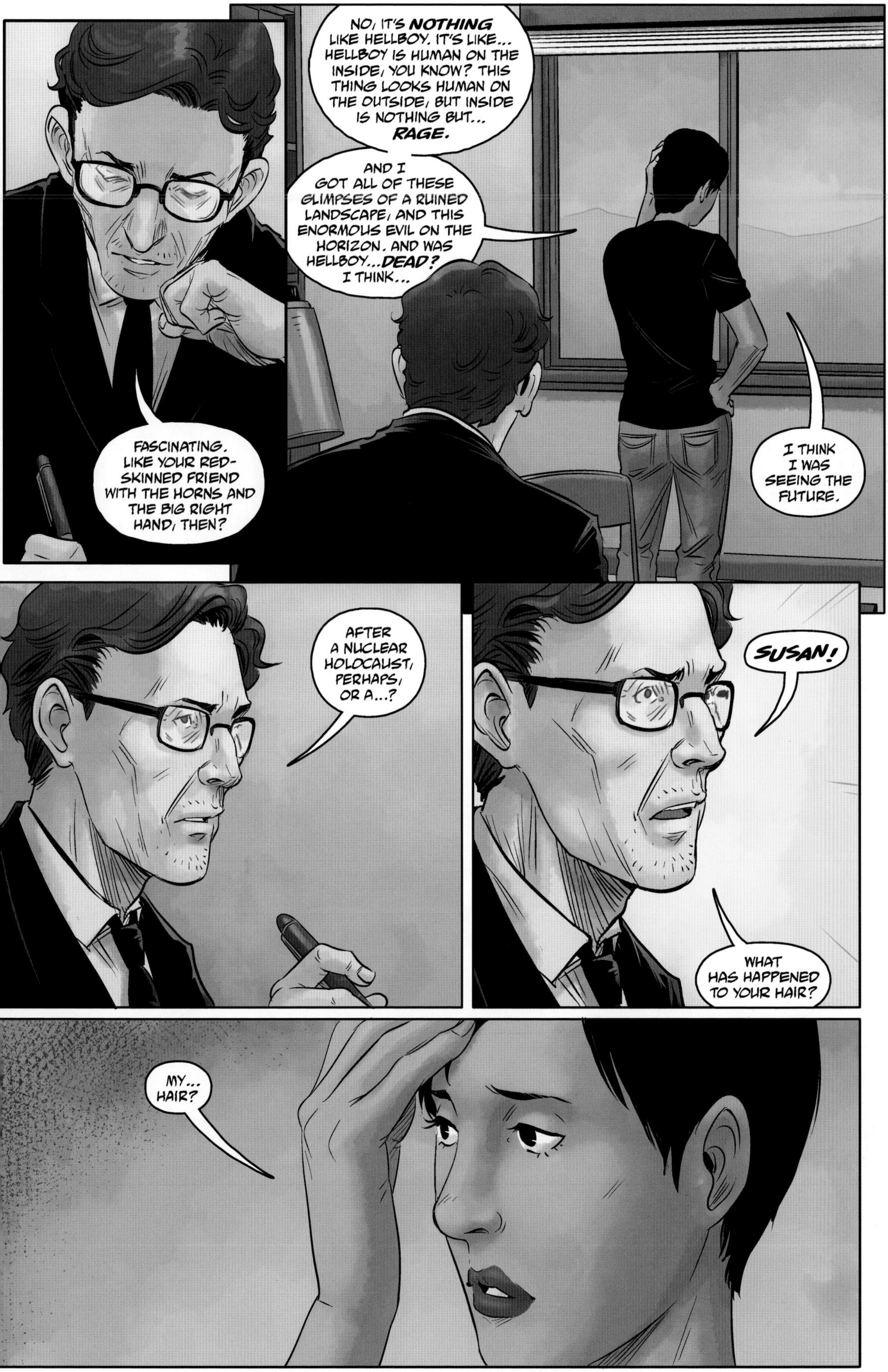
NO, IT'S NOTHING LIKE HELLBOY. IT'S LIKE... HELLBOY IS HUMAN ON THE INSIDE, YOU KNOW? THIS THING LOOKS HUMAN ON THE OUTSIDE, BUT INSIDE IS NOTHING BUT... RAGE.
FASCINATING. LIKE YOUR RED-SKINNED FRIEND WITH THE HORNS AND THE BIG RIGHT HAND, THEN?
AND I GOT ALL OF THESE GLIMPSES OF A RUINED LANDSCAPE, AND THIS ENORMOUS EVIL ON THE HORIZON. AND WAS HELLBOY...DEAD? I THINK...
I THINK I WAS SEEING THE FUTURE.
AFTER A NUCLEAR HOLOCAUST, PERHAPS, OR A...?
SUSAN!
WHAT HAS HAPPENED TO YOUR HAIR?
MY... HAIR?

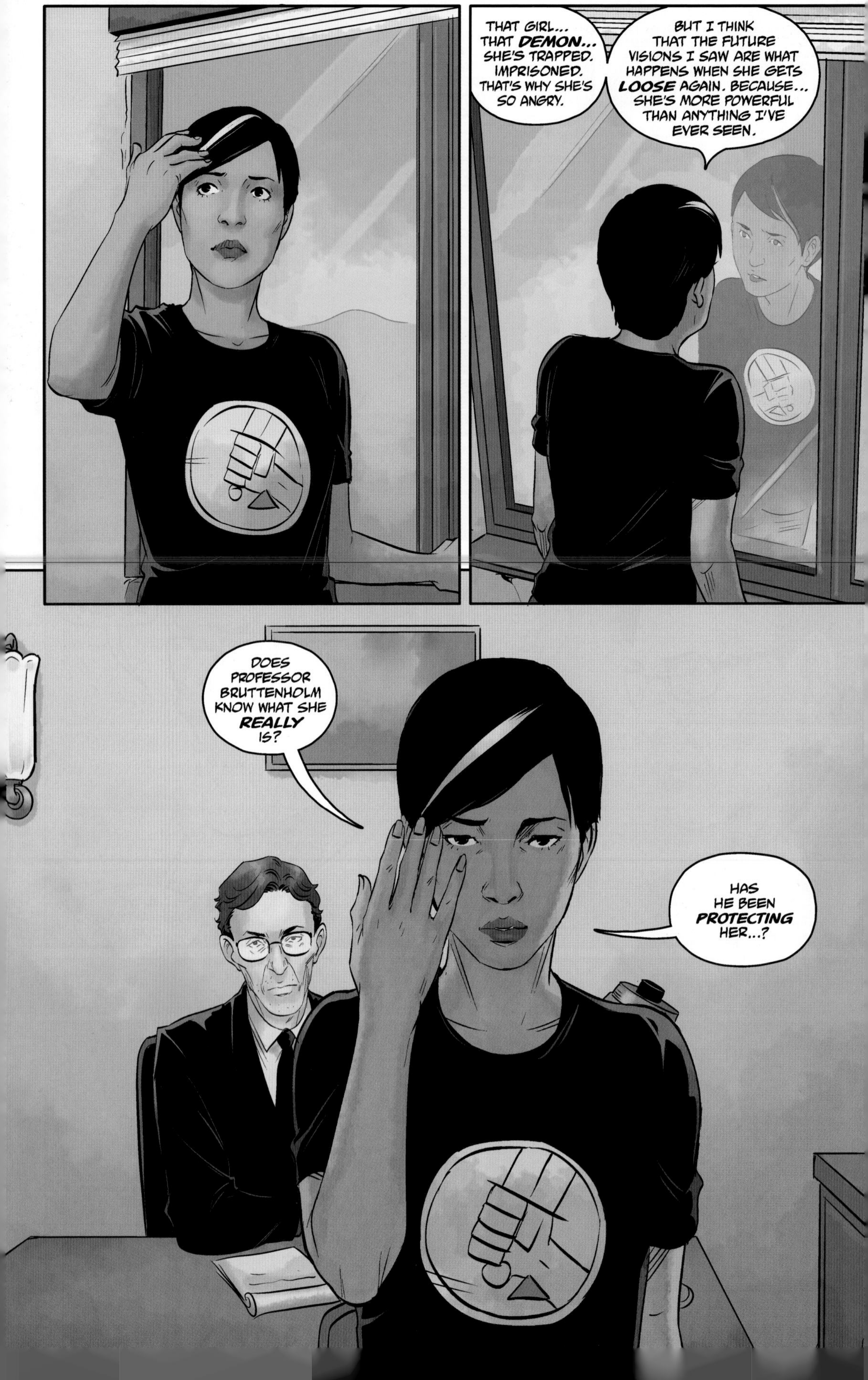
THAT GIRL... THAT DEMON... SHE'S TRAPPED. IMPRISONED. THAT'S WHY SHE'S SO ANGRY.
BUT I THINK THAT THE FUTURE VISIONS I SAW ARE WHAT HAPPENS WHEN SHE GETS LOOSE AGAIN. BECAUSE... SHE'S MORE POWERFUL THAN ANYTHING I'VE EVER SEEN.
DOES PROFESSOR BRUTTENHOLM KNOW WHAT SHE REALLY IS?
HAS HE BEEN PROTECTING HER...?

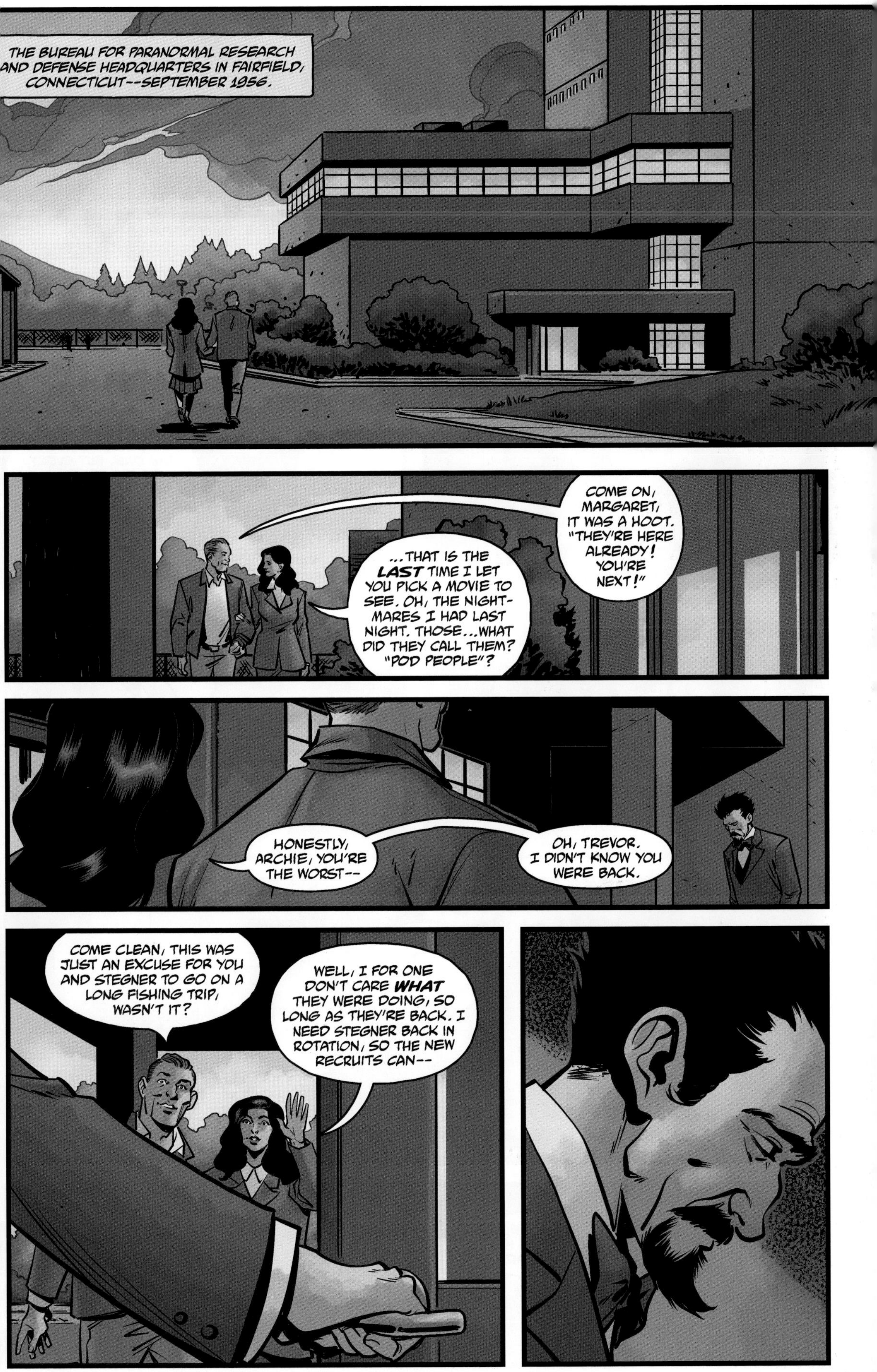
THE BUREAU FOR PARANORMAL RESEARCH AND DEFENSE HEADQUARTERS IN FAIRFIELD, CONNECTICUT--SEPTEMBER 1956.
...THAT IS THE LAST TIME I LET YOU PICK A MOVIE TO SEE. OH, THE NIGHT-MARES I HAD LAST NIGHT. THOSE...WHAT DID THEY CALL THEM? "POD PEOPLE"?
COME ON, MARGARET, IT WAS A HOOT. "THEY'RE HERE ALREADY! YOU'RE NEXT!"
HONESTLY, ARCHIE, YOU'RE THE WORST--
OH, TREVOR. I DIDN'T KNOW YOU WERE BACK.
COME CLEAN, THIS WAS JUST AN EXCUSE FOR YOU AND STEGNER TO GO ON A LONG FISHING TRIP, WASN'T IT?
WELL, I FOR ONE DON'T CARE WHAT THEY WERE DOING, SO LONG AS THEY'RE BACK. I NEED STEGNER BACK IN ROTATION, SO THE NEW RECRUITS CAN--

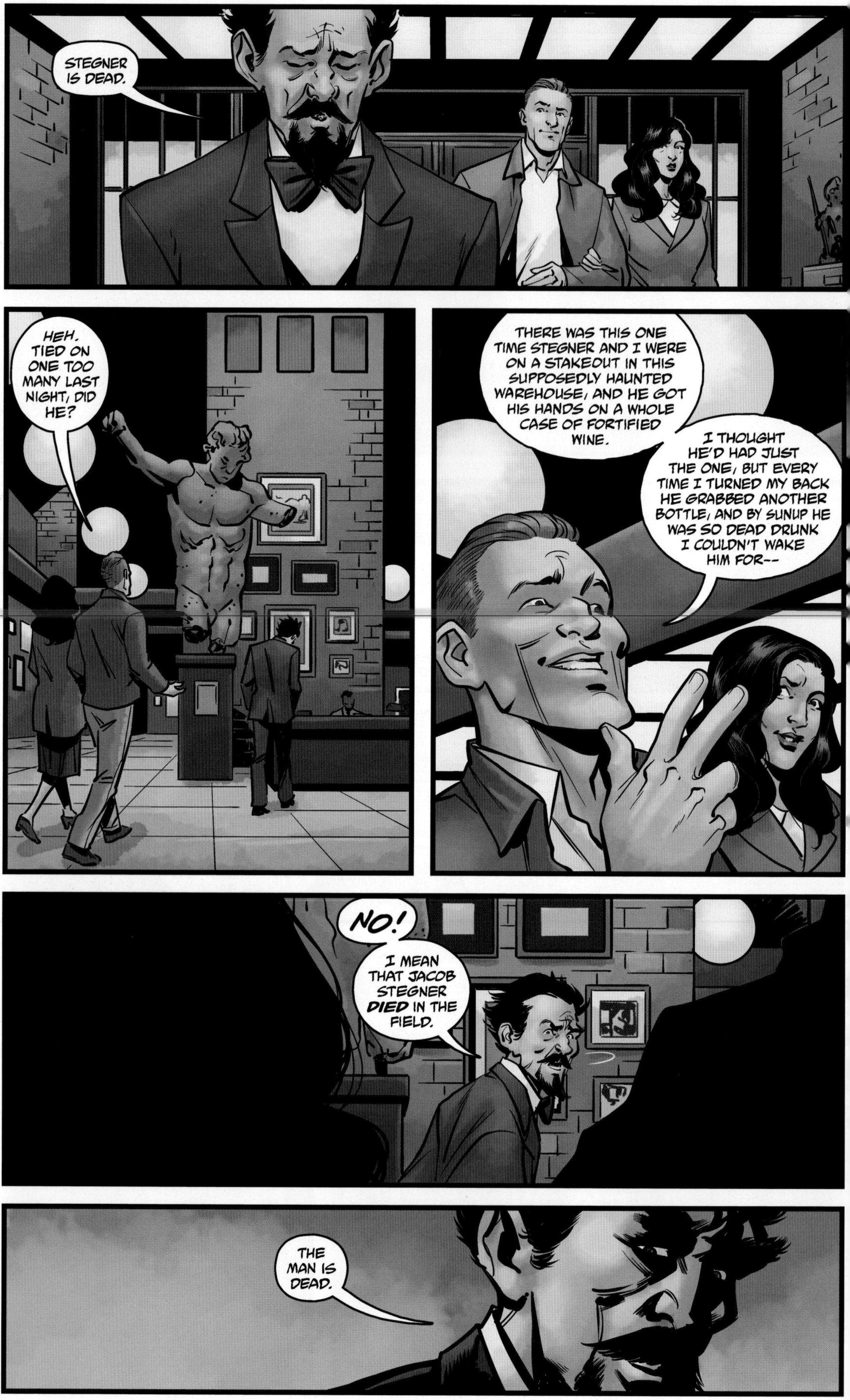
STEGNER IS DEAD.
HEH. TIED ON ONE TOO MANY LAST NIGHT, DID HE?
THERE WAS THIS ONE TIME STEGNER AND I WERE ON A STAKEOUT IN THIS SUPPOSEDLY HAUNTED WAREHOUSE, AND HE GOT HIS HANDS ON A WHOLE CASE OF FORTIFIED WINE.
I THOUGHT HE'D HAD JUST THE ONE, BUT EVERY TIME I TURNED MY BACK HE GRABBED ANOTHER BOTTLE, AND BY SUNUP HE WAS SO DEAD DRUNK I COULDN'T WAKE HIM FOR--
NO!
I MEAN THAT JACOB STEGNER DIED IN THE FIELD.
THE MAN IS DEAD.

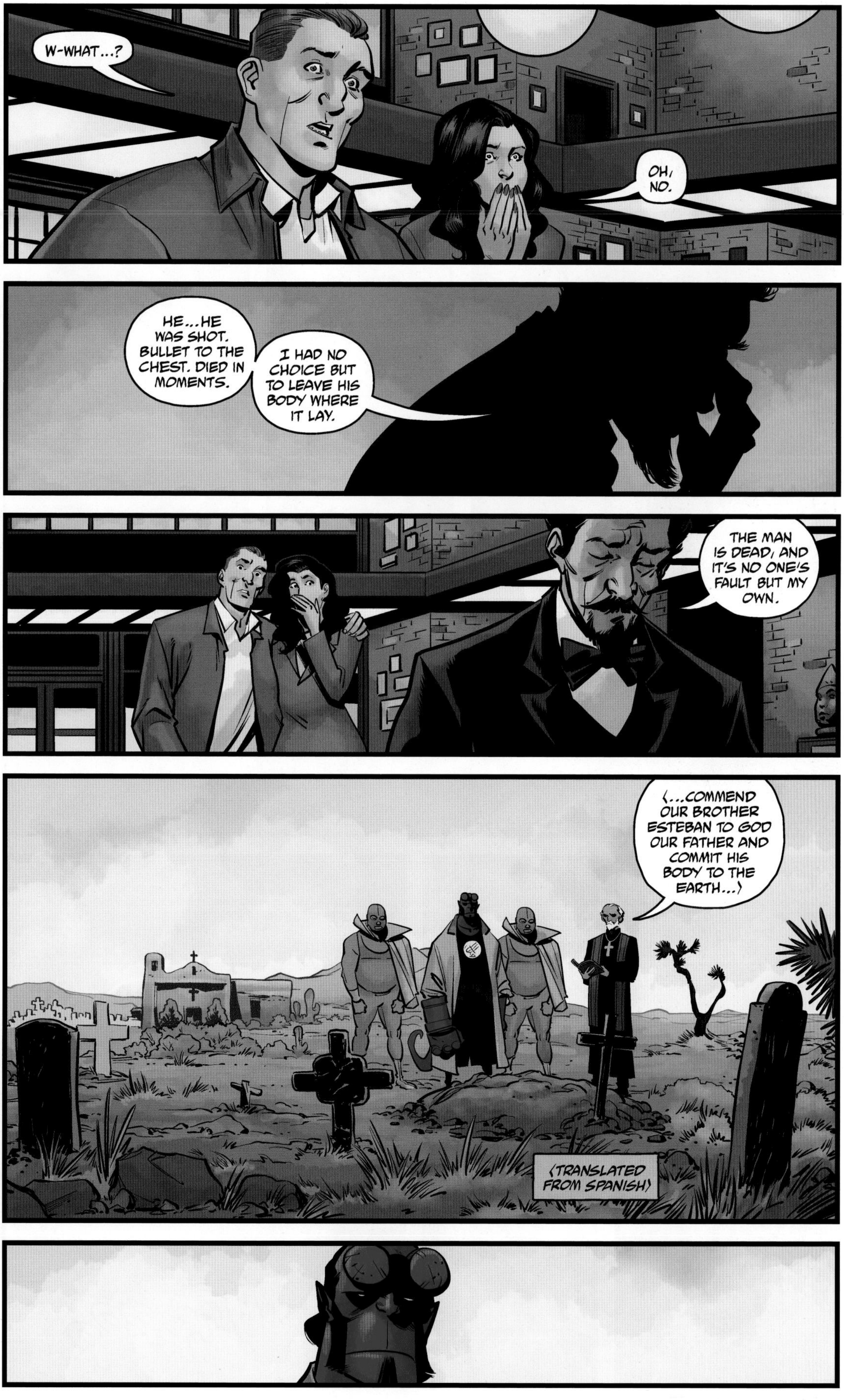
W-WHAT...?
OH, NO.
HE...HE WAS SHOT. BULLET TO THE CHEST. DIED IN MOMENTS.
I HAD NO CHOICE BUT TO LEAVE HIS BODY WHERE IT LAY.
THE MAN IS DEAD, AND IT'S NO ONE'S FAULT BUT MY OWN.
‹...COMMEND OUR BROTHER ESTEBAN TO GOD OUR FATHER AND COMMIT HIS BODY TO THE EARTH...›
‹TRANSLATED FROM SPANISH›

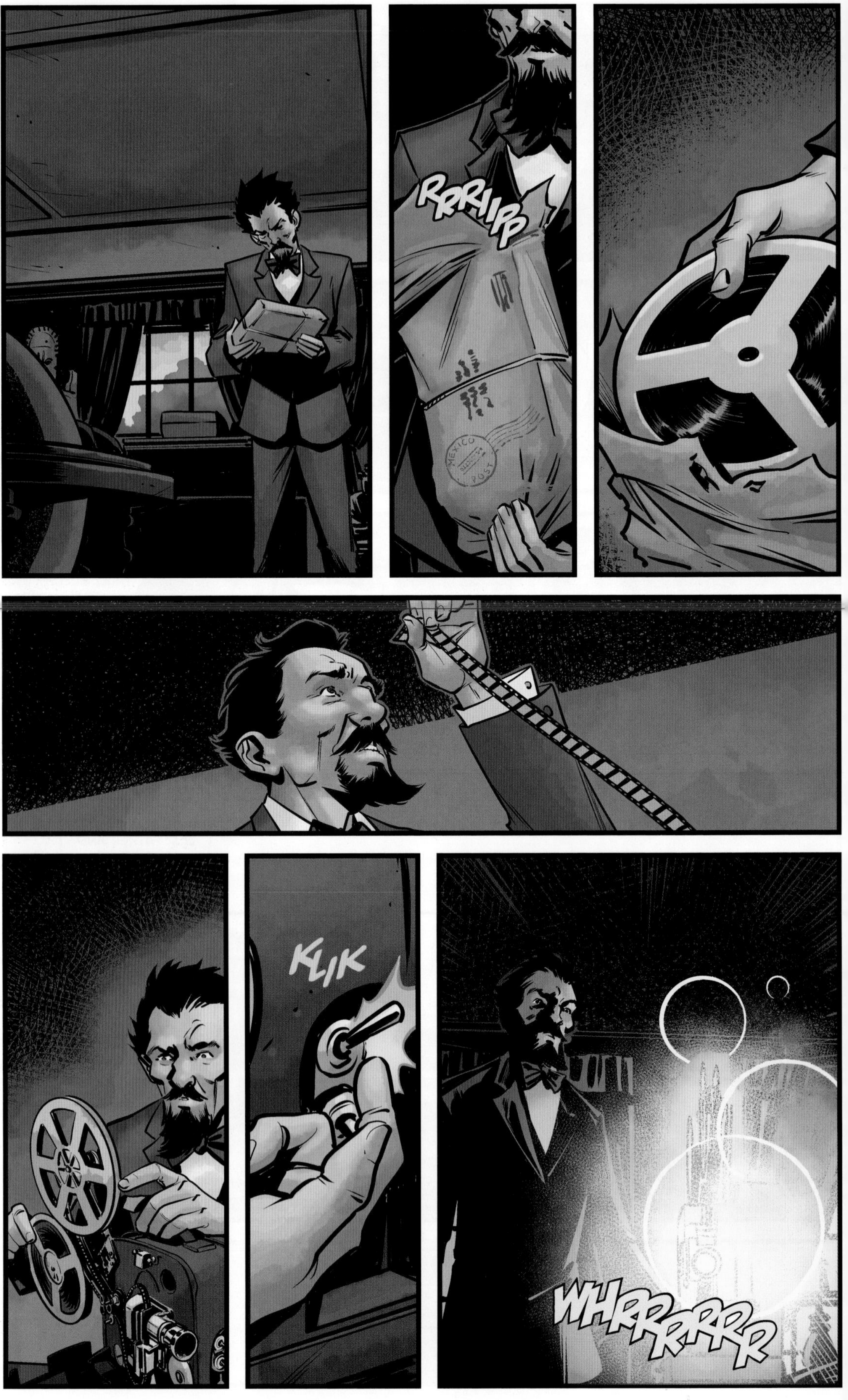
RRRIPP
MEXICO
POST
KLIK
WHRRRRRRR

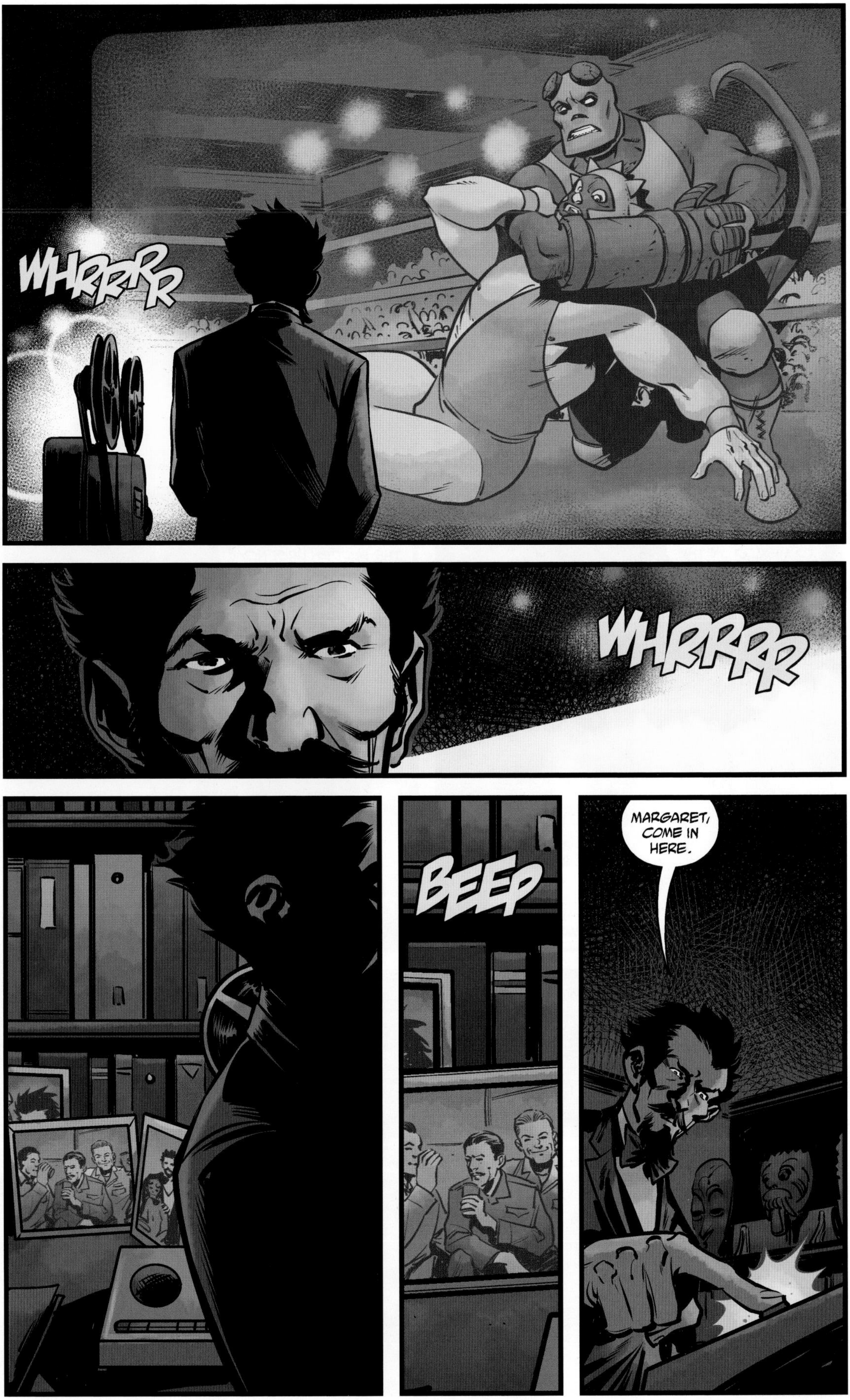
WHRRRR
WHRRRR
BEEP
MARGARET, COME IN HERE.

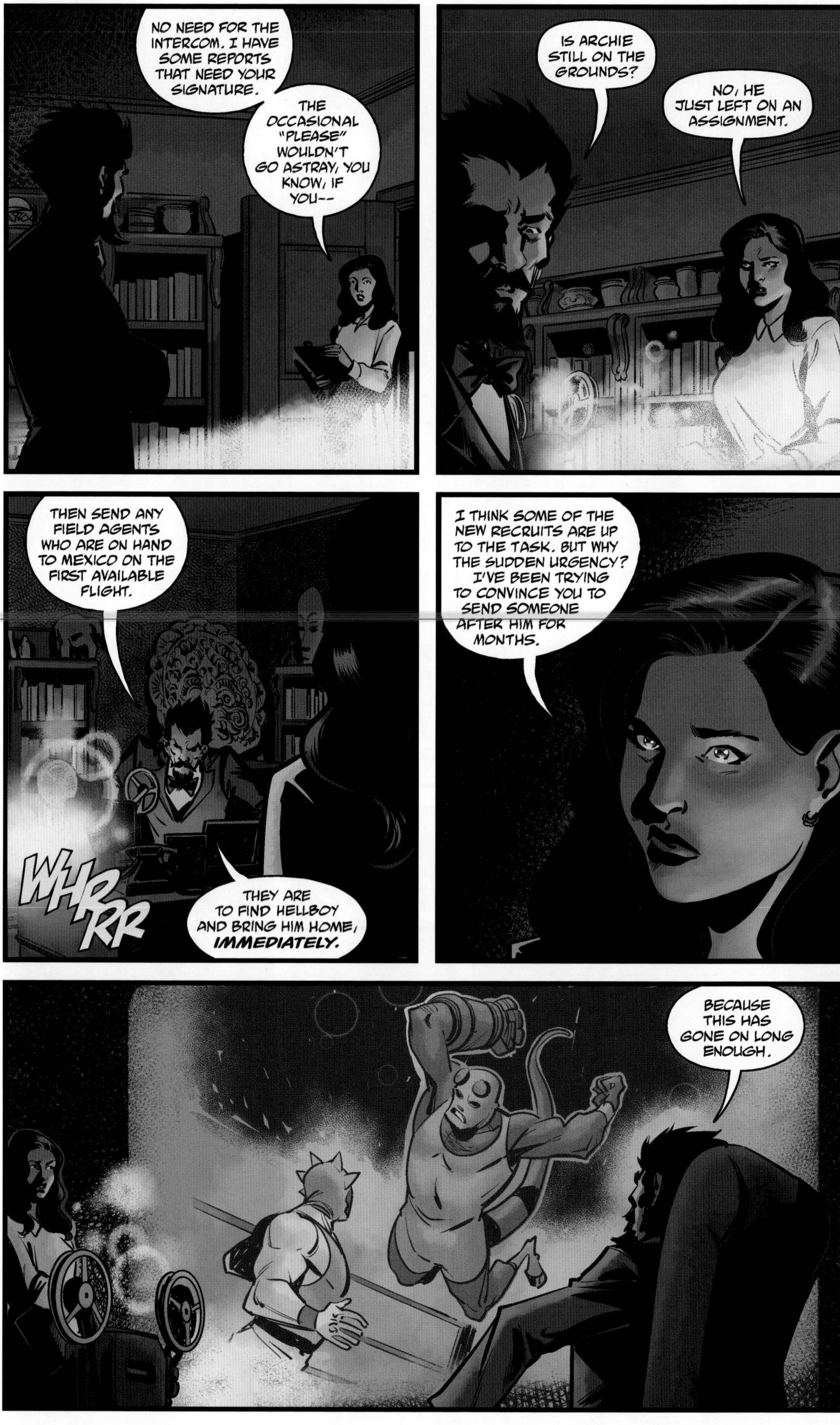
NO NEED FOR THE INTERCOM. I HAVE SOME REPORTS THAT NEED YOUR SIGNATURE.
THE OCCASIONAL "PLEASE" WOULDN'T GO ASTRAY, YOU KNOW, IF YOU--
IS ARCHIE STILL ON THE GROUNDS?
NO, HE JUST LEFT ON AN ASSIGNMENT.
THEN SEND ANY FIELD AGENTS WHO ARE ON HAND TO MEXICO ON THE FIRST AVAILABLE FLIGHT.
WHRRR
THEY ARE TO FIND HELLBOY AND BRING HIM HOME, ***IMMEDIATELY.***
I THINK SOME OF THE NEW RECRUITS ARE UP TO THE TASK. BUT WHY THE SUDDEN URGENCY? I'VE BEEN TRYING TO CONVINCE YOU TO SEND SOMEONE AFTER HIM FOR MONTHS.
BECAUSE THIS HAS GONE ON LONG ENOUGH.

CHAPTER FIVE

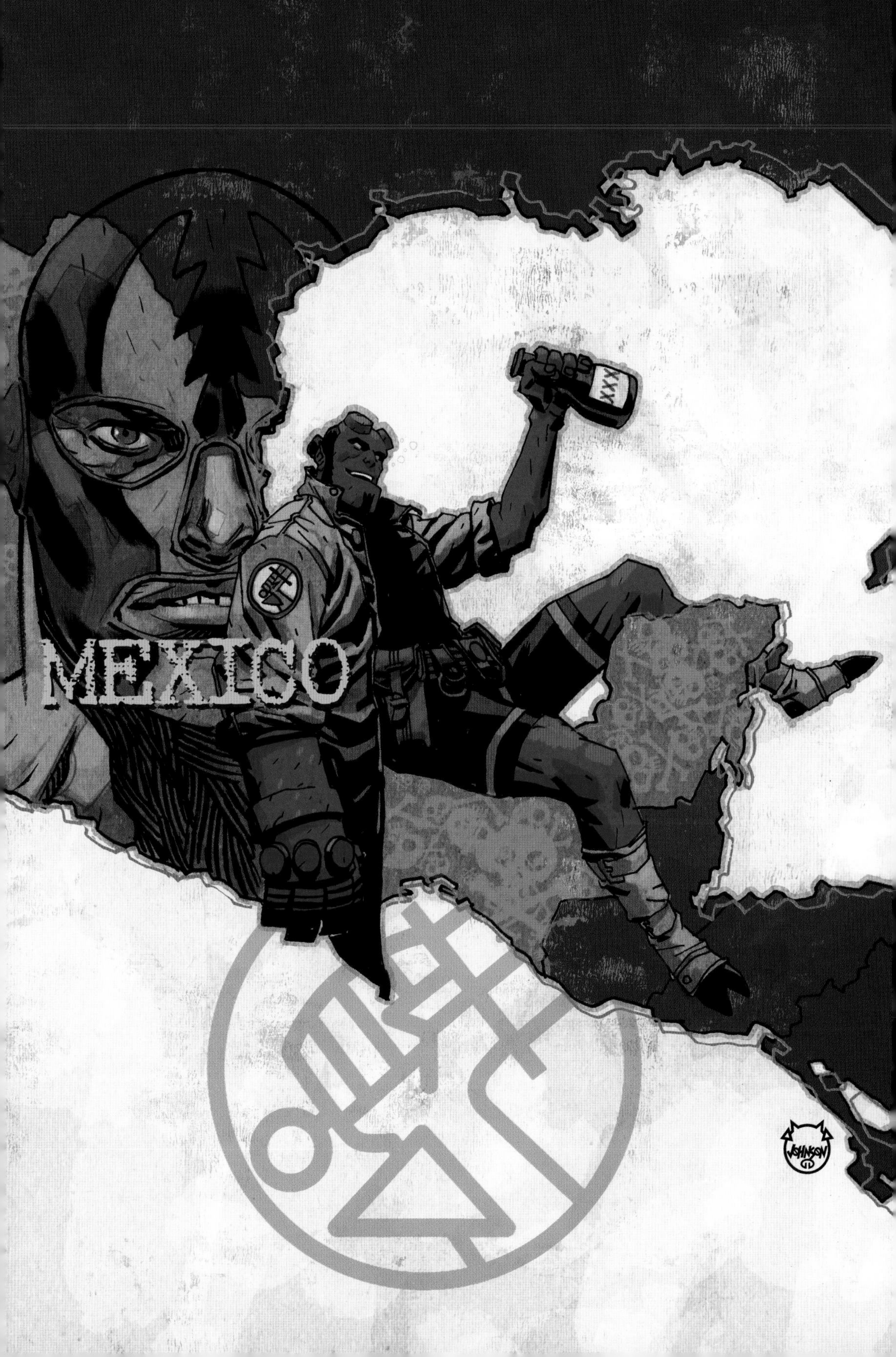
XXX
MEXICO

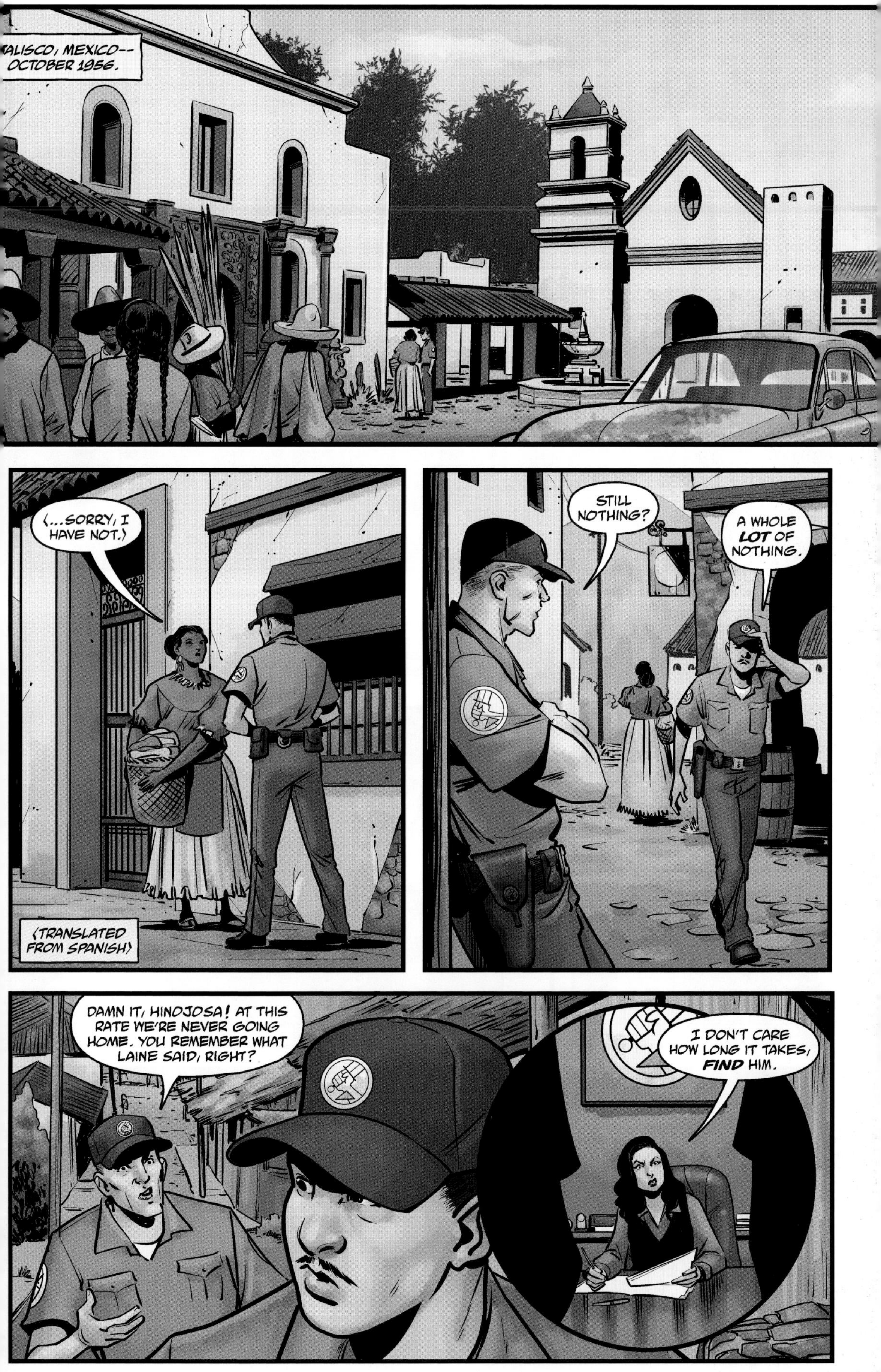
JALISCO, MEXICO--
OCTOBER 1956.
‹...SORRY, I HAVE NOT.›
‹TRANSLATED FROM SPANISH›
STILL NOTHING?
A WHOLE LOT OF NOTHING.
DAMN IT, HINOJOSA! AT THIS RATE WE'RE NEVER GOING HOME. YOU REMEMBER WHAT LAINE SAID, RIGHT?
I DON'T CARE HOW LONG IT TAKES, FIND HIM.

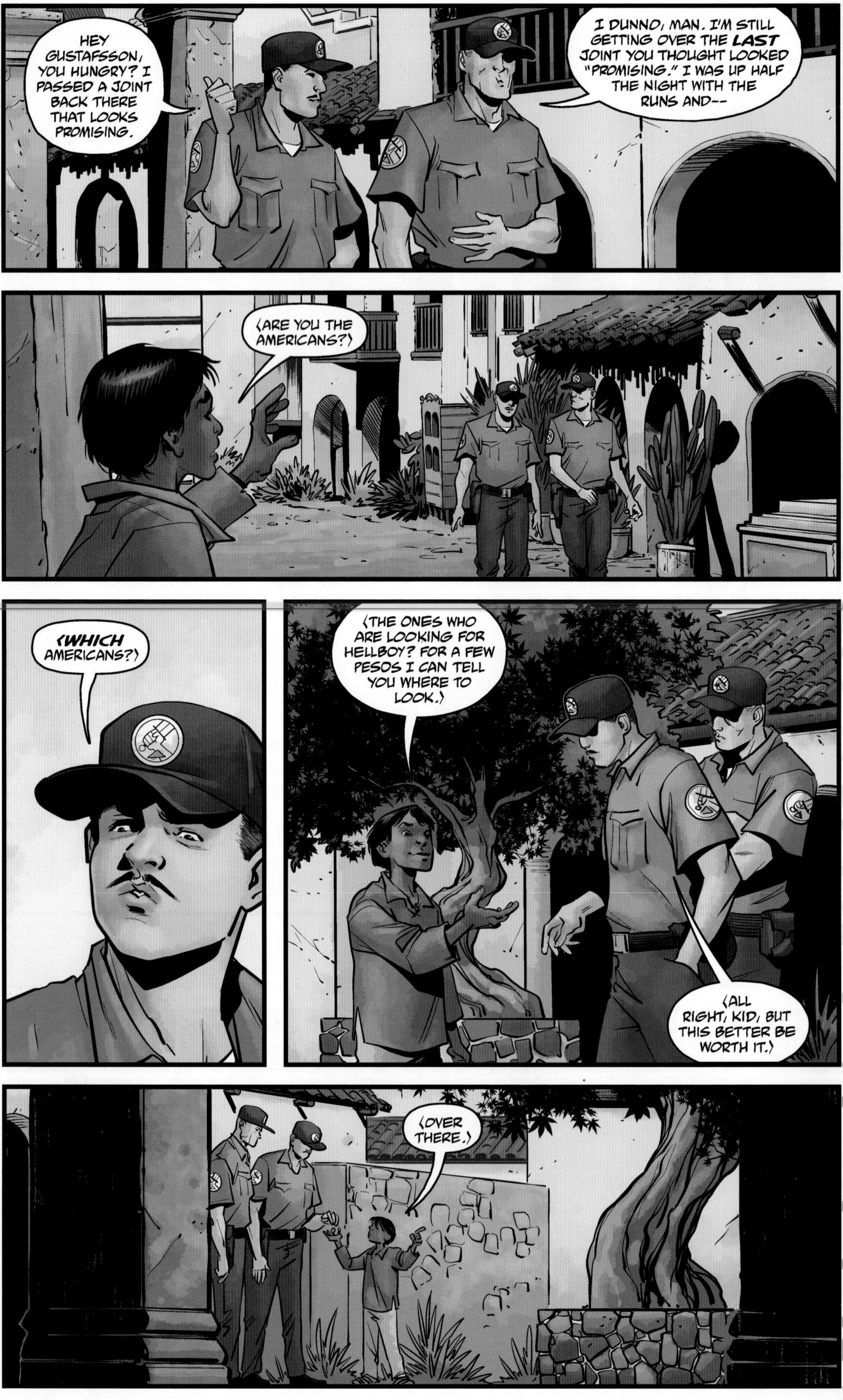
HEY GUSTAFSSON, YOU HUNGRY? I PASSED A JOINT BACK THERE THAT LOOKS PROMISING.
I DUNNO, MAN. I'M STILL GETTING OVER THE **LAST** JOINT YOU THOUGHT LOOKED "PROMISING." I WAS UP HALF THE NIGHT WITH THE RUNS AND--
‹ARE YOU THE AMERICANS?›
‹***WHICH*** AMERICANS?›
‹THE ONES WHO ARE LOOKING FOR HELLBOY? FOR A FEW PESOS I CAN TELL YOU WHERE TO LOOK.›
‹ALL RIGHT, KID, BUT THIS BETTER BE WORTH IT.›
‹OVER THERE.›

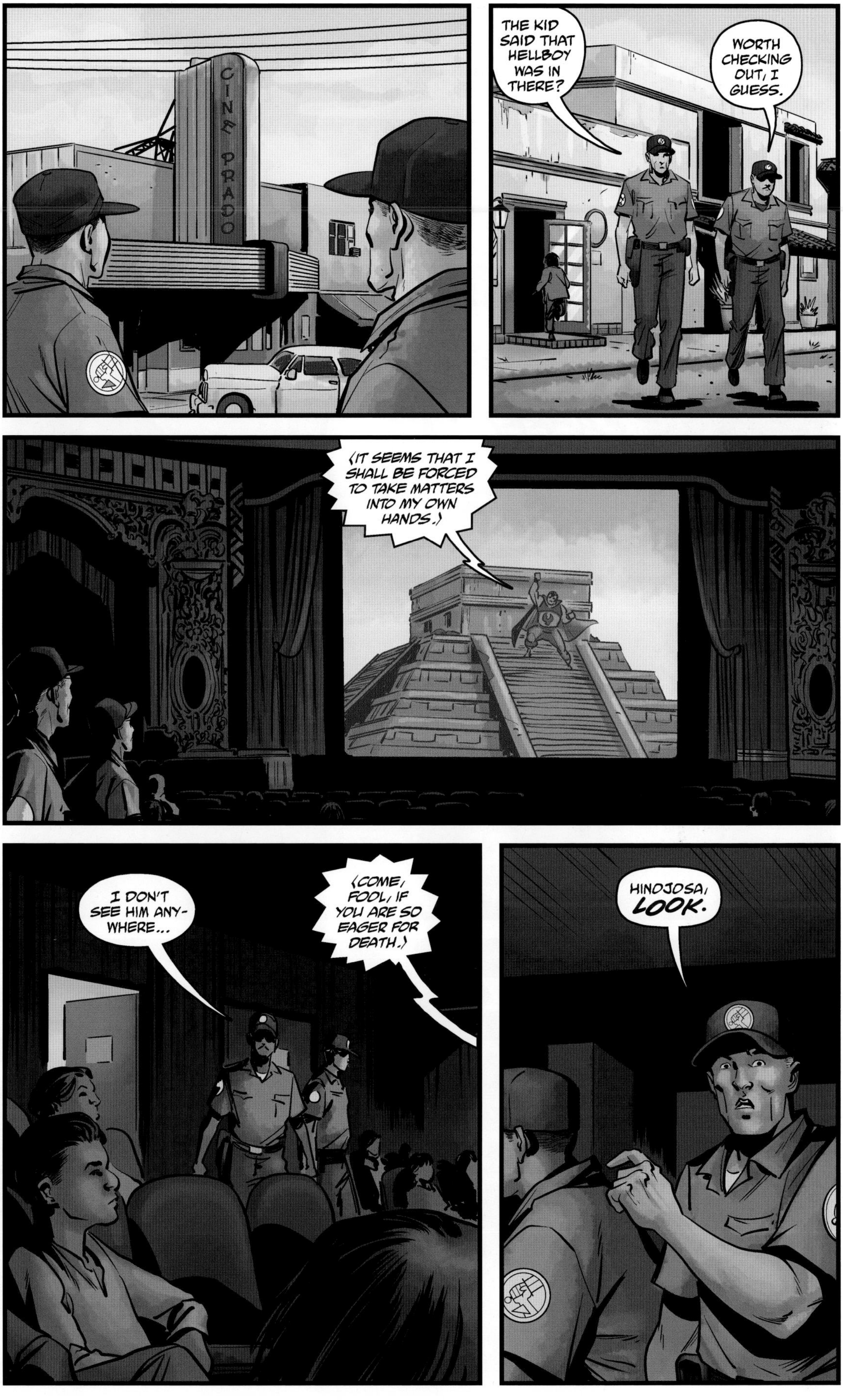
CINE PRADO
THE KID SAID THAT HELLBOY WAS IN THERE?
WORTH CHECKING OUT, I GUESS.
⟨IT SEEMS THAT I SHALL BE FORCED TO TAKE MATTERS INTO MY OWN HANDS.⟩
I DON'T SEE HIM ANY-WHERE...
⟨COME, FOOL, IF YOU ARE SO EAGER FOR DEATH.⟩
HINOJOSA, **LOOK.**

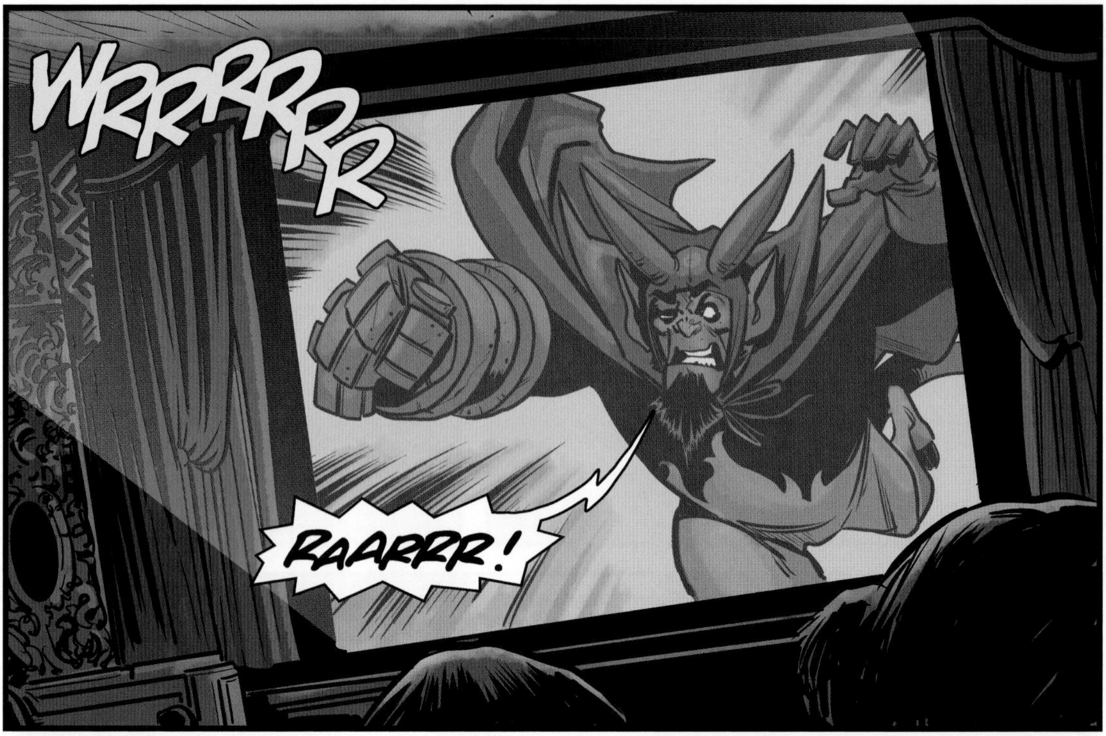
WRRRRRR
RAARRR!

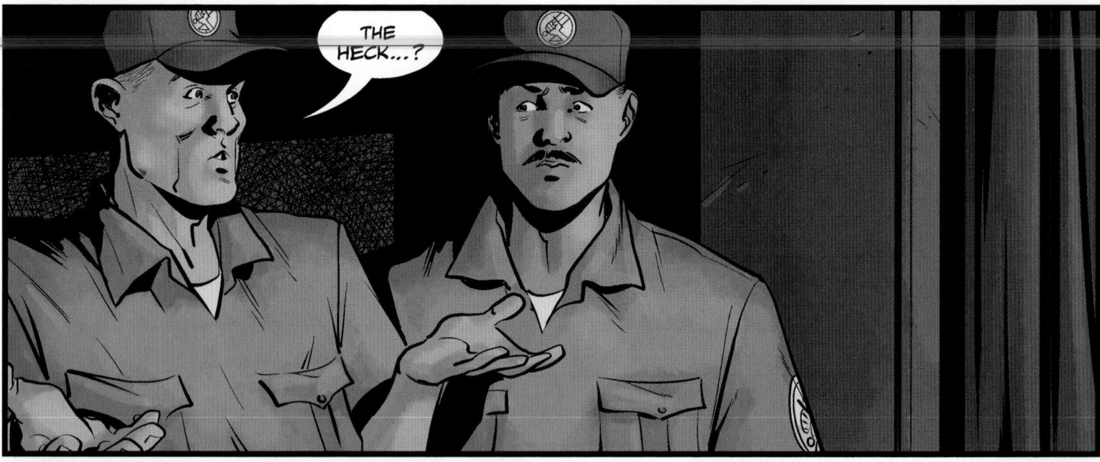
THE HECK...?

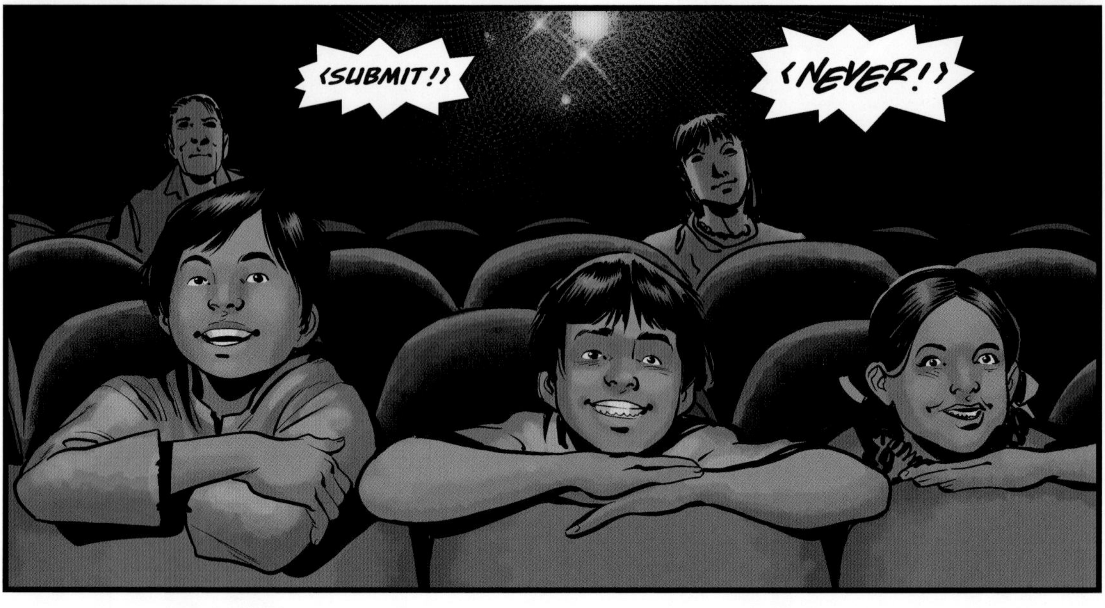
‹SUBMIT!›
‹NEVER!›

MEXICO CITY--
AUGUST 17, 1956.

I DON'T KNOW ABOUT THIS...

YOU SAY HE'S NEVER ACTED BEFORE?

COME ON, JEFE, JUST LOOK AT HIM AND TELL ME YOU CAN THINK OF A BETTER PERSON TO PLAY THE DEVIL!

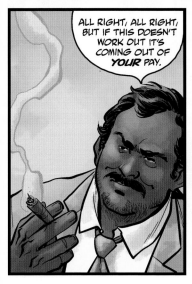

ALL RIGHT, ALL RIGHT, BUT IF THIS DOESN'T WORK OUT IT'S COMING OUT OF *YOUR* PAY.

HELLBOY, MY FRIEND, YOU'RE GOING TO BE A *STAR*.

YEAH ≥HIC≤ A STAR...

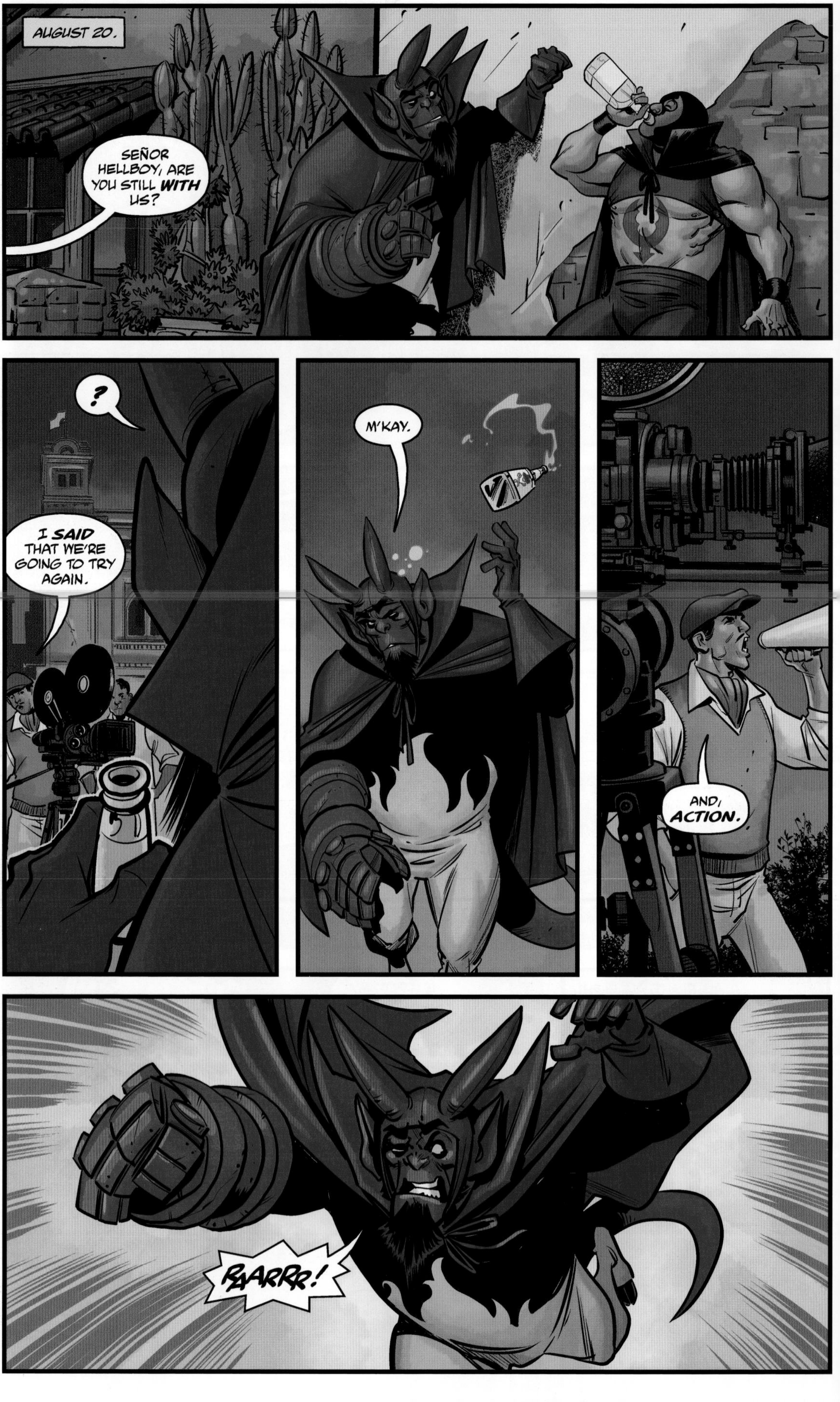
AUGUST 20.
SEÑOR HELLBOY, ARE YOU STILL WITH US?
?
I SAID THAT WE'RE GOING TO TRY AGAIN.
M'KAY.
AND, ACTION.
RAARRR!

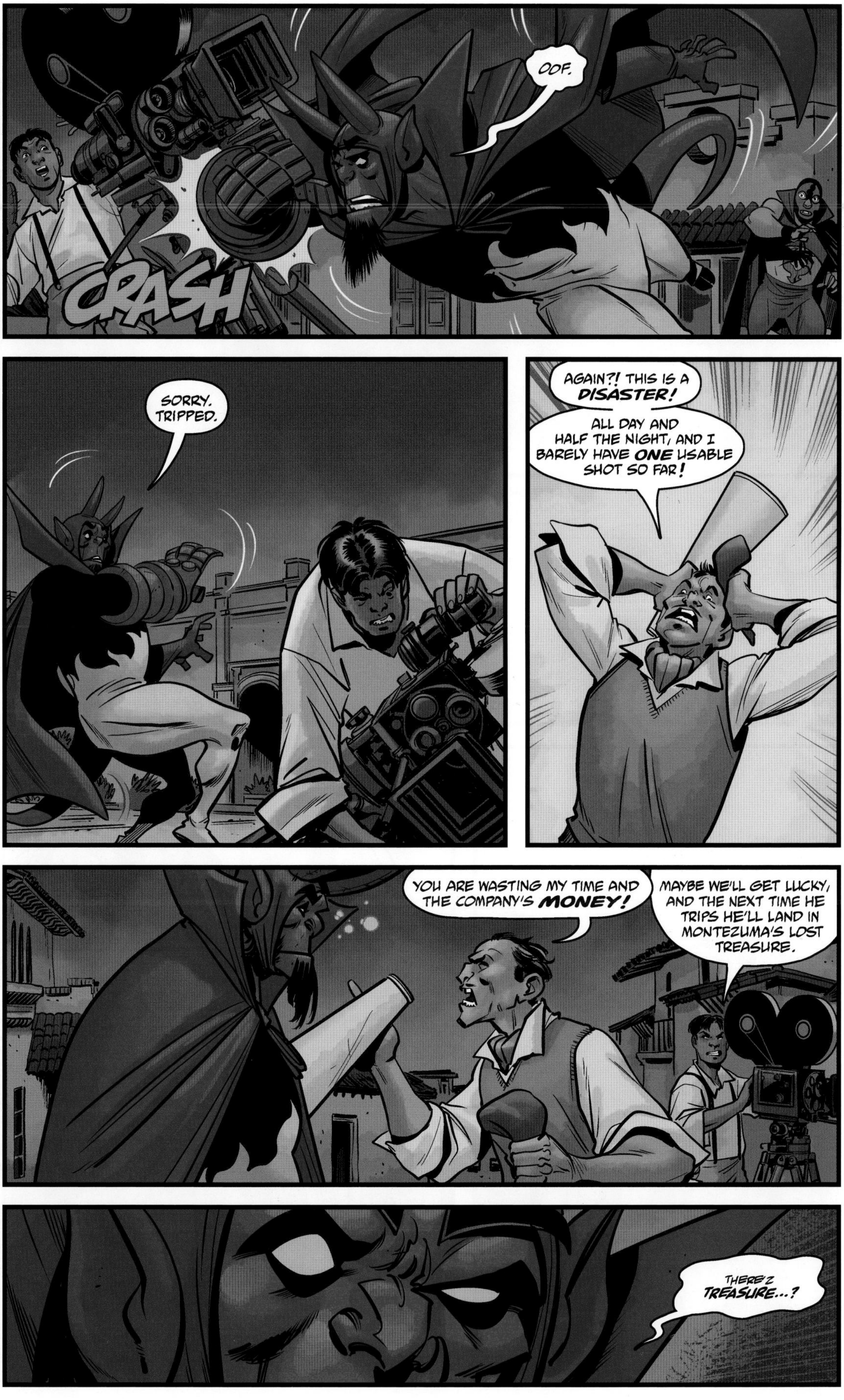
OOF.
CRASH
SORRY. TRIPPED.
AGAIN?! THIS IS A DISASTER!
ALL DAY AND HALF THE NIGHT, AND I BARELY HAVE ONE USABLE SHOT SO FAR!
YOU ARE WASTING MY TIME AND THE COMPANY'S MONEY!
MAYBE WE'LL GET LUCKY, AND THE NEXT TIME HE TRIPS HE'LL LAND IN MONTEZUMA'S LOST TREASURE.
THERE'Z TREASURE...?

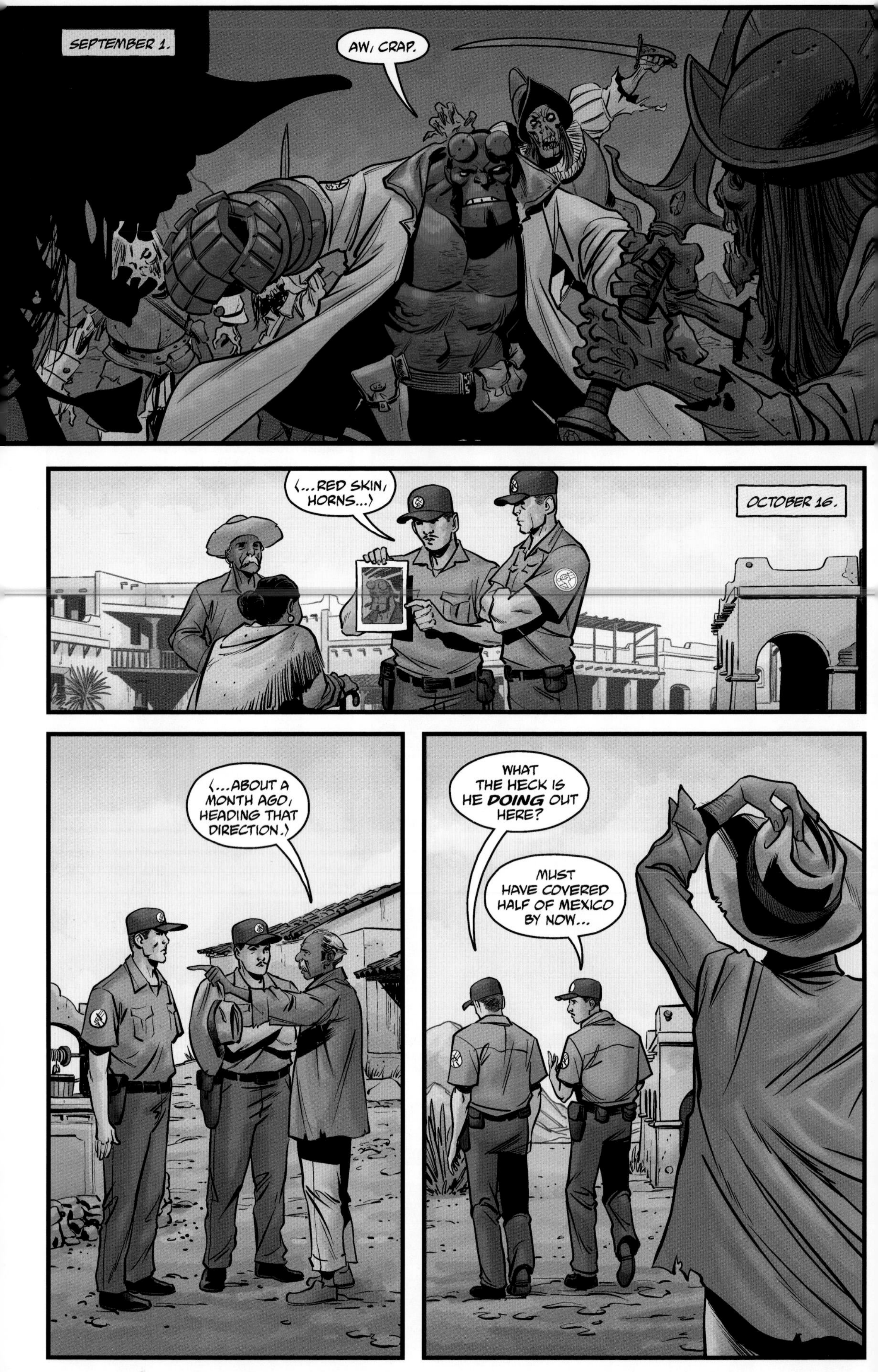
SEPTEMBER 1.
AW, CRAP.
‹...RED SKIN, HORNS...›
OCTOBER 16.
‹...ABOUT A MONTH AGO, HEADING THAT DIRECTION.›
WHAT THE HECK IS HE **DOING** OUT HERE?
MUST HAVE COVERED HALF OF MEXICO BY NOW...

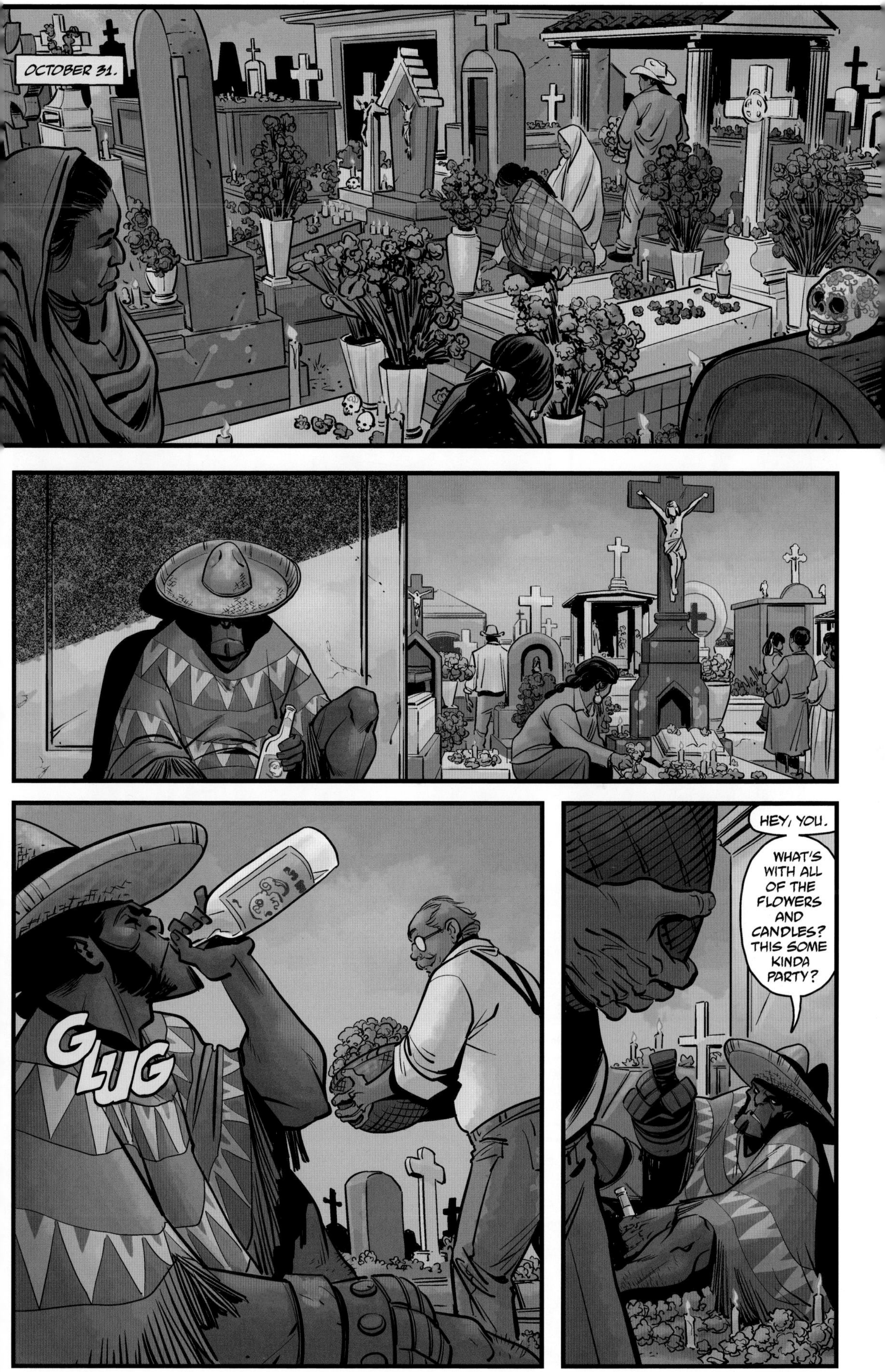
OCTOBER 31.
GLUG
HEY, YOU.
WHAT'S WITH ALL OF THE FLOWERS AND CANDLES? THIS SOME KINDA PARTY?

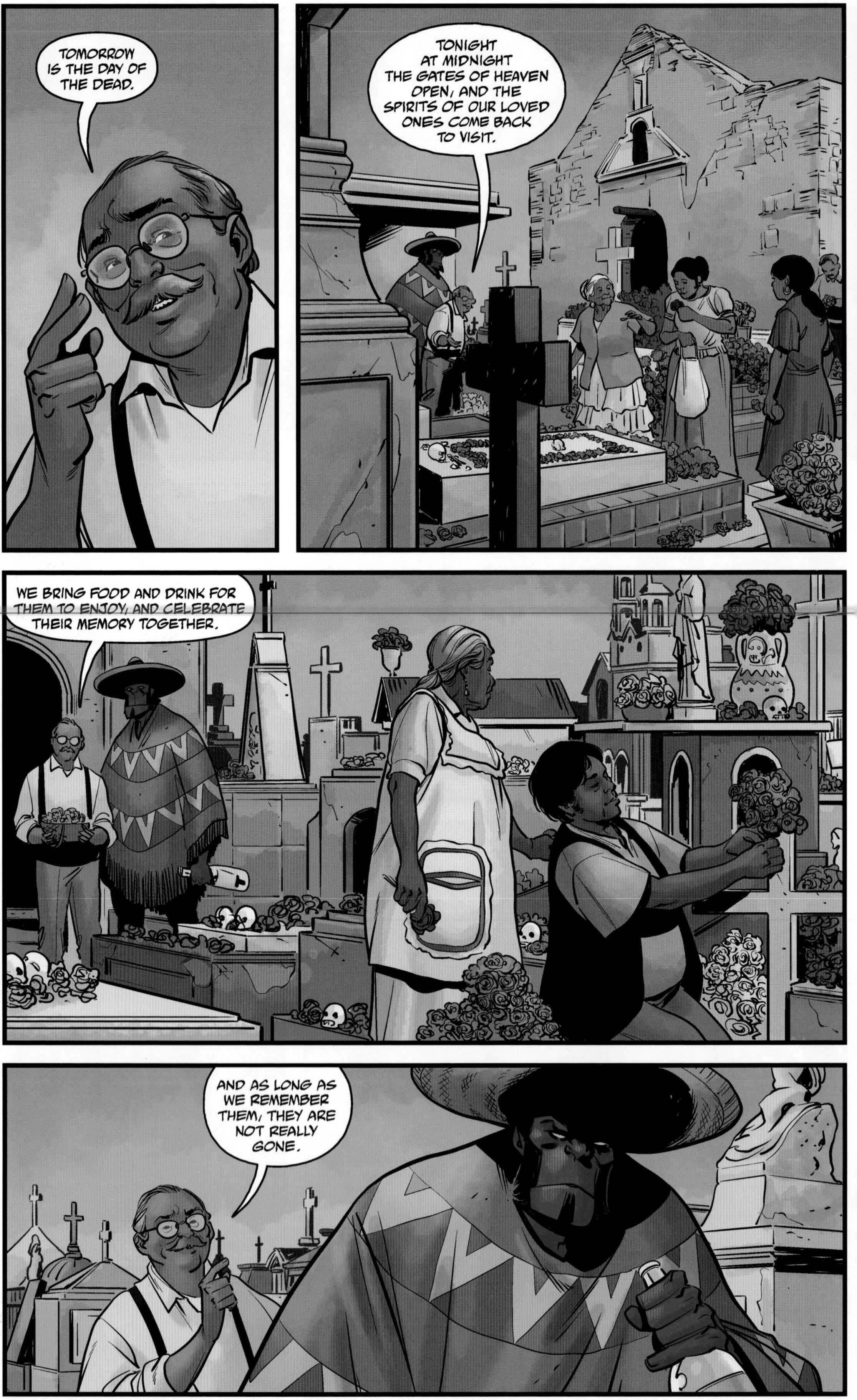
TOMORROW IS THE DAY OF THE DEAD.
TONIGHT AT MIDNIGHT THE GATES OF HEAVEN OPEN, AND THE SPIRITS OF OUR LOVED ONES COME BACK TO VISIT.
WE BRING FOOD AND DRINK FOR THEM TO ENJOY, AND CELEBRATE THEIR MEMORY TOGETHER.
AND AS LONG AS WE REMEMBER THEM, THEY ARE NOT REALLY GONE.

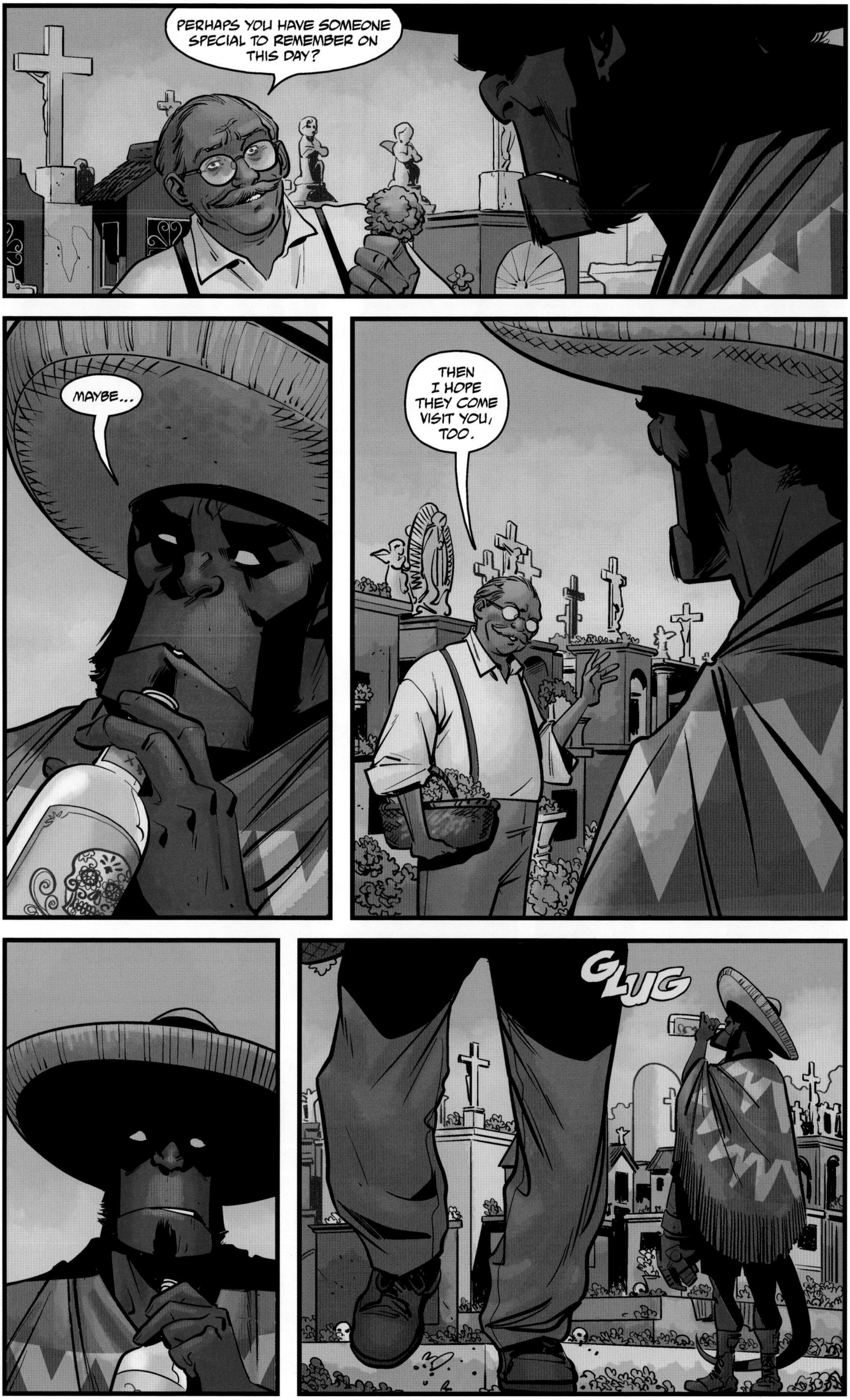
PERHAPS YOU HAVE SOMEONE SPECIAL TO REMEMBER ON THIS DAY?
MAYBE...
THEN I HOPE THEY COME VISIT YOU, TOO.
GLUG

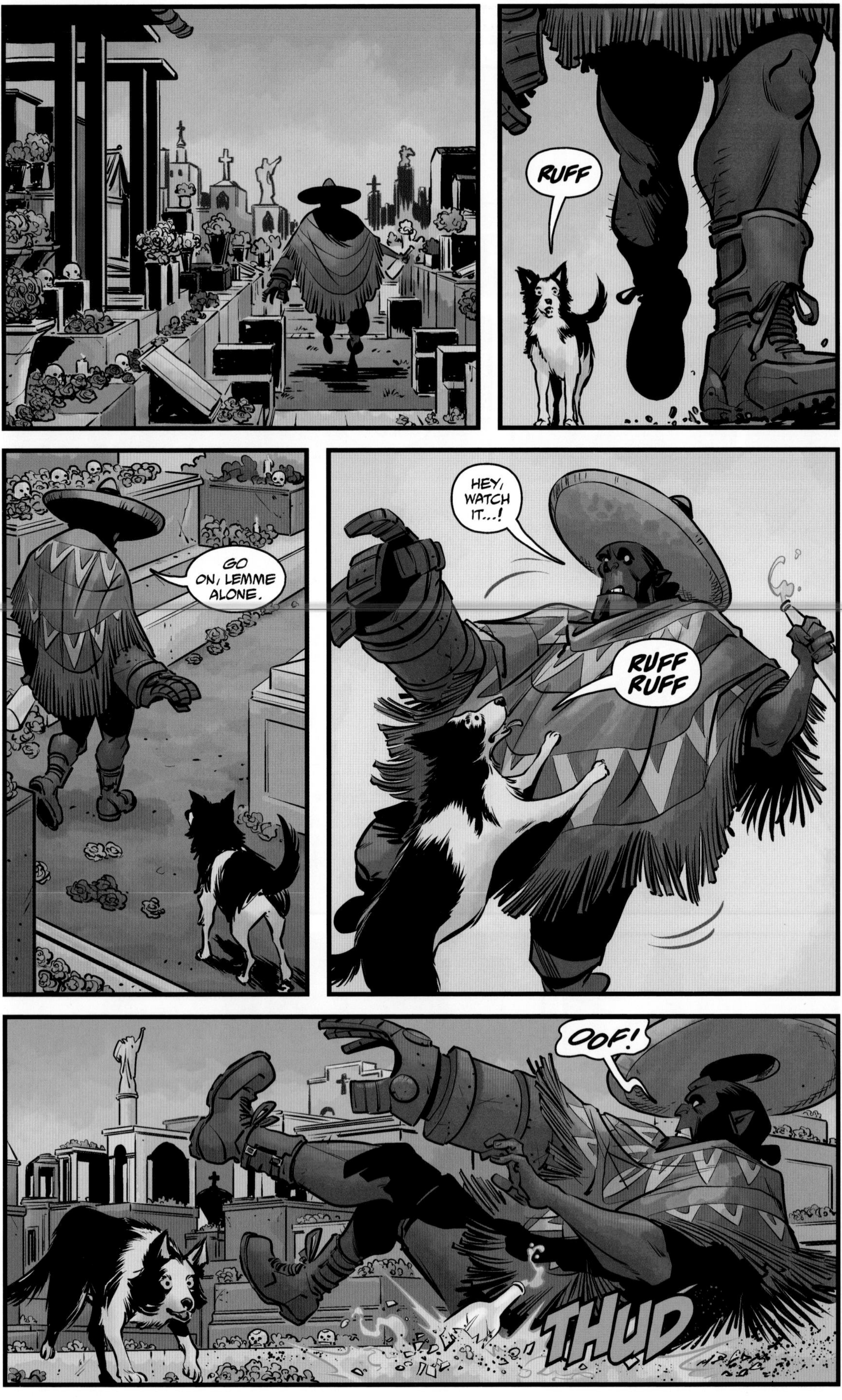
RUFF
GO ON, LEMME ALONE.
HEY, WATCH IT...!
RUFF RUFF
OOF!
THUD

SNIFF

SNIFF

YEAH, MAC USED TO GIVE ME THAT LOOK, TOO.

I'M SORRY, BOY, I DON'T HAVE ANY TREATS FOR YOU.

MAYBE YOU CAN GET SOMETHING FROM ONE OF THE GHOSTS, HUH?

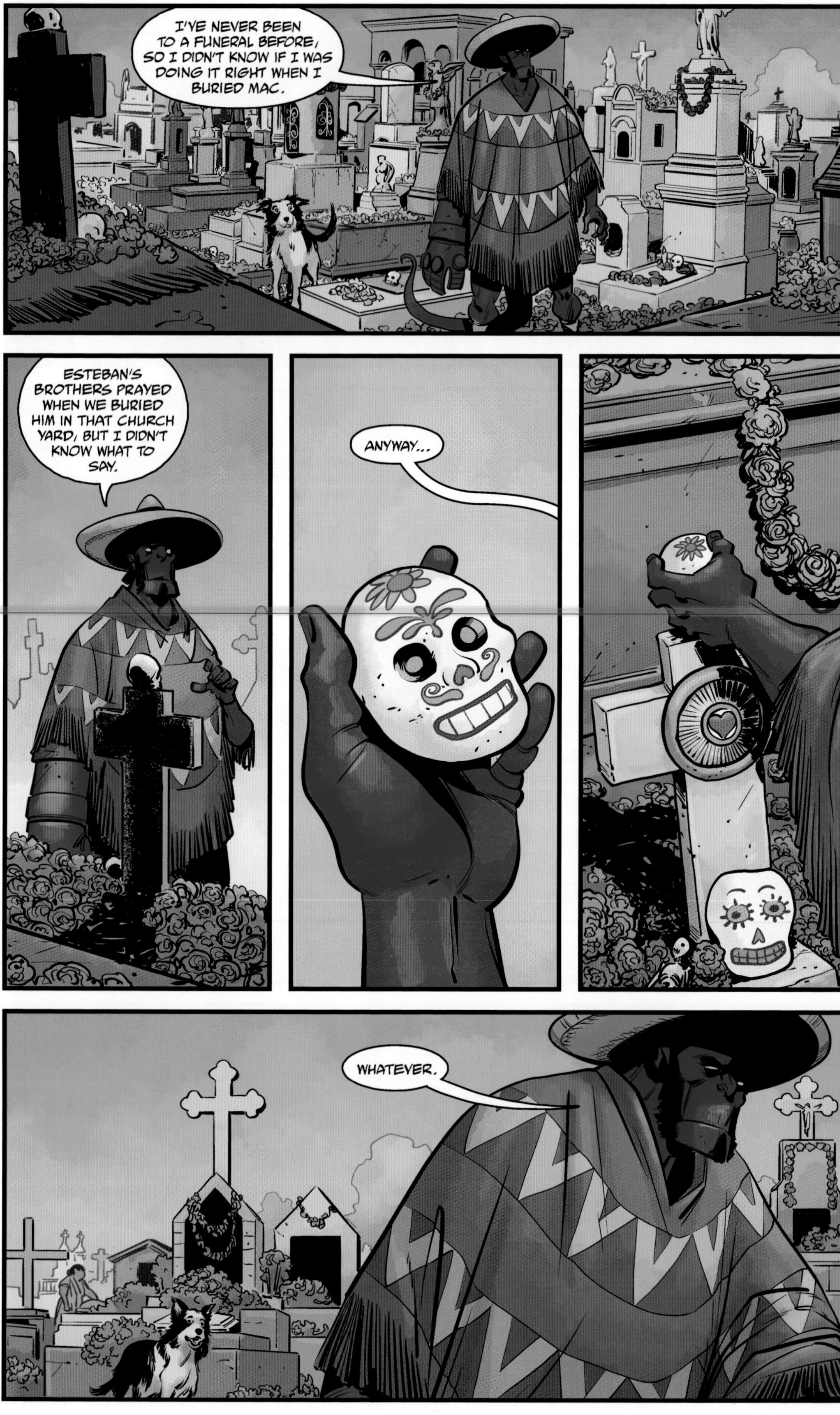
I'VE NEVER BEEN TO A FUNERAL BEFORE, SO I DIDN'T KNOW IF I WAS DOING IT RIGHT WHEN I BURIED MAC.
ESTEBAN'S BROTHERS PRAYED WHEN WE BURIED HIM IN THAT CHURCH YARD, BUT I DIDN'T KNOW WHAT TO SAY.
ANYWAY...
WHATEVER.

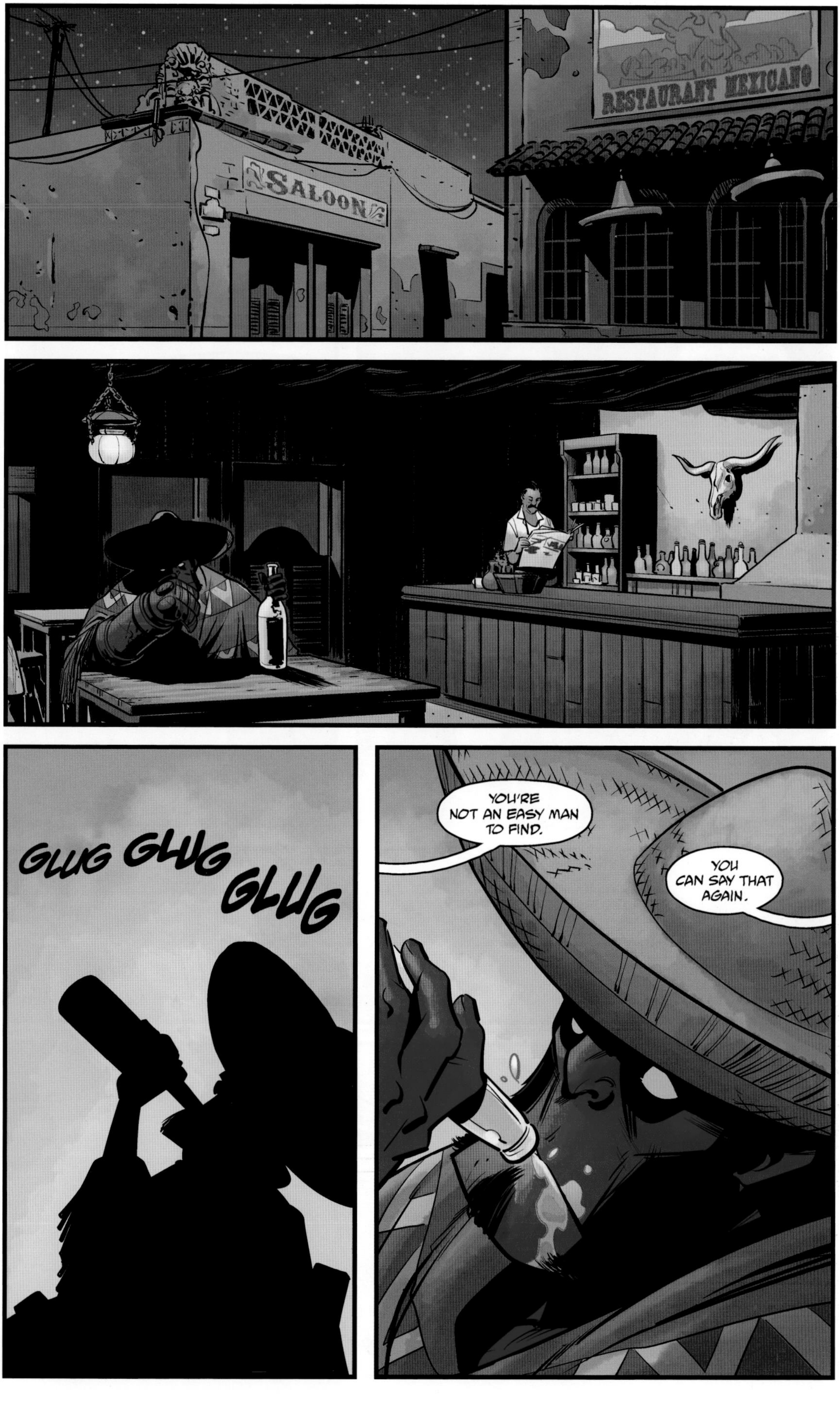
SALOON
RESTAURANT MEXICANO
GLUG GLUG GLUG
YOU'RE NOT AN EASY MAN TO FIND.
YOU CAN SAY THAT AGAIN.

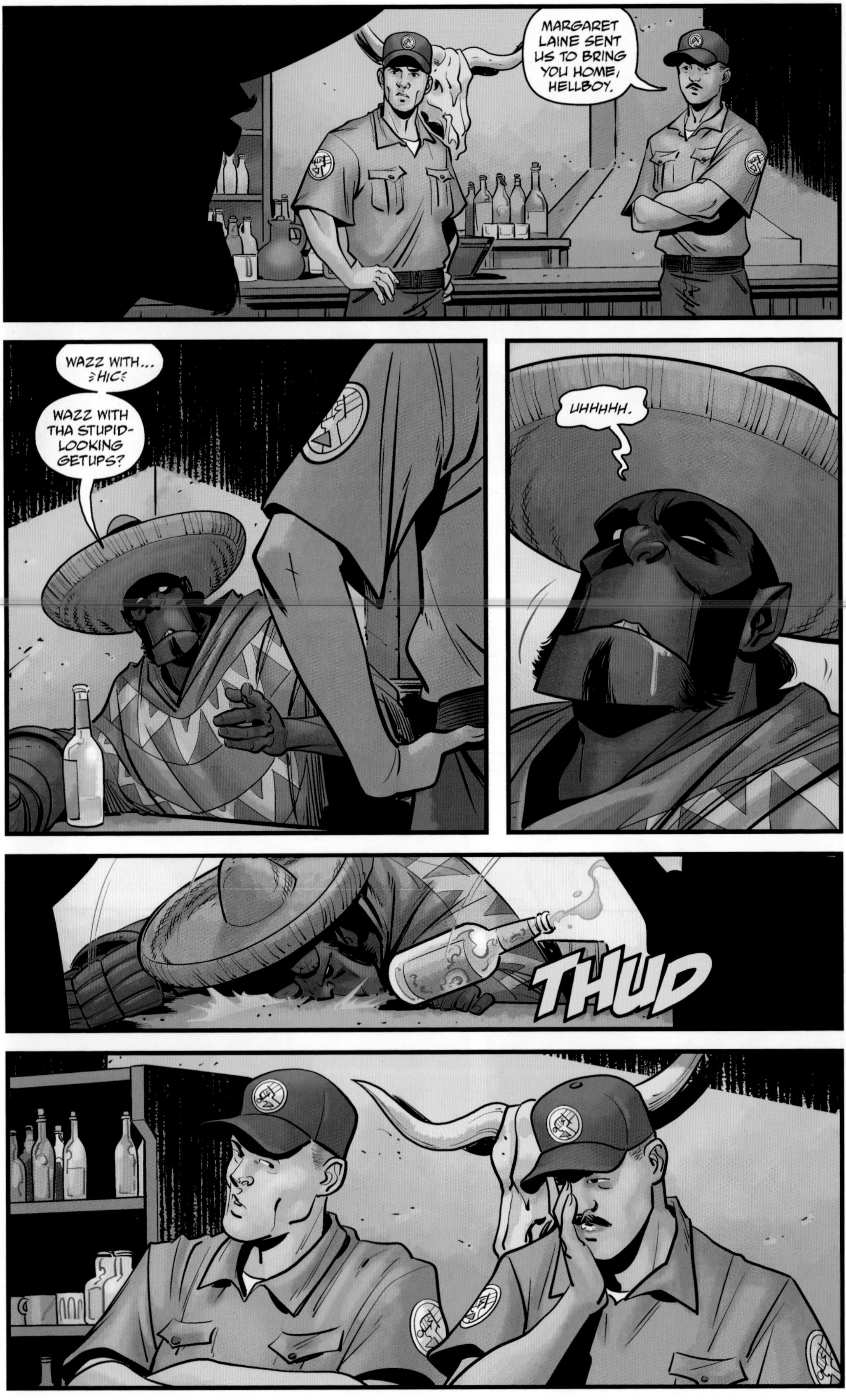
MARGARET LAINE SENT US TO BRING YOU HOME, HELLBOY.
WAZZ WITH... HIC
WAZZ WITH THA STUPID-LOOKING GETUPS?
UHHHHH.
THUD

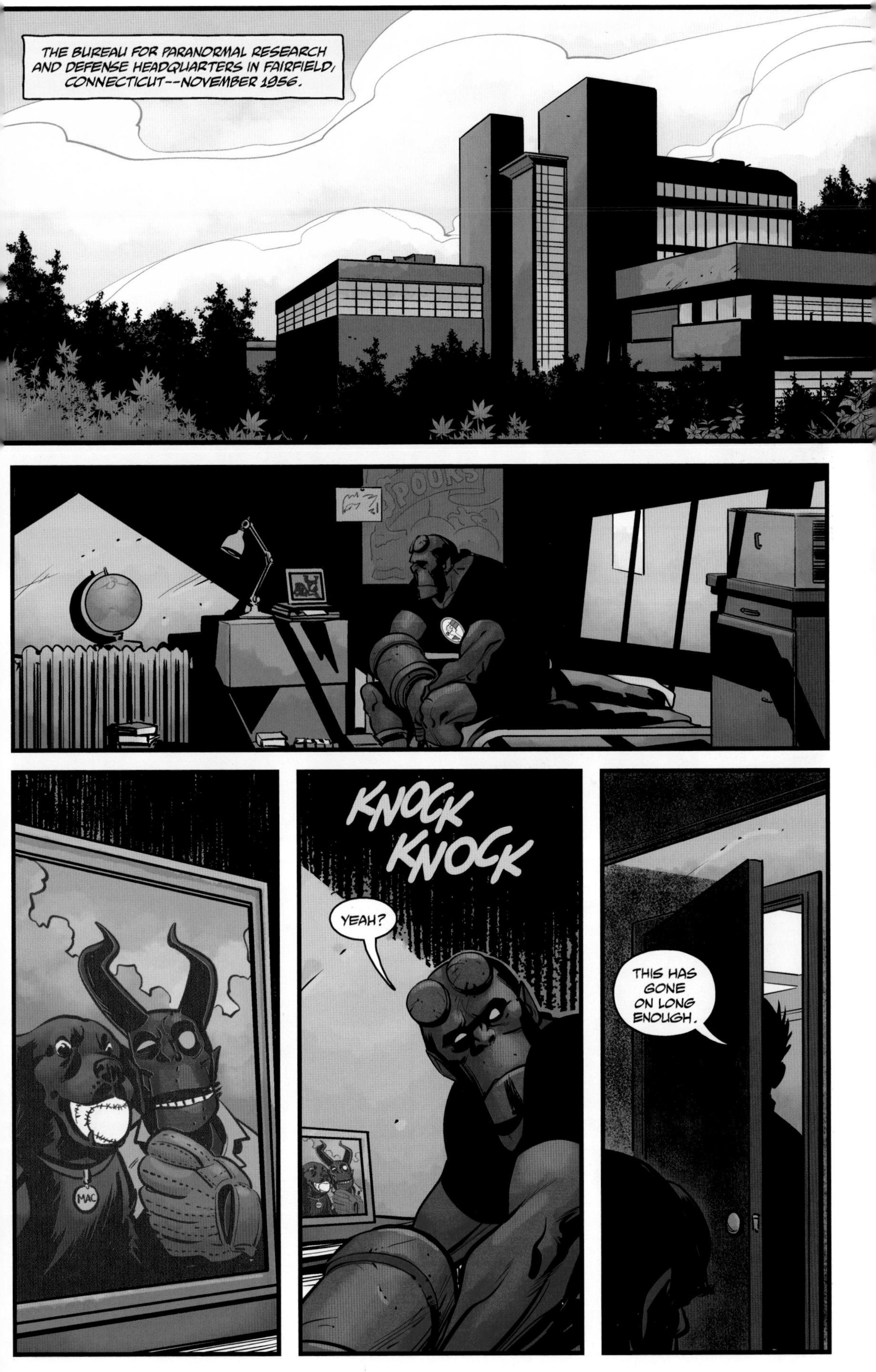
THE BUREAU FOR PARANORMAL RESEARCH AND DEFENSE HEADQUARTERS IN FAIRFIELD, CONNECTICUT--NOVEMBER 1956.
SPOOKS
MAC
KNOCK KNOCK
YEAH?
THIS HAS GONE ON LONG ENOUGH.

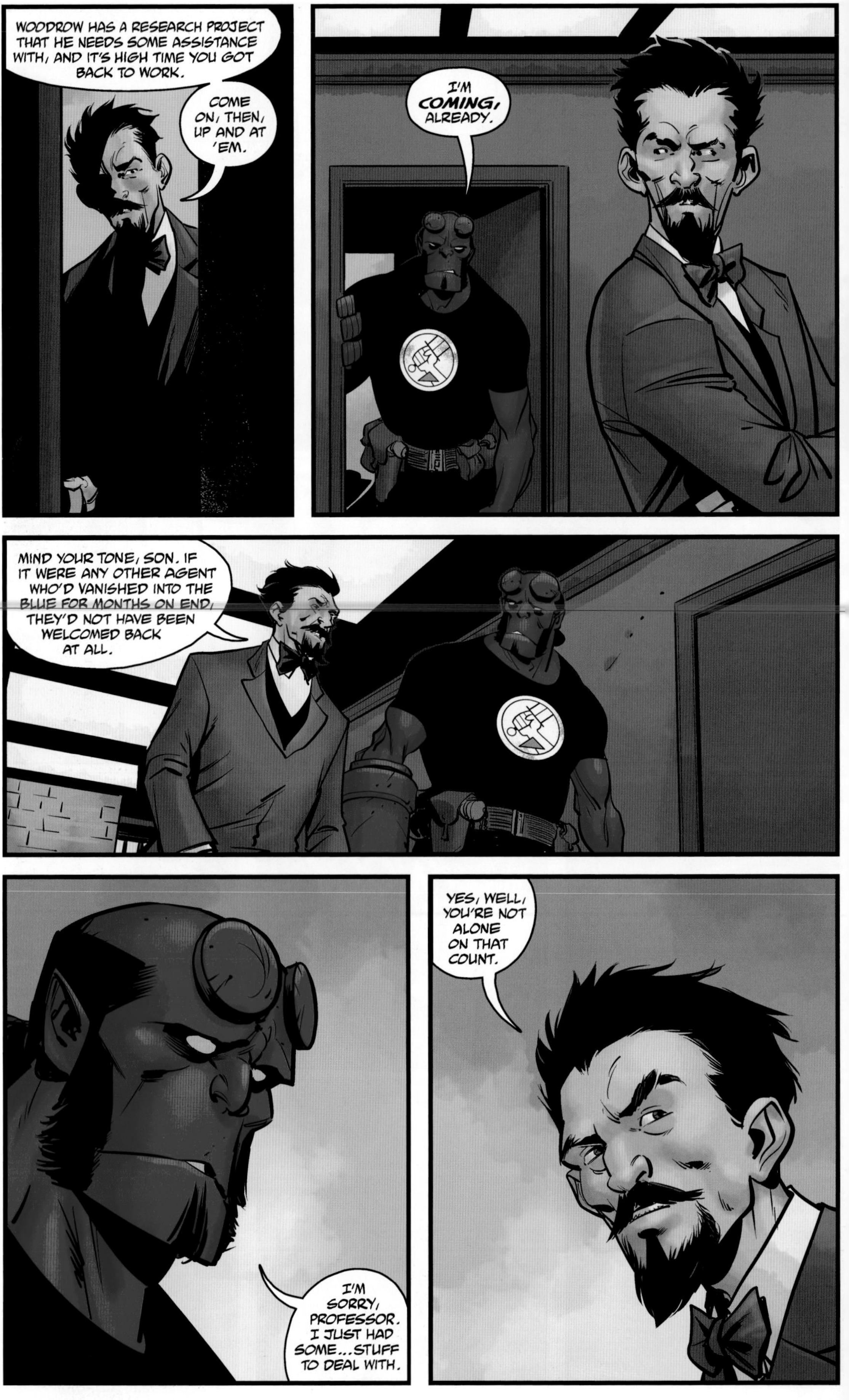

WOODROW HAS A RESEARCH PROJECT THAT HE NEEDS SOME ASSISTANCE WITH, AND IT'S HIGH TIME YOU GOT BACK TO WORK.
COME ON, THEN, UP AND AT 'EM.
I'M COMING, ALREADY.
MIND YOUR TONE, SON. IF IT WERE ANY OTHER AGENT WHO'D VANISHED INTO THE BLUE FOR MONTHS ON END, THEY'D NOT HAVE BEEN WELCOMED BACK AT ALL.
I'M SORRY, PROFESSOR. I JUST HAD SOME...STUFF TO DEAL WITH.
YES, WELL, YOU'RE NOT ALONE ON THAT COUNT.

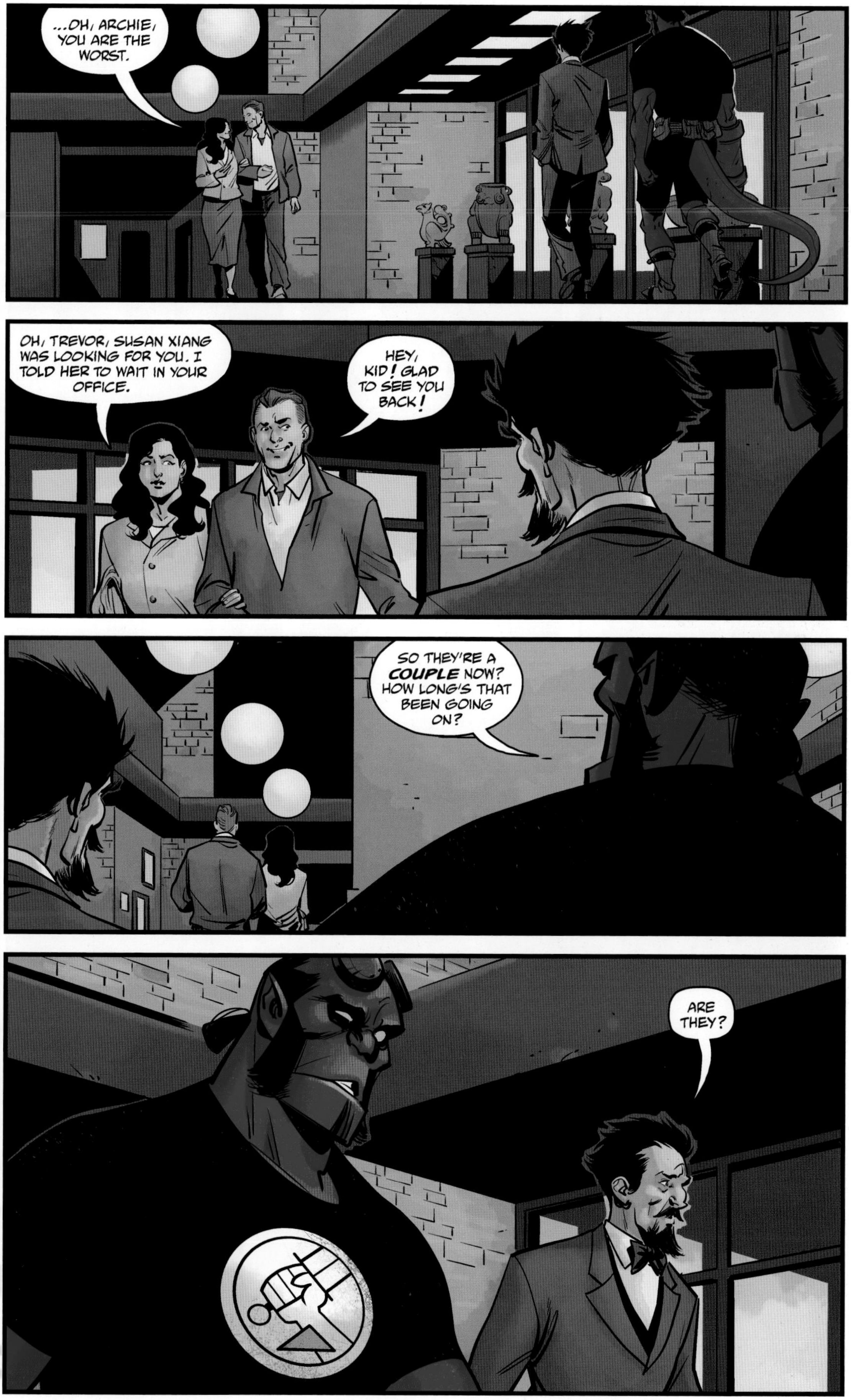
...OH, ARCHIE, YOU ARE THE WORST.
OH, TREVOR, SUSAN XIANG WAS LOOKING FOR YOU. I TOLD HER TO WAIT IN YOUR OFFICE.
HEY, KID! GLAD TO SEE YOU BACK!
SO THEY'RE A COUPLE NOW? HOW LONG'S THAT BEEN GOING ON?
ARE THEY?

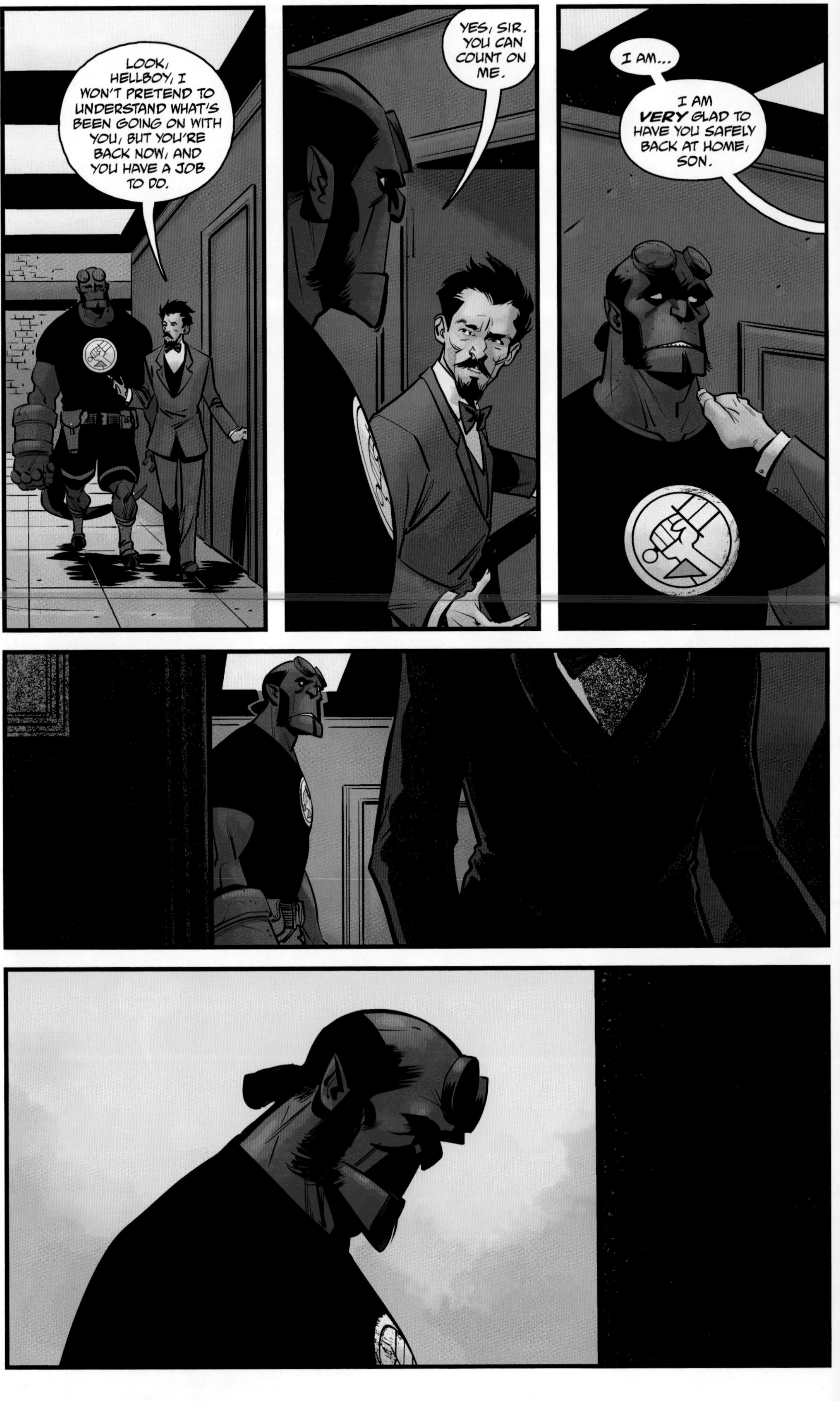
LOOK, HELLBOY, I WON'T PRETEND TO UNDERSTAND WHAT'S BEEN GOING ON WITH YOU, BUT YOU'RE BACK NOW, AND YOU HAVE A JOB TO DO.
YES, SIR. YOU CAN COUNT ON ME.
I AM...
I AM VERY GLAD TO HAVE YOU SAFELY BACK AT HOME, SON.

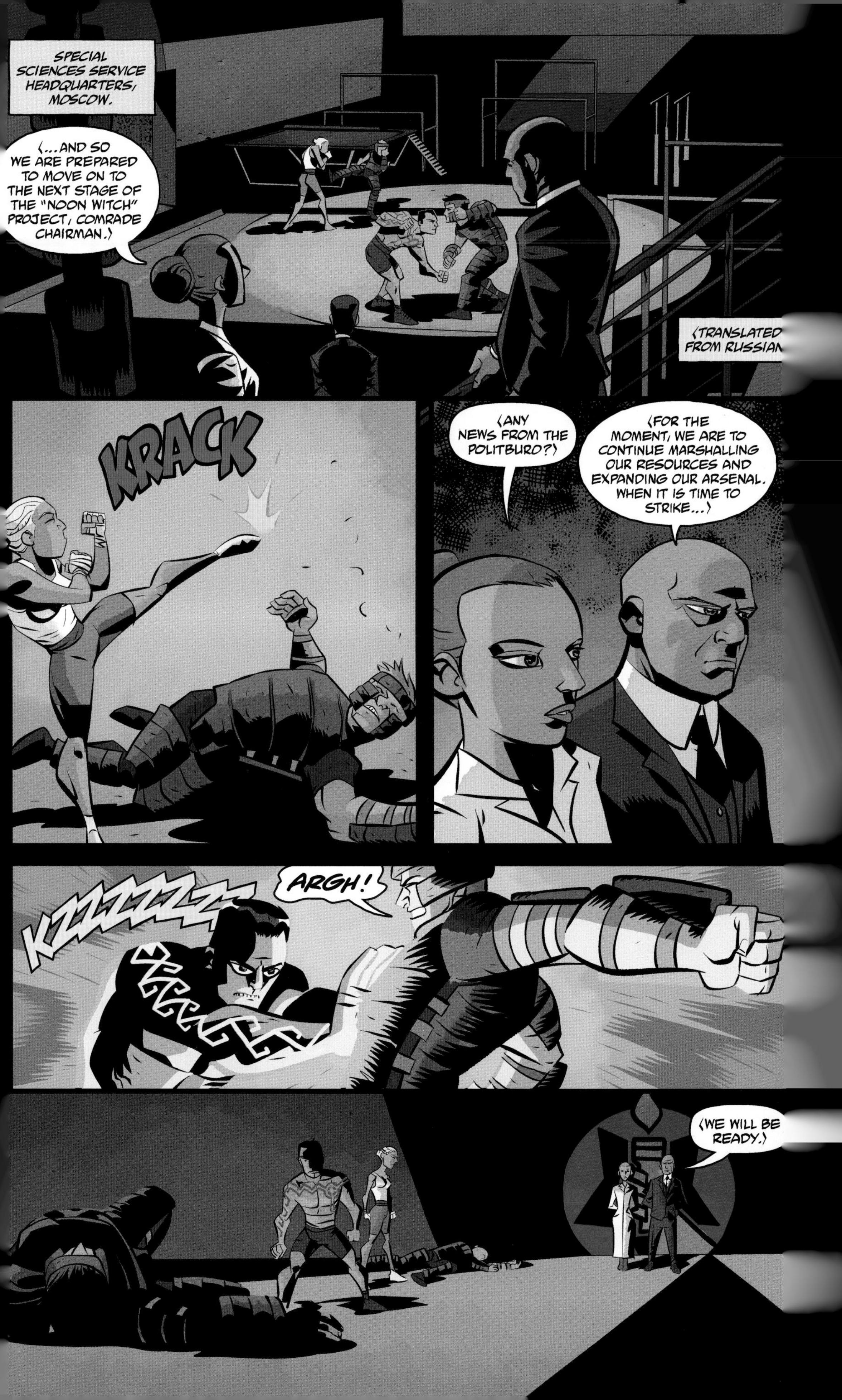
SPECIAL SCIENCES SERVICE HEADQUARTERS, MOSCOW.
⟨...AND SO WE ARE PREPARED TO MOVE ON TO THE NEXT STAGE OF THE "NOON WITCH" PROJECT, COMRADE CHAIRMAN.⟩
⟨TRANSLATED FROM RUSSIAN
KRACK
⟨ANY NEWS FROM THE POLITBURO?⟩
⟨FOR THE MOMENT, WE ARE TO CONTINUE MARSHALLING OUR RESOURCES AND EXPANDING OUR ARSENAL. WHEN IT IS TIME TO STRIKE...⟩
KZZZZZZZ
ARGH!
⟨WE WILL BE READY.⟩

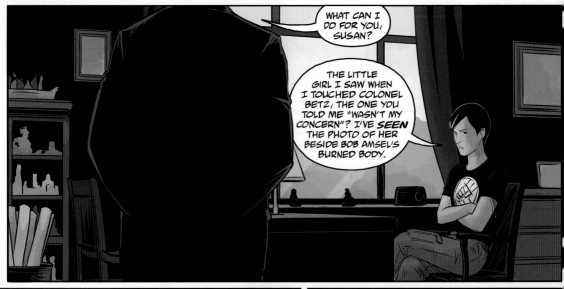

WHAT CAN I DO FOR YOU, SUSAN?

THE LITTLE GIRL I SAW WHEN I TOUCHED COLONEL BETZ, THE ONE YOU TOLD ME "WASN'T MY CONCERN"? I'VE *SEEN* THE PHOTO OF HER BESIDE BOB AMSEL'S BURNED BODY.

I HAD ANOTHER VISION OF HER A FEW WEEKS AGO, AND IT'S BEEN HAUNTING ME EVER SINCE. I CAN'T STOP THINKING ABOUT THE TERRIBLE POWER, THAT HORRIBLE RAGE...

LINNEBERG AND I HAVE BEEN DIGGING INTO IT, AND THE ONLY THING WE KNOW FOR SURE IS THAT IS *NOT* JUST SOME LITTLE GIRL.

YOU *KNOW* WHAT SHE REALLY IS, DON'T YOU? SO WHY ARE YOU KEEPING IT A SECRET?

YOU'RE... YOU'RE JUST GOING TO HAVE TO TRUST ME, SUSAN. I HAVE MY REASONS.

FINE, HAVE IT YOUR WAY. BUT LINNEBERG AND I ARE GOING TO KEEP LOOKING INTO THIS, AND WE *WILL* GET TO THE BOTTOM OF IT.

I PROMISE YOU THAT.

THE END

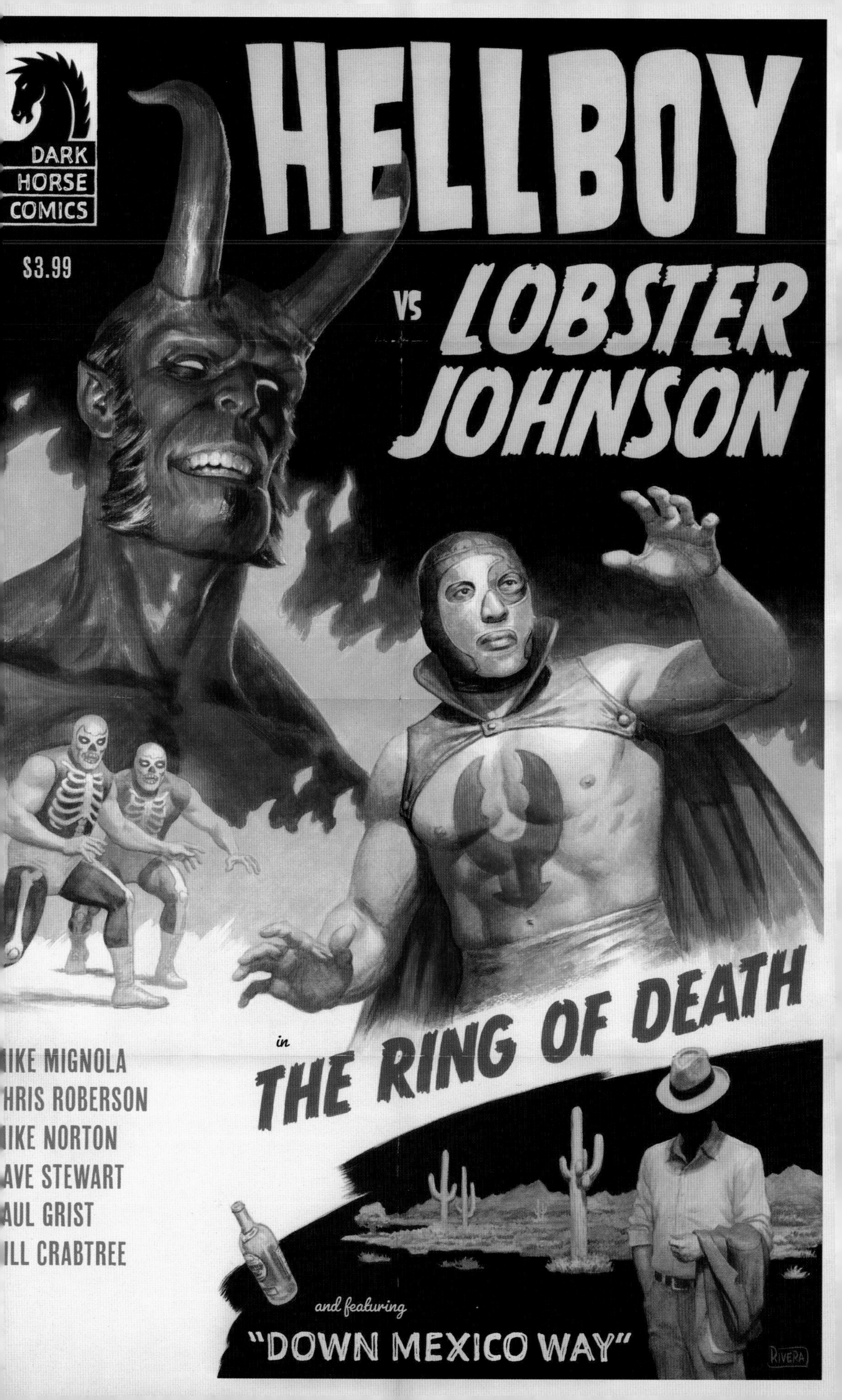
DARK HORSE COMICS
HELLBOY
$3.99
VS LOBSTER JOHNSON
IKE MIGNOLA
HRIS ROBERSON
IKE NORTON
AVE STEWART
AUL GRIST
ILL CRABTREE
in
THE RING OF DEATH
and featuring
"DOWN MEXICO WAY"
RIVERA

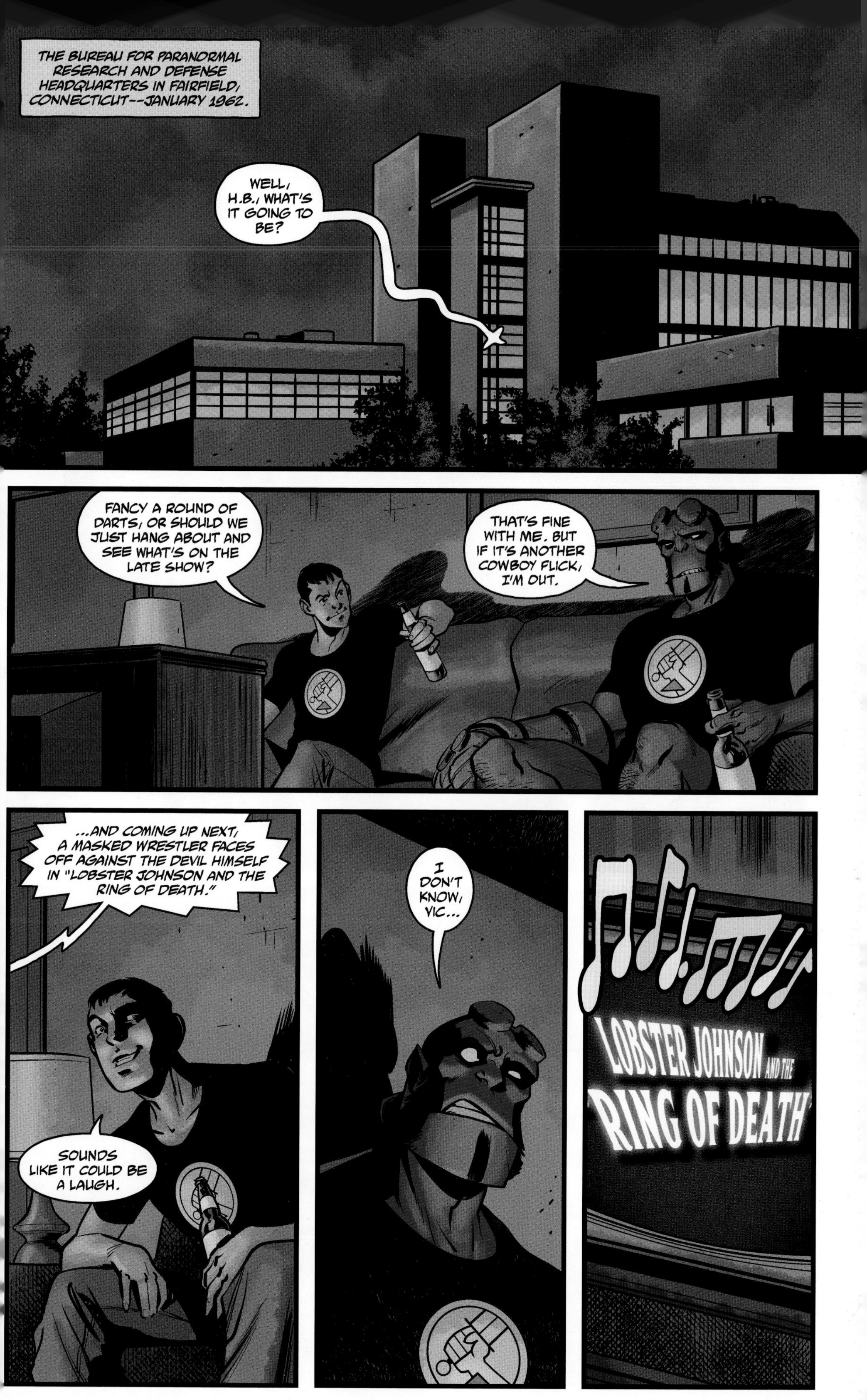
THE BUREAU FOR PARANORMAL RESEARCH AND DEFENSE HEADQUARTERS IN FAIRFIELD, CONNECTICUT--JANUARY 1962.
WELL, H.B., WHAT'S IT GOING TO BE?
FANCY A ROUND OF DARTS, OR SHOULD WE JUST HANG ABOUT AND SEE WHAT'S ON THE LATE SHOW?
THAT'S FINE WITH ME. BUT IF IT'S ANOTHER COWBOY FLICK, I'M OUT.
...AND COMING UP NEXT, A MASKED WRESTLER FACES OFF AGAINST THE DEVIL HIMSELF IN "LOBSTER JOHNSON AND THE RING OF DEATH."
SOUNDS LIKE IT COULD BE A LAUGH.
I DON'T KNOW, VIC...
LOBSTER JOHNSON AND THE RING OF DEATH

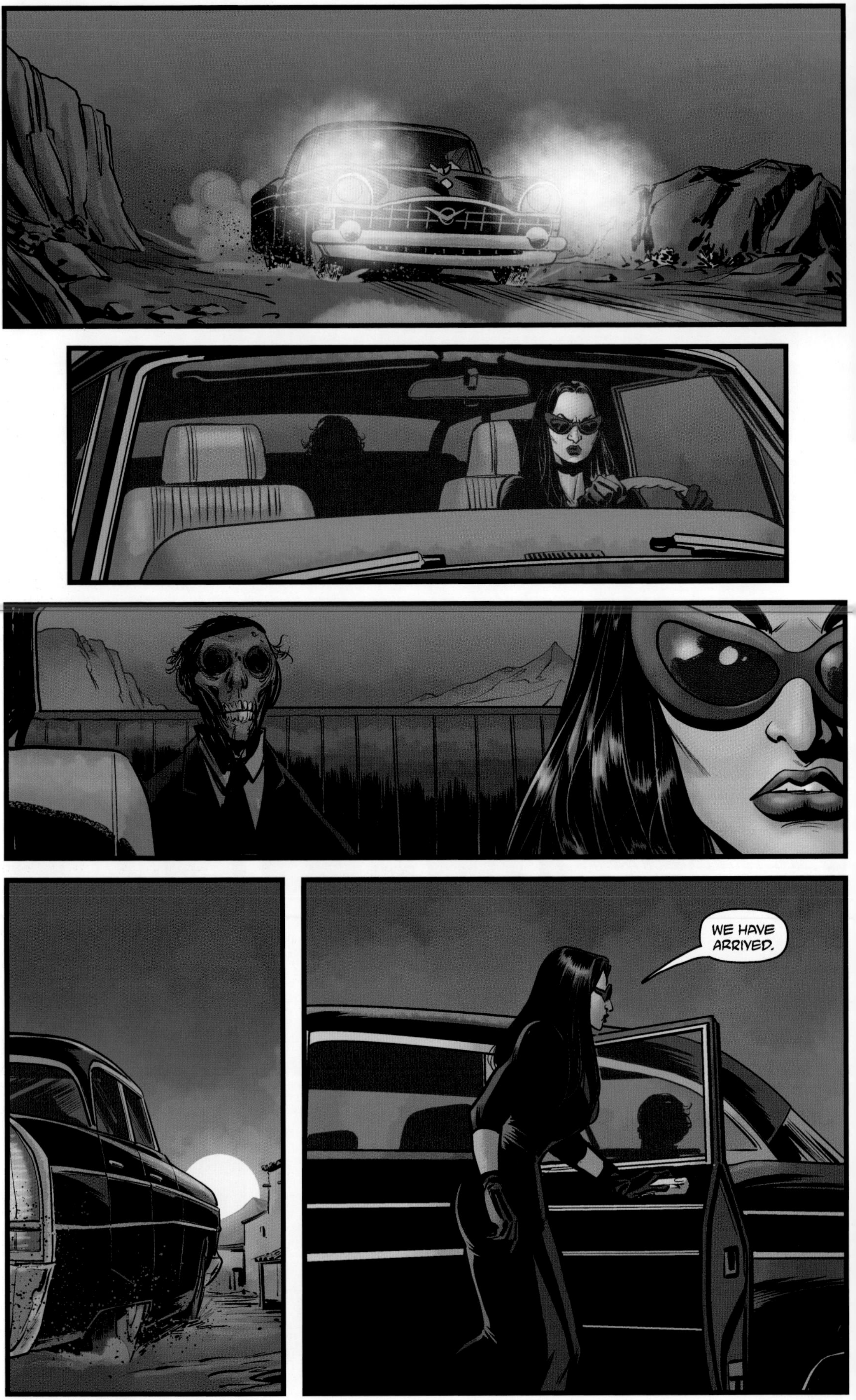
WE HAVE ARRIVED.

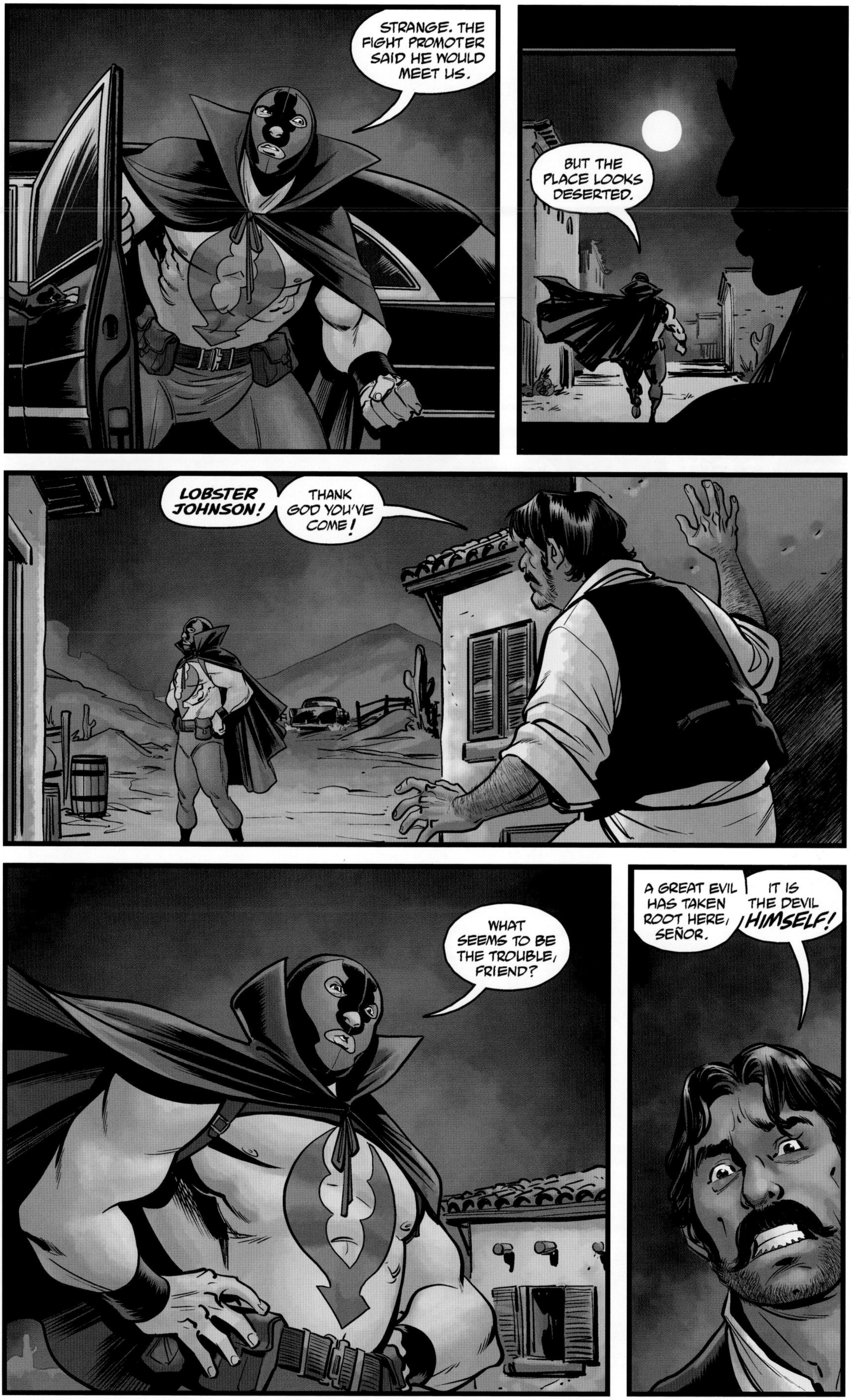
STRANGE. THE FIGHT PROMOTER SAID HE WOULD MEET US.
BUT THE PLACE LOOKS DESERTED.
LOBSTER JOHNSON!
THANK GOD YOU'VE COME!
WHAT SEEMS TO BE THE TROUBLE, FRIEND?
A GREAT EVIL HAS TAKEN ROOT HERE, SEÑOR.
IT IS THE DEVIL HIMSELF!

KNEEL, YOU DOGS!

BOW BEFORE YOUR **NEW** MASTER!

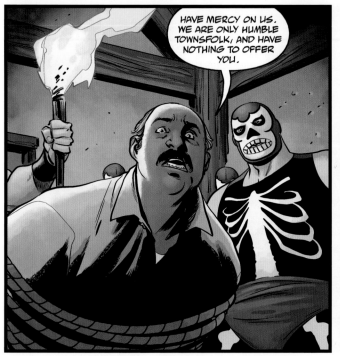

HAVE MERCY ON US. WE ARE ONLY HUMBLE TOWNSFOLK, AND HAVE NOTHING TO OFFER YOU.

AND PLEASE, DO NOT TAKE MY DAUGHTER OFELIA FROM US, I BEG YOU.

I AM NOT AFRAID, FATHER.

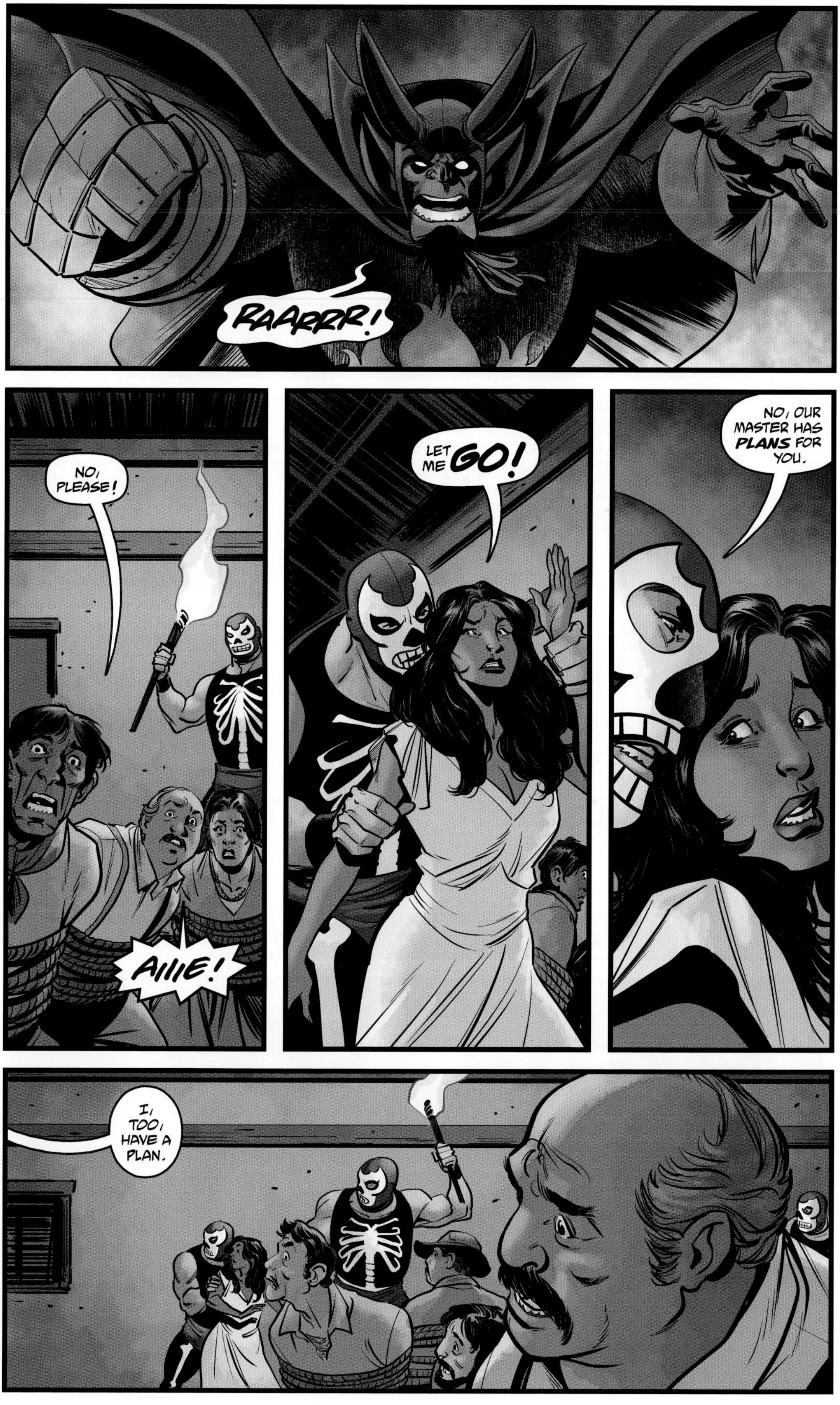
RAARRR!
NO, PLEASE!
AIIIE!
LET ME GO!
NO, OUR MASTER HAS PLANS FOR YOU.
I, TOO, HAVE A PLAN.

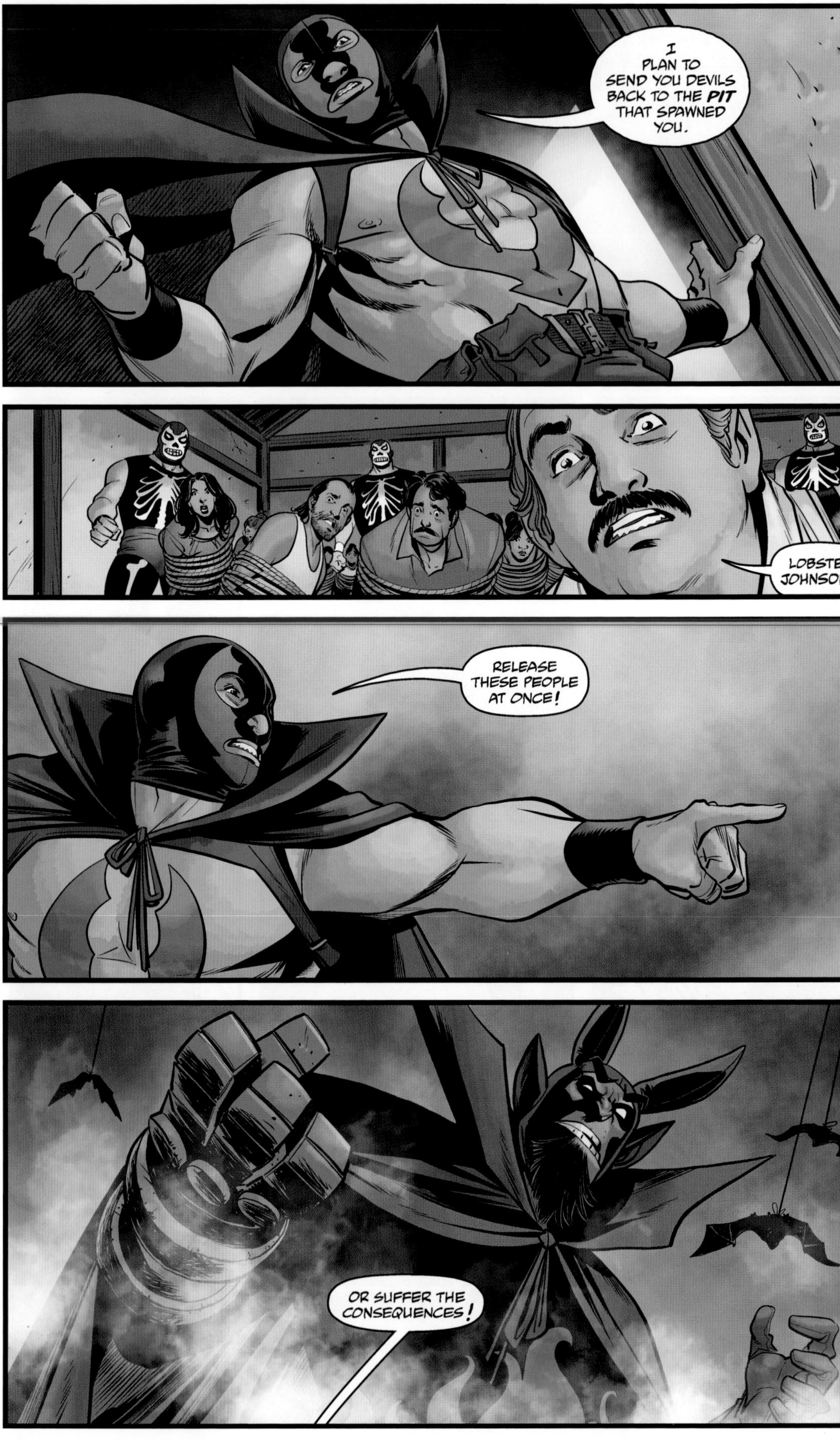
I PLAN TO SEND YOU DEVILS BACK TO THE PIT THAT SPAWNED YOU.
LOBSTER JOHNSON!
RELEASE THESE PEOPLE AT ONCE!
OR SUFFER THE CONSEQUENCES!

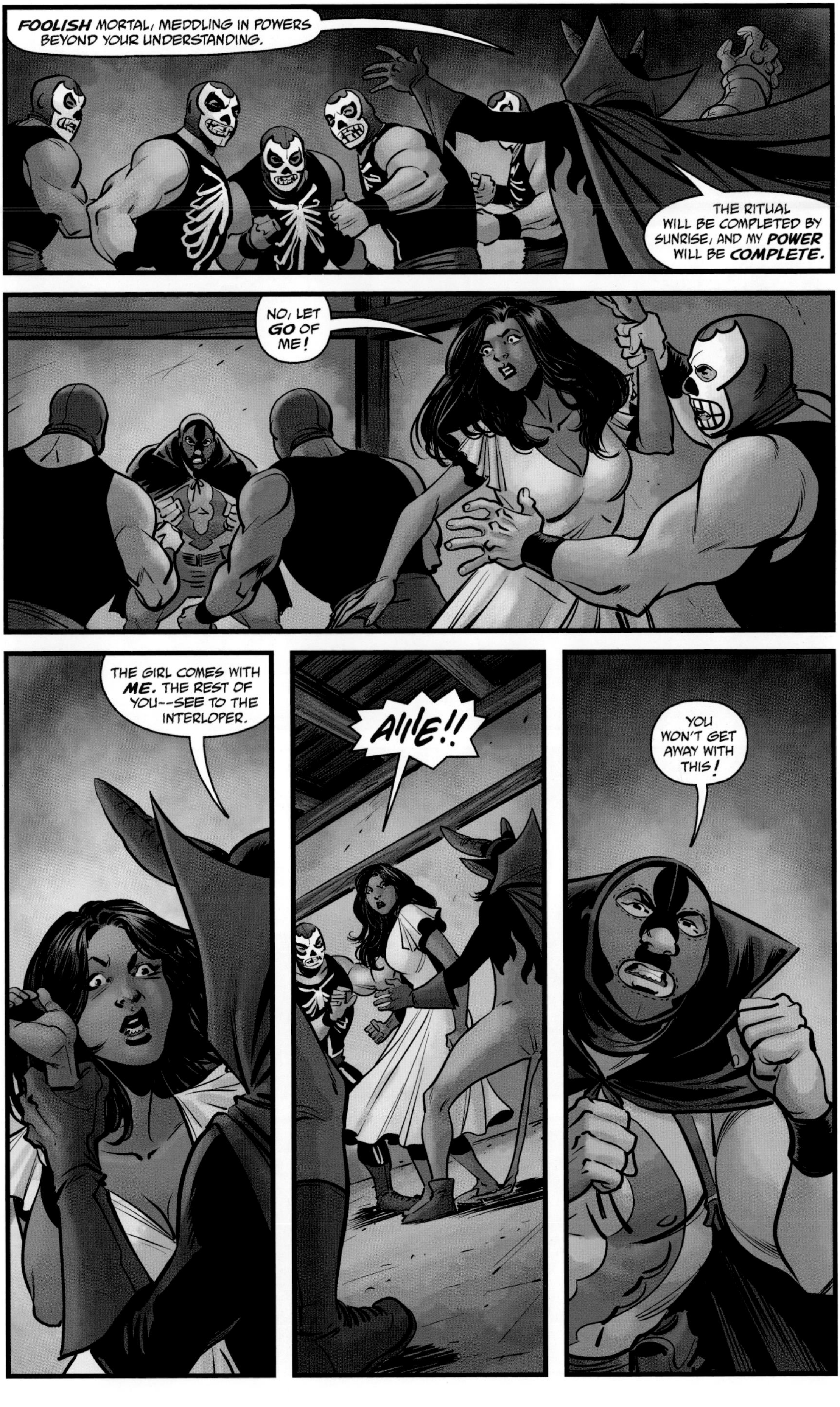

FOOLISH MORTAL, MEDDLING IN POWERS BEYOND YOUR UNDERSTANDING.
THE RITUAL WILL BE COMPLETED BY SUNRISE, AND MY POWER WILL BE COMPLETE.
NO, LET GO OF ME!
THE GIRL COMES WITH ME. THE REST OF YOU--SEE TO THE INTERLOPER.
AIIIE!!
YOU WON'T GET AWAY WITH THIS!

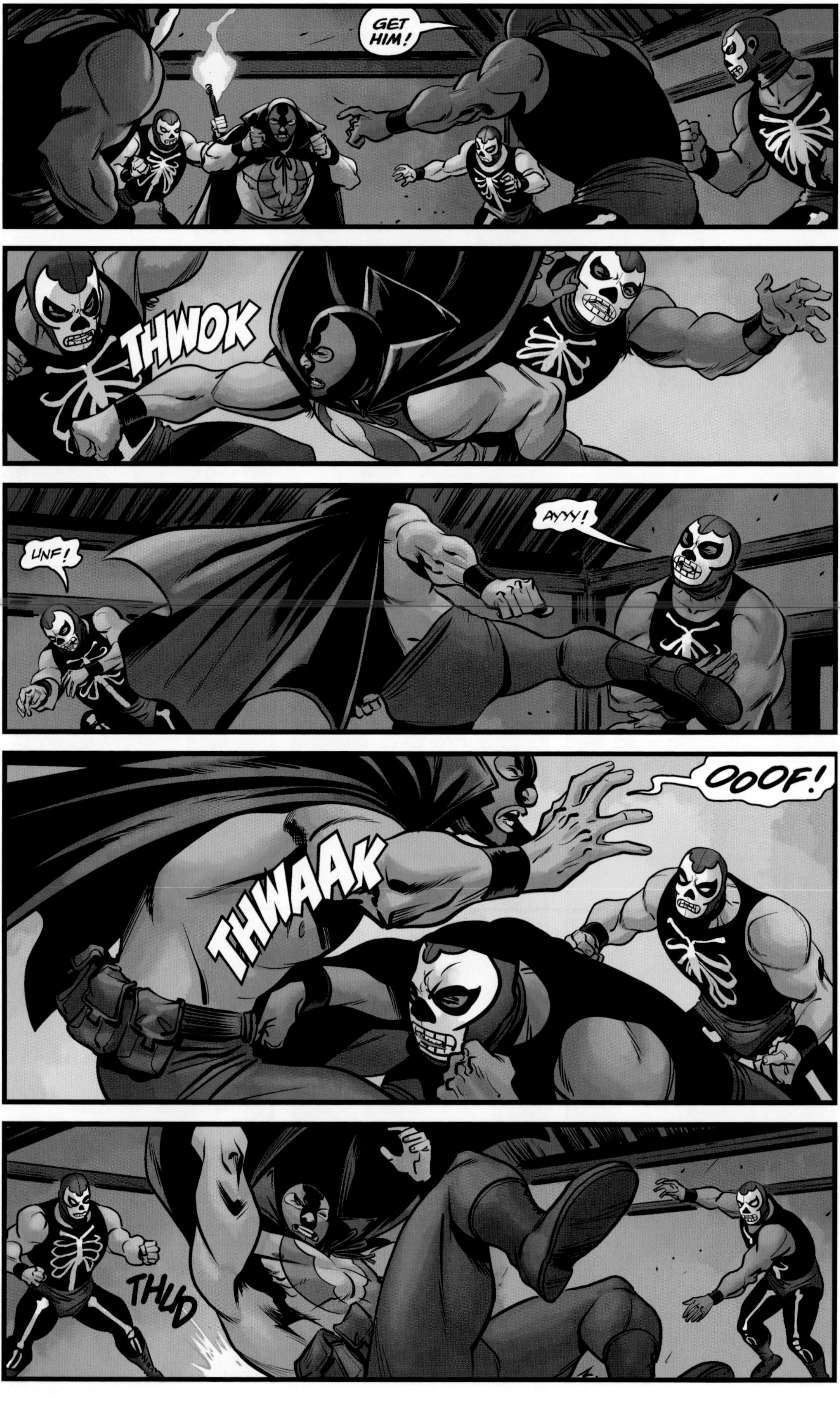

GET HIM!
THWOK
UNF!
AYYY!
OOOF!
THWAAK
THUD

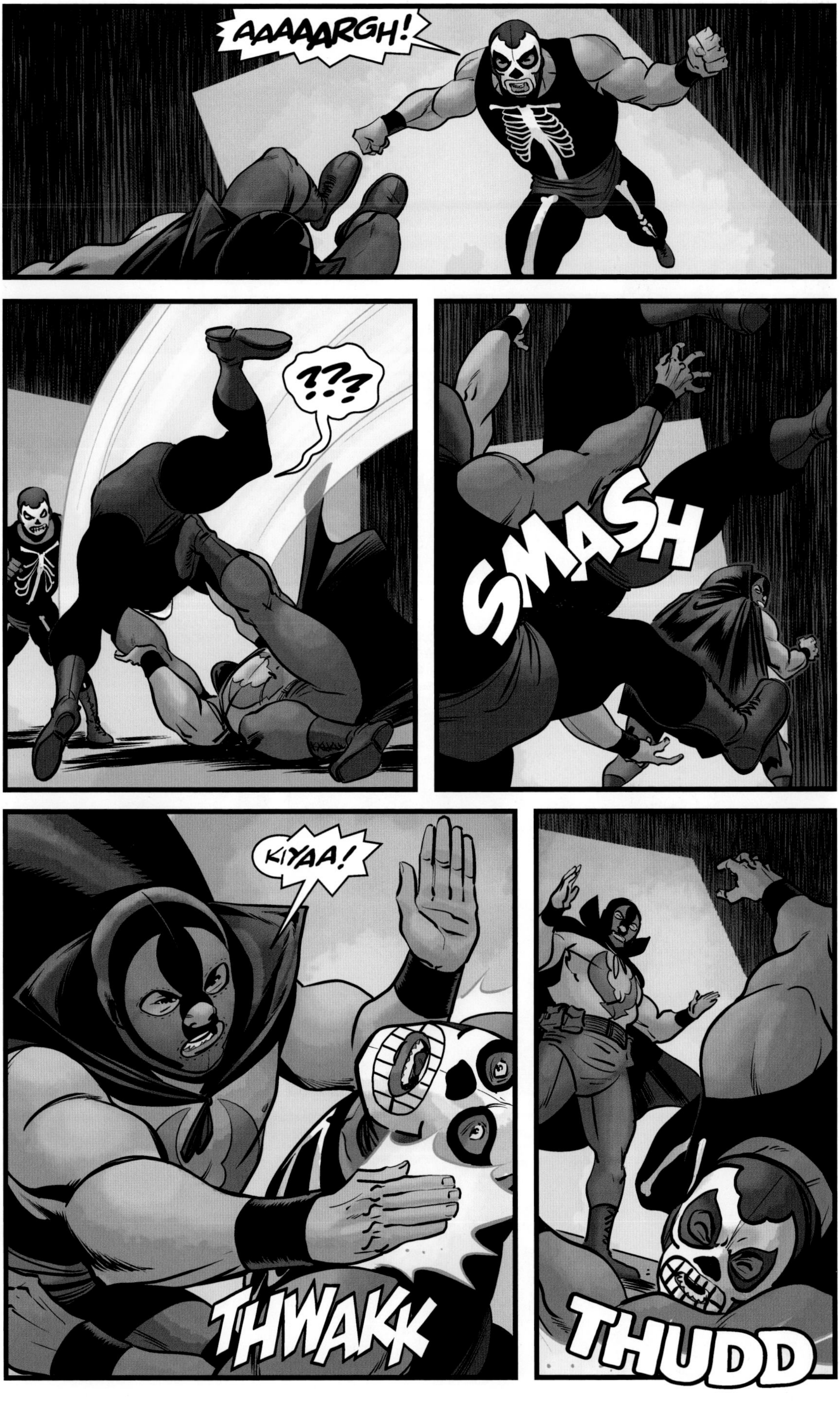
AAAAARGH!
???
SMASH
KIYAA!
THWAKK
THUDD

SO FALL ALL ENEMIES OF *JUSTICE.*

UHHHHHH

ARE YOU HURT, MAYOR?

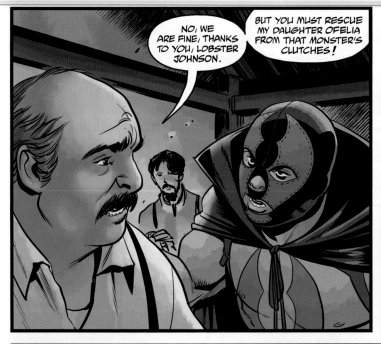

NO, WE ARE FINE, THANKS TO YOU, LOBSTER JOHNSON.

BUT YOU MUST RESCUE MY DAUGHTER OFELIA FROM THAT MONSTER'S CLUTCHES!

WHERE HAS HE TAKEN HER?

LEGENDS SPEAK OF A RUINED TEMPLE IN THE WOODS BEYOND THE VILLAGE, WHERE DARK RITES WERE PERFORMED IN ANCIENT TIMES...

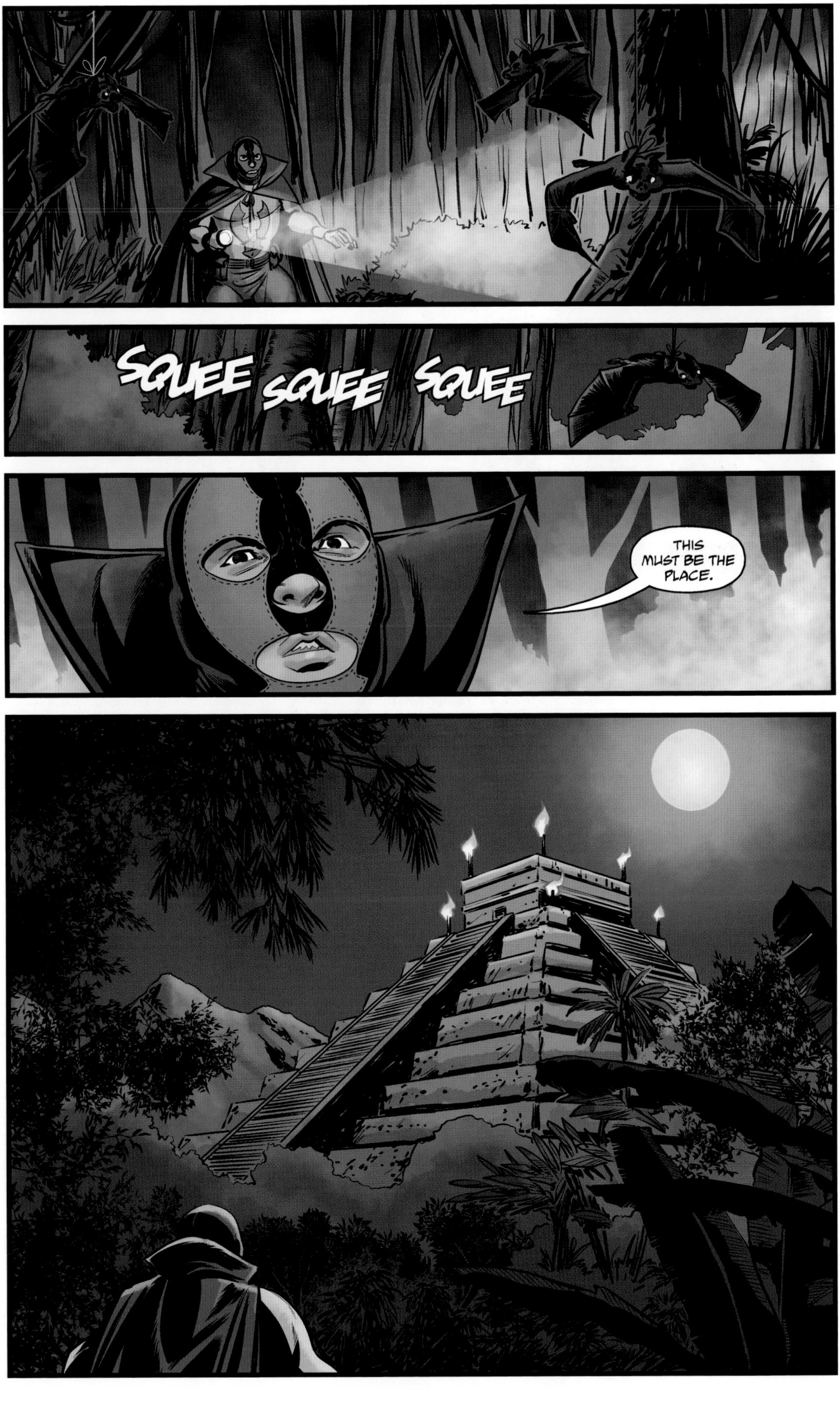
SQUEE SQUEE SQUEE
THIS MUST BE THE PLACE.

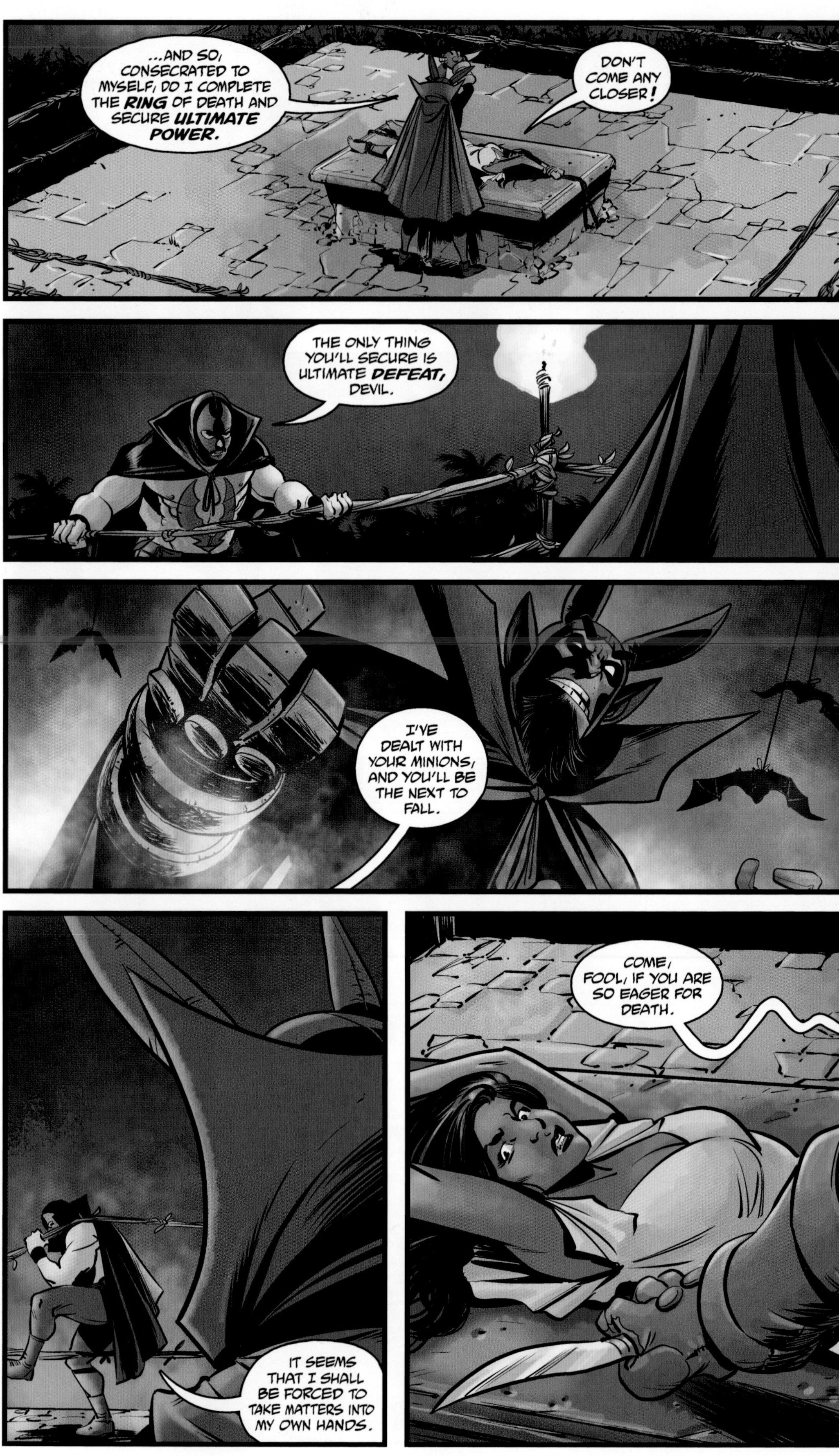
...AND SO, CONSECRATED TO MYSELF, DO I COMPLETE THE RING OF DEATH AND SECURE ULTIMATE POWER.
DON'T COME ANY CLOSER!
THE ONLY THING YOU'LL SECURE IS ULTIMATE DEFEAT, DEVIL.
I'VE DEALT WITH YOUR MINIONS, AND YOU'LL BE THE NEXT TO FALL.
IT SEEMS THAT I SHALL BE FORCED TO TAKE MATTERS INTO MY OWN HANDS.
COME, FOOL, IF YOU ARE SO EAGER FOR DEATH.

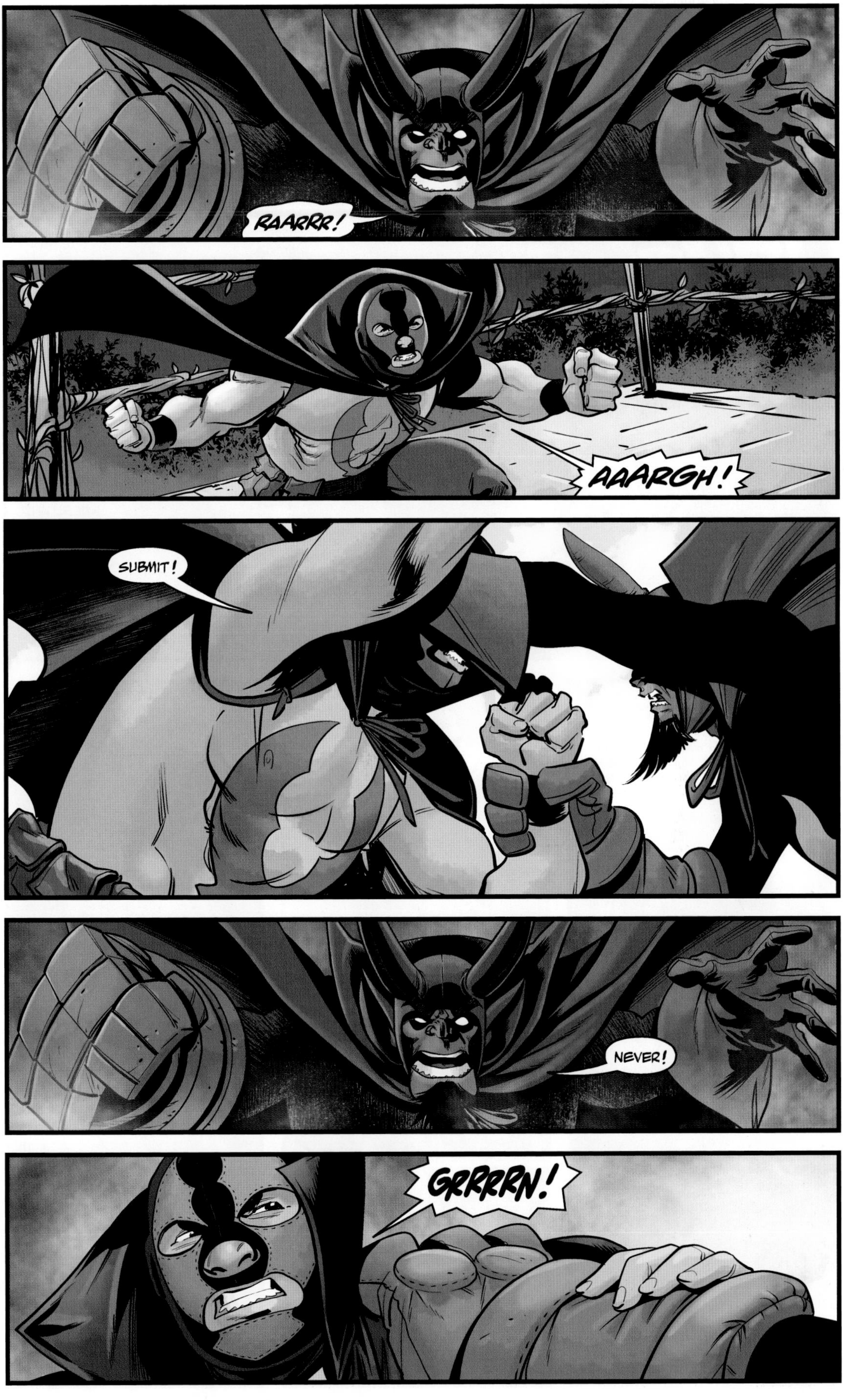
RAARRR!
AAARGH!
SUBMIT!
NEVER!
GRRRRN!

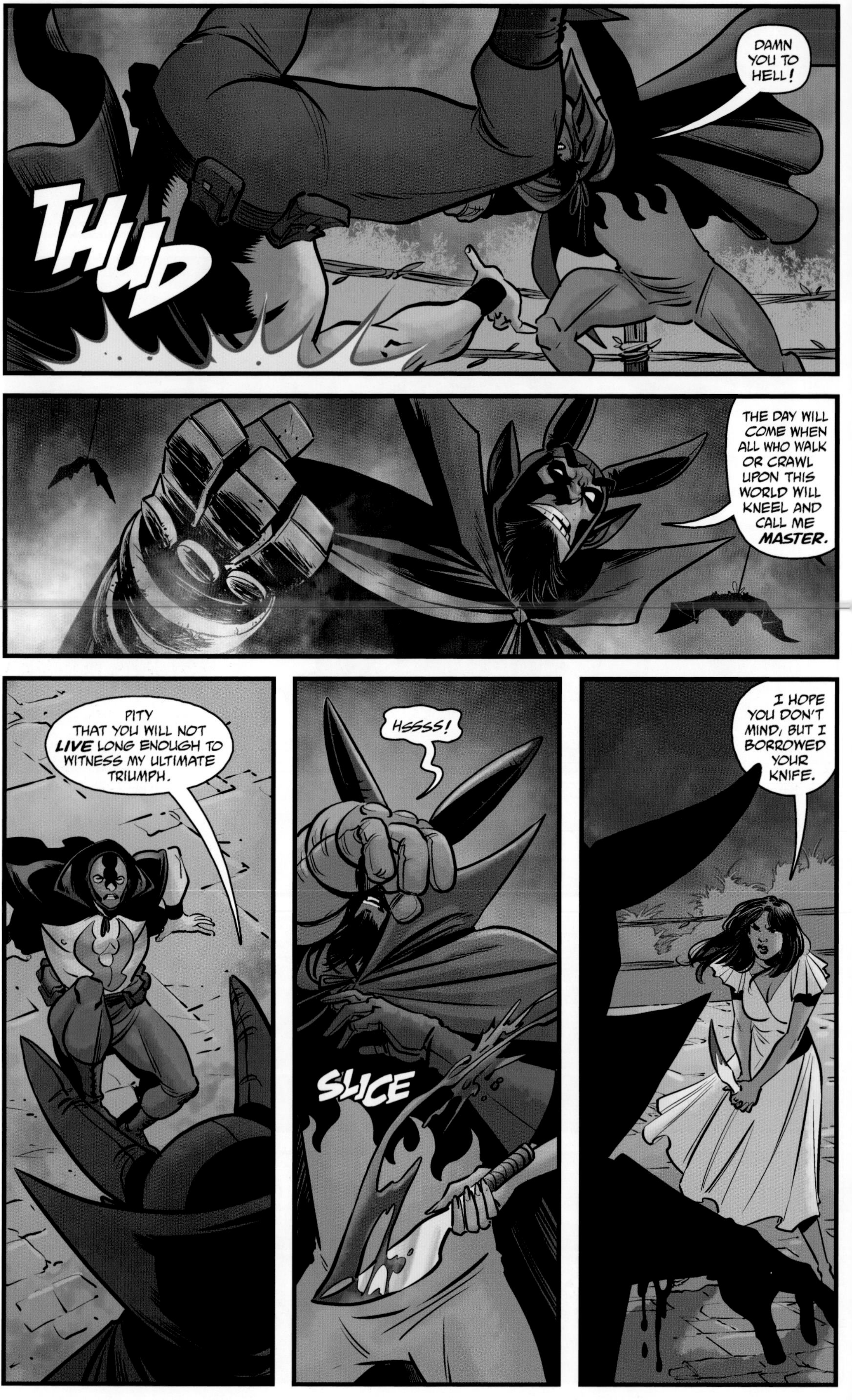
DAMN YOU TO HELL!
THUD
THE DAY WILL COME WHEN ALL WHO WALK OR CRAWL UPON THIS WORLD WILL KNEEL AND CALL ME **MASTER.**
PITY THAT YOU WILL NOT **LIVE** LONG ENOUGH TO WITNESS MY ULTIMATE TRIUMPH.
HSSSS!
SLICE
I HOPE YOU DON'T MIND, BUT I BORROWED YOUR KNIFE.

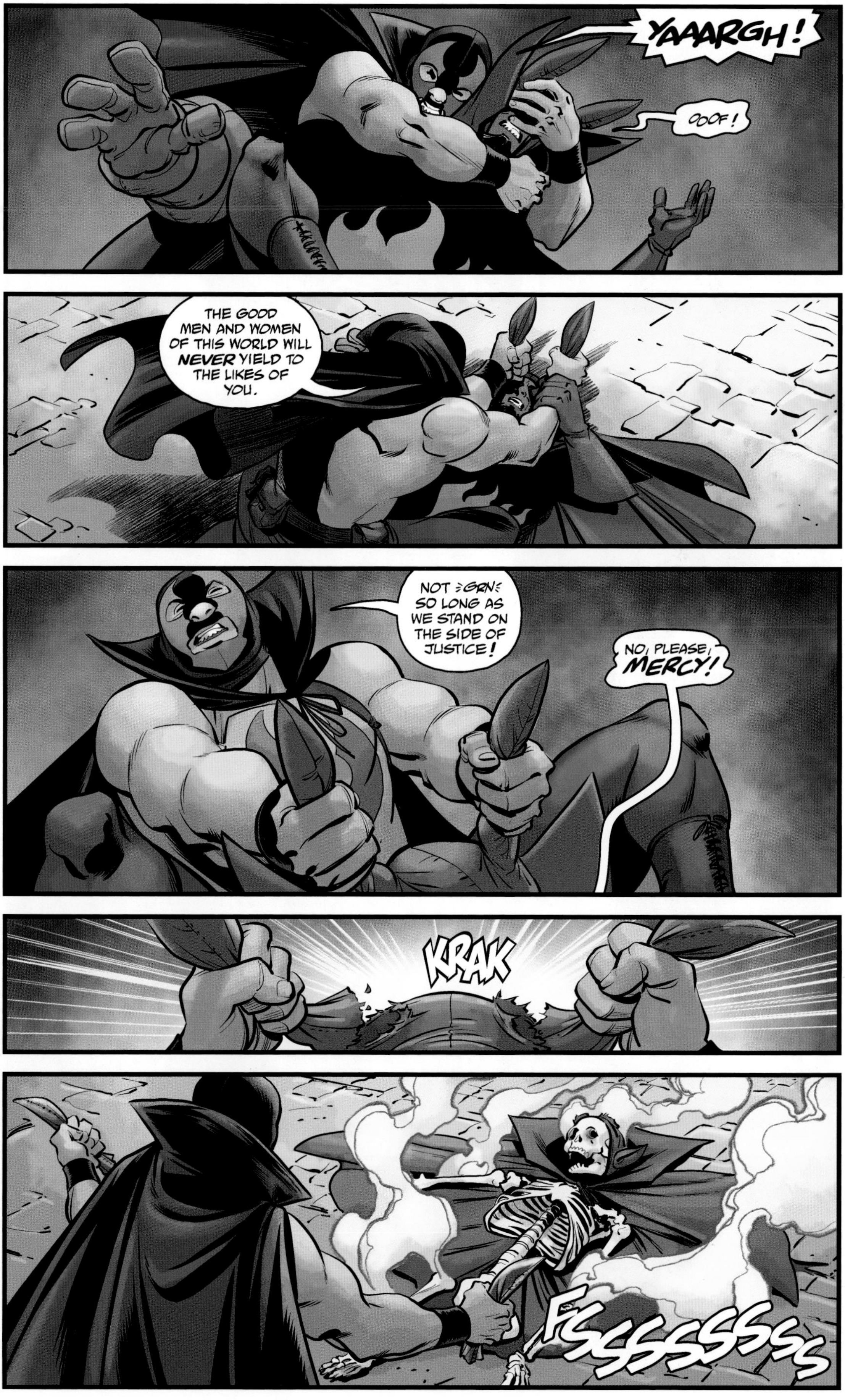
YAAARGH!
OOOF!
THE GOOD MEN AND WOMEN OF THIS WORLD WILL NEVER YIELD TO THE LIKES OF YOU.
NOT GRN SO LONG AS WE STAND ON THE SIDE OF JUSTICE!
NO, PLEASE, MERCY!
KRAK
FSSSSSSSSS

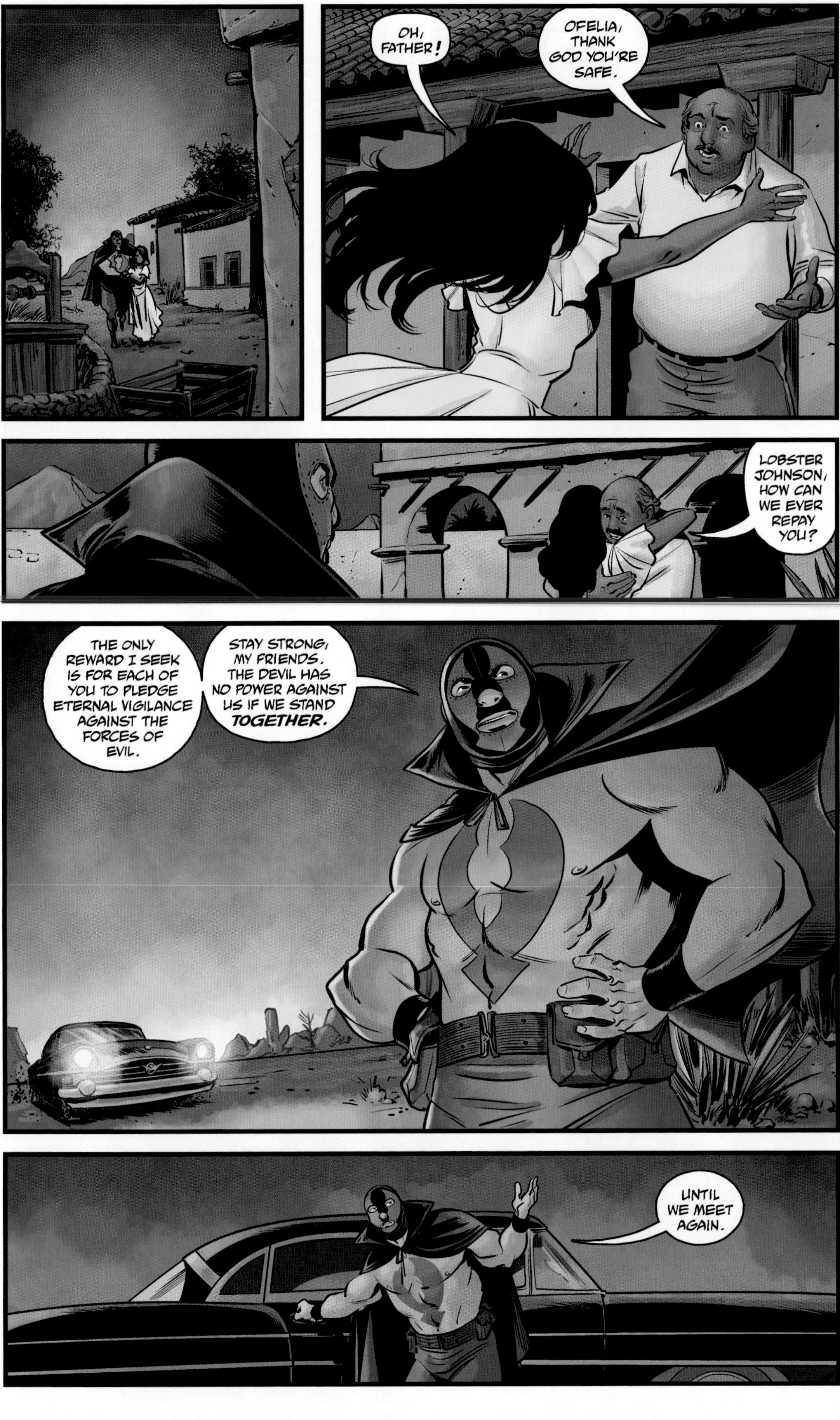
OH, FATHER!
OFELIA, THANK GOD YOU'RE SAFE.
LOBSTER JOHNSON, HOW CAN WE EVER REPAY YOU?
THE ONLY REWARD I SEEK IS FOR EACH OF YOU TO PLEDGE ETERNAL VIGILANCE AGAINST THE FORCES OF EVIL.
STAY STRONG, MY FRIENDS. THE DEVIL HAS NO POWER AGAINST US IF WE STAND *TOGETHER.*
UNTIL WE MEET AGAIN.

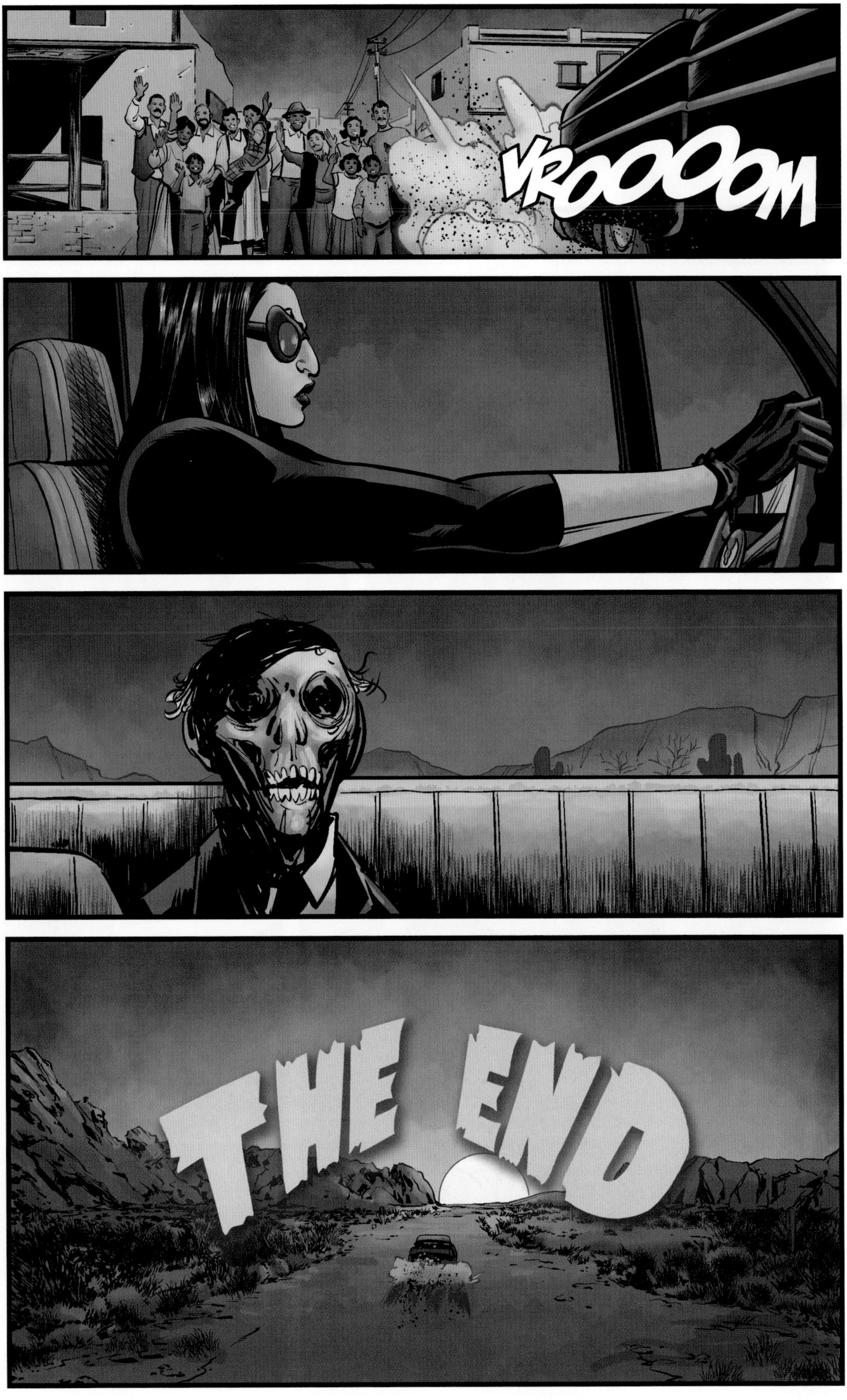
VROOOOOM
THE END

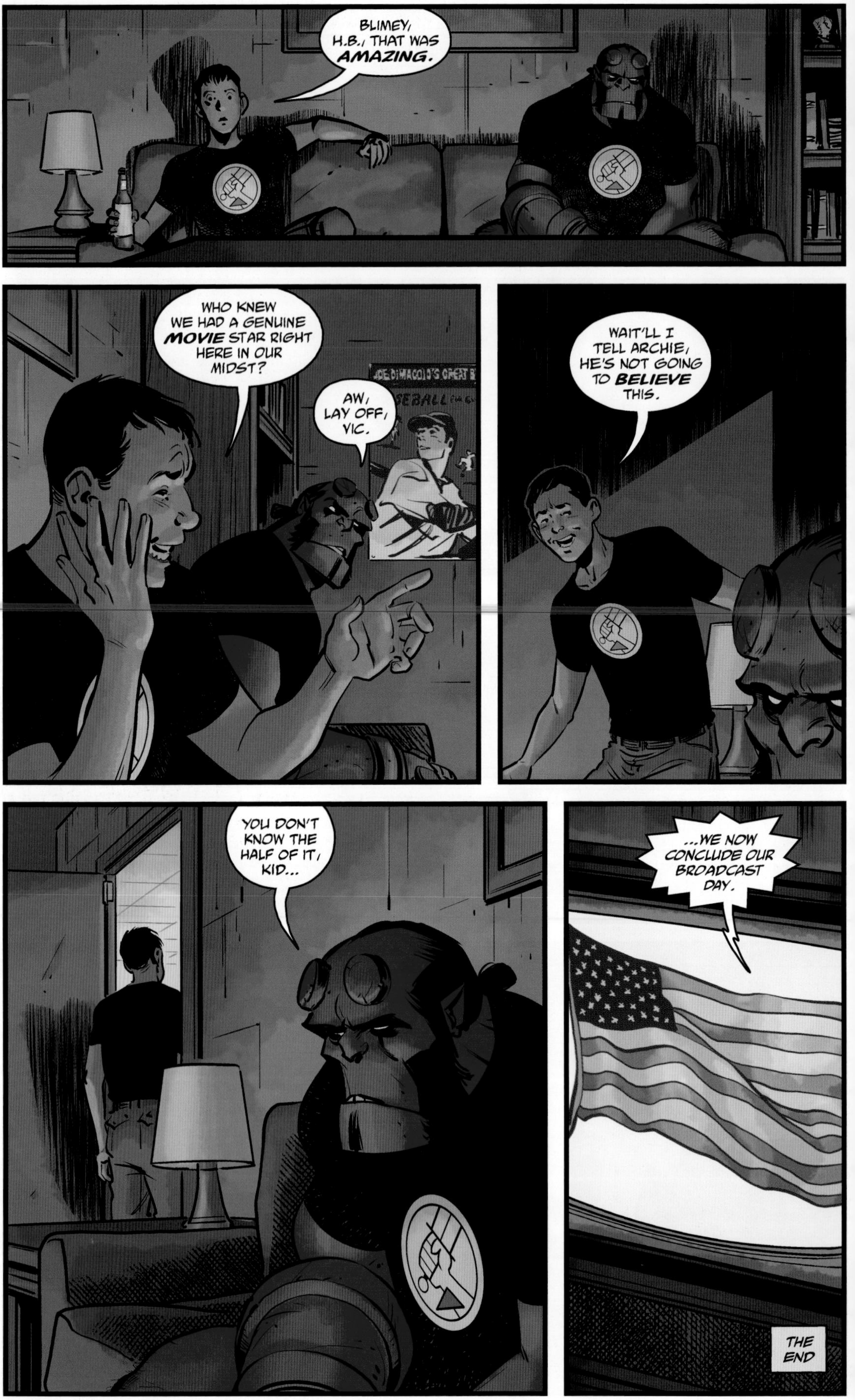

BLIMEY, H.B., THAT WAS AMAZING.
WHO KNEW WE HAD A GENUINE MOVIE STAR RIGHT HERE IN OUR MIDST?
AW, LAY OFF, VIC.
WAIT'LL I TELL ARCHIE, HE'S NOT GOING TO BELIEVE THIS.
YOU DON'T KNOW THE HALF OF IT, KID...
...WE NOW CONCLUDE OUR BROADCAST DAY.
THE END

Down Mexico Way

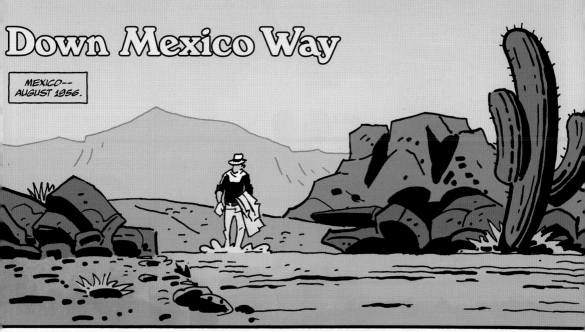

MEXICO--
AUGUST 1956.

The subject has been absent from his duties for some time now.

I have traveled to his last known position in search of him.

He was not difficult to locate.

AAAAND, ACTION.

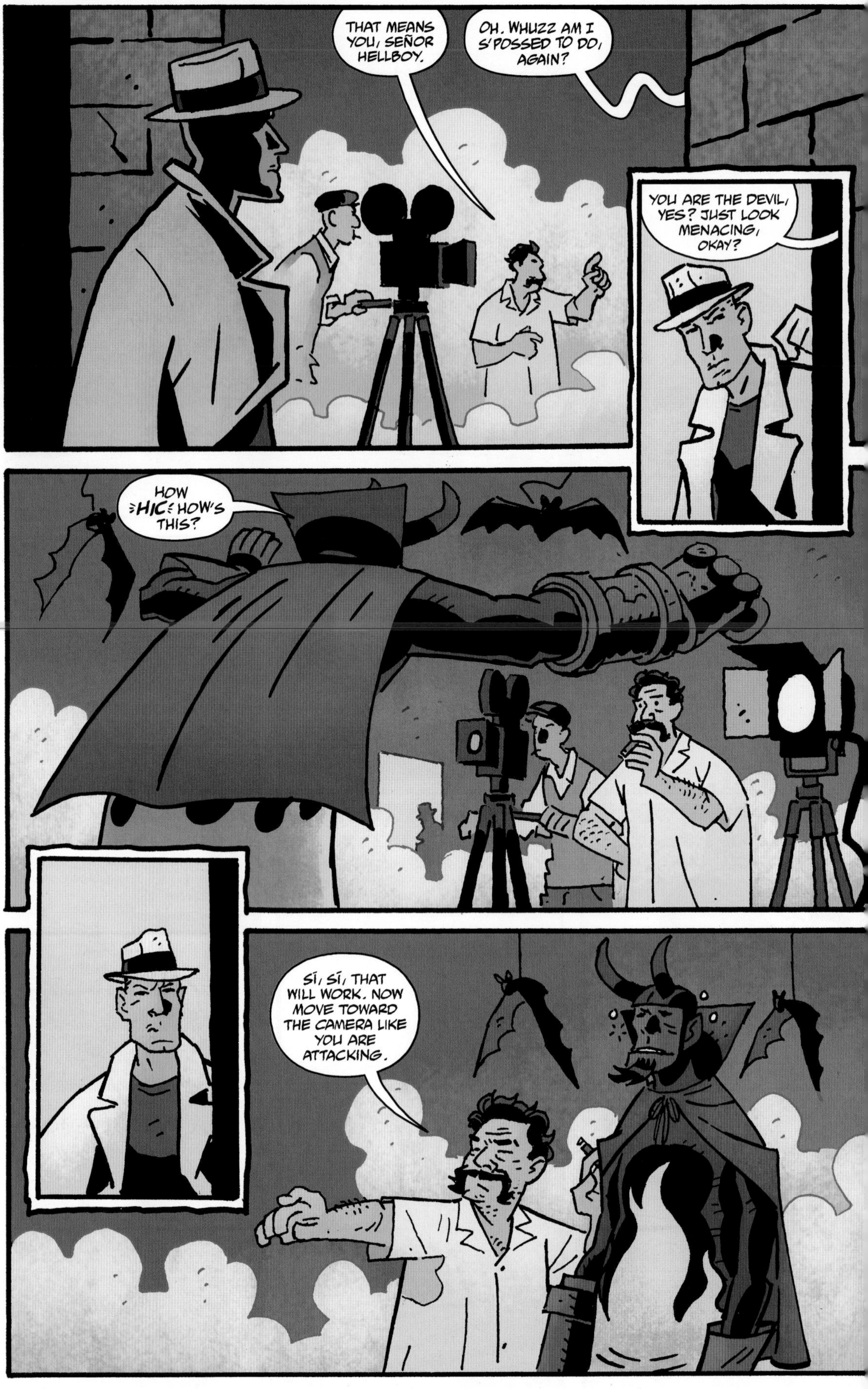
THAT MEANS YOU, SEÑOR HELLBOY.
OH. WHUZZ AM I S'POSSED TO DO, AGAIN?
YOU ARE THE DEVIL, YES? JUST LOOK MENACING, OKAY?
HOW *HIC* HOW'S THIS?
SÍ, SÍ, THAT WILL WORK. NOW MOVE TOWARD THE CAMERA LIKE YOU ARE ATTACKING.

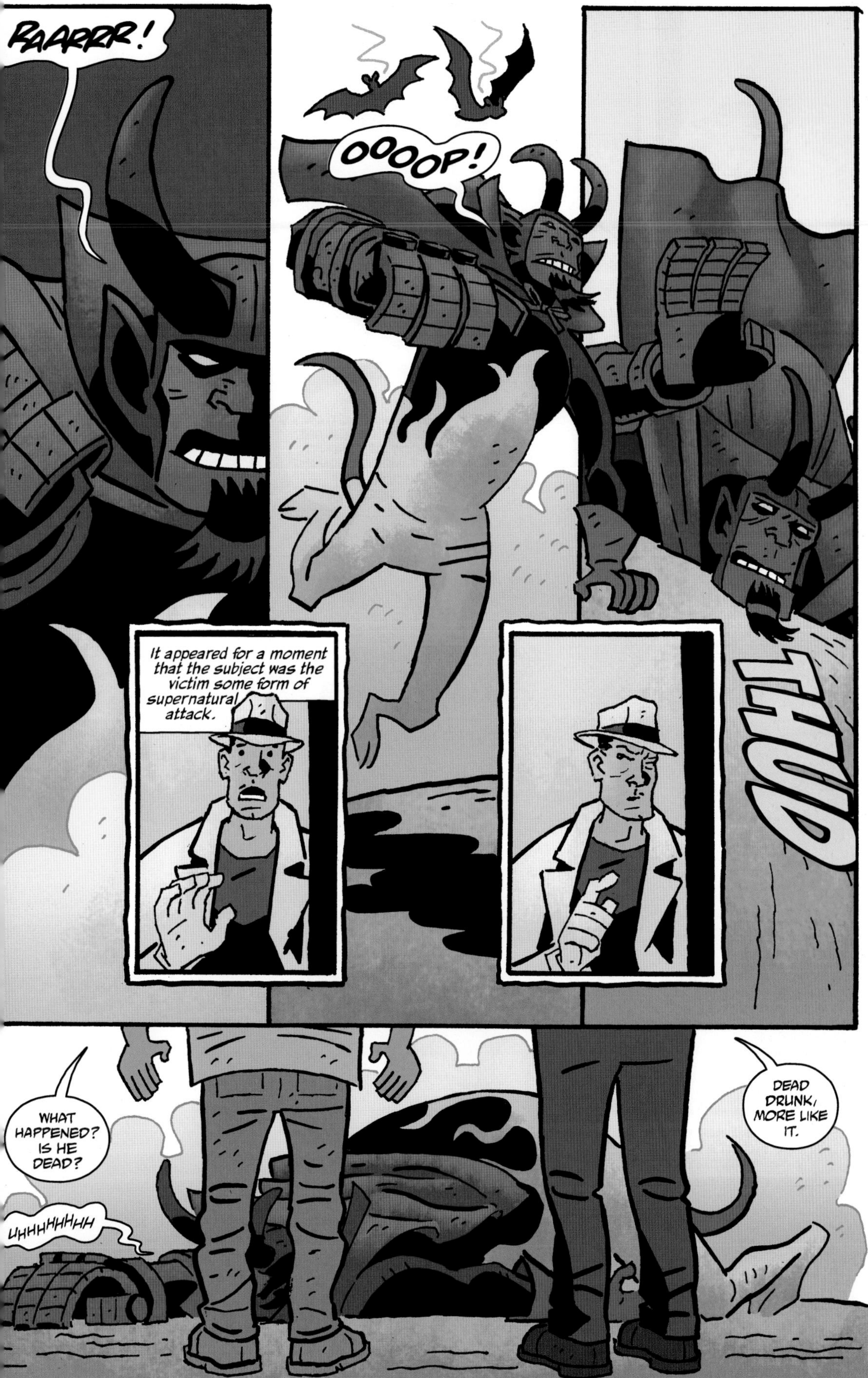
RAARRR!
OOOOP!
It appeared for a moment that the subject was the victim some form of supernatural attack.
THUD
WHAT HAPPENED? IS HE DEAD?
UHHHHHHHH
DEAD DRUNK, MORE LIKE IT.

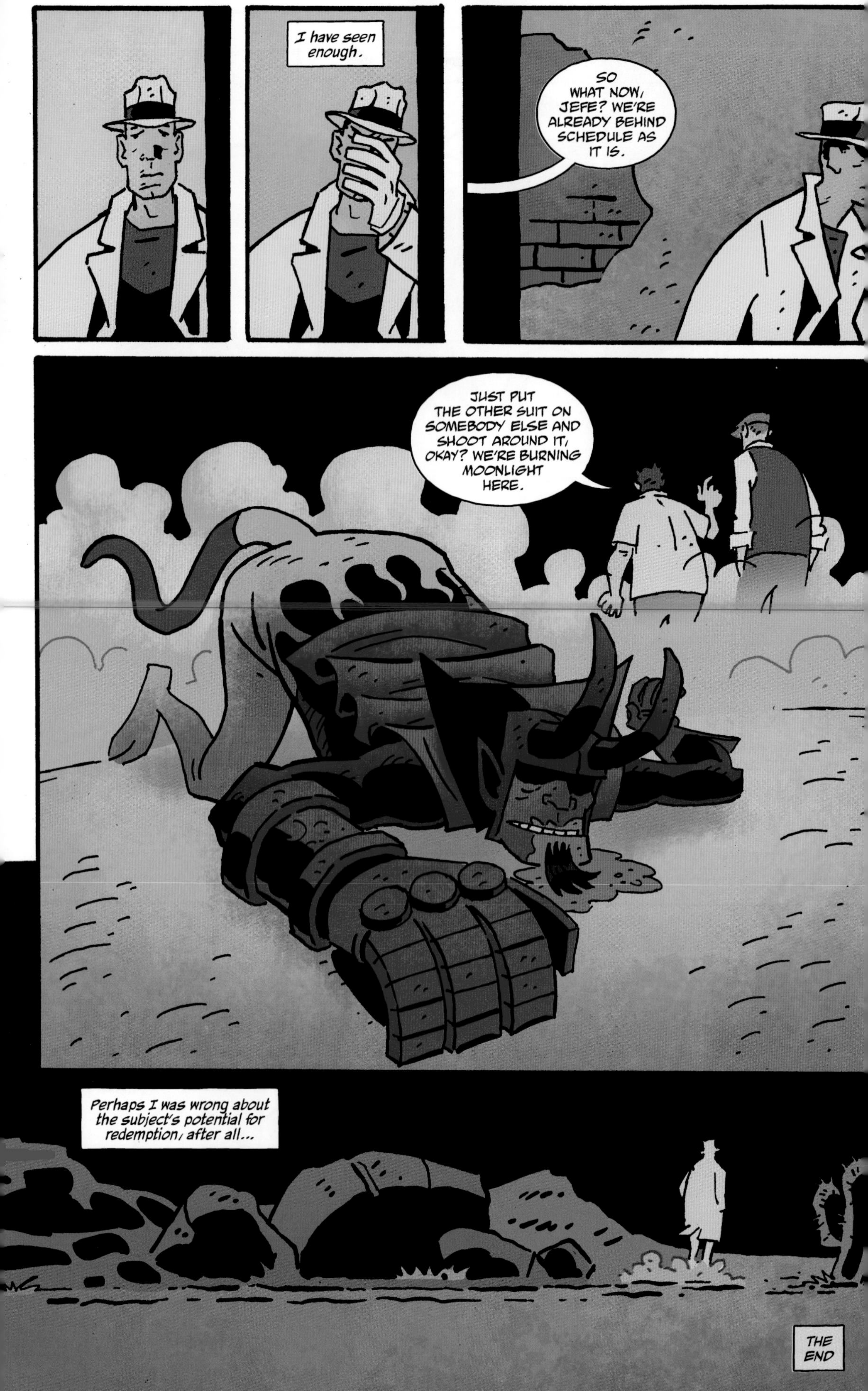
I have seen enough.
SO WHAT NOW, JEFE? WE'RE ALREADY BEHIND SCHEDULE AS IT IS.
JUST PUT THE OTHER SUIT ON SOMEBODY ELSE AND SHOOT AROUND IT, OKAY? WE'RE BURNING MOONLIGHT HERE.
Perhaps I was wrong about the subject's potential for redemption, after all...
THE END

HELLBOY ™

AND THE B.P.R.D. 1956

SKETCHBOOK

Notes by editor Katii O'Brien.

Mike Norton, who has drawn a few
B.P.R.D. issues in the past, got to design
Hellboy's costume for his brief turn as
the devil in a Mexican luchador movie.
This is a story we've been talking about
telling for a long time.

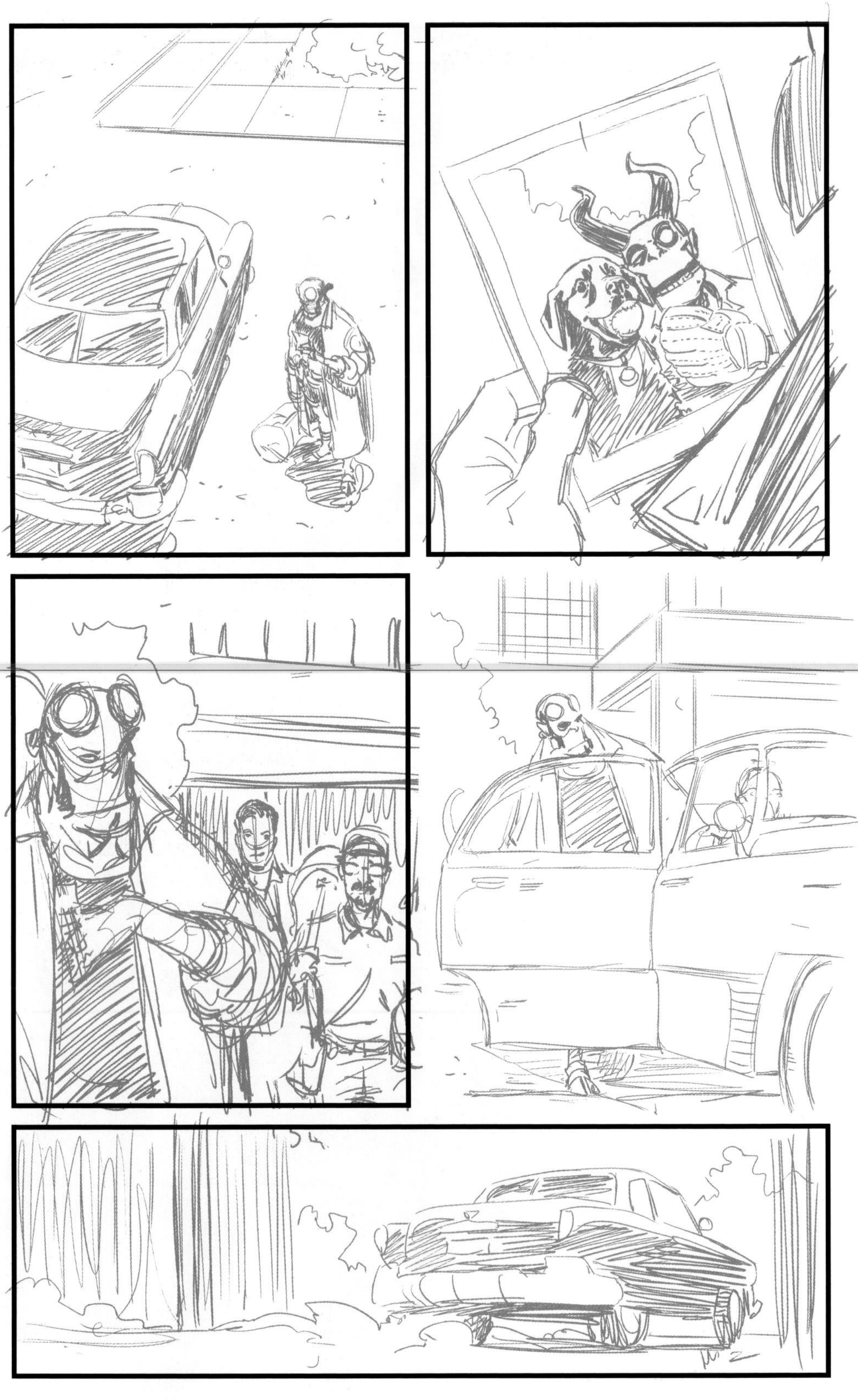

These pages and the next two feature some of Mike's rough layouts and inks from the first issue (*this spread*) and last issue *(following spread)* of the series.

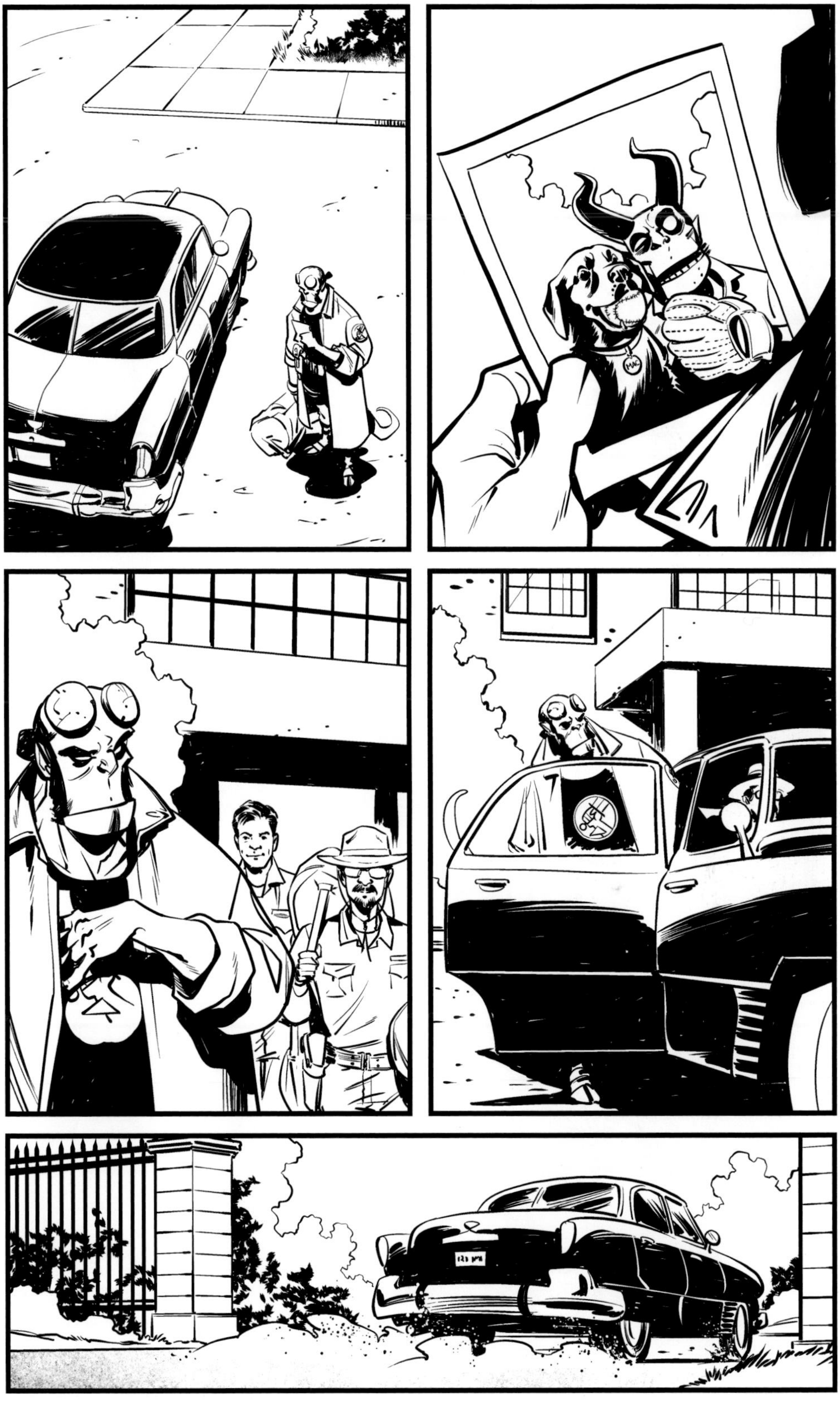

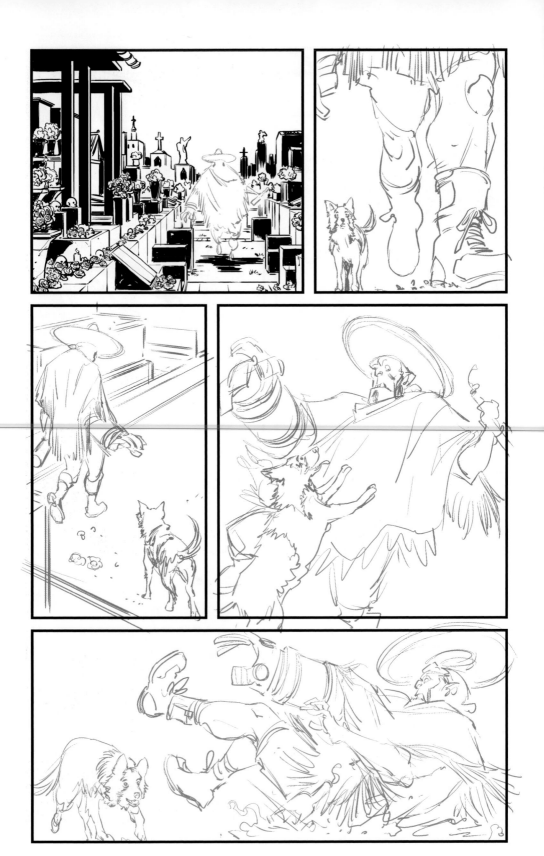

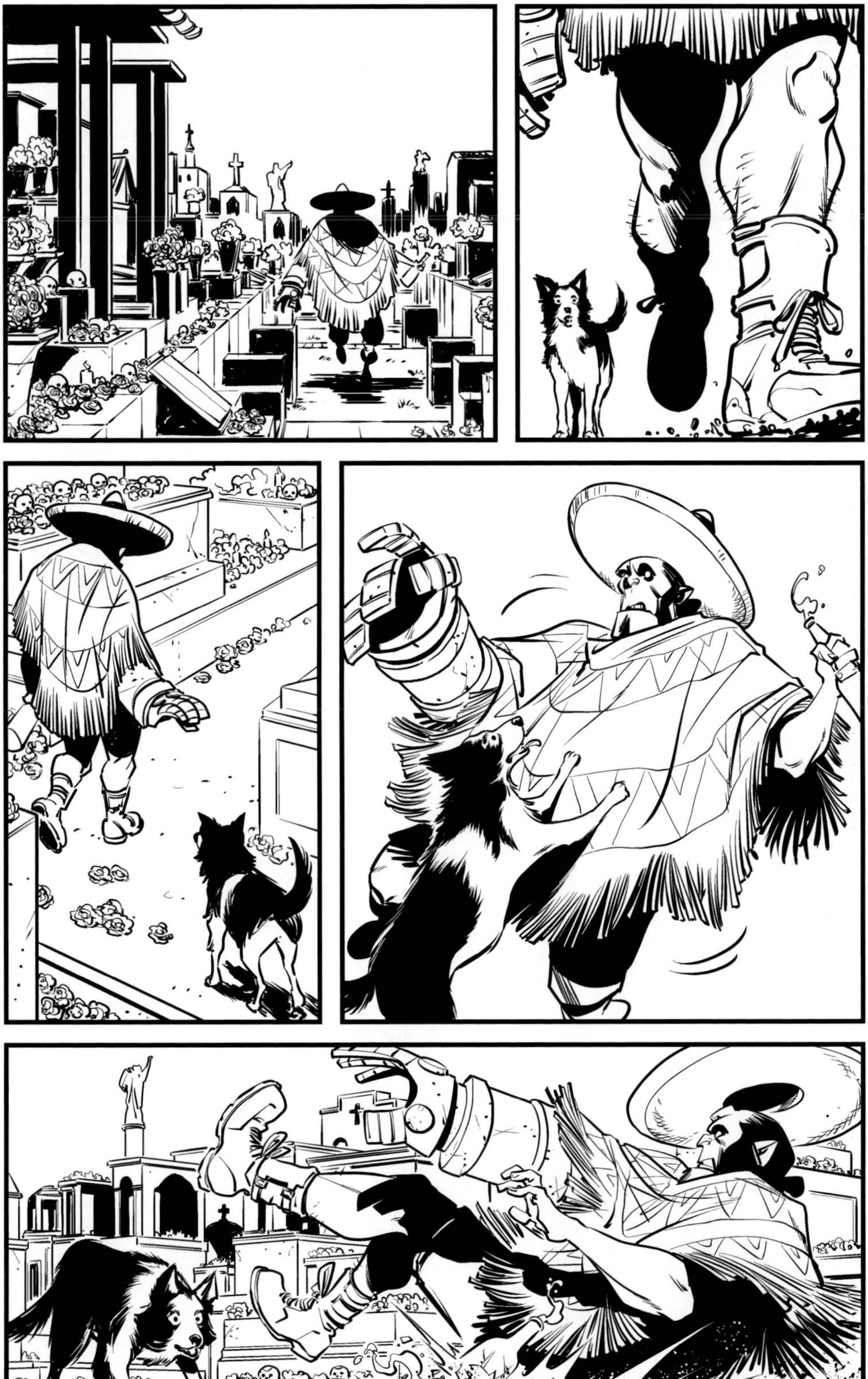

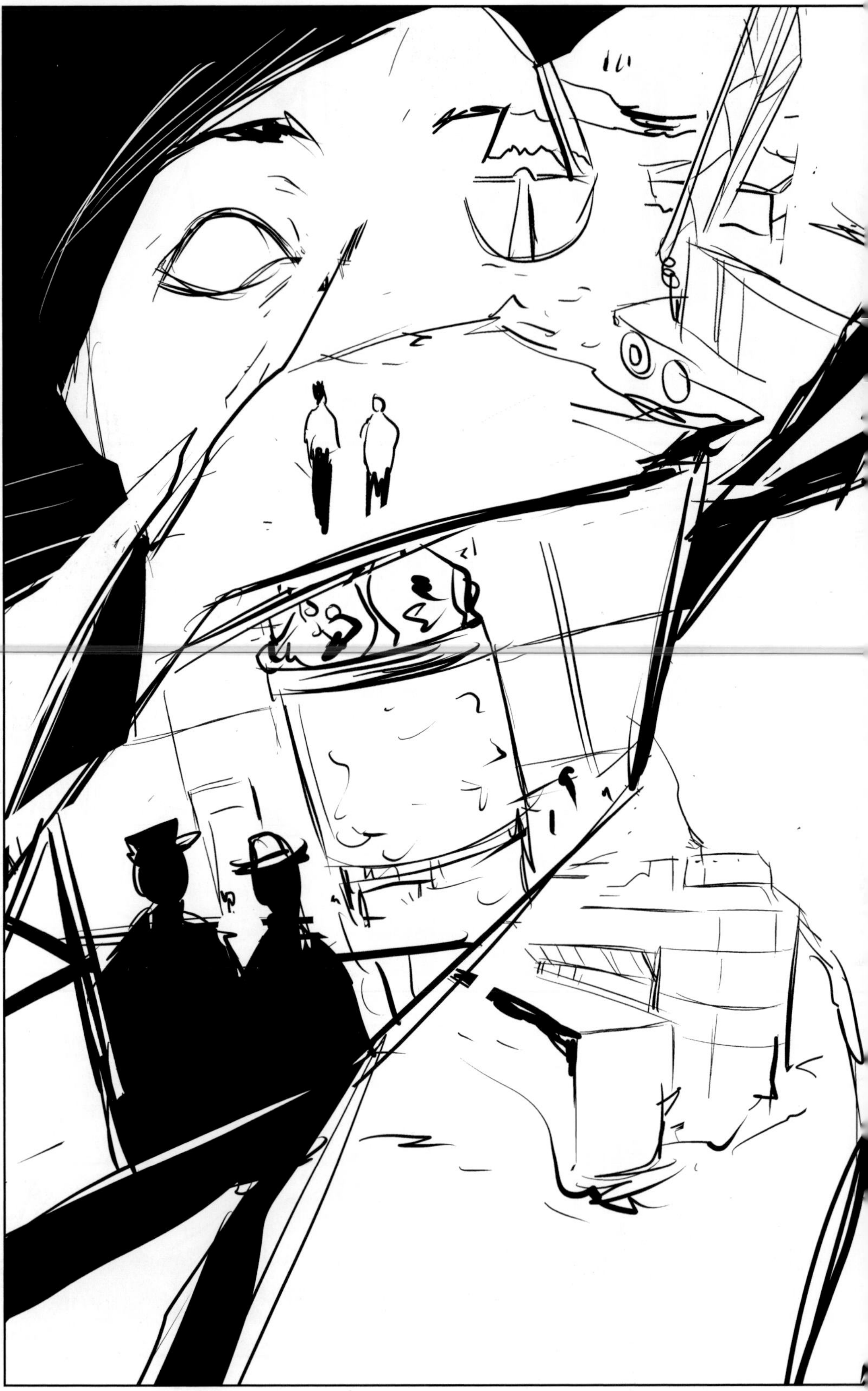

Yishan Li, newcomer to the Hellboy universe, drew Susan Xiang's story. Here is one of Sue's visions from issue #2, roughs on this spread and inks on the following one.

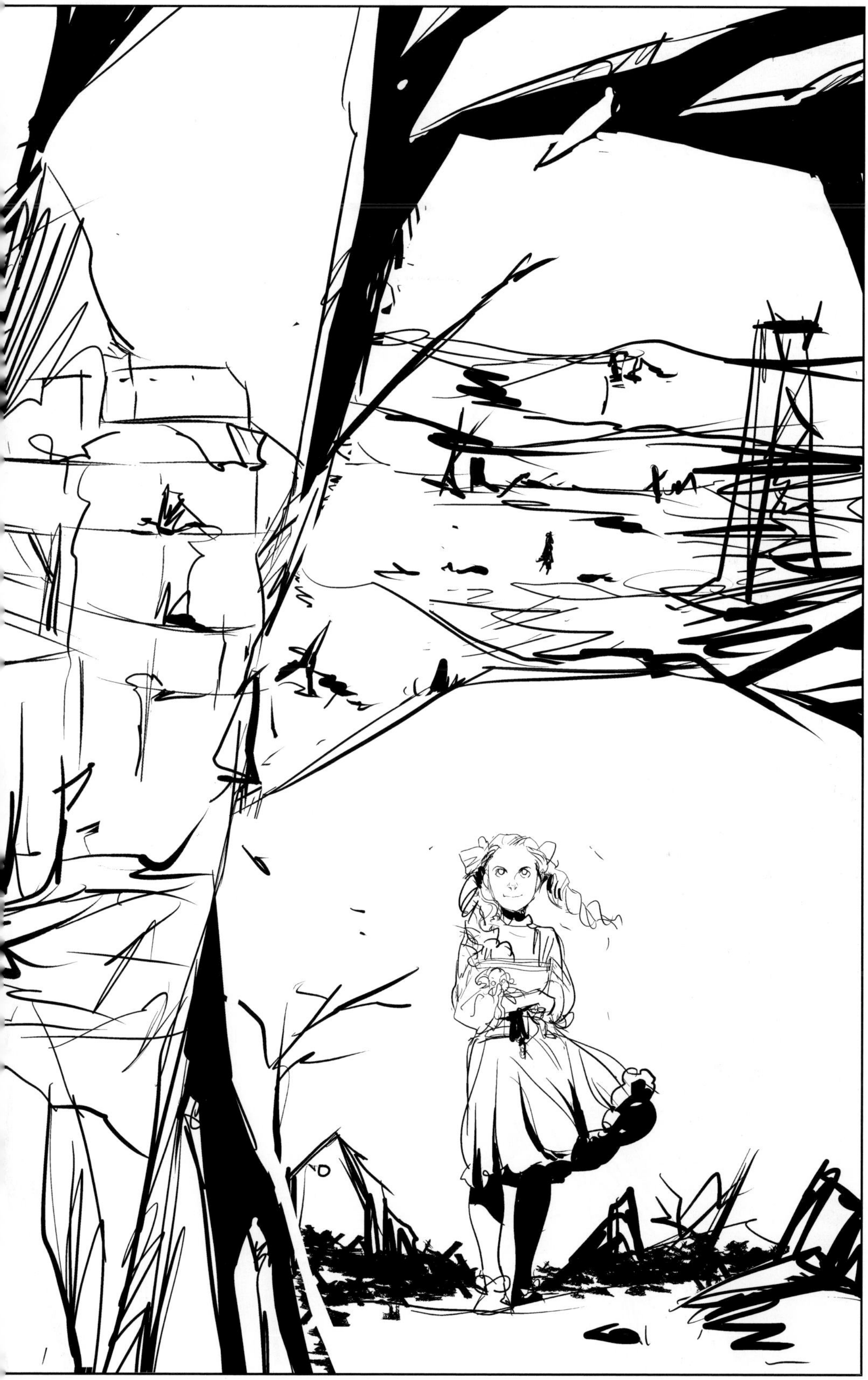

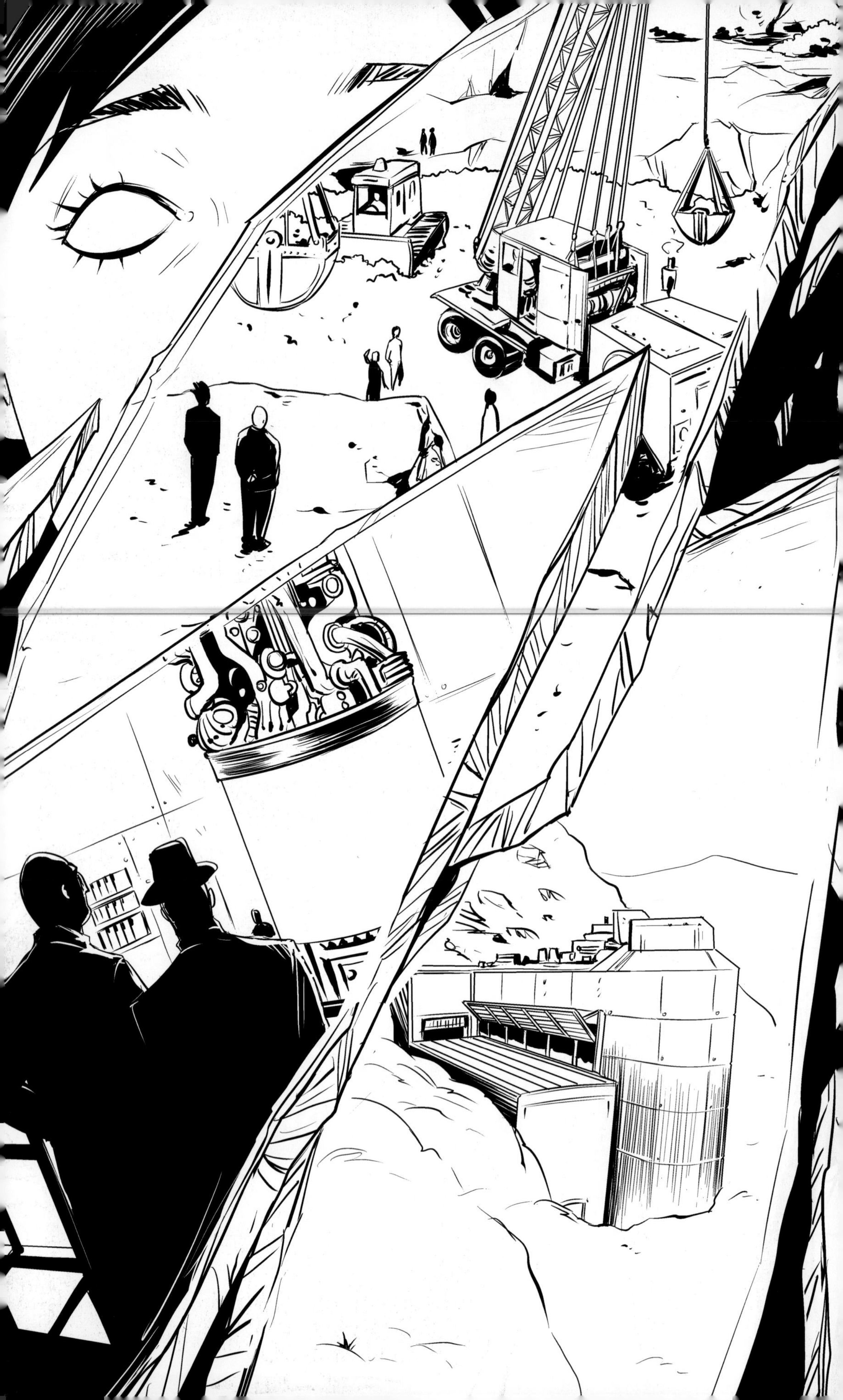

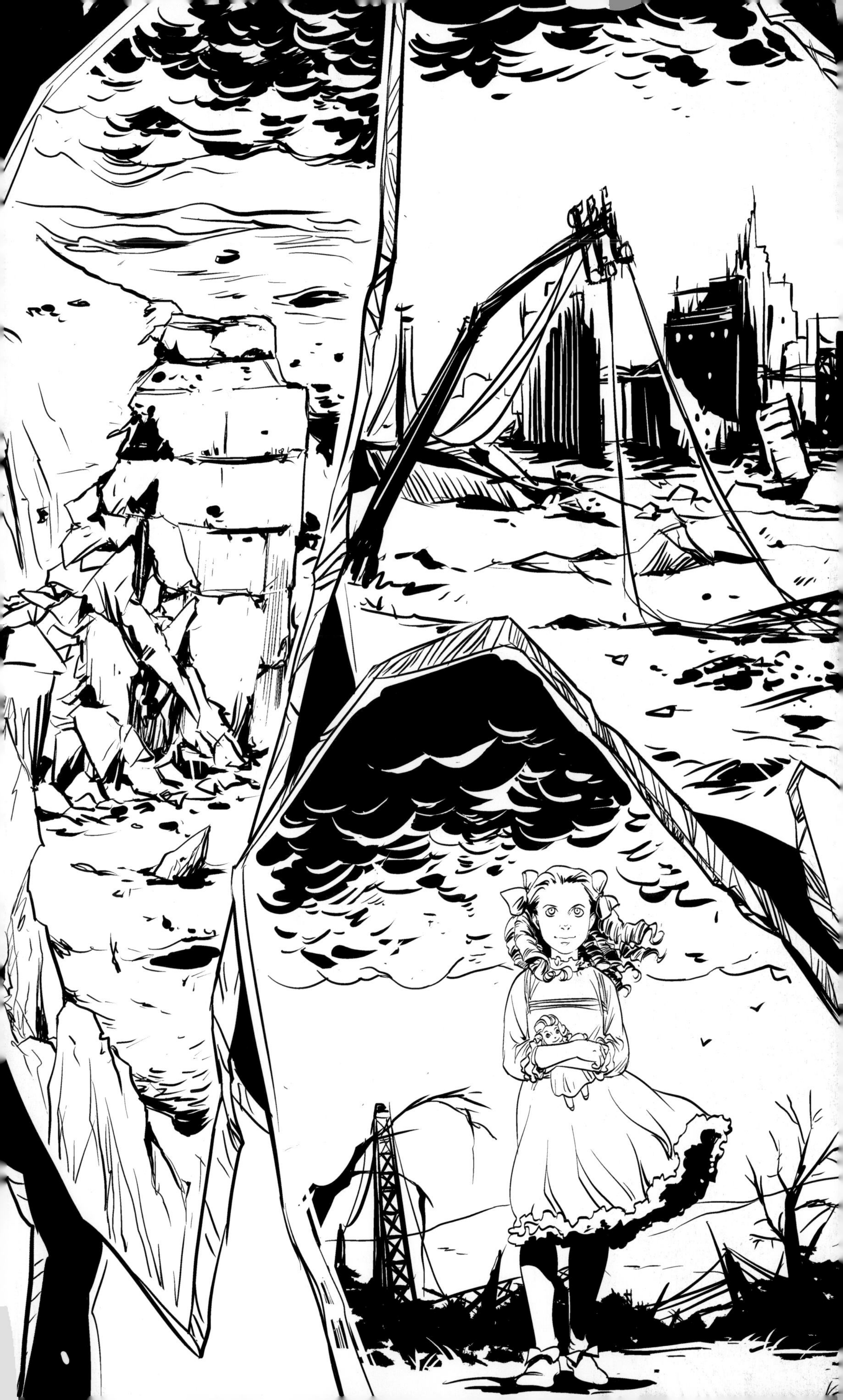

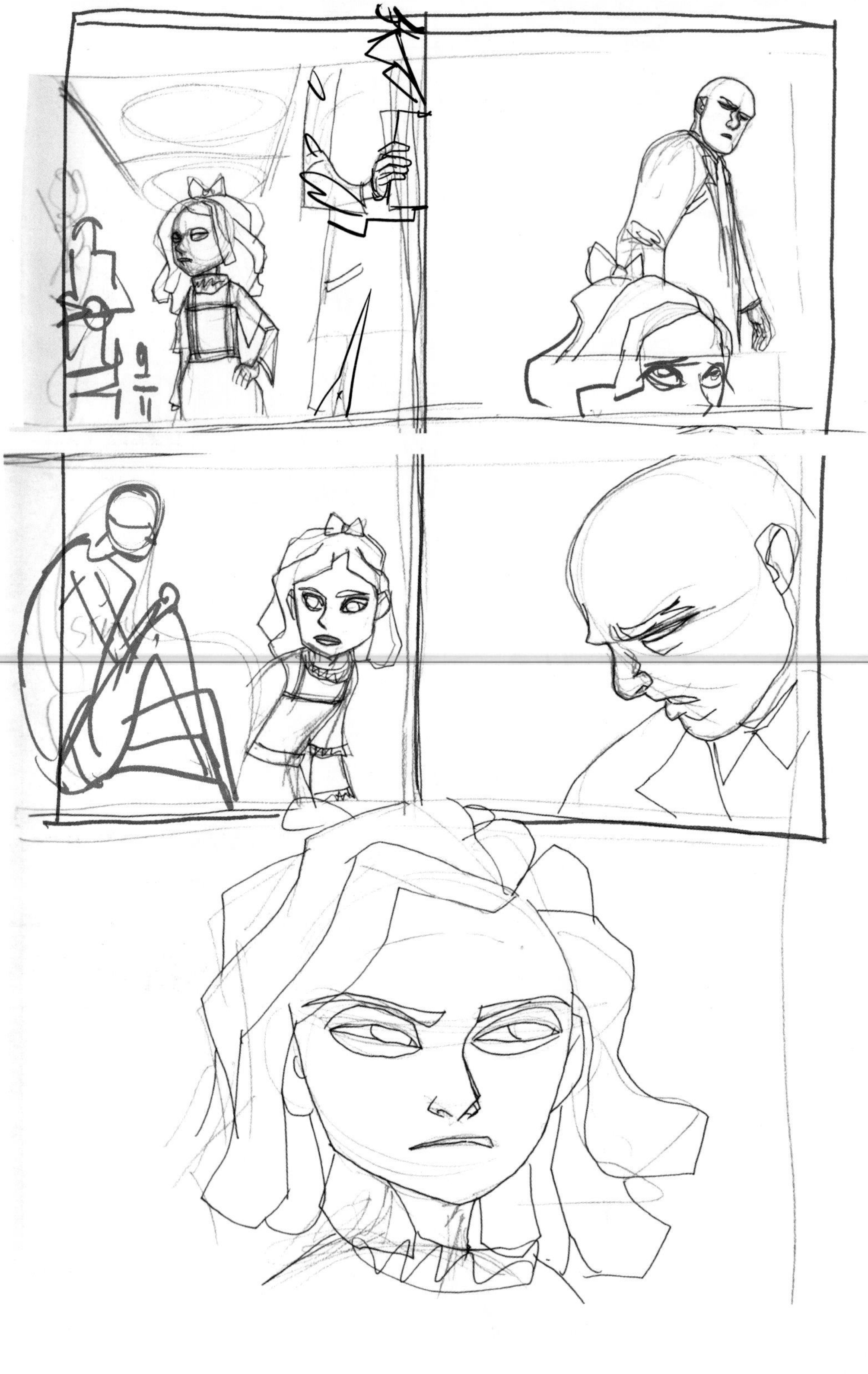

The Soviet story, centered on longtime villain Varvara, was drawn by *B.P.R.D.* and *Abe Sapien* artist Michael Avon Oeming. This spread is his layouts for the last two pages of the first issue, and the following spread is the final inks.

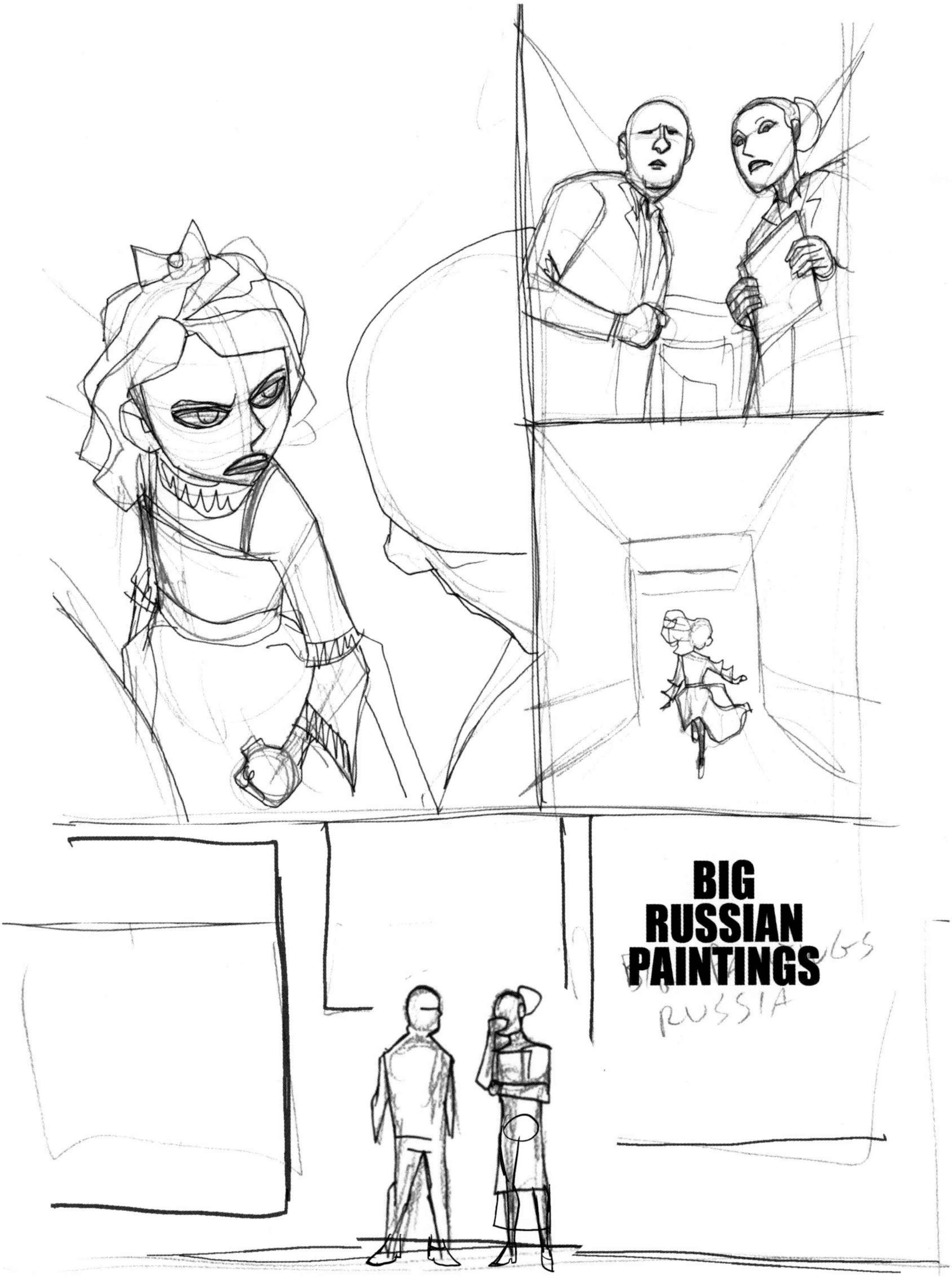
BIG
RUSSIAN
PAINTINGS
RUSSIA

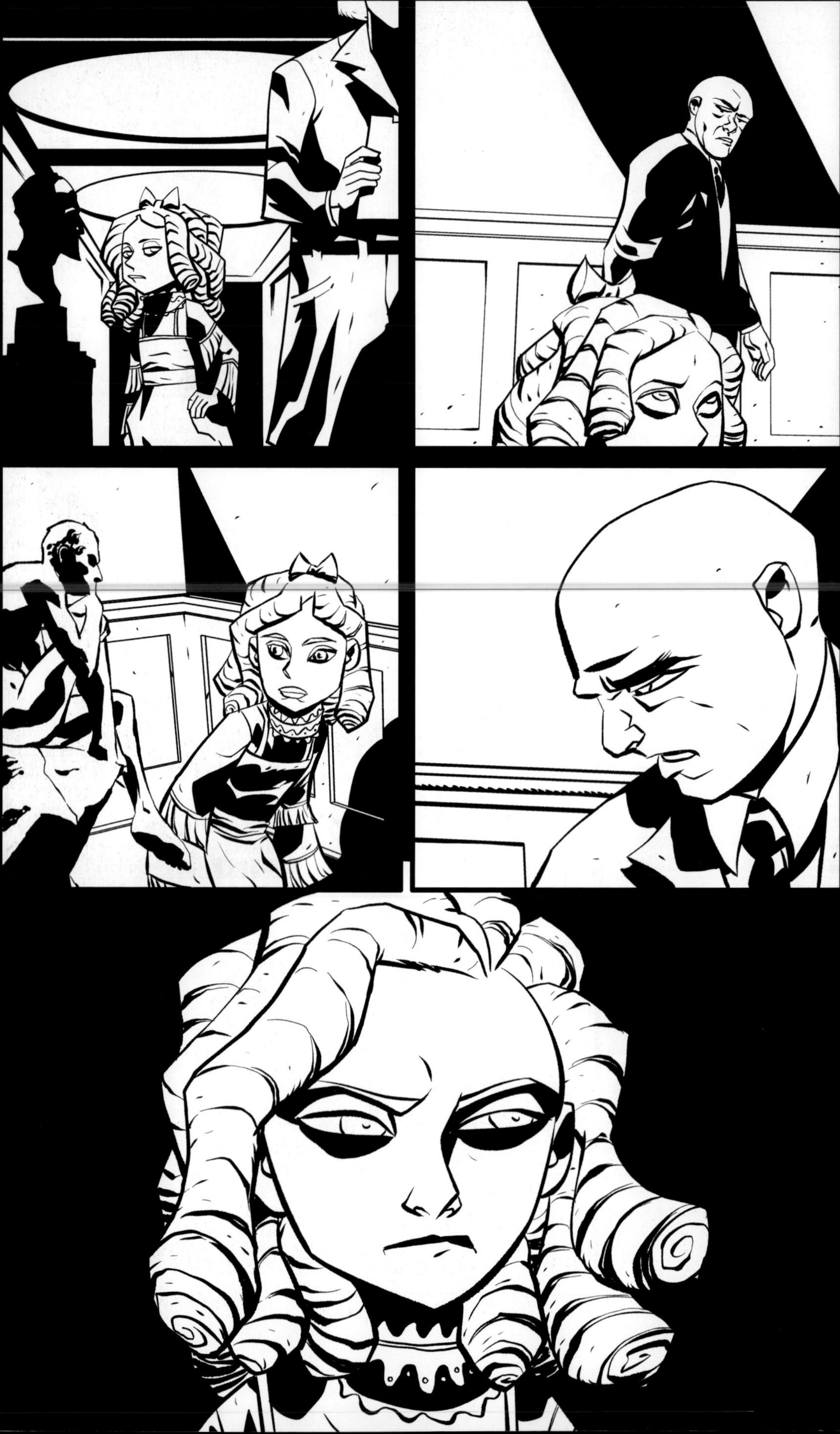

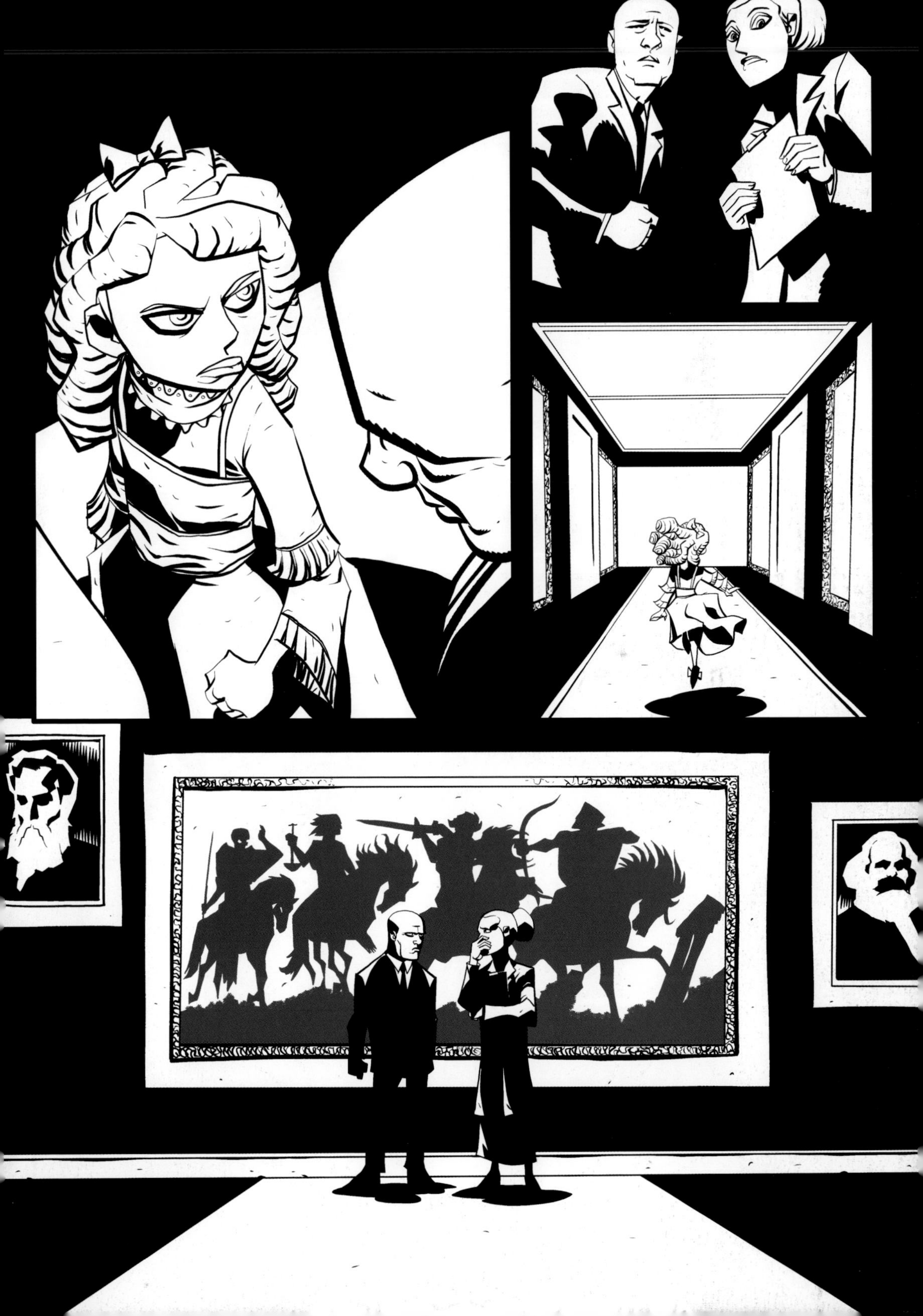

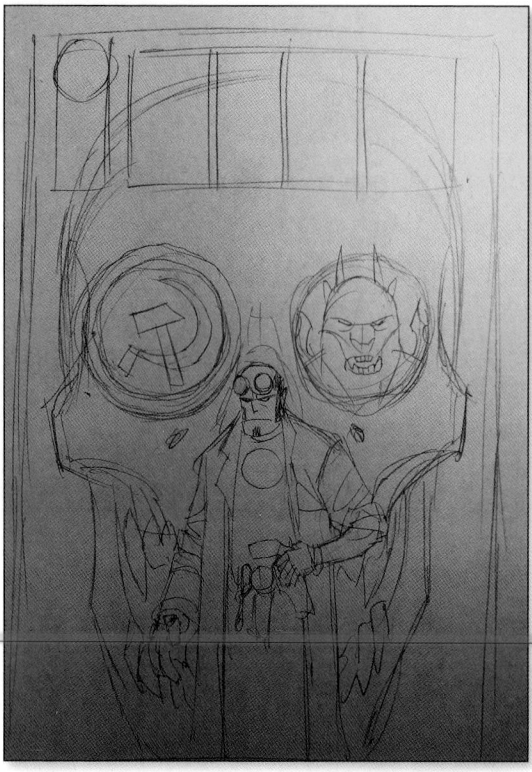

Dave Johnson did the covers for the main series. On this page are sketches for the covers for issue #1 (*left*) and issue #2 (*below*), and on the opposite page are sketches for issues #3–#5 (*top to bottom*).

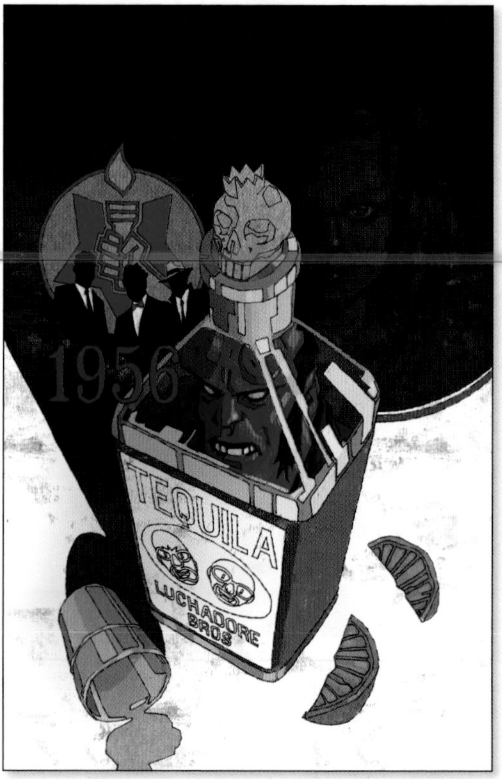
1956
TEQUILA
LUCHADORE
BROS

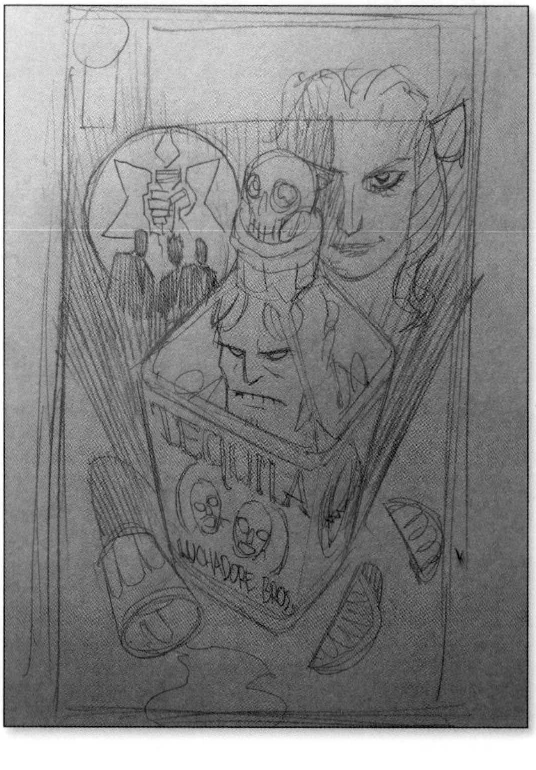
TEQUILA
LUCHADORE BROS

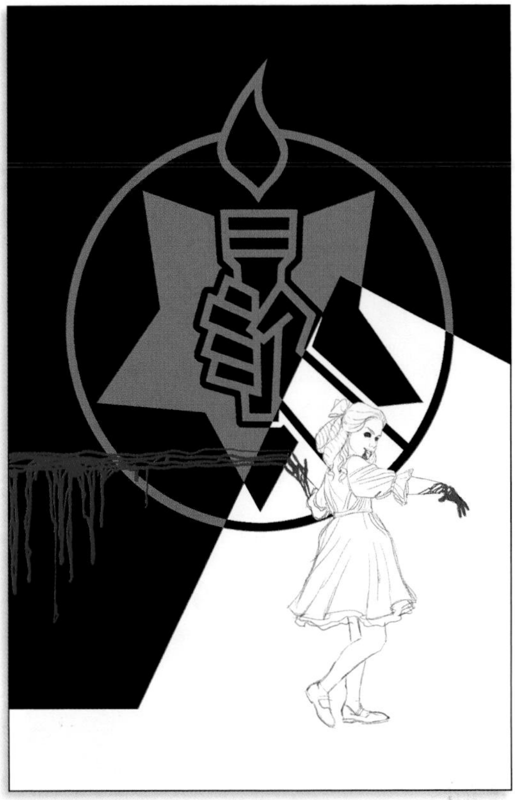

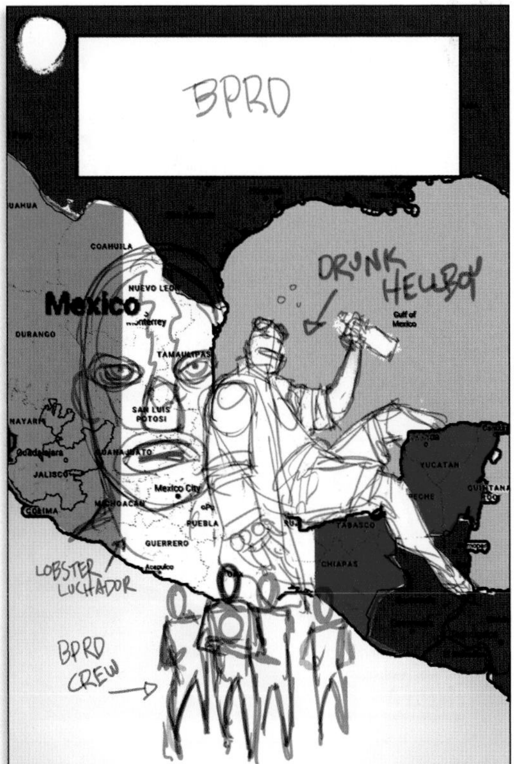
BPRD
Mexico
COAHUILA
DURANGO
SAN LUIS POTOSI
JALISCO
Mexico City
PUEBLA
GUERRERO
Gulf of Mexico
YUCATAN
TABASCO
CHIAPAS
DRUNK HELLBOY
LOBSTER LUCHADOR
BPRD CREW

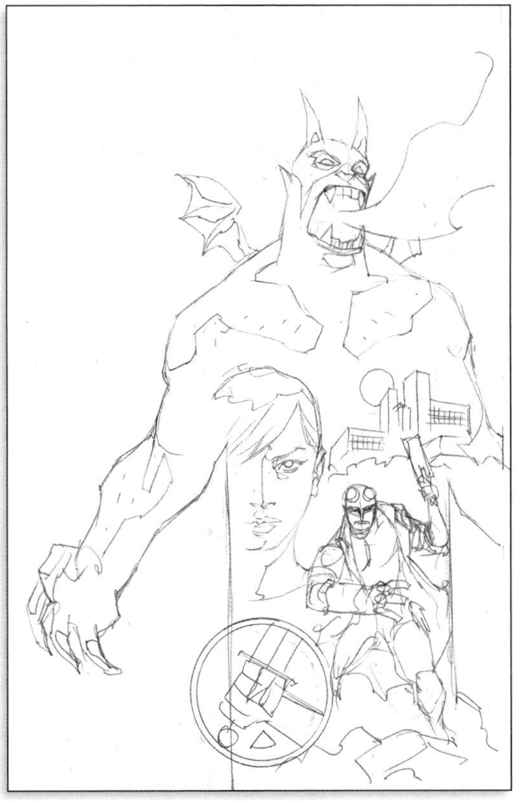

Paolo Rivera's process pieces for his painted cover to *Hellboy vs. Lobster Johnson: The Ring of Death*.

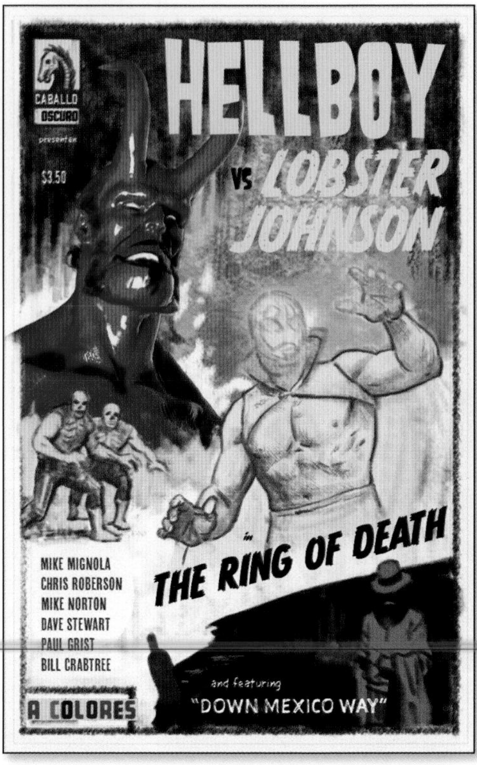

HELLBOY
CABALLO
OSCURO
presentan
$3.50
VS LOBSTER JOHNSON
THE RING OF DEATH
MIKE MIGNOLA
CHRIS ROBERSON
MIKE NORTON
DAVE STEWART
PAUL GRIST
BILL CRABTREE
A COLORES
and featuring
"DOWN MEXICO WAY"

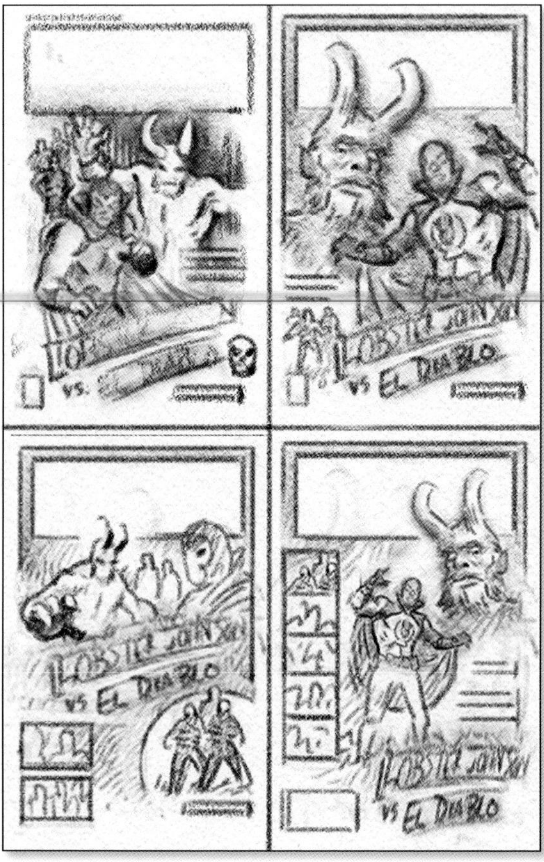

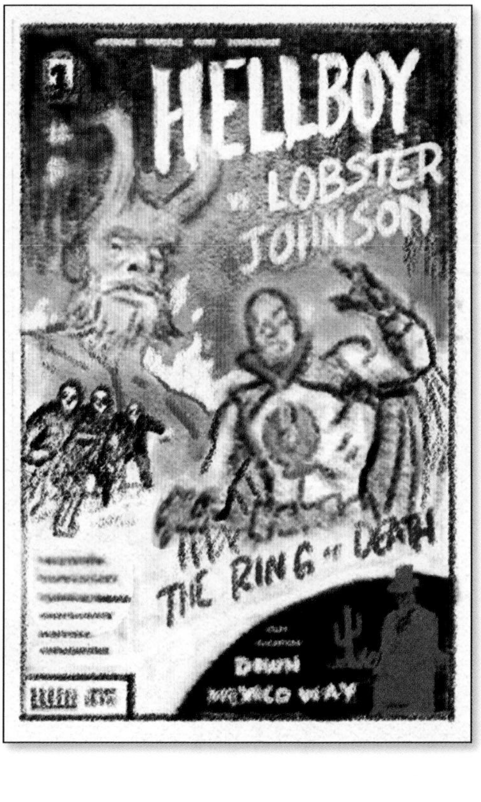

HELLBOY
vs LOBSTER JOHNSON
THE RING OF DEATH
DOWN
MEXICO WAY

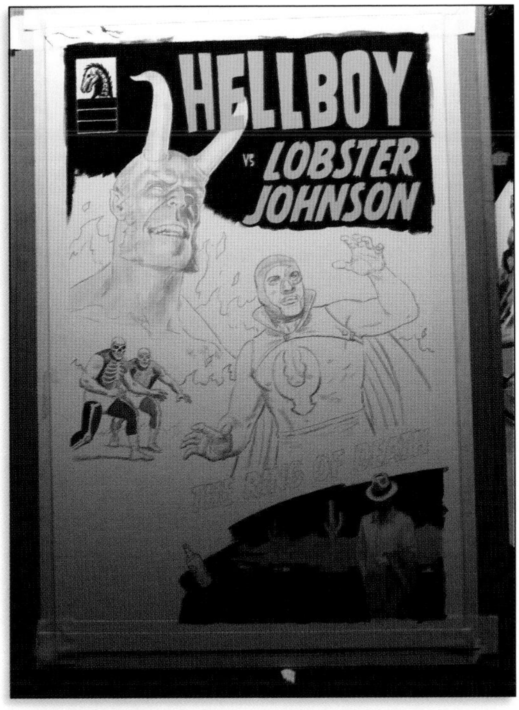
HELLBOY
vs
LOBSTER
JOHNSON

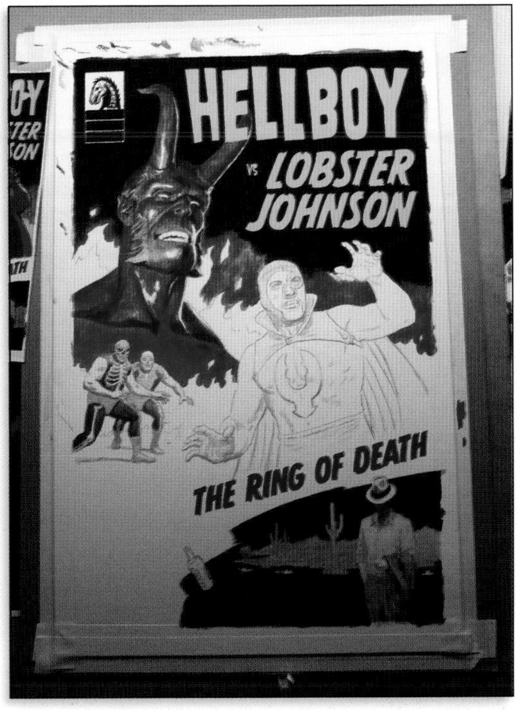
HELLBOY
vs
LOBSTER
JOHNSON
THE RING OF DEATH

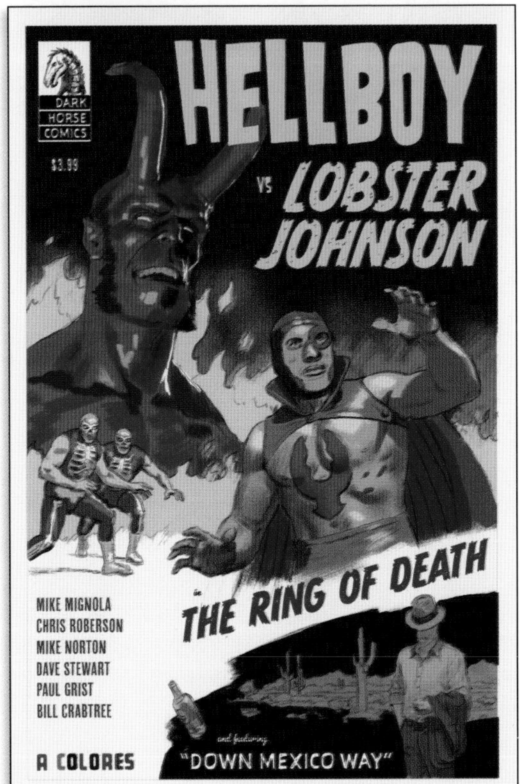
DARK
HORSE
COMICS
$3.99
HELLBOY
vs
LOBSTER
JOHNSON
in
THE RING OF DEATH
MIKE MIGNOLA
CHRIS ROBERSON
MIKE NORTON
DAVE STEWART
PAUL GRIST
BILL CRABTREE
and featuring
"DOWN MEXICO WAY"
A COLORES

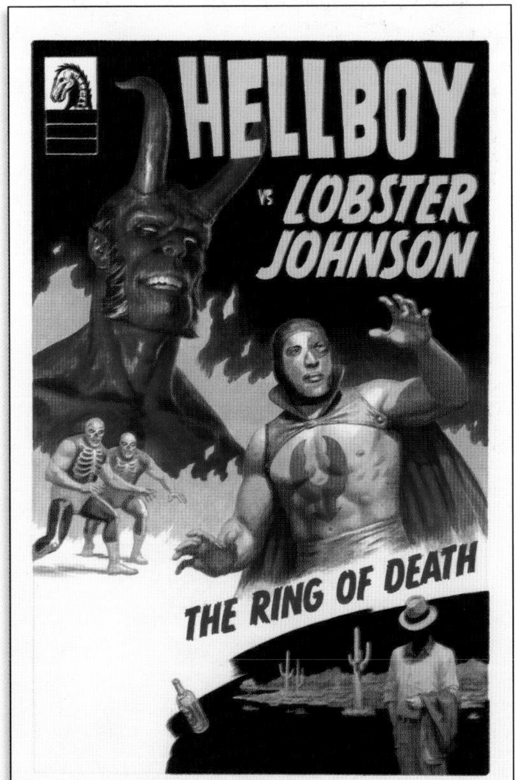
HELLBOY
vs
LOBSTER
JOHNSON
THE RING OF DEATH

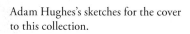
Adam Hughes's sketches for the cover
to this collection.

Also by MIKE MIGNOLA

HELLBOY™

by MIKE MIGNOLA

HELLBOY LIBRARY EDITION

VOLUME 1: Seed of Destruction and Wake the Devil
ISBN 978-1-59307-910-9 | $49.99

VOLUME 2: The Chained Coffin and The Right Hand of Doom
ISBN 978-1-59307-989-5 | $49.99

VOLUME 3: Conqueror Worm and Strange Places
ISBN 978-1-59582-352-6 | $49.99

VOLUME 4: The Crooked Man and The Troll Witch
with Richard Corben and others
ISBN 978-1-59582-658-9 | $49.99

VOLUME 5: Darkness Calls and The Wild Hunt
with Duncan Fegredo
ISBN 978-1-59582-886-6 | $49.99

VOLUME 6: The Storm and the Fury and The Bride of Hell
with Duncan Fegredo, Richard Corben, Kevin Nowlan, and Scott Hampton
ISBN 978-1-61655-133-9 | $49.99

HELLBOY IN HELL
ISBN 978-1-50670-363-3 | $49.99

HELLBOY OMNIBUS

VOLUME 1: Seed of Destruction
with John Byrne
ISBN 978-1-50670-666-5 | $24.99

VOLUME 2: Strange Places
with John Byrne
ISBN 978-1-50670-667-2 | $24.99

VOLUME 3: The Wild Hunt
with Duncan Fegredo
ISBN 978-1-50670-668-9 | $24.99

VOLUME 4: Hellboy In Hell
with Richard Corben and Gary Gianni
ISBN 978-1-50670-749-5 | $24.99

HELLBOY: THE COMPLETE SHORT STORIES

VOLUME 1
with John Byrne, Corben, Fegredo, and others
ISBN 978-1-50670-664-1 | $24.99

VOLUME 2
with Jason Shawn Alexander, P. Craig Russell, Corben, and others
ISBN 978-1-50670-665-8 | $24.99

HELLBOY: 25 YEARS OF COVERS
ISBN 978-1-50671-455-4 | $34.99

INTO THE SILENT SEA
with Gary Gianni
ISBN 978-1-50670-143-1 | $14.99

HELLBOY IN MEXICO
with Richard Corben, Fábio Moon, Gabriel Bá, and others
ISBN 978-1-61655-897-0 | $19.99

HELLBOY: THE FIRST 20 YEARS
ISBN 978-1-61655-353-1 | $19.99

GARY GIANNI'S MONSTERMEN AND OTHER SCARY STORIES
by Gary Gianni
ISBN 978-1-59582-829-3 | $24.99

HELLBOY: WEIRD TALES
ISBN 978-1-61655-510-8 | $24.99

HELLBOY: MASKS AND MONSTERS
with James Robinson and Scott Benefiel
ISBN 978-1-59582-567-4 | $17.99

HELLBOY: AN ASSORTMENT OF HORRORS
ISBN 978-1-50670-343-5 | $14.99

HELLBOY AND THE B.P.R.D.: 1952
with John Arcudi and Alex Maleev
ISBN 978-1-61655-660-0 | $19.99

HELLBOY AND THE B.P.R.D.: 1953
with Chris Roberson, Ben Stenbeck, Paolo Rivera, and Joe Rivera
ISBN 978-1-61655-967-0 | $19.99

HELLBOY AND THE B.P.R.D.: 1954
with Roberson, Corben, Churilla, and others
ISBN 978-1-50670-207-0 | $19.99

HELLBOY AND THE B.P.R.D.: 1955
with Roberson, Churilla, Rivera, and Shawn Martinbrough
ISBN 978-1-50670-531-6 | $19.99

HELLBOY AND THE B.P.R.D.: 1956
with Roberson, Mike Norton, Yishan Li, Michael Avon Oeming, and Paul Grist
ISBN 978-1-50671-105-8 | $19.99

THE HELLBOY 100 PROJECT
TPB: ISBN 978-1-61655-932-8 | $12.99
HC: ISBN 978-1-61655-933-5 | $24.99

NOVELS

HELLBOY: EMERALD HELL
by Tom Piccirilli
ISBN 978-1-59582-141-6 | $12.99

HELLBOY: THE ALL-SEEING EYE
by Mark Morris
ISBN 978-1-59582-142-3 | $12.99

HELLBOY: THE FIRE WOLVES
by Tim Lebbon
ISBN 978-1-59582-204-8 | $12.99

HELLBOY: THE ICE WOLVES
by Mark Chadbourn
ISBN 978-1-59582-205-5 | $12.99

AVAILABLE AT YOUR LOCAL COMICS SHOP OR BOOKSTORE! • To find a comics shop in your area, visit comicshoplocator.com.
For more information or to order direct visit DarkHorse.com or call 1-800-862-0052 Mon.–Fri. 9 a.m. to 5 p.m. Pacific Time.
Prices and availability subject to change without notice.

DarkHorse.com

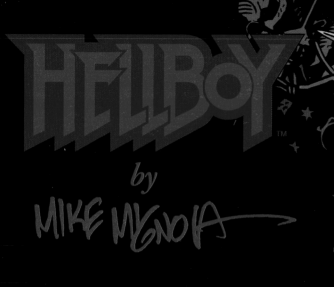

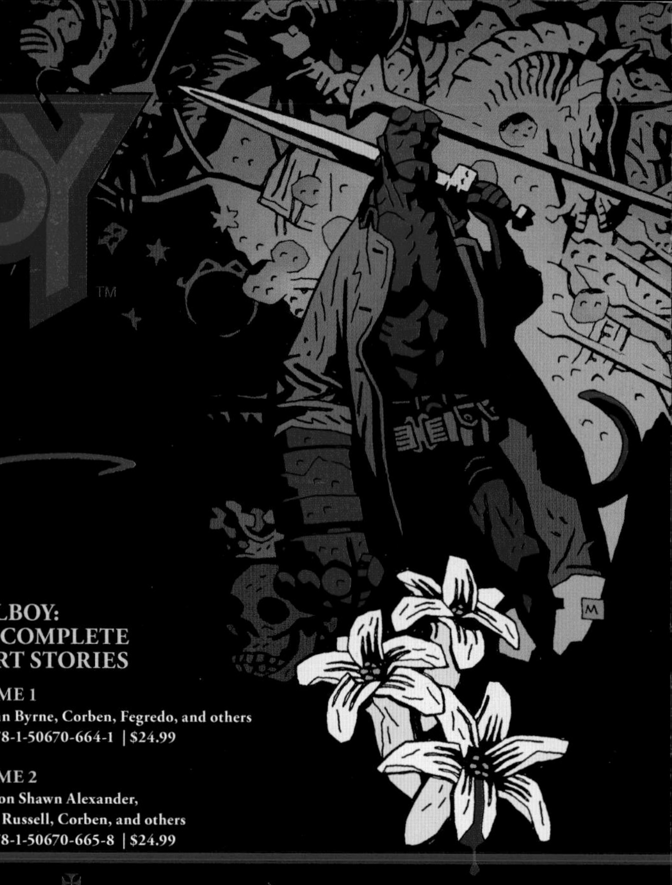